St Kilda Resettlement Genesis

PAUL SHARMAN

Copyright © 2017 Paul Sharman

All rights reserved.

ISBN-10: 1540844153
ISBN-13: 978-1540844156

DEDICATION

For all friends and colleagues who inspired me to write this novel.

CONTENTS

	Acknowledgments	i
1	Terrorism	1
2	Insurrection	20
3	Breakdown	34
4	Evacuation	64
5	Shooting Party	89
6	Arrival	108
7	Settling In	150
8	Bonxies	185
9	Changes	215
10	Relationships	245
11	Mothan	267
12	Climate Change	288
13	Blackhouse	301
14	Sheep	319
15	Stalkers	334
16	Tsunami	363
17	Slaughter	384
18	Revelation	412
19	Resurrection	427

ST KILDA RESETTLEMENT: GENESIS

20 Departure   455

ACKNOWLEDGMENTS

Thanks to friends and family for their support and forbearance during my writing of this novel. Thanks in particular to Kerensa de Ryck for providing the cover artwork.

This is a work of fiction. Names, characters, businesses, places, events and incidents are either the products of the author's imagination or used in a fictitious manner. Any resemblance to actual persons, living or dead, or actual events is purely coincidental.

1 TERRORISM

The explosions at Mullach Mor were barely audible over the relentless beat from the dance video blasting from the 60 inch plasma TV screen in the bar room. The only sign that anything was wrong was a temporary dip in electricity supply as the back-up generator inside the 1970s diesel power station burst into life. On top of the hill, the main communication mast toppled and fell short circuiting the nearby radomes. A few seconds later another explosion brought down the scaffolding of the elevated radome at Mullach Sgar.

Having heard the blasts, Derek raced from his room. He leapt into the dark blue Landrover parked outside, started it up and roared along the sea front toward the series of hairpin bends leading to the island summit and where he thought was the origin of the explosions. Skidding and almost losing control on the algae covered bend by the firepond, he crashed the Landrover down into low ratio before grinding at maximum possible speed up the series of 1:4 bends toward TOTH. Top of the hill, a military acronym still used by the civilian contractors running the radar tracking station on the summit where small missiles test-fired on the Hebrides Range were tracked; their performance assessed for use against unmanned drone aircraft in the escalating Mediterranean conflict zone. With Stornoway Coastguard closed there was no need for suicide. The bombers could execute their attack, destroy the island communications and make their getaway before the alarm was raised. Suicide would be better saved as a tactic for attacking a crowded city rather than an isolated Atlantic island that, for most of the infidel nation, existed only in its collective imagination. The military complex on South Uist was well protected but out here, 50 miles down range, the terrorists had taken advantage of an all too obvious security weakness.

The attack had been devastatingly simple. A series of small charges had cut the steel cables guying the north-east side of the mast while further synchronized charges cut the steelwork at the base of the tower. The remaining cables steered the falling steelwork onto newly refurbished radomes. Using a similar tactic, the broader tower on nearby Mullach Sgar had been felled using the weight of the radar installation on top as an effective lever.

The small fishing boat, hired in Stornoway, had anchored unseen in Glen Bay. Using the sheltered anchorage, away from the often gale-force south-easterly winds around St Kilda, the boat would not have seemed out of the ordinary sheltering from stormy conditions. On this night the moon was full and the sea calm, ideal conditions to land unnoticed from their small dingy and quietly trudge up Glen Mór to the top of the hill. With the island staff either in their rooms or drinking in the bar, the al-Qaeda inspired bombers from the mainland thought they would be unchallenged on the thousand foot ascent up Glen Mór. However Great Skuas dived at the moonlit heads of the unwelcome intruders to their nesting ground. Ornithology had not been forefront in planning the attack. The Bonxies struck unprotected heads and resulting curses were distinctly Scottish. Urban disaffection in Edinburgh and Glasgow had ripened many from the immigrant communities for indoctrination by a perversion of Islam that promised martyrdom in return for acts of political violence. Jihadists, they called themselves followed inflammatory words from on-line Mullahs based in the mountains of Pakistan. These mainly unemployed young men from the Central Belt took up secretive paramilitary training in the wetter mountain landscapes of Scotland now virtually independent from the absentee government in Westminster.

Finding island communications smashed, Derek, the MOD Base Supervisor began to shake. Like many working on the island, duty free alcohol had taken its toll. Opening the quarter bottle in the glove compartment he steadied his nerves with a dram before getting back into the Landrover. Derek set off to drive back to the Base for help. Without thinking he selected high ratio before putting the vehicle into gear and covered the flat road between Mullach Mór and the T-junction at Mullach Geal in record time. Turning down hill and nearly rolling the vehicle at the first hairpin he realized his mistake and tried to push the small gearshift back into low ratio on the move. Cursing at the protesting gearbox, Derek pushed the reduction gears into neutral. Before he could fully take in the speed of the now freewheeling Landrover, gravity slewed it into the next and sharper bend. Fear took hold and he flung himself across the front seat and tried to get head and shoulders into the passenger foot well. Uncontrolled, the Landrover hammered along the crash barrier until, at the end of the rails, it careered across the moor before dropping eighty feet to the quarry below. Derek died alone and unnoticed in the broken remains of the vehicle while his team were buying yet another cheap round at the bar. Only in the sober light of morning would the full horror and implication of the night's events become clear.

After breakfast, the small team of radar technicians waited outside the loading bay for the long wheel base Landrover to transport them to the top of the hill. Low cloud hid the previous night's devastation from view as they joked and shared cigarettes. Aware that communications were down, sorting the problem would have to take priority that morning. Maybe just a fuse or two, at worst a damaged cable somewhere out on the moor. Whatever the problem, they were experts and it shouldn't take them long to fix it.

By 9.00 am the six men had been waiting thirty minutes and still no sign of Derek. Keith suggested he checked Derek's room as they hadn't seen him in the Mess at breakfast either. He came back after a few minutes.

"Strange…he is not in his room and it doesn't look like

his bed's been slept in either. Well we had better get up to TOTH and fix things. I'll go and get the old Landrover from the garage."

"Hang on a minute, I'll go and check the medical wing. He might be in there for some reason."

Niall had a feeling that all might not be right and the duty nurse ought to know. He returned with her looking somewhat perplexed. Apparently Derek had been noticeably reclusive of late and she had been concerned considering his previous history of depression.

"I think we ought to treat this as a missing person incident," Sally suggested. The men looked surprised but agreed that finding Derek should be the morning's priority. Comms could wait for an hour or two.

"OK," she said. "I need you to go to the top of the hill. One to stay in the vehicle and three of you spread out and check the Cambir and Glen Mór. The other two work your way back over Conachair and across to Oiseval."

She sincerely hoped he had not taken his depression to the Gap, the scene of a fatal fall not many years previously when a day-tripper had deliberately jumped off the three hundred foot cliff.

The search party needed one man to stay in the vehicle and relay radio messages back to Sally. Due to the extreme topography, battery powered VHF handsets could not transmit from one side of the island to the other. Sally was to stay at the Base and be ready to receive Derek as a casualty should it be necessary. She did not consider it necessary to try and call for Coastguard assistance just yet, especially, since the closure of Stornoway they would have to fly from Aberdeen. If it turned out to be a false alarm the bill wouldn't be worth thinking about.

It was a squeeze getting all six of them into the old short wheel-base Landrover. The side facing bench seats had never proved popular, especially descending the 1:4 hill when the two foremost passengers felt the rest would end up on their laps. The rust streaked vehicle sprung to life readily enough though. Like all vehicles on St Kilda it was well maintained. For some of the shift mechanics, their work became a way of life. Certainly a few of the older men found unpaid overtime a more absorbing pastime than watching raunchy pop videos in the Puff-Inn.

The cloud-base on Conachair was just above the quarry. As the vehicle negotiated the first hairpin bend the mist became intermittent. Passing the historic Milking Stone on the right of the road, out of habit, Keith paused the vehicle at the adjoining track to the quarry. The large rock at the entrance to the quarry had historically been used to ensure good luck by St Kildan women returning from milking in Glen Mór. Mischievous spirits were supposedly associated with this isolated boulder and failure to make a deferential gesture was inviting trouble. Maybe the cattle would pick up mastitis or similar ill should they forget to pour a little fresh, creamy milk on the rock. Should the worst happen, the sick beast could be cured by application of poultice prepared from the small mauve flowered herb they called Mothan. Naturally antibiotic, the poultice was rubbed on the udder and good luck was also said to come to anyone who drank the milk from a cow that had eaten the herb. Climate change had brought mild, wetter winters to St Kilda and the insectivorous plant was flourishing even where heavy rains had leached nutrients from the soil. Mothan, or Butterwort, being a carnivorous plant survives poor growing conditions by trapping and digesting insects incautious enough to land on its sticky leaves.

Similar feelings of entrapment and assimilation into the landscape had led to several military personnel being removed from St Kilda on psychological grounds in recent years. A party of visiting geologists had recently tried to ascertain the limits of past glaciation and had chipped off a large sample for analysis back at the University of Edinburgh. Oblivious of their disrespect, the research had proved inconclusive. The island kept its secrets hidden and their research project had proved an expensive failure.

The mist lifted long enough for a clear view into the quarry and Derek's vehicle was spotted lying on its driver's side. Keith drove the old short wheel-base up the bumpy track to where Derek's Landrover lay wrecked. Diesel fuel and spilled battery acid had given the surrounding wet ground a toxic rainbow hue. The roof-bar rested on a large stone giving a view of the side window caked in dried blood from the swollen wound to Derek's right temple. A few flies were hovering around the sunroof, burst open by the impact. Derek's left arm curled over his head fixed in *rigor mortis*. There was no longer any need to go to the top of the hill. Keith radioed back to Sally who clearly heard and understood what they had found. She asked them to return to the Base and collect her and a stretcher from the medical wing. The party was subdued as they drove downhill, the vehicle skidding slightly at the slippery bend by the fire-pond. No one noticed the Great Skua alight on the wreckage of the Landrover as they drove away from the quarry.

Sally returned to the quarry with Keith and Niall. They would have to upright the Landrover before she could remove Derek's body. Aidan had volunteered to drive the Case loader up to the quarry and very carefully placed the forks underneath the Landrover. Assisted by its position lying against the Milking Stone, the twisted vehicle rocked over onto four wheels. Derek's body, frozen in a semi-fetal position, fell back across the front seats. The hand bent over to protect his head before he died was swollen and bruised from the blood that had drained into it overnight. It was not going to be easy to place his contorted body on the stretcher. There was going to be no easy way to do this Sally advised. They should place him, distorted as he was, in the back of the Landrover. With the two men in front she would sit in the back with him to try and prevent his stiffened body from toppling and further injury. She would call the Coastguard for help when they returned to the medical wing.

They had all been shocked by Derek's death and were half way back to the Base when Niall remembered all communications on the island were down for an as yet unascertained reason. Sally knew that the island's topography had in the past prevented VHF transmission to the Coastguard when they had been based at Stornoway. She had always telephoned for help in the past but now the microwave telephone link was down their only chance was that a VHF handset would be able to transmit a call for assistance from the top of the hill.

Turning round at the helipad they briefly called the others waiting by the loading bay. The radio message advised they would be going to the top of the hill to try and transmit a message to the Coastguard asking for assistance. Sally wasn't sure whether this would work but it was worth a try.

Keith drove the rusting Landrover with its grim passenger up through the hairpin bends into the low cloud. It was the silence up there that alerted him to the fact something was wrong. The wind always blew on top of the hill and the whistle from the communication mast anchor cables could be heard many yards before reaching the radar station. Today even with a fresh wind gusting to force six, through the mist, they could hear nothing. Approaching the office building, he had to break hard to avoid the tangled steel and cables lying across the road.

"What? Oh shit!" The reason for comms failure became

immediately apparent. Keith stopped the Landrover and ran to the fallen mast. He was a specialist radar technician and was so appalled he briefly forgot about Derek's body lying curled and stiff in the back of the vehicle.

Sally pulled the collar up on her light nurses' jacket and walked over to him. "OK, Keith. Now we know what happened but not how. Presumably Derek came up here to investigate last night before crashing on the way down." She placed her hand gently on Keith's arm. "For now, let's see if we can get the Coastguard out to help us before even thinking about repairing this mess."

Sally picked up the VHF handset from its cradle on the dashboard. Out of habit she called *'Stornoway Coastguard, Stornoway Coastguard....this is Kilda Base. We have an emergency....please respond.....over?'* She repeated the message several times before remembering Stornoway Coastguard had been decommissioned. It was only when she called *"Mayday, Mayday'"* on channel 16 that the self-styled Mujahedin group heard and relayed her request for help to Aberdeen. By this time, the small hired fishing boat was nearly back to Stornoway where they could reclaim their deposit and celebrate a successful trip. Their pretense of an overnight fishing trip had to look realistic so they had returned slowly to arrive back mid-morning. It was with grim relish they heard the emergency call over the boat's own VHF set. Omar, his name only recently adopted, replied at once and giving their precise location used the boat's far powerful transmitter to alert the Coastguard to a fatality at St Kilda. Smiling he realized that in relaying the alert he had acquired a good alibi, should the need arise.

The Sikorsky S-92 lifted off from Aberdeen Heliport at 10.30 that morning crossing the Grampian region before heading out over the Minches and onward to St Kilda. The pilot acidly remarking that since moving the operation to the east coast it took at least forty-five minutes longer to respond to the Western Isles. But as the casualty sounded very much dead, admitting it wasn't a very original comment, he quipped that he wasn't going to get any deader!

It was nearly an hour later when the Coastguard helicopter touched down at St Kilda's helipad. Sally and the team of radar technicians were waiting in the ironically termed International Airport Lounge, a small concrete building at the head of the landing craft slipway. Derek's body remained curled in the back of the elderly Landrover. His limbs had begun to soften which made it easier for the Coastguard paramedics to place him in the strong Cordura body-bag. The corpse was examined and an initial report form filled out. Obvious injuries were noted including his missing left eye and scratched face. Sally was surprised she had not noticed this earlier. Neither had Keith or Niall when they found him dead earlier that morning. "Bloody Bonxies," she muttered under her breath.

The Skua had entered the wrecked Landrover through its open sunroof. Only Sally's swift attendance had prevented any further carrion feeding. The large brown predatory sea-birds had returned to the island some thirty years after it had been evacuated in 1930. Hated by the St Kildans as egg thieves stealing their living, the ground nesting Skuas had been persecuted and completely driven from the island by the 19th century. As if remembering their historic persecution, present day Bonxies attacked all, particularly male, intruders to their nesting grounds. Year on year, the rising Soay Sheep on the island sustained the population of these aggressive birds. Hunting like wolves, the lambs were easy pickings. Like crows with a rabbit, they always took out the eyes first, then ham-stringing their blinded victim before ripping out its living stomach.

The Minister for Defense Procurement was incandescent.

He had not long approved another multi-million pound budget to maintain the Hebrides Range. The South Uist complex was the only site in the UK where the MOD could safely test tactical missiles and was by far the largest employer on the Western Isles. Time and time again he had received reports of alcohol abuse on the Range but had always passed the problem back down for local management to deal with. The current situation was a legacy of military occupation when, given the opportunity to cheaply drink yourself to oblivion, you weren't considered a man if you didn't do so. The subsidized drink culture had remained even though regular servicemen were, by then, rarely seen at St Kilda. Crown exemption was a perk confirming the island's popularity as a posting to get cheaply plastered but they had really done it this time. A drink related fatality and an unchallenged terrorist attack. Ironically it seemed the deceased supervisor, an acknowledged alcoholic, had been the only one sober enough to respond that night. The initial report confirmed the rest of the men were drinking in the bar and military security at the remote tracking station had long been ignored by the civilian contractors running the Base. At the recent defense review there had been talk of St Kilda's tracking capability being operated from the Aberporth Range, hundreds of miles to the south. With the Watchkeeper program successfully up and running the Aberporth team had proved their worth admirably. If they could safely operate unmanned high altitude long endurance drones, the Minister was struggling to find a convincing reason to continue funding staff at St Kilda with obvious psychological problems. Isolating a small male community and providing them with cheap alcohol made no sense at all and was a health and safety liability for the MOD. If Aberporth were clever enough to detect dolphins playing with targets twenty miles away and avoid blowing them out of the water, how could he justify supporting human resources at an outdated Cold War tracking station with inherent mental health issues.

The men had seen it coming. Three months after the attack the news came almost as a relief. At least they now knew their periods of isolation on Britain's remotest habitable island were coming to an end. The Puff-Inn had been the first facility to close. With serial histories of alcohol related accidents the bar closure was inevitable. It had to be expected, as it had been so many times before, but this time with ministerial condemnation the closure wasn't going to be the usual fortnight's restriction. This was going to be permanent.

Mainland Scotland had at last begun to get on top of alcohol problems the nation had been struggling with for years. While the mainland had begun to follow the rest of the UK and adopt socially responsible drinking patterns, the still marginalized Western Isles maintained destructive drinking habits. It was as if they were still trying to exorcise ingrained memories of forced Clearance which had socially devastated the region one hundred and fifty years earlier.

St Kilda had escaped the Highland Clearances. The sheep barons had considered it more trouble than it was worth to closely manage flocks fifty miles out in the Atlantic. However, seen through the dialectic of the Cold War there had been something heroic about managing men out there. Oil was cheap and plentiful and the diesel fired power station underpinned the transient community. The thirty minute helicopter flight took away the discomfort of the crossing for the men. All but the handful who operated the landing craft shuttling back and forth across some of the most difficult waters in western Europe arrived by helicopter. In 1930, St Kildans had evacuated at their own request. No helicopter or power station for them, the community had become too elderly to any longer cope with the hardships of their remote island existence.

The Base employees were similarly ageing. The average was around forty-eight and with several approaching retirement St Kilda had become a very unattractive place for younger employees. Not simply the age differences within an unbalanced team, but coming from the mainland a lot of the young men and occasional young women had been appalled to find heavy drinking still very much evident in spite of drug and alcohol awareness advice rammed home during their formative education. The Scottish Government had given priority to cutting down alcohol and drug related social problems but at St Kilda, unacceptable drinking habits were still found to be the norm for their older colleagues. Peer pressure to drink ensnared young and old alike.

For the younger men, Cold War fears of their older colleagues were hard to comprehend. The young men simply had no need for psychological wilderness to escape the sum of all fears. Theirs was an imminent world and threats to be feared were from terrorist attack. Suicide bombers killing or maiming hundreds in the Braehead Centre or on Prince's Street were tangible concerns. Mutually assured destruction should nuclear armed nations of east and west square up to each other were considered history. For these young people the sum of all their fears was to go through the educational system to find themselves unwanted by an economic system favoring unmanned production systems over full time employment. Technicians were always going to be in demand but, as they saw it, due to the irresponsibility of the middle-aged, highly educated young adults faced very uncertain employment paths, especially in the Western Isles.

Each time the bar had been temporarily closed there had been assertions that the Base would lose valued employees due to catch all measures punishing an innocent majority for the irresponsible behavior of the guilty few. This time, however, the terrorists had highlighted systemic rather than personal failings and, if they were to be honest, the demolition of the tracking station opened an honorable way out of the trap many of the men found themselves caught in. The island was comparable to a human pressure cooker. A couple of dozen men with infrequent female company on an orbiting space station would have fared little better than the radar operators at St Kilda. They were going home to locations as far flung as the Channel Islands and Malta. A few of the older men reacted to the closure with sadness. Away from strained relationships or chaotic mainland lives, St Kilda had become as much their island home as it had been for the thirty-six elderly evacuees departing aboard HMS *Harebell* on August 29th 1930. It seemed the 1957 military re-occupation was coming to a similar end. The military presence had become outdated along with its ageing staff.

The impending departure of the MOD from physical occupation of the island presented the Western Isles Trust with more than one conundrum. The rent would still be paid until the Base complex was demolished and the ground restored as far as possible to its original condition. The tracking station infrastructure could be repaired, updated and remain on Mullach Mor and Mullach Sgar to be remotely operated from Aberporth but human accommodation was no longer to be considered priority. For the MOD, annual savings had to be considered against the cost of demolition and removal of waste building material from St Kilda. For many years, The Trust had insisted on military structures being painted olive green to minimize their visual impact on the World Heritage Site. For visitors the buildings were a sensitive issue. Tourists came to have their pre-conceptions confirmed. Visitor information generally excluded any reference to the 1970s military base, on older maps cartographers had specifically excluded it. The first sight on landing from the day-boat at St Kilda had been the dilapidated accommodation block and diesel power station. Campers spent their nights in Britain's most remote tent site illuminated by the glare of sodium lights listening to the throb of heavy generator engines. A far call from the remote Utopia promised by the tourist industry. Since the Land Reform Act of 2003, many overnight visitors voted with their feet and took their tents over the ridge and wild-camped on the far side of the island. The slog over the top of the hill worth it for a peaceful night's sleep away from the noise of the Base. Modernization of the facilities had included the sinking of a new borehole at An Lag. Far better than the unreliable well dug in 1957, crystal clear water now regularly overflowed onto the already boggy ground making the corrie a haven for the damp loving insectivorous plant Mothan.

The service agreement between MOD and the Western Isles Trust had provided the island Rangers with electricity and potable water supplies. They also had access to medical assistance should it be required. On the odd occasion a visitor injured themselves, first aid was always to hand. The twice weekly helicopter flight from Benbecula brought mail and groceries from Balivanich and a feeling of being in contact with the outside world. On days when bad weather prevented the helicopter flight, isolation seeped into the consciousness of those waiting for news from outside. Since the destruction of the communication mast internet access had ceased although the microwave telephone link had been restored to pre-digital standards. The technicians were relieved the power-station had not been the terrorists' target.

Without MOD facilities the Trust staff would find island life difficult. Not impossible but with supplies coming by tourist boat in summer and Coastguard assistance a telephone call away the situation hadn't been too bad. There were rarely any Trust staff on St Kilda during winter months, it being deemed unnecessary to maintain a presence during the time of frequent storms and few visitors. However as a responsible employer, the Western Isles Trust was obliged to concur with national health and safety at work regulations. While the MOD was on the island, access to medical facilities, clean water, electricity and regular supplies were possible. Once the military left this could not be guaranteed and the Trust human resources manager was also beginning to have qualms regarding the mental health issues of keeping staff for extended periods on the island.

Concerns over dilapidated military buildings and staff facilities were not the only items on the agenda for the meeting in Edinburgh. At the Extra-ordinary General Meeting the Regional Factor had another big issue with which to juggle. The elephant in the room was the reform to the Common Agricultural Policy. Since 2004 emphasis had been placed on environmental cross compliance in return for agricultural subsidy. The Europe wide policy of supporting small farmers to stay on the land had been much abused but since Irishman Ray MacSharry had held the post of European Commissioner for Agriculture there had been funding for environmental conservation within the EC, particularly in the economically disadvantaged areas of the west. The Hebrides became prime candidate for financial assistance for agriculture, nature conservation and community development. The EU Habitats Directive was at the heart of a greening political imperative in the early 21st century. Funding was made available for co-financing of conservation projects. St Kilda had attracted funding for its Rangers, administered through Scottish Natural Heritage, but since global recession the situation was changing. The six-yearly review was rapidly approaching and SNH had advised that co-funding of conservation at St Kilda was likely to cease due to changing European social imperatives.

Social needs of Europe's agricultural community, especially the remnant small communities had never been quite forgotten. In fact they were the hidden and disadvantaged sector of rural society the Common Agricultural Policy had been set up to protect back in 1957. Due to the current chaotic economic situation, the time seemed ripe to get back to basics. Funding of nature conservation, seemingly so important in the late 20th century now seemed, like Cold War military outposts, to be outdated. Brussels was arguing that European social funds should be used for supporting human society rather than nature which, from the Brussels viewpoint, was considered quite able to look after itself. After all were not Europe's most precious habitats a result of previous human management? Greater emphasis was going to be placed on supporting small farmers to manage their lands in a sustainable manner. Gone were the days of unlimited inputs of fossil energy in the form of cheap diesel and artificial fertilizer. There was a brave new reality ahead, an almost back to the future mind-set was coming where everyone would have to live within their means and within sustainable natural resources.

The Western Isles Trust was, for all practical intents and purposes bankrupt. That was the unavoidable conclusion to be drawn from the Extraordinary General Meeting. For all the work of the marketing consultants, the sale of property and the letting of holiday cottages, income from membership and investments in such straitened economic times were not going to make the books balance. Further staffing cuts were going to be inevitable, particularly at outlying properties away from Scotland's economic centers.

"With Common Agricultural Policy reformed yet again, that fund is simply not going to be available to us. CAP once again insists European money is used to support agricultural communities to keep them on the land. Nature conservation has to take second place; cross-compliance will shortly be a thing of the past." The Trust Director made her point to stunned local managers.

"To be honest, in order for the Property to remain viable, we will need a small farmer to support on St Kilda. We certainly have enough sheep there to qualify but we have to turn away from the island being an open air laboratory to becoming a viable agricultural holding once more."

The St Kilda Manager rose to her feet. Josephine Miller was employed to juggling funding from Scottish Natural Heritage, Historic Scotland and rents from the MOD to finance conservation of the St Kilda World Heritage Site. Now the rug was being pulled out from under her feet. CAP reforms meant funding to SNH would be targeted at social wildlife projects. Historic Scotland had been struggling for years since austerity measures had shelved the UK Heritage Bill leaving archaeologists at St Kilda struggling for their share from the common pot. "If funding is only going to be available to support a viable agricultural tenant," she asked, "what is going to happen about the Trust's obligations toward maintenance of World Heritage status on the islands?"

The Director continued her speech. "As you are no doubt aware, World Heritage status is simply an accolade for the Trust. It does not bring any funding and actually adds to our financial burden. I, for one, would be happy to see St Kilda returned to viable human occupation following a remit of sustainable agriculture. We may have a World Heritage Site on our hands but unless that brings in funding we might as well forget it." The Director paused allowing Josephine to speak.

"If the future management aim for St Kilda is to support a viable agricultural community, where does that leave me? I am an archaeologist not a farmer. I also employ rangers and archaeologists to protect the wildlife and cultural heritage, what about that small community?"

The Director continued but to Josephine it felt like the decision to stop funding her work had already been taken. "We have to follow the funding trail and adapt our management accordingly. Otherwise, we won't be able to run a tea-shop, let alone a World Heritage Site. We have gone into this quite thoroughly and decided on a new set of objectives for managing St Kilda."

"But where does that leave me?" The St Kilda Manager was becoming stressed.

"As you already are aware, your post is up for review this December so we ask you to be flexible and consider other opportunities. You have done a great job handling the logistical nightmare that has been St Kilda. An enthusiastic agricultural tenant on the island will make management so much easier. However we will still need someone to keep an overview on the integrity of our archaeological resource. To be honest, it's not really my area. I feel there is no imminent threat to the natural resources of the island that we can realistically manage. Climate change is beyond our control so we will adopt an approach of managed retreat. We will just have to wait and see what happens. However, what we are proposing today is to employ a custodian family to effectively resettle, repopulate St Kilda and, at least on paper, try and make a living from the sheep flocks already there. Yes, I know it's hardly likely to be an economic flyer considering the distance to market, etc. but the enterprise, unlikely as it might appear, will bring in much needed European funding until the economic climate picks up. The custodian will be given the strict tenancy condition to protect the island's archaeology and you, hopefully as our consultant, will be contracted to make sure that happens. It remains essential that, like everyone else involved with St Kilda, in protecting our natural and archaeological heritage the custodian maintains an objective distance. There will still be a policy of minimum intervention in the natural processes on the archipelago. As before, the Trust's impact on the island's internationally precious fabric must be kept to an absolute minimum."

Josephine seemed preoccupied. "So you are telling me that my post is effectively to be made redundant in December?" The strain was beginning to show around her eyes. She long been suffering ill health brought on by continuing and increasing overwork, while refusing to delegate responsibility for St Kilda. Her personal attachment had always made delegation a difficult prospect. It sank home that she was now being asked to hand over completely.

"In so many words," the Director replied, "yes." The meeting closed with a return to the usual friendliness between colleagues but the dark bags under her eyes betrayed the intense stress Josephine was experiencing. After living and working on the island, direct management of St Kilda was being taken out of her hands. The Director came over and with a sympathetic and genuinely friendly smile quietly asked her to give priority to placing an appropriate advertisement in the Scottish national press. Now that it seemed likely the MOD would pull out of their lease, the Trust had to pander to Holyrood nationalism or risk further alienation from the Scottish population. Quite bluntly, unless the Western Isles Trust moved their goal-posts there would be no more funding for any of their jobs.

2 INSURRECTION

The riots of 2011 had been just the beginning. Urban society was collapsing with rural hinterlands in denial. The riots had become an annual event spreading further each year. No longer confined to run down areas of industrial towns and cities of England, Scotland was now being affected. Edinburgh's quiescence reflected the nation's failure to gain independence from Westminster rule and that summer saw street violence on a scale unseen since the Porteous Riots of 1736. The 2005 G8 troubles had been mainly intelligent protest from middle class student perception of global injustices of the capitalist system. Nothing prepared the city for hundreds of rioters running amok smashing and looting their way down Princes Street and into the Waverly Shopping Centre.

The 'Edinburgh Bubble' had finally burst. That year the Fringe festival had been cautioned not to satirize English riots. Joke of the devil and he is bound to appear was the advice of the local authorities. Never the less in true Fringe tradition the riots were engaged with cynicism aimed at disempowerment rather than encouragement. The disbelieving guests evacuated from the Balmoral Hotel watched in bewilderment as the Princes Mall roof garden became the muster point for Edinburgh's disaffected as the looting began.

Whether it really was the vast sum spent extending Edinburgh's showpiece tramway, only history will tell. Had, as several city councilors remarked, the original £800 million spent on completing the green public transport project been spent on improving social housing stocks and job creation, these riots may not have occurred with the ferocity they had. Prince's Street businesses, already affected by construction work delays, could ill afford the night of terror that scared both locals and tourists away from Scotland's premier shopping street.

"Well, I am glad most of you made it in this morning. Last night's events were certainly something else." His eyes betrayed an excitement not universally shared by his students as Dr David Williams greeted his first year geography students at the start of their 10.00 am lecture. He continued, "Let me remind you that Geography is the study of processes and patterns of human and natural systems on the earth's surface and their interaction. In your studies you will be bringing together disciplines from both natural and social sciences to help understand the causes and consequences of the world's major environmental problems, such as acid deposition, deforestation, overgrazing, debt, climate change and food supply. Yes, I know I am quoting the Prospectus here but it is important you realize that last night's riots cannot be understood in isolation from any or all of the above."

Making eye contact around the room he noticed one female student looking slightly pale. "I do appreciate that for some of you a night on the town may have turned into something more than you had bargained for, but remember for those of you out last night you were participant observers."

The pale student looked squarely at him, pushing back her long fair hair. "We were not participants! We were scared, Dr Williams. No doubt you watched all this from your TV at home. You need to be reminded we are lucky to be able to afford a bed-sit and paying for a TV license is out of the question. It's a complete non-starter. We are broke and, if we were involved in the riot, that's why!"

Murmurs of assent trickled around the room but intervening promptly, Dave Williams picked up where he left off. "OK, point taken – but as you progress with your studies, maybe later research, you will need to learn the trick of objectively distancing yourself in order to study events in which you deliberately or, as last night, accidentally I hope, find yourself. It is not an easy technique and can at first feel somewhat schizophrenic. What I haven't told you so far is that I sat up into the small hours last night completely rewriting my lecture plan for today. I consider the riots to be a seminal point in our nation's redevelopment and the fact that they erupted close by the Walter Scott Monument hardly a coincidence. So – let's please keep further comments constructive and I will now outline my plan for today's session."

Walking over to the podium at the side of the stage, Dave Williams picked up the remote and switched on the ceiling mounted projector. The first slide appeared on the screen behind him. His text was superimposed over an easily recognizable tourist brochure photo of Edinburgh as the Athens of the North.

"First we will examine the history of rioting in Edinburgh. We will then look at Edinburgh rioting in contemporary context. Then we need to examine what went wrong and what societal repercussions we can expect. Finally we need to think of a research methodology that will enable us to study events that we are inevitably going to be participants in."

He clicked to the next slide with the photo of Georgian Edinburgh superimposed with the simple word *Riots?*

"OK – somebody tell me about the history of rioting in Edinburgh?" The room stayed silent for a moment before the more enthusiastic students began to confer with each other. Finally one young man raised his hand and referred to the G8 riots in 2005.

"Thank you Jim, the 2005 G8 riots represent protest against perceived inequalities of global capitalism, rather than Scottish or local Edinburgh issues. Can anyone come up with anything else, particularly at a more local level?"

Silence returned as puzzled students began to realize the significance of the previous night's riots. Aware of the time constraint on the morning lecture, Dave Williams enlightened his audience. "Your silence completely makes the point for me – history records no riot in Edinburgh since the building of the New Town that you see in my slides. Briefly, there were riots around the time of the Acts of Union of 1706 and 1707 and during the 1745 Jacobite rising. Nothing recorded since the building of the New Town, so why should that be?"

Luke raised his hand, "Were the people too happy to riot?"

"I doubt it given everything else the population had to deal with – disease, poverty, crime, not that much different from today. No I think there is more to it. Look at the slide and tell me what you see there."

Luke replied, "I see classical buildings, like you see in London and Bath."

"And in Dublin", Dave Williams added. "What I want you all to think about is whether Edinburgh's architecture made the population happy or did it have another function?"

Jim came back, "weren't these buildings representative of money and power?"

"You are getting close, Jim. You are right that the architecture of these buildings was intended to impress, but mainly to impress other wealthy landowners. I doubt they were built to impress the general population, though. Think about Edinburgh as a focus for resistance during the Jacobite uprising against London centered Hanoverian monarchy. Dublin gives us a clue....."

Emma, who had begun with her complaint against

student poverty was becoming interested. "I think I am getting it – these new buildings in Edinburgh and Dublin are the same as those built by the Georgians in London. George III was Hanoverian and if his style of buildings were put up elsewhere, everything would look like London. Is that right?"

Dr Williams was looking pleased. "You are very nearly there, Emma. Tell me, why would the Hanoverians want other cities of the newly United Kingdom to look like London?"

Silence again. "I'll tell you. The reason they wanted the major cities to look like London was to spread their ideas and system of social values away from the Capital. They wanted Hanoverian seeds to grow and flourish across the nation and to do that they had to create fertile ground. Not only Hanoverian ideas and social values but economic values too. Think about it – when you go on holiday, if you can afford to, Emma, do you find it easier to go to a back street café or do you go to the local MacDonald's? You might struggle to find Pedro's Café but as we all know, the Golden Arches are instantly recognizable and, to many, comforting places to head for in unfamiliar surroundings. The Golden Arches get our money, eh?"

He let the point sink in. The students were beginning to discuss with each other, a good sign so Dave moved on. "Getting back to Georgian Edinburgh what I am suggesting is that the architecture of New Town made those with money feel comfortable. The neo-Classical architecture represented a social and economic network that connected money and ideas across the United Kingdom and across most of Europe and into developing colonies around the world. Think about the White House that, those of us with televisions, see on the news each night. Yes, think of the present day White House as the spider in the center of a neo-classical web still very alive today. Long distance control is another way of looking at it, social control across time and space via your TV set. Back in the eighteenth and nineteenth centuries it was London at the center of the web; ideas and money flowing back and forth along architectural song-lines for want of a better description. The money side of things is pretty obvious, just think of house prices around Edinburgh. I think you will agree it is more comfortable to live in Georgian New Town than some outlying housing estates but you certainly have to pay for that privilege. So what about the flow of ideas? What ideas can you associate with neo-classical Edinburgh? I have mentioned the term neo-classical rather than classical several times what is the difference?"

Gordon raised his hand, "Neo means new so neo-classical must mean new classical."

"That's it, Gordon", Dave continued, "the Hanoverians admired Classical Greece and Rome considering their time a golden age of reason, a time when men were free to think objectively, away from superstition and family responsibilities. Based on the city states of the Mediterranean the thinkers of the time became detached from the increasingly depredated earth from which they drew their resources. Classical and neo-Classical ideology detached from the earth that nourished it. Compare the great classical philosophers with the likes of Robert Adam, David Hume and scientists like James Watt. Archimedes and Watt would have shared a lot of common ground – and common architecture."

Emma looked agitated. "You have mentioned these famous men, but what of the women of the time? I can't think of any famous classical women other than the fantastical Cleopatra or Helen of Troy and when it comes to neo-classical women, all I can think of are pathetic characters out of Jane Austin. These men detached themselves from genuine female values too. It's disgusting, this is a men's story leaving women written out of history. Talk about men only!"

"Brilliant Emma! You're nearly there." Dave Williams was enjoying this, getting the students sitting up beside him on his favorite hobby horse.

"The architecture of Edinburgh New Town arguably represents a men only view of the world. Objective, detached from the confusing ways of women, away from squalling children, away from muddy connections to the land and those laboring to pay for it all".

"Hang on a minute, wasn't that the time of the slave plantations?" Luke re-joined the debate. "I remember seeing the film *Amazing Grace*. Most of industrial Glasgow was built on the back of the slave trade."

"Quite right, Luke, so what does that say about enlightened Edinburgh, standing aloof in the east, away from the industrial powerhouse?"

"I suppose it means that here in Edinburgh our riches could have come through Glasgow which in turn got its riches from slavery in the West Indies".

"Yes", replied Dave. "Some argue there are those in Scotland still reaping the benefits of slavery, while black people still have to bear the pain, not that you are likely to find many black people feeling comfortable amongst the neo-classical architecture of Edinburgh New Town."

Emma contributed with a cautious question. "You say Edinburgh was enlightened – what exactly do you mean?"

"Edinburgh was the seat of Scottish Enlightenment; representative of a movement based on science and reason that spread across Europe and her colonies during the eighteenth and nineteenth centuries. A hub in a socio-economic network represented by neo-classical architecture you see across much of the developed world today, and also by the trees, parks and gardens associated with it. However I'll leave neo-classical horticulture for another time. We will stick to the built environment today and consider how it enabled an ambience that prevented rioting for over two hundred years, that is until last night." Dave paused for effect again. "Having dismissed God as prime mover in the universe, the rational humanists of the Scottish Enlightenment rejected any authority that could not be justified by reason. They held to an optimistic belief in the ability of man, not woman, to effect changes for the better in society and views of nature guided only by reason. So in plastering the once rebellious capital city of Scotland with neo-classical adornments, our city fathers believed they were emanating rational values based on an architecture of reason. It was a kind of social contract between the city and its people. The city provided a stable and reasonable environment and in return the people supported and protected the architecture that controlled that stable environment. A self-regenerating, but exclusive system based on detachment from, for the city fathers, the harsher realities of life. Nazi Germany coined the phrase freedom from freedom. Did neo-classical Edinburgh offer a freedom from the freedom to be distracted by raw emotion? Does neo-classical architecture generate social harmony or does it smother dissent? There is of course a flip side to all this. If the so called network of freedom was dependent for its existence on profits from slavery, high priced exclusivity and the free flow of capital one could argue that the working classes or those without capital to invest couldn't be part of this enlightened system."

"Or without a white willy!" Emma was nearly out of her seat with indignation as the dark side of the Enlightenment struck home.

"Thanks for that, Emma!" Dave Williams' eyes betrayed his amusement in spite of frowning professional disapproval. "I was going to add, also without approved religious practices. Even God had to pass a DBS check! The Free Church of Scotland was started here in Edinburgh to get away from state control of our religious as well as physical landscapes."

"Bloody nutters, they are", quipped Luke.

"Thank you Luke!" This time his disapproval was genuine. "Luke. I need to remind you of the University's equality and diversity policy. I don't want to hear comments like that again in my sessions. Is that clear?"

"Sorry, Dr Williams but their disapproval of singing and dancing seems so harsh and …" He was cut short.

"Luke, before you say any more I suggest you read up on the subject or better still go along to one of their services before making sweeping statements on a subject you obviously know very little about."

With the students somewhat subdued by Dave's reprimand the lecture continued in a more formal manner.

"To get back to the subject, I am asking you to consider why there has been no recorded rioting in Edinburgh for over two hundred years. I propose it to be connected with the neo-classical architecture and an unwritten social contract engineered to support Hanoverian domination of Scotland. However the freedom from freedom it generated included freedom from worldviews challenging to Hanoverian hegemony. Religion was tightly controlled by the state and the views of women, laborers or anyone without capital to invest in the system were discounted. So called freedom was based on income from colonialism and slavery and threads in this tapestry ran through most of Europe and into North America, Australia and a host of other European colonies. As I touched on earlier the great lowland estates and parklands of Britain and her colonies represent neo-classical economy. If you are interested read up on the absentee landlords from the south and highland clearances; not such a benign paternalism there."

"Sorry, getting off my hobby horse for a moment, why was there no Edinburgh riot for two hundred years – Jim?"

"Well it looks like dissent was smothered by neo-classical architecture and reasonableness. No raw emotion allowed in the Athens of the North. It must have been a very tense place to live, especially for the poor and soul destroying for women – but one question. What happens if you can't actually see the architecture, Dr Williams?"

Dave Williams thought for a moment before he answered. "Now that's a very good point. There are probably at least two answers depending on what you mean by *see*. It is well known that after dark Edinburgh had a dangerous reputation. Tourists flock to be titillated by ghost stories, Burke and Hare body snatchers, and the lascivious activities of ladies of the night. That's just it – architecture needs to be seen or it loses its power. Why do you think that before the current recession our significant neo-classical buildings were floodlit after dark? I suggest it is not simply to dramatize the city but to prolong the neo-classical contract into the night. An all seeing eye maintaining law and order so that you lot have the freedom to go out and spend money clubbing or whatever it is you get up to."

Emma snorted. Dave waited until her suppressed giggle dissipated before continuing. "Jim asked what happens when you can't see the architecture. Well, when the lights go out you stay in and money stops flowing, apart from the dubious black economy flourishing once again in St Cuthbert's Kirkyard. There is another form of blindness to the architecture. We don't *see* it when it loses relevance to our lives. I am sure you will have heard of the cultural change that took place at the end of the twentieth century – I lived through it. It seemed one minute everything was under control. From cradle to grave the welfare state looked after you. You went to school, university, got a good job, good pension and died, nice and simple. I entered the post-modern era you were all born into, coming from a cozy, safe post-war world into the uncertainties and insecurities of the free market economy. Now look what's happened, no job security and a meritocracy even more brutal than the aristocracy it replaced. At least paternalism found a use for you even if it was only as cannon fodder for much of the 20th century."

Emma was about to interrupt. "Yes I know, Emma. Please let me finish. You are going to tell me about women chained to the kitchen sink, national baby milk and so on, right?" She nodded, "It sounds like a man's world to me."

"Sounds like Nina Simone to me but then I really am showing my age!" Dave Williams continued, "We have taken the lid off Pandora's Box after sitting on it for two hundred years, that's what's happened and now we are facing freedom and its consequences. You were all born into a world of genuine but mainly unstructured opportunity. The internet has flourished bringing a plethora of influence where, previously, city life had been played out according to neo-classical rules. Now, you never go out without mobile phone, I-pods for your personal music, you take your landscapes with you. In the bad old days of my youth you listened to whatever was delivered to you on the radio or TV and before that if you wanted free music, but not free choice, it was the band in the park. All very structured for you. You think you have choice but every choice is monitored, every download noted while the capitalist matrix twists and turns to make money out of you at every opportunity. Thinking about music, the power of neo-classical architecture didn't just extend into parks and gardens, it possessed souls through classical music, strictly formulaic to achieve the desired effect. Jazz emerged at the start of the twentieth century and its discordant notes marked the beginning of the end for neo-classicism. Think of associations with black music, how does Rap fit with the architecture of New Town?"

"There is an exception though. We all know the National Monument on Calton Hill. It was never completed as a building but holds immense neo-classical power elevated above the city and close by the government buildings. What happens there at the end of April?"

The students became surprisingly focused at the implication of what he was saying. Again, Emma looked perplexed. "But that doesn't make sense, I took part in the last Beltane Fire Festival. It was fantastic but, if I am getting this right, surely neo-classical architecture would never facilitate a Pagan event?"

"Think about it Emma. What makes it so exiting?"

She continued, "It....it's the thrill of doing something so wild, even naughty, in front of the National Monument. We were barely clothed and all that drinking and partying that went on......I am getting a bit confused."

Dave Williams had chosen his moment well. "The architecture or should I say, the neo-classical *spirit of place*, allowed you to cavort the night away for a very good reason. Within a city controlled by architectural Prozac there has to be some form of release – especially for young people, dare I suggest especially for young women? In allowing you to have your Beltane Festival at the most significant neo-classical site in Edinburgh, the city keeps control over you. The city has created a space on Calton Hill for all manner of protest and in doing so keeps the city safe from challenges of freedom of expression."

"But we love acting out on Calton Hill, Dave. We are not being controlled.....are we?"

"Emma, by *acting out* on Calton Hill you are drawing in the spirit of place, acknowledging its power. It's like being caught in a spider web without knowing it. Tom Paine the eighteenth century republican recognized the effect remarking how all public life ends up being a puppet show in front of a sublime edifice of tradition. He wrote *Rights of Man* in protest to all this but it took Mary Wollstonecraft to offer her *Vindication of the Rights of Women* in 1792 to remind the neo-classical world that it was smothering the female viewpoint.

Challenging stuff for New Town and it took local hero Rabbie Burns to calm troubled waters. Read his *Rights of Woman* and see what you think. He wrote his poem after seeing the London actress Louisa Fontanelle, who is known to have performed in both Edinburgh and Dumfries. Needless to say he became smitten with her stage persona, doubtless crafted to appeal to wealthier male theatre-goers. You see – the power lines go round in circles, there is little chance of escape once caught in the patriarchal system."

"I am sorry Dr. Williams but this really is too much. You are telling me that at Beltane, on Calton Hill, we are all being encouraged to perpetuate Edinburgh's patriarchy?" Emma was looking darkly at him.

"I am afraid so; you think you are escaping but really you are just winding the patriarchal spider web tighter around yourselves up there. Not just you but the Hindus in October. The Hindu Dusshera festival is encouraged in autumn but not your Samhain which is accommodated elsewhere. The Beltane Fire Festival is drawn in, absorbed by the National Monument but absorption of Samhain as well could become too much for the neo-classical spirit of Calton Hill to swallow."

"Christ! It really is a man's world. Fuck………" Emma picked up her notepad and bag and with tears of anger clambered to the end of the bench. She left the lecture theatre, slamming the self-closing door behind her.

Sensing rightly that his point had been made, Dave Williams turned to his audience already collecting their effects, ready to leave for their coffee break. "Before you depart for coffee, I'll leave you with one last quote,

> *But I, being poor, have only my dreams,*
> *I have spread my dreams under your feet,*
> *Tread softly because you tread on my dreams*

W. B. Yeats 1899

See you all, I hope, in thirty minutes and we will conclude this morning's session by working out a methodology for researching power of place in Edinburgh New Town."

3 BREAKDOWN

Dave sat at the kitchen table reading the previous day's *Scotsman*. He had been at home all week, unemployed for the first time in his teaching career. His personal performance review had not gone well. He had been called in by the Head of the Geography to discuss his previous year's work, expecting her to go through the usual motions, setting achievable targets for the next academic year and mandatory minor criticisms to keep him on his toes. He hadn't expected to be told that as an Associate member of the academic staff he would not be required in October. The problem, implied at first then blatantly placed before him to explain, was his field work investigation into power of place in Edinburgh's New Town.

What had he been thinking to send students out to lift the lid on Edinburgh's darker side like that? It should have been obvious that problems would come from raising a specter everyone knew existed but also helped sustain tourist commerce in the city. Dave's point that that was exactly the outcome he had intended was brushed aside. He had been told his 1990s psycho-geography approach was outdated and not going to of any use to students looking to gain a foothold in tourism management in the 21st century. The geography students, many needing to hold down part-time jobs, were now paying high tuition fees in the expectation of landing worthwhile jobs managing Edinburgh's townscape as a tourist attraction. The darker side was for the Social Services to deal with, not tourism students.

It was the criticism that his methods were outdated that really stung Dave Williams. As a student himself, he had been more than enthusiastic about delving beneath the skin of

Britain's landscape. The subtle mechanisms of control that encouraged public access and participation in Neo-classical public space eased the flow of capital but excluded those without resources to take part in the performance. Public performance had been built on foreign and internal urban slavery. Two hundred years ago, women and working classes were not considered worthy of any role other than to support the system. Driven into the recesses of the city, economically undesirables only appeared after dark. As the 20th century progressed, flood-lighting extended the hours of architectural control. Undesirable or challenging members of society sought resort away from well-lit shopping streets. At the edges of the New Town surveillance through the all seeing eye of the CCTV camera protected economically important architecture. Since economic collapse floodlighting had become a luxury the city could barely afford and Neo-classical control was losing its grip.

His line manager barely allowed him to finish. He had been shocked that she had shown no interest in the feminist angle of his argument. He was being dismissed as another outdated socialist geographer and should concentrate his efforts on achieving a vocational rather than philosophical outcome for his students. There was also the matter of a complaint from Jobson's department store regarding students annoying shoppers. Two students had presented needing help at the drop-in clinic near St Cuthbert's and there had been an alleged incident of some kind of drug taking on Calton Hill. One bright female student had dropped out from the course following research in St. Cuthbert's Kirkyard. She had also heard of students trespassing in Charlotte Square. It was not going to happen again; in future students would be trained to become employable and not be wasting their time exposing phenomenon likely to drive trade away from Edinburgh rather than draw it in.

Dave had protested this would mean a return to Tyler

style vocational education. It had been appropriate following the Second World War when the nation needed students trained to fulfil roles aiding economic and social recovery, hardly applicable today. His manager had had difficulty remaining calm after that point in the meeting.

"Exactly, Dr Williams! That is exactly the point I am trying to get you to see. In case you hadn't noticed we are in the grips of a recession equally as bad as that of the 1920s. The social consequences may be worse given the speed of communications now. The BBC cannot broadcast things are getting better while a plethora of social problems is broadcast and discussed across social media every minute of the day. I'll concede you have a valid point but it is not one this University can afford to support. We need student tuition fees to keep our heads above water. We are a business like any other and have to provide what our customers demand. What the customer wants today is a job at the end of their three years with us. I am afraid, to that extent, I have decided to advertise for a new member of staff experienced in the business side of tourism management. I know that might sound blinkered to you but as a senior manager I have to think of the financial viability of the department. We will pay you for an extra month to help over the interim but we will not be asking you to return to teach in Martinmas." The University had reverted to a traditional four term academic year based on the quarter days to reflect its Scottish identity.

Dave walked home in a state of shock; effectively he had been fired. Alternate emotions of anger, disbelief and panic bubbled up inside him. Was that it, he thought. The end of his teaching career? He had gone into this line of work after graduating as a mature student ten years earlier. His previous employment in the English Midlands had disappeared along with the motor industry that supported so much of the UK heartlands. He had liked Scotland, the malaise of ageism refreshingly absent in the emerging nation shaking off centuries of southern domination. Now the south had caught up with him again. He had met his now wife Deborah a couple of years after moving to Edinburgh. She already had two daughters from a previous marriage. Erica, the elder girl had had a troubling teenage period with alcohol and drug experimentation. Her mother had forcefully advised her to have a termination following unexpected pregnancy at the age of seventeen. Anne, the younger, was by contrast a studious girl and now at the age of sixteen, to her mother's relief, showed no inclination to follow her elder sister's fall from grace. Anne was becoming a knowledgeable naturalist and her idea of heaven was a bird-watching trip to the Isle of May. She had been too young at the time to appreciate the long term implications of her elder sister's difficult experience, though the budding scientist in her might have appreciated the wholesale immersion in Erica's personal experimenting.

Deborah taught at the Castlemount High School. It was not a school of high academic achievement but she felt she played her part in producing well rounded young people prepared to take their place in the industrial zones of the Central Belt. Not like Dave, she had often thought, with his head in the clouds and getting passionate about left-wing issues more relevant to the 1970s than in the twenty-first century. Notwithstanding they had had a good marriage, not of opposites but of complimentary individuals. There were times in class when a smirk crossed her face remembering the physical aspect of their relationship from the previous night. He might be an academic but he certainly knew how to press the right buttons when the situation demanded. Dave might have his head in the clouds but he was a good man, stepfather and mentor for her two daughters since their own Dad left them in the lurch. She hadn't intended to marry again but in Edinburgh social expectations had proved too strong to resist.

Dave had almost dismissed reading the Jobs section of the *Scotsman* classified pages. He wasn't interested in the increasing number of vacancies for care-workers to look after Edinburgh's ageing society. There were enough unemployed youngsters to train for that role. Another paper there, he thought; how the elderly become parasites on the young rather than support them in the twenty-first century. Not a lot of point if his University days were over though. He almost missed the Western Isles Trust advert being so convinced there would be nothing of interest in the classified job section. The advert almost glowed among the adverts for care-work. The Trust wanted a custodian family for St Kilda and they would give preference to a couple with children over the age of sixteen, meaning beyond the age of compulsory education. He cut the advert from the paper and pinned it to the kitchen notice-board, hoping Deborah would find it and be similarly excited about the prospect when she came in that evening.

Erica was the first to come in that evening. She worked part-time in the Fir Cone café and loved its bohemian ambience. It proved interesting when she and her step-father faced across the counter. Her standard response when the occasion arose was friendly teasing of the man few recognized as her stepfather.

"What can I get for you this evening, Sir?" She knew Dave would appreciate the inference but also knew he wouldn't misinterpret the tease for anything more. It was a private joke between the two of them and not to be mentioned in front of Deborah.

Erica noticed the clipping on the notice-board immediately, wondering if Dave was serious. She knew her mother would immediately pour cold water on the idea. She was almost always dismissive of anything unconventional and it only been her strong maternal instinct to protect Erica that had kept her in the family. Disapproving of almost everything Erica had been up to in her late teens, the pregnancy had been the last straw. She had accompanied Erica to the family planning clinic and subsequent psychological interviews until the abortion had been carried out. Procedure had always been Deborah's strong point but following the termination and Erica brought back home, her maternal conscience raised itself. Partly regretting having organized Erica's abortion she had felt compassion for her first daughter deprived of a strong father figure. Had her first husband lived up to his parental responsibilities, Erica's might have been spared her confused teenage years. Dave might not be that strong, but he was a good man and related well with girls. He had ticked enough boxes for her to invite him into the family.

Erica physically recovered quickly enough but the psychological wound never really healed. She had other relationships and took exceptional care to avoid pregnancy when the situation arose. She also became very assertive, practically aggressive with men who would not or could not see beyond her sexual attractiveness. Tall and on the slim side with short, boyish hair, her androgynous look collected many admirers. Romantic in more ways than her demeanor suggested, few would accept Erica for the intelligent and practical minded young woman she had become. Both Erica and her mother held Dave in high regard for turning her around and away from a potentially chaotic and uncertain future.

Anne was just Anne, contentedly wrapped up in her own world. The scientist of the family, she had been interested in natural history since meeting a hedgehog at the bottom of the garden she explored as a small girl. She had been so excited when Deborah had produced a pocket guide to the wildlife of Britain and sent her out to look for and identify whatever else might be in the garden. Deborah had to go out and bring her in, protesting, for supper that summer evening. The mold for Anne's naturalist future had been set.

Anne had been too young to really understand why Erica made frequent visits to the clinic or why she hid in her room for weeks after the final appointment. The usually ebullient

Erica was not herself but Anne paid her little attention compared to the attention she gave the varied plants and animals she encountered with book and magnifying glass in hand. Dave had given her a pair of binoculars for her twelfth birthday precipitating her enthusiasm for identifying and trying to understand the lives of all things feathered. One thing Dave had noted with a twinge of concern was her independent nature. Nothing he could really put his finger on but she never really seemed to engage with him. He had never seen her cry. Even when the family cat was run down outside in the street. Anne had calmly picked up the broken, still warm body and buried it behind the shed. On the odd times he had to remonstrate with her over some minor domestic transgression she quietly accepted his discipline. Unlike Erica, there was never any challenge. It was if since the departure of her biological father she had since detached from the emotional world around her. Totally confident in her own ability to live in a world without the ups and downs of her volatile elder sister she became, if he was to put it kindly, an enigma to him. Less kindly he wondered if she was simply blanking him out. Ignoring him as a man, this trait might possibly lead her into trouble in future relationships. He would have to watch out for that if and when she became interested in the opposite sex. Dave was no fool in these matters and had seen a few of his apparently hardened female students crack under similar strains. It was part of being a good teacher to be able to reflect but in the case of Anne, was he simply barking up the wrong tree? Was it just a male need to be noticed, to be taken seriously by females indifferent to him? Teaching certainly taught him life was far more complicated than he had ever imagined.

Deborah came in about 6.30pm having planned her work for the following day. She hadn't really had enough time to prepare but it felt important to her not to bring work home other than in exceptional circumstances. Her lessons were mainly a rehash of previous years' material so as a seasoned high school teacher she found it easier than when she first started. As long as she could convince the kids her lessons would take them down a route to future employment, she could keep their attention. She had often joked Dave wouldn't last five minutes with her young students. His philosophizing about everything and rarely getting straight to the point would lead to riots in the secondary classroom. Not a term she would encourage nowadays of course. It genuinely upset her that Dave had become unemployed but she noticed the advert for Custodian at St Kilda with incredulity, choosing not to mention it until they were alone.

Dave had prepared the family evening meal for 7.00pm. It gave Erica just enough time to get to the Fir Cone for her shift. Anne was as usual reading in her room, a plant identification volume open at the page describing Butterwort. Insectivorous plants had always fascinated her and the author explained that in Gaelic speaking regions Butterwort, known there as Mothan, was valued for healing and divinatory properties. She was engrossed in her reading but came down readily when called for dinner. The girls preferred vegetarian food though Dave and Deborah were fine about whatever they ate as long as it was produced without cruelty. He was waiting for one of them to mention the advert but it only came up in Erica's hurried goodbye as she left for the Fir Cone.

"Cool idea about St Kilda, Daddy," she quipped wrapping her scarf around and pulling her woolly hat down over her ears. It was getting very cold outside. Anne was miles away, no doubt thinking of some bird or other, he assumed. Quietly she was actually hoping against all hope they really would go to St Kilda, that island of birds she thought she would only ever be able to dream about visiting. Deborah simply looked at him saying she would talk to him about the idea later. She didn't want to pull apart yet another of Dave's impractical dreams in front of the girls. Erica had gone out and Anne was in her room, head in another natural history book, thought her mother. A good time to talk to Dave about this St Kilda idea.

Dave was sat at the kitchen table with a glass of red wine reading the *Scotsman* through again. In his excitement seeing the Western Isles Trust advertisement he had neglected to take in much else. His dream of imminent departure had created a sense of urgency to catch up on what was happening in the troubled nation before he took his family away from it all. He was sure this could be the opportunity of a lifetime and he was also sure that many others dreaming of a new life at the 'edge of the world' would apply. Deborah poured herself a glass and sat down opposite him. He looked up sensing her need to talk.

"Dave," she began. "I know you have always dreamed of getting away from it all, so I am assuming you are serious about wanting to apply for the St Kilda job – if that's what you can call it? But, have you thought about the rest of us. I am sure Anne would be delighted but Erica seems happy now. She has sorted herself out and is building a decent life for herself at last. It may be hard for me at school sometimes but basically I am doing well and we both know we need my salary now you have lost yours." Her last words stung Dave. He had never been unemployed before, apart from brief summer spells waiting for teaching contracts to start in the autumn. Her argument could not be challenged though. That is unless they gave up their present lifestyle.

Dave's argument was based around the premise that staying as they were, in a city where they were all going to hell in a hand cart, was not an attractive option. Why not make the change and leave the city behind them and breathe the clean air of freedom out at St Kilda? He was looking forward to being hands on again, remembering his younger years working as a gardener and forester, not that there were either gardens or forests at St Kilda now. He ought to at least be able to start a vegetable patch though.

"David!" Deborah snapped him back to their warm kitchen in Edinburgh. "You are not listening to what I am saying, are you? If you want to apply, then by all means go ahead. I suppose it will tick a box for your Job Seekers Allowance obligations, but don't expect me to support you in this. In the unlikely event of you being accepted you will be out there on your own, or maybe just you and Anne, who I know would jump at the chance."

The fact that Dave was seriously contemplating this move made Deborah realize that even after being with him for several years he had never lost his youthful romanticism. A radical romantic was what he used to call himself; neither a digger nor a dreamer, but a dreaming digger. There was a danger he would dig himself into a dream so deep he would be buried but of course he couldn't, or wouldn't, see that side of the argument.

"Debs, this is important to me and I am going to apply. I can't just sit here doing nothing while life passes me by. I also know I can't expect you to blindly follow me in this. I don't like the idea of going out there on my own, or just with Anne, but I need to apply. I need someone to take me seriously now the University has given up on me."

Deborah left the kitchen to settle down to watch a TV program in the living room. Dave took his lap-top from its bag for the first time in days and began to compose his application, determined but also uneasy about the effect that following his dream might have on the family.

The completed applications began to arrive in the Inverness office within a few days. Enthusiastic telephone enquiries were referred back to the advertisement insisting all applications were to be in writing. There were applications ranging from those wanting to reinstate the islands agricultural economy to building an eco-tourism business. Some even suggested reverting to the now illegal practice of egg harvesting. Citing their climbing qualifications they also demonstrated complete ignorance of bird protection legislation. Others wanted to renovate the cottages and start a new Utopia on the island, living in harmony with the seasons and in peace and love with their neighbors. They too displayed ignorance of statutory protection for the internationally cherished archaeological resource at St Kilda. They were also in blissful denial or ignorance of the fact that living in harmony with the seasons would also mean being exposed to the vagaries of the north Atlantic. What the St Kilda Manager was looking for was someone with practical abilities, was psychologically realistic about remote living and with a supportive personal relationship. She didn't want a desperate loner likely to jump off a cliff after a few months. Neither did she want anyone determined to build New Jerusalem at St Kilda, riding roughshod over statutory protections the Trust was barely able to comply with let alone enforce.

Josephine Miller read the application from Dave Williams with interest. Dr Williams was an academic and a professional Geographer. There should be no impractical nonsense and he would respect the islands statutory designations. Without strict adherence to procedures dictated by those designations all hope of future funding would be lost. Also as an academic, she thought, he probably wouldn't want to start any heavy work moving stones around but would, in the absence of a paid warden, be happy to continue accurate recording of archaeological change and natural events. In his application he made scant reference to family though he had mentioned a teenage daughter very keen on bird-watching, she would have to ask about his family situation at interview.

Other applicants seemed to be mainly adventurous young families thinking St Kilda would be an ideal place to resettle. There had been similar social projects to resettle isolated areas of the west with young families, particularly in Ireland. This had been partly successful but many families had drifted back to the cities after a few years. Schooling was always the problem; on reaching secondary school age the children had to board away from home making nonsense of the resettlement ideal. State education required all children to go through the system regardless of where their families lived. St Kilda would be just such an example. Schooling would be next to impossible and medical facilities difficult. She didn't want to wind the island clock back to 1930, there was no sense in contemplating such an idea. Josephine also noted there had been an application from Sally MacDonald one of the recent MOD nurses. She was in her late thirties, fit and eager to go back to the island. She did make a somewhat feminist reference to the island community having been ruined by male dominance and wanting to rekindle family life there. This, in Josephine's opinion, unrealistic ambition could not be allowed to proceed but on the positive side her enthusiastic knowledge of the island and paramedic skills would be of great benefit to whoever might be custodian. The medical wing in the empty base had simply been mothballed and only perishable items would have become unusable since the power had been turned off. A small generator had been left on island and could be brought back into service for the custodian family as and when the need arose.

She needed a third candidate before setting up the interview day, someone with the strength of character to survive life on a remote island and with skills in practical self-reliance. Her mind had almost been made up, she wanted Dave and Sally but Human Resources demanded she choose from three candidates. Going back over the discarded applications she stopped at one from Steve Brown. This application had come from south-east England about as far away from St Kilda as you could imagine in the UK, but he was an avid ornithologist and his field observation skills should be transferable to archaeological recording. He was in his thirties too and had been a St Kilda volunteer in the past. He was looking for a fresh start away from the rat-race of the London area. Yes, he would do as candidate number three and while none appeared one-hundred percent perfect they were good enough to show her boss, the island Factor, that she was doing her job properly.

Dave was pleased to receive the interview invite letter but it put him in a quandary with Deborah. He knew this was not just another of his dreams; he really wanted this to happen but was realistic enough to know he needed family support to do it. He could conceive of going to the island with Erica and Anne but not really of leaving Deborah behind. Complex feelings arose when he thought of the scenario. He really felt excited about the prospect of living life as he felt it was meant to be lived. He loved the idea of working with his hands out on Britain's remotest habitable island, providing for his wife and family as had generations of islanders before. His two daughters were enthusiastic and he knew Erica had her head very firmly screwed on now. Anne was the scientist in the family and he could leave the record keeping to her. It was just a matter of convincing Deborah. At home she was the bread-winner now and in spite of this being a perfectly acceptable situation in mainland society, he dreamt of going back to what he saw as a more fundamental way of life. A way of life where he could be head of his family, the provider and leader through adversity. He didn't envisage his family as chattels, of course, but being patriarch of his family did hold an appeal, he couldn't deny it. Back in Edinburgh and unemployed he occasionally felt the pyramid was reversed, the three busy women in his family had begun to make him feel irrelevant.

Deborah Williams left Castlemount High School around 7pm that evening. Even though it was getting late there were still a few cars belonging to younger teachers in the car park.

Frost had already formed on roofs and windscreens of the more exposed vehicles. She opened the door to her Toyota hatchback placing her heavy bag on the passenger seat and started the engine. Turning the heater controls to full heat and demist she knew that the interior of this small modern car would quickly warm up while she scraped ice from the windscreen outside. The two youths watching knew that too and also knew they would have no chance of stealing the vehicle without the key being already turned in the ignition switch, such was the security system on this model.

One youth walked over to Deborah and engaged her in conversation trying out the age-old routine of asking for spare change to get a meal that night. Instead of stimulating her maternal instincts, Deborah became irritated and though not what the young man expected, his distraction achieved the desired result. Deborah turned to face him and challenge his right to be on the school premises at that time of the evening. The second youth saw his chance and jumped in the driving seat. Deborah reacted in an instant and ran around the car to reach for the driver side door. The first youth had jumped into the passenger seat and the car sped off with Deborah's hand still gripping the driver-side door-handle. She screamed as her wrist broke forcing her to release as the car sped away.

"You fucking bastards!" She screamed and screamed over again while clutching her broken wrist to her chest with her good hand. The noise and unprofessional swearing brought out one of her younger colleagues who led her inside, uncontrollably sobbing, and sat her down to administer first-aid. The triangular bandage and sling proved a real-time challenge for the younger teacher. In first-aid classes no one wore a thick overcoat as did Deborah that evening. The Police and Ambulance service were called but only the Ambulance arrived. The overstretched Police control room operator said she would send an officer to Deborah's home to take a statement as soon as one was available. Car-jacking was not apparently considered serious enough to warrant immediate response for a constabulary decimated by staffing cuts.

The Ambulance paramedic was happy enough with the young teacher's first-aid for the broken wrist and Deborah was led to the emergency vehicle and driven to the Royal Infirmary. Though in considerable pain when they arrived she was asked to wait while a junior doctor was found to come and attend to her. Meanwhile if she would just go to reception and provide all the necessary details, she would be seen as soon as possible. After giving her details, she returned to the waiting area and thought to ring Dave to tell him what had happened. That wasn't going to be easy, she quickly realized, as her mobile phone had been in the bag left on the car passenger seat. She expected the bastards had pocketed that and thrown everything else out of the window. Her pupil's class-work was no doubt lying in a gutter somewhere in the so called cultural heartland of Scotland. She had had enough of Edinburgh's so called culture and she was sick of the endless tension of teaching, trying to get through to teenagers whose only spark of enthusiasm had been for the recent riots. Had the car-park lights not been switched off to conserve energy she reckoned those two boys would never have had the nerve to take her car like that. The CCTV system was out of order, had been for months, and they probably knew that too.

She returned to the reception desk and asked to use a phone to ring Dave. She was directed to the hospital shop where she could purchase a pre-paid phone card and then use one of the public phones in the lobby hallway. It cost her five pounds to make the call to Dave to tell him what had happened and why she would be late. Shocked and still in considerable pain it occurred to her that it actually felt good to let the man in her life take responsibility that evening.

By the time Dave arrived in his own car, an elderly Peugeot estate, she had been X-rayed and the wrist put in a back slab, a half-plaster cast to allow for swelling and supported by a fresh sling. She wouldn't be returning to work for a few weeks the young doctor advised. If ever, thought Deborah. She just wanted to be home and feeling cared for.

The following morning felt like a Sunday to both of them. Dave got up around 8.00 and made tea in the kitchen. Anne had just left for school. At sixteen she was beginning to consider her own future options and she had told her parents there was a careers fair that morning. Erica, after working into the small hours at the Fir Cone, was still fast asleep. Dave smiled as he heard gentle snoring from her room as he crossed the landing. After all that happened just over a year before he was glad she had come through and was still with them. Anne would be alright, he instinctively knew that, but with Erica it had been a close call.

He brought the tea tray back up to their room and climbed back into bed. Deborah usually poured the tea but this morning he was going to do it. One small step toward asserting his future, he thought whimsically. He passed the cup to her and noticed the smell of stress on her breath. It was a smell he had once put down to throat infections but had learned from worried students the smell indicated extreme duress. He had not expected to experience this with Deborah.

"Debs, are you OK?" Stupid question really with her right forearm plastered and bandaged but at a deeper level her breath smell indicated something was very wrong.

"Dave, I can't go back. I've had it." The pain hadn't been too bad that night but her shocked mind had kept her awake and she needed to talk. "I have tried and tried at Castlemount but, in spite of all my efforts, I get mugged in my own schoolyard, probably by ex-pupils. Something's changed, I don't think I can face going back."

Dave put his own cup back down on the bedside table. "You'll be OK in a couple of weeks. Treat this as an extra holiday. It will be Christmas soon and you'll have a few extra weeks off before Spring term starts." It was a platitude, he knew that, but he also recognized the small sign that maybe Deborah would come round and support his St Kilda idea.

Deborah thought of all the lesson planning and preparation that would have to be done before then and it would be unlikely the supply teachers would have brought her pupils to the point in the scheme of work she had intended by Christmas. Being a teacher was like being a task master keeping her reluctant pupils on an educational treadmill and they would jump off given any opportunity. The pupils of Castlemount would make short work of any fresh young teacher asked to cover in her absence. But what if they related better to the pupils' age-group than she did? Would she actually have a job to go back to? How on earth would they pay their mortgage with them both out of work? That morning it suddenly seemed all too much and she dropped her half empty cup into the duvet and burst into tears. Suddenly sitting up straight, she turned to Dave. "Dave, I want to go to the interview with you." He looked surprised, he hadn't actually broached the subject with her but she had obviously read the letter put back in the envelope on the kitchen windowsill.

"I really mean this Dave, I want us to go there, I want to support you, be your wife in a new venture for us. I just don't want to be here in this bloody city anymore!"

"OK, OK, one thing at a time, Debs." The force behind Deborah's support for him was unsettling. This was no dream, she really did want to support him on St Kilda but the responsibility that inferred scared him more than he had expected. "I'll ring the Western Isles Trust later." Deborah looked him squarely in the eye, "Do it this morning, Dave, please?"

Josephine Miller, recovered from her traumatic St Kilda management meeting, was surprised but pleased when Dave rang to ask if his wife could attend the interview with him. Apparently she really wanted to support him in the custodian role and their two post-school age daughters would be coming too if he got the job.

Sally MacDonald had also been in touch too, offering her services as a long-term volunteer if she didn't get the custodian role. This was getting better and better, she thought. Just a pity they had to put Steve through the interview process when she already had the personnel she wanted, in the bag so to speak. The interviews had been scheduled for the following Thursday. A quick decision was needed as she hoped to have a custodian in place in the Spring. Three months without anyone on the island was risky but over the stormy winter months sea-borne squatters would be unlikely.

Steve Brown was amazed to be offered an interview. He was somewhat of a loner spending much of his spare time, between mundane casual jobs, out bird-watching on the Cuckmere Estuary in East Sussex. Even so the thought of leaving his home area for the far north-west felt daunting. Getting himself together to make the interview in Edinburgh the following Thursday was going to prove a challenge. He would have to fly from Gatwick. The Western Isles Trust were thankfully offering to pay interview expenses, unlike many organizations since the recession started. The internal flight would get him there and back the same day so no need for overnight accommodation. He hated the thought of staying in a cheap hotel or guest house, having to face complete strangers across the breakfast table.

For Dave the interview meant a short trip across town, no problem, he assured himself. Sally had to make the easy journey by train from Glasgow. They were both unaware of the challenges facing Steve five hundred miles to the south, totally oblivious of what life on St Kilda would really be like.

Dave and Deborah duly arrived at the Trust head office at 0930 and were shown into the board room. They sat together with the St Kilda Manager and the Factor across a dauntingly large table. Even so the two Western Isles Trust managers made an effort to make them feel relaxed and initial conversation over coffee was easy. The background situation regarding the departure of the MOD and the financial implication for the Trust at St Kilda was candidly explained by the Factor. They were told there were to be three candidates that day and that they hoped to be able come to a decision by the end of Friday, letting the successful applicant know over the weekend. Josephine emphasized the unique responsibility being custodian for St Kilda would entail. It was not going to be a paid position but all living expenses would be found. Tourists would be returning after Easter and, as custodians, they would be free to make whatever arrangements they liked with the day boat operators who came over from Harris. As voluntary custodians they would be allowed to engage in small freelance activity keeping within the statutory constraints, of course. It was vitally important for Trust that sea-bird recording be continued as a condition of Scottish Natural Heritage funding. Had they all a good head for heights and a common sense attitude towards danger? Likewise it was important that remote sheep flocks on Soay and Boreray be monitored. There was a high powered telescope on the island sufficient for that duty. Above all the main duty was to interpret the island to summer visitors and keep a running record of archaeological features on the island. It was again imperative that changes be reported immediately as a condition of Historic Scotland financial support. Under no circumstances was the custodian to make any material changes at St Kilda or to introduce any alien plant or animal species.

"So that means no pets, I am afraid to say." Dave nodded as though miles away, but in reality inwardly digesting what he was being told.

"You will have access to all facilities on the island, though of course certain military structures, including the power station, will not be within your remit. They will be periodically checked by the Capabilities Manager from the Hebrides Range. Medical facilities are in place and I am hoping to engage a former MOD nurse to live and work with you. She knows the island well and has all necessary skills should you need medical attention."

Turning to Deborah she continued. "Now, Mrs. Williams, can you tell me about your family and what commitments they have regarding education, jobs and so on. I assume there is no longer statutory obligation for school attendance?"

"That's right," Deborah replied. "We have two daughters, Erica is twenty-three and Anne is sixteen coming on seventeen soon. Erica has a casual job behind a bar in town, the Fir Cone café. Do you know it?"

The St Kilda Manager nodded, it had been a favorite haunt of hers in the past. You could just make out the marks of past nose and multiple ear piercings suggesting Josephine had had a less conventional past than her present position implied.

"Anne would be leaving school next summer anyway and she has already said she would jump at the chance to continue her ornithology interests at St Kilda. They are both great girls, quite different in many ways but as sisters they would support each other come what may and support Dave and I throughout our time on the island. Anne would be just the girl for the sea-bird recording, it would be right up her street."

Josephine had already made up her mind to offer the Williams family the post. "Accommodation on the island would be in the recently refurbished Manse. There is a standby generator which can supply your electricity. All you would have to do is keep the diesel tank topped up. It would be up to you to start it up whenever it was needed. Everything in the Manse is run from electricity, no other heat source being a condition imposed by Historic Scotland." Josephine was beginning to make this opportunity sound quite complicated. No just going out there to live a simple life. There were no useable vehicles and only one road servicing radar installations at the top of the hill. The simple constraint of not making any material changes was beginning to sound like a major complication, thought Dave.

Deborah felt happy enough with domestic arrangements, they were going to be her responsibility. She did wonder about food supplies but Josephine put her mind at rest.

"You will find literally tons of tinned food in the Base kitchen area and large amounts of dried food. Admittedly fresh vegetables could be a problem but you can make arrangements with the day boat operators to help you with fresh supplies. I have no problem with a bit of fishing if you want to supplement your diet."

"No collecting birds' eggs then?" Dave joked. "No!" came Josephine's less jokey reply.

She continued, "Travel out will be our responsibility. The successful applicant family will sail from Harris at our expense. To start with you shouldn't need much. Sleeping bags might be an idea before you get the bedding aired. There will have been no heat in the Manse since the departure of the MOD a few weeks ago. I have checked and the telephone and internet service are still functioning so you can get in touch for advice anytime, should you need to. There will be plenty of things to ask about in the first few days and I can't think of all possibilities right now. We need someone to be able to start in the Spring and be able to adapt in situ, so to speak."

The Factor glanced at his watch. "We do have to interview a couple of others today so I think it's time to draw things to a close, for now. We hope to make a decision later today or tomorrow at the latest. I have just one last question, "If offered the position of voluntary custodian would you accept?"

Considering their recent experiences of life in Edinburgh, riots, unemployment and violent crime there was no question. Dave and Deborah both agreed that if offered the position they would accept immediately and be ready to go out to St Kilda as soon as feasible. Deborah did think about what they would do with their house but considering the housing shortage in the city, letting should not be a problem. The letting could be arranged through an estate agent and the rent would more than cover their mortgage. This was a once in a lifetime opportunity and they were going to seize it. They had no further questions though no doubt there would be plenty more in the coming weeks if they were appointed.

The two managers conferred for a few minutes. There were no obvious problems with the Williams as custodian family. Colin, the Factor had noticed Dave deep in thought, almost absent while his wife was speaking. Could be a sign either way, but so far so good, he thought.

Sally turned up for interview at 11.00 prompt. She had been waiting outside since 10.15 and had overheard a fair amount of the Williams' interview. They sounded as if they were certain to get the main position but as she had said in her application, she could happily be a long term volunteer on the island. It seemed crazy, she thought, to turn down her intimate knowledge of the place and her medical training.

She sat down in the chair still slightly warm where Dave had left it. "Hello again, Sally." Josephine greeted her warmly. They knew each other from earlier days at St Kilda. She remembered Sally as keeping herself to herself away from working hours. She was never one for socializing in the bar, a bit of a loner, probably not that well suited to leading a resettlement party. She had no close family either. They both knew the psychological perils embedded in St Kilda's evacuated landscape but it was good Sally had offered herself in a voluntary role. With her local knowledge and medical skills she would be good support for the custodian, but not as custodian herself.

"Let me get this right, Sally. You have withdrawn your application to be custodian but instead are offering your services as long-term volunteer?"

"Yes, I feel I don't have the personal support needed to be custodian but feel that for the right person or family I could give support. I know the place intimately and have the right medical skills to assist in almost any situation that might arise. Almost the only thing I didn't manage to do in my years on St Kilda was to act as midwife, not very likely in a predominantly male community."

"Well you never know, Sally." Josephine thought about the two young women likely arriving with Dave and Deborah Williams in the spring. She was reminded of the occasional female volunteer having gone back to the mainland pregnant after a few weeks in the male dominated island community. There had been tensions whenever any of the guys got emotionally involved, tensions that were felt right across the one-sided community. The combination of cheap alcohol, bored men and excitable young women in holiday mode was just asking for trouble but pleasures generally seemed to outweigh any resultant pain. Outcomes were not always painful, most of the few women working on the island had had a fling at some time or other. Away from mainland social constraints, St Kilda was known for being a place to let your hair down, for dropping inhibitions. Even the Wee Frees had come to the island in the 19th century to escape secular constraints on the mainland. That extra fifty miles beyond the Outer Hebrides made all the difference. Some things would never change and resettlement was going to prove an interesting experiment.

Sally's interview ended amicably and Josephine was satisfied things were dropping into place for the resettlement plan she had in mind. There was just the question of engaging a naturalist to compliment the custodian family.

Steve Brown was due for interview thirty minutes after Sally left but after twenty-five minutes there was no sign of him. Back in Sussex, Steve had been having serious qualms about St Kilda. He loved the birds, the wide open spaces and solitude. It was the latter that concerned him. In crowded south-east England people were known to go out of their way to avoid having to communicate with each other. Like so many others in the south of England, Steve preferred to be safely locked inside a shell of his own making. Maybe it was of the landscape's making? In the carefully manicured landscape of the South Downs National Park nature was controlled, encouraged on human terms only. Southern ecology had cultural parameters. At St Kilda, engaging with the natural world was likely to prove physically hazardous and people were likely to be more genuinely social in a challenging and potentially dangerous environment. Steve was someone most would consider a loner, though he himself failed to recognize this. He could interact with those around him as well as anyone as long as it was in a structured context. He fell down when interactions took a personal direction and it was this possibility that frightened him. In his sea-side town flat he could retreat from close personal involvement, preferring to interact with so called friends on social network websites. On the small island of St Kilda he would most likely be forced into situations where close contact and engagement with real rather than virtual social situations would be unavoidable. Dreams of working as naturalist on a remote island were easier to leave as just dreams. Reality would likely prove too difficult. Steve was never going to find out having failed to attend the interview. Even making a telephone call to withdraw his application had proved too difficult.

Josephine spoke to Colin. "It doesn't look like Steve Brown is going to turn up. Shall we simply propose the Williams and Sally to HR?"

Josephine was secretly relieved not to have to put Steve through an interview for a position she had no intention of offering him. Anne Williams looked a strong minded and strong bodied lass and was keen to be a volunteer naturalist and her sister Erica had the maturity to cope with whatever life threw at her. That was Josephine's opinion and after a brief discussion on practicalities, the two managers agreed that Dave Williams, his wife, daughters and Sally MacDonald would be an ideal combination for the position. The Williams as custodian family supported by Sally as general assistant and paramedic should the need arise. Accommodation would be simple with the Williams in the Manse and Sally MacDonald in the Factors House up on the village street. All that remained was for them all to get to know each other before committing to months, if not years in each other's company on the island. Josephine and Colin decided that after formally offering them their positions they should all meet together socially.

Deborah opened the envelope bearing the WIT logo. It had dropped through their letter box less than twenty-four hours after the Trust interview. Dave had popped out to the newsagents but she would give him the news when he got back. They would tell the girls when they got out of bed, but Anne had already noted her mother's excitement and felt a supreme satisfaction that she would at last be going to the place she had only imagined could be her home. Erica was still fast asleep after working into the small hours at the Fir Cone.

Dave had no job to give up, Deborah, with some

trepidation, was thinking about her resignation letter to Castlemount High. Anne, she knew would be delighted at the prospect but Erica was a slight unknown. Since her abortion she had matured into a confident young woman, seemingly capable and adaptable but, she had noticed, Erica hid her real feelings behind a mask of projected confidence. She had been though a harrowing year and Deborah felt sure the scars had not yet completely healed. Erica had shown enthusiasm when Dave first suggested this life changing experience for them. Now there was going to be the matter of letting their Edinburgh house to pay the mortgage while they were away. There were several local estate agents who could handle that for them so no real problem there. Just a plethora of questions to ask about practicalities concerning supplies, bedding, communication and so on. She could ask those questions at the informal social evening Josephine suggested they should attend the following Friday night.

Deborah had been slightly surprised at Dave's somewhat qualified reaction to the news that that they had been offered the custodian post. It was as if he had gone through the motions of getting this far but now the dream was in their grasp he felt uneasy about it. She thought it was typical of him to opt for the dream rather than the reality of going to St Kilda, but she was determined they were going to follow this through for the girls' sake as much as their own.

Sally Macdonald received her letter around the same time and was immediately looking forward to leaving the small flat she rented in Glasgow. She could pack all that mattered to her into a large rucksack and a couple of suitcases. With barely a month passed since ending her last shift on the island, returning there seemed perfectly normal. She had earned a good salary as nurse but this time it would be unpaid. This was going to take some explaining to the Jobcentre but she would be available for work, as they requested, within one and a half hour's travelling time from home. That ruled out just about everything from St Kilda. Still that was life and she was going to make the most of this opportunity with no rent to pay and all else found. She was looking forward to meeting the Williams family on Friday. The thought occurred that past demographics were going to be reversed at St Kilda. Four women and one man occupying the island, another imbalance but one she imagined more in favor of sustainable community life. This was going to be a good resettlement, she determined.

The social evening had been organized by arrangement with the successful applicants. Josephine was surprised that they had chosen the Fir Cone but then again she was pleased they hadn't chosen a high class venue in New Town either. Dave and Deborah arrived around seven-thirty and chatted with Erica and Anne who had been there since six. Not quite a night off for Erica but she was easy about it, the Fir Cone being effectively a second home for her. Sally arrived just after eight, apologizing profusely for the lateness of her train from Glasgow. Apparently the early winter cold had frozen points somewhere along the line. Josephine had been there since six-thirty and had been quietly working away in a corner of the bar. She closed her lap-top and greeted the Williams as new found friends. Josephine was genuinely happy that after an absence of almost a century there would be family life at St Kilda again. She bought them all drinks though she was careful to keep away from alcohol herself. It was going to be an important evening and she needed to keep her antennae finely tuned for any hint of dissonance. Josephine bought Sally a drink as soon as she sat down with them and the socializing process began.

The women chatted like old friends, though Josephine noted Deborah was taking in the implications of this adventure in a considered as much as an enthusiastic way. She was being as realistic as she could about the opportunity being offered her family. Dave was being a little reticent and not adding much to the women's conversation. Josephine actually had to prompt him for his opinion on a couple of occasions. It seemed to her that he was disengaging and letting the women take the lead in planning the resettlement.

"Come on, Dad. We are going to need your input as well. St Kilda wouldn't be the same without a man!" Erica had chosen her irony carefully. Josephine was happy that Dave had laughed at his daughter's joke at his expense. It was a good sign but had he reacted angrily she would have had concerns over her decision to appoint him.

Dave Williams relaxed after that and entered the discussions enthusiastically. The history of the island was brought up by Sally and the way the community had had been brow beaten into submission by Free Church Ministers, the fun of living replaced by endless hard work and servitude to a demanding male God. Dave chose his moment and with a twinkle in his eye, joked that 'his' women had better behave themselves or Lady Grange's House could be put to use once again. Josephine made no comment but Sally knew that Lady Grange had been exiled on St Kilda for questioning her husband's politics during Scotland's Jacobite rebellion. Josephine noted a darker expression passing briefly before Sally regained her bubbly enthusiasm for the adventure. Deborah appeared the pragmatic member of the group. Anne was enraptured at the prospect of recording St Kilda's bird life and as the youngest member of the party, Josephine hoped, little affected by more adult convolutions. Erica, after initial cheeriness, now appeared deep in thought. That could be a good sign too, thought Josephine. Erica is taking the prospect of life on St Kilda seriously. Erica was in fact suddenly feeling very homesick at the prospect of leaving social life at the Fir Cone behind. When one of the customers she knew better from the other side of the bar asked when the Fir Cone crowd could arrange to visit she felt much better. After the student debacle on Calton Hill, her friend Dan had continued to use the Fir Cone and though things remained tense between them he and Dave were still on speaking terms although his plying other students with hallucinogenic mushrooms had played no small part in Dave's dismissal from the Geography department.

"See you at St Kilda, Erica!" Dan's cheery promise saw a second dark expression flicker cross Sally's face as she joked with the other women at the table. This time Dave stood up to buy a round and invited Dan to join them. With his long dark hair tied back in a ponytail, dark stubble and athletic build Dave could see why his female students had more often than not made fools of themselves over him. However, in these changed circumstances he would be glad of some male support at a table of enthusiastic women. Dan and Erica had been friends for some time but as far as Dave knew there had never been any romantic involvement between them. Since the abortion, Erica had shown no inclination for physical closeness or, he had noticed on more than one occasion, close emotional connection with any of the/ men in her life and that included him, her father. The jokes and innuendoes were there to cover up lingering effects of the shattering of her girlish innocence and withdrawal from studies at Edinburgh College of Art. Looking at her now, animated and enlivened at the prospect of St Kilda and chatting happily with Dan about it, Dave felt proud to be her stepfather. Josephine noted that Deborah was exhibiting subtle signs of concern over plans being discussed for Dan to visit the following summer, when his own studies were completed.

The group chatted on amicably and Josephine bought another round making sure to stay sober herself. Not just the matter of driving but she wanted to remain sensitive to the nuances however subtle. Dan had been an unexpected development but he seemed a positive addition to the dynamic. An obvious friend of Erica's and a support for Dave in the face of the female bonding that was going on. In her enthusiasm, Sally had forgotten to leave in time to get back to

Waverley Station for her train to Glasgow. Luckily Deborah offered to put her up on the settee for the night at their place. The evening came to a natural end around eleven when an involuntary yawn from Anne suggested it was time to close. Josephine shook hands with everyone, including Dan, and bid them good night. She would be in touch regarding travel arrangements over the coming week. She wanted everything firmly in place before the birds and tourists returned in April.

Arriving back with Sally in tow, the Williams saw their home in a new light. The presently unaffordable mortgage insignificant compared to the warmth and security their centrally heated home offered on such a cold night. Sally was especially appreciative having missed the train back to her unheated flat in Glasgow. She stroked the cat snoozing contentedly on the settee where she would shortly be making her own bed. No-one had mentioned pets during the evening but if the past protocols had any bearing the cat would have to be left behind. Josephine would no doubt remind them of this later.

Erica had stayed on at the Fir Cone and Anne went straight to her room after they had returned. She would sit up into the small hours contacting virtual friends around the world on social media. Deborah fell asleep almost immediately but after they got into bed, Dave could not sleep running the events of the previous month through his head over and over again. In his day, students would have enjoyed and benefitted from the research exercise. He just couldn't fathom why it had all gone so badly wrong. Probing under Edinburgh's genteel skin had scared the students so much he had been dismissed from the department. Had society changed so much since his own student days? As Dave turned over to sleep next to Deborah he comforted himself with the thought that at St Kilda, at least, the landscape would be fresh and honest.

4 EVACUATION

The village always looked bleak at this time of the year. The grass growing along the street cropped short by hungry sheep. Now several weeks after the autumn equinox, brown tinged moorland framed the green fields between the empty village and the sea. The late greenness a legacy of excessive manuring with seabird offal and domestic waste in the nineteenth century. Nothing had been wasted, human waste and kitchen scrapings valued as much as the cattle dung collected from the byres each winter. As the population aged, peat ash contributed less to the nutritious compost spread over the fields. The nitrogenous waste from the byres began to lose its potash balance as fewer villagers found the necessary strength to collect peats for the hearth fires in the final few years of occupancy. Climbing 1400 feet to the nearest peat beds on Mullach Mór had stretched beyond the physical abilities of most. Over the latter years of the nineteenth century, fit young adults drifted away in search of an easier life. Had they stayed at home to take their part in the community, the future could have been sustainable. Following the First World War the few young men still at St Kilda were tempted away by the tales of soldiers stationed on the island. Young women too, left with their more worldly new partners. It had been a genuinely sad day when on August 29th 1930, the few remaining villagers left for good. The final straw had been the death of one of the few young mothers on the island having died of appendicitis. The community had been unable to get medical help in time. The family names are commemorated on discretely placed pieces of slate inside the remains of their former homes, quickly devastated by winter storms following the evacuation. Look closely and preservation becomes apparent, ruined cottages stand for eternity uninhabitable but still recognizable for the homes they once were.

By the early 21st century, the Trust had sympathetically restored six of the cottages to accommodate conservation volunteers, building contractors and the odd tourist party. The sheep researchers, on island for around nine months of the year considered their rented cottages as second homes. The island lies in the path of regular, deep Atlantic depressions and the habitable cottages required increasing protection from the elements, winter storms seemed to be increasing in intensity as the climate changed. The phenomenon of the North Atlantic Oscillation meant that sooner or later, the jet stream would move and the weather patterns change for better or for worse. The Warden always had to consider the worst case scenario when closing the cottages down for the winter. As well as a thorough cleaning, felt roofs had to be re-proofed and the wire ties holding them down repaired. Inside anything perishable had to be removed and furniture either removed from contact with the floor or protected by placing wooden legs inside cut off plastic bottles. Tables wore waterproof boots to protect their wooden legs from water trickling through the walls and settling on the concrete floors. Just one of the problems inherent to the modernized 19th century cottages still battling against rather than existing with the environment. Another problem for the Victorian builders had been and still was, the wind. With idyllic summer views across the bay, in winter the cottages stood four square against south-easterly gales. At the end of September, the Warden boarded the windows against elemental forces rarely experienced on the mainland. Chipped and eroded paint on these boards bears witness to the relentless ferocity of the winter at St Kilda. In between the boarded up 'white' houses with pitched roofs and clean rooms with chimneys stand 1830s 'black' houses. For the modernizing St Kildans, vernacular, almost timeless, Hebridean blackhouses evolved with the landscape of the Western Isles and evolved to withstand almost everything the North Atlantic weather systems could throw at them. Oval in shape, these self-built homes had double skinned dry stone walls filled with rammed earth, the roofs were thatched and, most importantly, orientated end on to the prevailing gales. The irregular surfaces of the walls helped to break the force of the wind and in the living space a central hearth sent smoke up to preserve the thatch. Due to the smoke, these cottages were indeed black inside and, with the house cow over wintering on the lower side of the cottage, tourists often reported having to clamber over the dung heap also added to by the human occupants, when invited inside. Each year thatch was repaired or replaced, the discarded material removed adding to the village compost system.

Very little remained of the old village, the nucleated clachan, found by the English philanthropist who arrived in 1812. Avoiding the Mediterranean warzone, his romantic cruise brought Thomas Dyke Acland to discover a remote and superstitious British community living in what he imagined to be illiterate squalor and poverty. The cash free independent community had also come to the attention of the Church of Scotland.

Not long after Acland's visit Dr John MacDonald landed in Glen Bay on a missionary visit to the community. He was to report back to the Church of Scotland in Edinburgh and concurred with Acland that the lives of the inhabitants were in need of improvement, not just physically and agriculturally but also spiritually. Through his radical preaching, Dr John MacDonald came to be known as the Apostle of the North. At St Kilda he found what he considered a semi-pagan community ripe for evangelical conversion. Dr John MacDonald raised money to build a church and Manse and appointed Reverend Neil Mackenzie as the resident minister. Enabled by outside money and Mackenzie's missionary zeal the St Kildans were persuaded to abandon their vernacular and sustainable way of life in favor of a fundamental and puritan vision of the world around them. Architectural design, written scripture and a cash economy were readily adopted by the easily converted and generally enthusiastic St Kildans.

For the Reverend Mackenzie the re-housing project epitomized the manly virtue of hard work without desire for physical gain or female approbation. The social tensions and confusion brought by this nineteenth century restructuring of once egalitarian village life sowed seeds leading to voluntary evacuation in 1930.

In 1843 the Free Church decision to break away from the secular Church of Scotland took place in the neo-classical church of St. Andrew in the New Town of Edinburgh. The final insult came with the congregation being told, that in challenging the Enlightenment, the more devout Christian attendees in the Edinburgh assembly had no more effect than the kick of a well bred horse. Like other contemporary movements, out at St Kilda, the Free Church of Scotland sought to build a religious community away from fear of scientific contradiction. At first resisted by the landlord, Macleod of Dunvegan, it took the departure of eight families on 13th November 1852 for Macleod to allow the Free Church foothold in the community. Taking advantage of their landlord's assisted passage scheme to leave Macleod lands in the Hebrides, they were not victims of Highland Clearance. Rather the eight families sought sanctuary in Australia where they could enact their religious beliefs without, what they considered, growing secular persecution. The ill-fated attempt to escape from St Kilda led to many of the thirty-six voyagers dying from modern diseases from which their isolated lives had afforded them no immunity and away from the island's medicinal herbs, particularly Mothan, they had no way to treat the simplest of their ailments as they headed toward a new life away from the unhappiness of their island home. Like flies caught on the leaves of Mothan, there would be no escape for the St Kildans.

Economic depression meant the Macleod estate could ill afford to lose any more of its productive tenants and the Free Church was allowed a foothold at St Kilda. The Free Church was to compound patriarchal management of the island into the early 20th century when the loss of young adults to the mainland made the community unviable. The ageing cottagers, predominantly women, evacuated their village in 1930 for what they thought would be an easier life in the west Highlands.

With the villagers gone, the island became first a private then a designated National Nature Reserve. Like the Free Church ministers before them, twentieth century scientists wished to work without interruption or fear of contradiction. Film maker Michael Powell was discouraged from filming on St Kilda for fear of encouraging exiled villagers to return seeking employment in return for local knowledge. Free thinking St Kildans were henceforth to be confined to postcard and myth. Julian Huxley, a naturalist arriving with the military advance party in 1957, encountered one such returned native and recorded *Homo sapiens* (1) on his species list. Such was the academic detachment from the human life that preceded scientific and military occupation of the island in 1957. The Enlightened and supposedly objective scientists were now detaching themselves from fear of cultural contradiction at St Kilda as had the Free Church elders not much over a hundred years before them. Male detachment had failed before and would fail again.

Operation Hardrock, an appropriate name for the Cold War invasion, reflected a vision that saw St Kilda as just that, a hard rock 50 miles out from South Uist. A place for military detachment, for manly activities without too many soft distractions. Operation Hardrock came just five years before the Cuban Missile Crisis when any thinking person in the UK feared annihilation, caught in an east-west nuclear stand-off. Out on the edge of the UK, St Kilda provided both a listening station in the north Atlantic and a down range monitoring station for tactical missiles test fired from South Uist. In the 19th century St Kilda was considered the *Ultima Thule,* an imagined sanctuary at the edge of the British world. With the nation under threat of nuclear Armageddon, the late 20th century saw this vision managed by the former National Trust for Scotland. Visitors arriving at the jetty after an arduous three hour crossing from Harris would admit to considering themselves pilgrims to an island reverberating with echoes of lost Utopia. Members of the current day Free Church saw themselves as truer pilgrims to the emptied village where the small Kirk, still consecrated, held the occasional service for those wishing to reconnect with a purer Christianity. On the occasion of the eightieth anniversary of the evacuation in 2010, Free Church members from Lewis arrived once more to worship, their congregation connecting with the wildness of ocean, the seals and seabirds as had, they perceived, the islanders a century before.

It is said that tourists look only for that which conforms to their expectations while the traveler explores the reality of the destination. The RAF arrived in 1957. Their personnel travelling to the island by helicopter shuttle from Benbecula. It was important staff did not stay on the island long enough to become new natives but for the young men working with heavy machinery to build the new road, St Kilda was no tourist destination. At the end of the working day, the empty reality of St Kilda crept in like the winter damp trickling through the thin walls of the Victorian cottages.

Operation Hardrock began with a tented village developing into the quick build concrete complex that was to stagger on beyond its expected 50 year lifespan. With the exception of the Manse, no thought was given to reusing the cottages other than crushed as aggregate for concrete mixing. New buildings were thrown up but by the time the MOD evacuated, the buildings as were their recent occupants, were already crumbling. Sprayed concrete was disintegrating and wire mesh exposed to the salt laden winds accelerating the corrosion of St Kilda's military folly. The belief that mutually assured destruction was the key to peace in an enlightened world had for nearly a century consciously ignored family values that could have maintained life on the island. With the prohibitive cost of running a diesel fueled power-station and deteriorating mental health of the workforce the British government deemed there was no other option but to close the Base.

Military occupation had spawned a culture sustainable for a few months at the most. The emptied landscape made bearable through subsidized alcohol and in later years, internet and multi-channel satellite TV. Side effects were alcohol dependency and lack of female company for the men who worked there. Lack of female company had led to tension, sometimes physical confrontation, when the Trust's female conservation volunteers first appeared. In response transitory females often formed distrustful cliques, suspicious of insincere male attention. For the older men, an easier option was to drink in the bar and watch uncomplicated dance divas gyrate across the huge plasma television screen in the Puff-Inn. Although unsustainable, the retreat of the military from their self-imposed Dystopia created a new set of problems for the Western Isles Trust.

The plan had always been to evacuate the equipment by the end of September, before the weather broke and winter sea conditions made landing craft crossings impossible. The world had been a very different place in 1957 when the MOD launched their occupation. In the second decade of twenty-first century the UK found itself in a subordinate position compared to the successful new economies of Asia. Even the once powerful United States had managed to adapt and work with rather than against a world they had previously sought to dominate by trade or military might. In Britain, without political impact or effective military power, the ongoing economic crisis led to newly commissioned naval shipping being sold off to defray sovereign debt. The scrapping of newly completed Nimrod surveillance aircraft had been just the beginning of the scale-down of UK armed forces.

In the last week of October the RFA *Mounts Bay* anchored inside the shelter of Village Bay. Her sister ship the *Largs Bay* had already been sold for service with the Australian Navy. That had been a result of the Defense Review of 2010. The only other available transport had been the *MV Randaberg*, successor to the red and white liveried *MV Elektron* lost in a North Sea storm a couple of years before. The commercial owners of the brand new *MV Ranadberg* had declined to send their flagship to St Kilda given the inglorious history of *MV Elektron* running aground at St Kilda in 2000. The *Elektron* had subsequently and mysteriously lost power and had to be towed back to port in hurricane conditions. Salvage costs had come close to making the owners insolvent. Since that event commercial landing craft operators would demand a premium before quoting for working in the unpredictable conditions at St Kilda where, increasingly, violent winds could rise on the clearest of days.

The RAF Chinook had arrived the day before and only managed to land at St Kilda's small heliport with some difficulty. Even such a large helicopter had been severely buffeted by turbulent gusts spinning down from Conachair. Only the sudden reversal of the windsock prepared the helicopter's pilot for the unexpected wind blast unsettling their landing. On the morning of the evacuation, the pilot was prepared for unpredictable gusts unlike the previous afternoon when a blast of turbulent air had nearly slammed the large machine into the steep slopes of Mullach Sgar just after take-off.

Bill and Archie were watching the aircraft lift off, its

cargo net loaded with sixty years of military paraphernalia, and land it on the heaving deck of the *Mounts Bay*. "I never thought I would see this day, Archie. This island has had its ups and downs but I'm going to miss the old place."

"Not me, Bill" he replied. "And my missus will be glad to see me home a bit more." Archie had only worked there month on, month off for a couple of years while Bill had been there since 1989. Some men had adapted but for many, posting to St Kilda had led to breakdowns either mental or marital, sometimes both.

The Chinook had begun to take the island vehicles across to the *Mounts Bay*. The two small vans and three Landrovers had been all in a day's work for the pilot from RAF Odiham. The big Case 821E wheeled loader was a different matter. Having pushed many stranded landing craft off the beach it was now itself in need of assistance from the Chinook and its cargo nets. After some deliberation, the decision had been taken to drive the Case onto doubled up steel sand ladders that had lain almost unused since 1957. Equally vintage steel chains were fitted with five ton hooks and locked onto the four corners of the impromptu cradle. The weight of the chains meant that four men were needed to stand cheek to jowl on the cab roof to attach the chains to cargo hooks on galvanized steel cables lowered from the Chinook hovering a safe distance above them. With the chains attached, the men jumped down and watched from the safety of the concrete 'Airport Lounge'. The men gasped and swore as the Chinook tried to lift off with the familiar Case twisting and swinging beneath. Even with two 4,868-horsepower Honeywell engines at full power the CH-47F heavy lift helicopter was at its operational limit with the jury rigged payload swinging in gusting winds that again seemed to have come out of nowhere. At full power the Chinook staggered the half mile over the water toward the *Mounts Bay*. In spite of the load being spread across four corners of the Case, the pilot had severe misgivings about this job.

Concentrating hard and only just managing to lift the Case up to landing deck level the pilot hadn't seen the large water devil spinning across the bay toward the ship. A particularly powerful down draft sent a spinning column of spray driving toward the Chinook and its unwieldy load. For the rusting 1950s chains the sudden twist of the Case proved too much and a welded link near the hook attached to the front of the nearside sand ladders gave way. The Case tilted and, on three chains, swung violently into the raised accommodation decks forward of the loading cranes. Several cabins on levels 3 and 4 were badly damaged and the Case fell heavily onto the landing deck where it narrowly avoided demolishing one of the ship's cranes. For the Chinook pilot this was going to a bad day. For the Captain of the *Mounts Bay*, he had begun to wish he had never sailed for St Kilda.

The chains and sand ladders still attached to the Chinook had become entangled with the cranes and the pilot decided to jettison the improvised hoist and leave the *Mounts Bay* crew to sort out the mess. Radio traffic between the bridge and the Chinook had been clearly heard in the Base. It had not been pleasant listening even if confined to precise military phraseology. The Case was a write-off but, apart from loss of heavy duty steel cables, the Chinook was unscathed. The Captain of RFA *Mounts Bay* was going to have to write an embarrassing report concerning around a million pounds worth of damage to his ship already earmarked to join the *Largs Bay* in Australia the following spring.

"Well, that's fucked it Archie." As acting Base Supervisor, Bill had seen many minor disasters and near misses at St Kilda in his thirty year service. The previous Supervisor's fatal Landrover crash had been the worst but no one had witnessed the accident apart from the Bonxies, he quipped grimly. The wreck of the Case, thanks to the RAF's cocked-up Chinook airlift had been most dramatic and in full view of the few remaining employees on the island. Hovering safely beyond Levenish, away from still aggressively turbulent winds, the Chinook pilot radioed that after the incident with the Case he had to return to Benbecula to refuel. He would then be flying back to Hampshire for hoist repairs, giving him time to think how to explain the loss of four heavy steel cables and cargo hooks, one Case forward loader and a million pounds worth of damage to the RFA *Mounts Bay*.

The accident with the Case had been the last straw for the MOD and it was decided to cut their losses and abandon the remaining equipment at St Kilda. After all it wasn't going anywhere. The Trust would no doubt complain but considering their practical need for MOD logistics, there wasn't much they could do about it. No organization could afford to stand on high-horse principles ignoring economic realities anymore. At the end of the day St Kilda was owned by the Western Isles Trust and the MOD only tenants and, if they did a flit, at the end of the day it was the landlord's problem.

Bill and Archie were joined by Sally then duty nurse on her final monthly shift. Scratching her head she commented it was a pity the end had to be marked by such a fiasco. The logistics personnel had always prided themselves on handling their equipment professionally. Forwarding turntable trailers onto rolling landing craft had been no mean feat, nor had driving the old Case down from TOTH, negotiating the hairpin bends without so much as a scratch. Just recently, a mobile crane had had a few scary moments up there operated by a civilian driver. The Case had come to the rescue and connected with a heavy tow chain the MOD driver had put the loader into low ratio and acted as a brake engine while the ungainly crane made its precarious descent down the twisting mountain road. She had heard of so many feats of men and machines since 1957. As one of the paramedics she had also treated many accidents when men and machines had not always worked in harmony. One accident she remembered well was the time a drunken airman, on her watch, fell off the top of the sea defense wall twenty feet onto the rocks below. A young woman conservation volunteer had been skinny-dipping on a warm midsummer night. The word had got around and the men poured out of the Puff-Inn to the cliff edge like lemmings to watch her and the airman went straight over. That was the story going round Harris anyway. It was yet another believable story from an unbelievable island.

"You coming to the bar tonight, Sal?" Bill asked. "It's going to be your last chance before we close down the power station."

Sally MacDonald was rarely seen in the bar. Apart from a disproportionate amount of her professional time having been spent on alcohol relate accidents she found the male bar room banter depressing and the perpetual dancing girls on the TV pathetic. She preferred to spend her evenings in her own quarters socializing with the occasional female Trust volunteer.

"OK, just for once I will, Bill. Can't see me coming to much harm with you and Archie there!" Sally was known to make the occasional exception.

"Rodger and Roz will be there too and I reckon Keith and John will turn up. It's the last night for all of us."

Rodger the cook and his assistant, Roz had been coming to St Kilda for years. He had previously worked in the Army Catering Corps in locations across Europe and the Middle East. Roz had come to work on St Kilda following break-up of her marriage in Glasgow. She preferred her month on St Kilda to the month spent in a lonely bed-sit back in town. Keith was the senior radar technician on the island and had been busy supervising the dismantling of sensitive tracking equipment for Chinook transport to the *Mounts Bay*. John turned his hand to many jobs on island from simple plumbing to cleaning and decorating. He had lately been responsible for ordering supplies and receiving deliveries arriving on the weekly supply helicopter service. There had been no landing craft since August due to strong winds driving heavy seas from the north. Now the Warden had been made redundant it would have been up to him to have set the traps and watch out for rats when the landing craft dropped its ramp on the beach. Rats had never been known on the island but there was always a first time. The large St Kilda Field Mouse confused a few of the visitors but unlike rats they posed little threat to ground nesting seabirds. Anyone who spent more than a few hours on the island knew that Great Skuas, the Bonxies, were the real problem, slaughtering Puffins and other smaller seabirds to feed their ever growing numbers. They took lambs too but with statutory protection there was little that could be done. John despised these large brown predators and would have given almost anything for a 20 gauge shotgun and an endless supply of cartridges. It was rumored he had taken his Sunday walks into Glen Mór to 'accidentally' tread on eggs of ground nesting Bonxies. John generally loved all birds but not Great Skuas.

The last remaining staff met in the Puff-Inn around 8.30 that evening. There hadn't been much clearing up after the evening meal in the canteen. Not like the heady days a few summers before when there had been around fifty men to cater for. Roz made a special effort to make the bar homely. It wasn't often a woman's touch could prevail in this male social bastion. The pool tables hadn't been used much in the final months after they had been told the Base was being closed down. At her request the large plasma screen TV was turned off and she had brought her own CD player and gentler music to play that evening. She had placed small tea-lights on each table. The effect was almost magical. Multitudes of model Puffins, Puffin murals and all manner of Puffin related artefacts appeared to come to life in the flickering candlelight. It felt good to be able to express her creative side instead of consistently having to weather storms of male banter across the bar.

Sally was the first to arrive. Roz heard her footsteps coming down the corridor from the nurse's quarter before she hesitatingly opened the door into the bar. "Oh, my...Roz. You have made this lovely. How many are coming tonight?"

"Well, there's me and you," she laughed. "Bill and Archie, Keith, John and, of course, Rodger." Roz and Rodger had got on like brother and sister since he arrived to replace Janet, the previous head cook. Janet had retired the previous year after accepting the posting on St Kilda following an acrimonious divorce. In her spare time, Janet became a successful artist inspired by the land and seascapes around her. She had retired to South Uist to concentrate on her painting and be closer to her children. Rodger came in next. Collapsing into a deep armchair and staring at the blank screen. "Sorry Rodge, no TV tonight, not even football." Roz teased him as he was known for dressing up in Glasgow Rangers colors whenever his team's matches were televised. He jokingly protested but, on this their last night on the island, there was no need for bravado. It was going to be an emotional evening for all of them. The other four came in together and Roz took up her position behind the bar. It was usual for catering staff to do a stint behind the bar in addition to kitchen and canteen work. With such small numbers they had decided to share the cleaning duties between them rather than leave it all to Roz and Rodger.

"Here we are then, the Last of the St Kildans......"

Bill was being ironic as usual though this time he meant it. Everyone had a drink, even Sally, as they sat round the table under the picture window looking out over Village Bay. It had seemed a strange juxtaposition with the large plasma screen TV next to the window framing one of the best known world heritage views in Europe. Roz put on one of her CDs and with drinks in hand the small group began to relax and for once open up to each other.

The lights of the *Mounts Bay* looked like a small industrial complex shining across the waters. They could see the wrecked Case had been put back on its wheels and somehow maneuvered away from the damaged accommodation decks. Not a good ending for their beloved Case, thought Archie, but he had to concede the guys on the ship must have worked hard to get it upright even with the help of the cranes.

Without the sound of the TV the rumbling of the diesel power station a hundred yards away could be faintly heard inside. It had been installed back in the 1970s and, for the men, was the beating heart of St Kilda. Landing craft shuttled back and forth over the years bringing diesel fuel to keep the island's life blood flowing. Bill had often wondered why it hadn't been replaced with wind turbines. After all St Kilda had limitless wind energy to draw on rather than rely on fossil fuel. Apparently it was something to do with the island's world heritage status. The seascape would be affected as visitors approached from Harris. St Kilda wouldn't look so wild and remote for the tourists but then the diesel power station always came as a shock when they landed. Campers often complained about the continuous rumble of the engines through the night, not to mention the bright lights around the buildings.

The lights were no problem this time of the year but in late summer, the Warden was always asking for them to be turned off. The steady rumble and bright lights attracted young sea birds leaving their burrows at night. They fledglings left at night to avoid predation but after weeks in dark underground nests were drawn to lights around the Base. The Warden would go out at dawn, catch the Pufflings and whatever else turned up before Skuas spotted the youngsters and kept them in cardboard boxes before release from the jetty in the evening. There would be no more need for that after the generator engines were shut down for the final time in the morning. There would be some good equipment left behind now the Chinook airlift had been abandoned. The remaining personnel would be picked up by a *Mounts Bay* RIB. The Base had its own rigid hulled inflatable boat but that had already been airlifted aboard.

"Hey Bill!' where've you gone?" Rodger snapped him back from his thoughts.

Roz passed round a bowl of mixed nuts. Sally was looking a bit uncomfortable. She was happier in her professional role and mixing in an intimate group took her out of her comfort zone. She took a deep drink from her glass and found herself speaking from the heart for maybe the first time on the island.

"This place, it could have been so good here...." Roz noticed the changed tone in Sally's voice and her moistening eyes. "These cottages, deliberately standing empty where there could have been families, could have been some life in this village. There would have been enough work on the Base or TOTH for a couple of families. Instead what do we have? St Kilda might as well be an oil-rig rather than a place where people have, and still could, live, love and grow old together. They could be real homes again."

"Hold on, Sal. That's a bit hard isn't it? We have had a good time here, though sometimes I have gone near stir crazy when the helicopter's been late. Then when I am home and the wife's getting at me I'm glad to be back." Rodger was never shy to respond when he felt criticized. In spite of his bluster he had a sensitive side.

"That's just it Rodger. No one ever stays here long enough to make it their home. We do a month on and a month off. No-one is encouraged to stay here, this place should be resettled and given some life again."

Sally's argument had been raised before. Archaeologists working on the island often commented that they found it hard to contextualize what they were doing when the clock had been deliberately stopped at the end of August 1930. Sally had thought about that too, perceiving an island frustrated by consciously blocked opportunity. A lot of the men suffering from alcohol induced depression had passed through her consulting room. They thought St Kilda a place of doom. She had seen several of the guys come to her in tears saying they could stand it no longer and she had to arrange quick evacuation for their psychological well-being. Enlightenment dialectic continued to echo on the island long after the rest of the UK had seen sense by working toward social equality and diversity. Sally hadn't mixed much on an informal basis. She was known well enough as the woman to see for a cut finger or a bad back. Occasional tea and sympathy but she had kept her personal side well hidden, only Roz had noticed she had never honestly opened up. Now with an unaccustomed drink in her hand, she was ready to explode.

"Just look at this place, it's completely unsustainable! It's only the alcohol that keeps you men sane, if that's not a contradiction in terms. The drink is so cheap here, if it was at mainland prices it wouldn't be quite so bad. The place is killing you all and you just don't see it! There's so much free energy here, wind and wave power unmatched anywhere else in the UK but what do we do? Preserve this, conserve that and all the time bring in ship loads of diesel, it's completely mad. The birds are dying because of climate change and still we burn diesel day and night. We are drinking ourselves stupid in an open air museum and walking around in an open air laboratory that we are not allowed to touch. Too tell you the truth I am fucking glad the Base is closing. Until there's some real life here, I for one will never be coming back."

The rest of the room watched astounded as Sally threw down her glass and ran out of the bar in tears. "Fuck me!' said Rodger. "She must have been bottling that up for years." Roz gave him a knowing look. "Just leave it, Rodge. Let her go and cry it out. I'm sure she'll be OK in the morning."

"Aye, but she has a point though." Bill was the oldest employee on the island. In his early sixties he wasn't going to do anything but take retirement when he left the island. The younger men returned to their glasses and suggested they put the TV back on. Roz conceded defeat but left her tea-light candles on the table. The younger men relaxed without the need for too much thought or conversation as the driving beat of dance music returned to the bar to smother the rumble of the power station. Pouting girls pranced provocatively out of reach for their entertainment. "You boys won't be seeing them again after we shut the power down tomorrow." As usual, Bill had the last word on matters aired in the bar.

Having never been enthusiastic for MTV or the many copy-cat channels, Bill and Archie left early to return to their respective rooms. Roz asked the other two to turn the TV off when they left and retired to her own room. As was the time honored custom in the Puff-Inn she sold a couple of rounds, albeit small ones, before bringing down the shutters for the last time.

After breakfast Bill and Archie walked across the tired lawn toward the power station. Architecturally it could have been designed by Porsche in the 1970s, a modernist icon of a time when oil was cheap and seemingly inexhaustible. A couple of years previous it had been shut down for major servicing and the replacement generator brought by landing craft had been just a quarter of the size. In the last year most visitors had arrived on-board cruise ships heading to or from Arctic destinations. In the northern winter they headed south to the Antarctic, their crews commenting on the similarity of St Kilda's monolithic power station to those in Greenland and

South Georgia.

The power-station emitted its comforting rumble twenty-four hours a day, seven days a week and it was now about to fall silent, may be forever. The feral Soay sheep always began their daily grazing routine around the power-station. The turf on the south side of the building was cropped bare and, until the alpha females gave the subtle signal to move, the sheep lay down contentedly, chewing cud in the morning sunshine. Only when the weather turned wet and windy did they take shelter on the north side of the building, joining a mix of tired seabirds, some having been drawn to walkway lights the night before.

"They're going to miss us, Bill." Archie had a soft spot for the sheep.

"Aye, they won't know what to do without you, Archie." Bill was nothing if not pragmatic. He was resigned to the end of his job and getting home to South Uist. At his age there would be no more work but Archie, having come from a farming background, would most likely find work with the RSPB project to conserve farmland birds through sustainable farming in the Hebrides. Thank goodness the MOD was still going to favor human life on the islands, he thought. The Hebrides Range was staying open as a source of employment for the younger men and their families. The future of the Balivanich camp, directly linked to the St Kilda operation looked more precarious. Bill and Archie began their close-down work and silence fell surprisingly quickly. Rodger employed a portable diesel generator to operate a minimum service for the canteen. The guys would still need lunch before they left. The plan had been to drain down the fuel lines and ensure all remaining diesel would be stored in the tanks near the helipad. Fire risk with diesel fuel was considered minimal but always a possibility. In the limited time available they simply turned off the fuel valves where the pipes entered the building. They didn't even have time to drain down the water cooling system. Through heat exchangers waste heat was transferred into heating pipes around the base. One small token toward sustainability, Bill thought ruefully. A pity the MOD had never built the wind turbines he had dreamed of maintaining since realizing the unsustainability of diesel power generation on the island.

As a final gesture Bill and Archie made a thorough job of topping up all the vital fluids of the power-station, greasing whatever still had to be greased in a digital age. They swept the generator hall floor and tidied the small office and tool store. When they left around 11.30 the closedown had begun to feel like a routine maintenance event but locking the doors behind them, the unaccustomed silence indicated finality. There was no need to turn off already extinguished lights. The two men walked over to the quadrant housing the KGB offices. Kilda Generating Board, the name had been thought up long before Bill had worked there and the workshop and garage area nicknamed Red Square. Fire assembly notices put up in the restored cottages told occupants to gather at Red Square. Not the best of instructions, Bill had thought, but everyone working on the island knew what it meant. The intention had been to take all the tools away with them but it wasn't going to happen now. All the vehicles had gone with the exception of the rusty bulldozer that had probably been there since Operation Hardrock. The large Romney hut that passed for a sports hall had collapsed the previous year. Strong winds had made short work of the corrugated iron structure and this winter's storms would certainly see the curved sheets blow away to join remains of galvanized roof sheets blown into burns and gullies from roofs of then new cottages in the 1860s.

12.30pm and time for lunch. Bill and Angus walked over to the canteen to join the others for their last meal at St Kilda. It seemed somewhat odd that in spite of their small company, lunch appeared just as usual. They walked along the counter helping themselves from the hot buffet. The small generator outside the back door could be heard working overtime and then suddenly spluttered to a halt.

"Sodding Hell!" Rodger had trouble to cope with the machine's insatiable demand for fuel since Bill and Angus had closed down the power-station. He went outside and topped up the small tank on top of the air-cooled engine. Thankfully, he thought, he wouldn't be doing this again tonight. In fact they would hardly have time to clear up before donning their protective immersion suits ready for the short RIB crossing out to the *Mounts Bay*. With the heating system shut down it was already beginning to feel cold. The heat from the one functioning cooker barely noticeable in the gathering chill of the damp autumn afternoon.

Rodger had prepared one vegetarian meal for Sally. He was glad she wasn't Vegan too, he thought. That would have been problematic. Sally had appeared for lunch, though had been noticeably missing at breakfast. Pre-empting further embarrassment she apologized for her previous night's outburst. "I really am sorry for my behavior last night. Think I really should join in with the rest of you more often and not bottle things up so much."

Inwardly, Roz agreed. The men nodded but let the issue wash past them without comment. "Don't let it get you down, Sal. It's this island, we all blow up sometimes. Real storm in a tea-cup place, as we all know, eh?"

"Thanks, Roz." Sally was genuinely grateful for Roz's tactful understanding of what it was like to be a woman frustrated on an island where male indifference smothered the opportunities women perceived. With lunch finished and no more essential work to complete all but Rodger and Roz went to pack their personal belongings and get ready for departure. The men had their own personal immersion suits so no need to struggle into outfits too large or too small which had often been the case for newer employees. Rodger and Roz quickly managed to wash the crockery by hand, there being neither time nor power for the dishwasher. Plates and cups were stacked to dry and the floor given a cursory mop. That was as far as it went that afternoon. Roz thought that whoever followed them would find a *Mary Celeste* kitchen when they arrived. She couldn't quite believe no one would be taking over when they finished their shift.

Rodger was still struggling to zip-up his extra-extra-large immersion suit when the RIB left the *Mounts Bay*. Bouncing across the choppy swell the open craft soon reached relative calm in the lee of the jetty. The skipper checked his watch before jumping ashore to tie the craft to the mooring bollards. The small group of six remaining Base employees had already carried their luggage down the historic slipway. Once the best in the Hebrides or so they had been told. Seal pups certainly liked to sunbathe on it in the Spring but now just the odd sheep trotted down to nibble at seaweed washed up on the strand line. Sheep adapted to eating seaweed survived winter hardship better than those dependent on more conventional grazing.

There had been no vehicle to transport their belongings down the steep flagstone slipway. It was never easy at the best of times and a sudden squall had brought with it a shower of rain making the slope particularly treacherous. Carrying their rucksacks and suitcases down to the jetty steps and the waiting RIB, Bill was reminded of an old archive film he had seen of the first evacuation in 1930. Here they were again carrying their belongings down the self-same slipway to a waiting boat. There was absolutely no chance of getting the *Mounts Bay* anywhere near the jetty of course. It was the RIB or nothing. Passing their bags down to the skipper, he stacked them between the seats. The craft was designed to carry twelve so there was plenty of space. The steps had always been tricky and, with the warden gone, untreated algae had made them very slippery. Bill slipped and hit the back of his head on the concrete steps. He picked himself up seemingly unhurt but quickly became aware of slight double vision. Sally had been right behind him, her hands full with her own luggage and unable to save his fall.

"Shit! Oh, fucking shit!" Sally's second public outburst in twenty four hours betrayed her nervous tension. She couldn't get off St Kilda quick enough and now it seemed there was another casualty for her to deal with. It was lucky he hadn't fallen into the sea, the red life rings had long been put into store. For some reason the warden had seemed more concerned about them not being washed away in bad weather than be available in case of emergency, but still that was Trust business. A remote manager had given the instruction but it made no sense to her to put away lifesaving equipment for the winter, precisely the time it was most likely to be needed. On top of swearing, she wanted to scream with frustration.

Bill had mild concussion and would soon be OK. She told him he had hurt his dignity more than anything else and the small party took their places in the RIB. The skipper pulled away from the jetty, heading out to the *Mounts Bay*, sheltering from the swell beside the promontory of Dun. This finger of rock and turf had been attached to the main island of Hirta three hundred years ago but the sea broke through one dramatic February night creating the most recent island in the St Kildan archipelago. Out in the open, the swell caused the fast RIB to bounce across the bay slowing only as it approached the rear of *Mounts Bay*. The purpose built pontoon took the small boat and its passengers into a different, almost industrial world and, once inside the warren of warm corridors, apart from the movement of the swell, being on board felt barely distinguishable from any military land base.

The officer who met the embarking St Kilda team informed them they would be sailing at 18.00 and directed them to the spacious Mess to relax and wait for their evening meal. Clearing condensation from the windows, Bill looked back across Village Bay, toward the jetty they had left only a few minutes before. The end had come swiftly, St Kilda was once again evacuated and that night would lie empty for only the second time since 1957. There had been a brief evacuation in the winter of 2014/15 when hurricane force winds had blown down the geodesic domes covering the radar equipment on top of the hill. Today's squalls seemed to have blown over and in the evening light the diesel power-station stood silent, an icon of modernity grey against the darkening brown winter slopes of Conachair. The olive green Base buildings were less distinguishable, the Trust had insisted on the subdued color scheme and now only the Factor's House and the refurbished Minister's Manse stood out white as darkness fell.

The younger members of the group seemed happy to be leaving and were already up and exploring the mess deck. Bill sat by the window and pondered on this the second major evacuation in a hundred years. The island really was empty now, just a few Fulmars still swirling around the cliff tops, all other sea-birds having left by the end of September. Even the Bonxies had left, their young well fed on smaller birds and carrion. There would be no more easy pickings until the spring lambs played among the Mothan in An Lag. Bill smiled at the effect the new borehole had on the flora there. Mothan flourished where the water overflowed. As a diabetic he rarely touched alcohol and the sweetly tainted tap water had had no effect on him. As such, he had been unaware of the subtle perceptual changes that had taken place in the minds of his alcohol drinking colleagues. The Base had been left in a hurry, not just because of the Chinook and Case fiasco but because of an approaching deep Atlantic depression forecast for sea areas Rockall and Malin. This was likely to bring Force Nine south easterly gales to the Hebrides sea area before it dissipated over the mainland. Even for a large ship, like the RFA *Mounts Bay*, Village Bay was no place to be caught in a strong south-easterly. Sheltered on all sides except from the open south-east, Village Bay had seen many wrecks in the shortly predicted sea conditions.

At 18.00 sharp, the large ship raised its anchor and with a parting blast from its horn the Captain began the night sailing to Loch Carnon. As the ship pulled away, Bill pondered on the end of another era for St Kilda. Cradling her coffee, Sally considered how it might have been, how her life might have panned out on the island had women been allowed their full role in the twentieth century community. The others were simply glad to be going home. Queuing at the buffet counter, Rodger was glad to be on the consumer side for once, joking with Roz, who was unusually subdued, about what they would be getting up to back in Glasgow. Rodger had already assumed that their friendship would continue back on the mainland. As for Archie, it looked like a return to farm-work on the crofts of South Uist. He had an interview with the RSPB the following week. Sally was considering joining the bank nursing team in the Uists for NHS Scotland rather than stay in Glasgow and the rest of the St Kilda employees were to be absorbed into the existing Hebrides Range workforce. She had heard the Western Isles Trust had already placed their advert in the Scottish national press for a custodian family to take up residence at St Kilda.

5 SHOOTING PARTY

Snow had been falling heavily in the Cairngorms. Cold weather had come early and the mountain hares had not completed their seasonal transition from brown to white making them easy prey for Golden Eagles watching from above. As top predators, the eagles were a success story in an area ecologically degraded by two centuries of field sports. The native Caledonian forest had also become moribund due to grazing from the excessive population of Red Deer. For two centuries, much of Scotland's greatest mountain landscape had been carefully managed to perpetuate high numbers of deer and Red Grouse for the autumn shooting season. Scottish Natural Heritage had previously been able to pull in European funding under the EC Habitats Directive to regenerate the native forest ecosystem dominated by Scots Pine. However, away from managed regeneration areas ancient trees fell to die alone among the grass and bracken that should have been full of vigorous young seedling trees. Red Squirrels took a fair number of pine seeds but intensive deer grazing was the prime cause of the failing regeneration of the once widespread Caledonian Forest.

European money paid for deer proof fencing to be erected protecting river valleys from excessive grazing and inside the fences the ecosystem was recovering. High fences however proved an obstacle to hill walkers and a death trap for Black Grouse blindly flying into the high tensile steel strands. They also looked very ugly and with a mission to re-wild their Cairngorm estate, one enlightened conservation organization had taken the controversial decision to remove fences and discourage deer by other methods. To the ecologists re-introduction of the wolf, absent for four hundred years would have been the obvious answer. They knew that idea would be a non-starter due to opposition from the upland farming community and commercial deer stalking interests. Tourism was already beginning to suffer through declining deer numbers in the Cairngorms. This particular estate had taken a zero tolerance approach to deer in the unfenced regeneration zones, they were simply shot on sight, as vermin, with no closed season. Scottish Natural Heritage had licensed year round slaughter and to the local human community it seemed natural science experimentation was taking priority over livelihoods dependent on field sports, or so the Press was reporting.

It was obvious to the Scottish Game Keepers Association that with intensive culling on the estate a vacuum would be created drawing in deer from surrounding estates, in turn reducing deer numbers available for their stalking clients. There would be a considerable reduction in income as wealthy shooters began to seek out sport elsewhere. The experiment proved a failure and, with deer being drawn in from the open moor to shelter in the regenerating forest, numbers on the Estate actually increased. To complicate management further, SNH funding to the Estate was conditional on deer numbers being reduced to a level sustainable within the forest ecosystem.

The corporate group from Canary Wharf had chartered their small plane from London City Airport and were looking forward to catching the Red Hind shooting season in November. Stag shooting had closed in Scotland but continued for a few weeks longer down on Exmoor where milder conditions prevailed. Even in south-west England snows had come unusually early to the moors. The Cairngorms were encountering winter conditions rarely experienced before mid-January.

The Estate stalkers were in position, their white overalls

improvised camouflage for the snowy conditions. The small team of marksmen lay in wait watching for the deer to break cover. Their rifles were fitted with sound moderators to minimize disturbance to both winter walkers and protected wildlife. On the other side of the plantation Estate workers stood in line, clearly visible on the snow covered hill side. The nominated leader of the group waited until he received the VHF radio message that the stalkers were in position. Raising his arm he waved silently to the rest of the team strung in a line across the hill side. The beaters entered the forest, as far as possible keeping to their line to minimize sheltering deer running back past them. It proved hard work crossing snow filled ditches and clambering over fallen timber; the plantation had been allowed to, in forestry terms, deteriorate to a semi-natural condition. Nervous deer bolted in front of the line of men and women struggling through deep snow among the trees. Calling and shouting they drove the fearful deer forward into the designated killing zone. The thuds of shots hitting their targets were barely audible in the wintry landscape as, one after another, fleeing deer were silently gunned down. When the killing was finished the carcasses were loaded onto the stalkers' soft-tracked all-terrain vehicle to be taken for processing in the Estate deer larder. Income from the sale of carcasses to game dealers was hoped to offset the expected reduction in Estate funding from SNH. For weekend walkers and cross-country skiers from Aberdeen, the only signs of conservationist slaughter were blood stains in the snow and the odd cartridge case missed by the stalkers clearing up before returning to their vehicles.

Complaints were vociferous. Even employed stalkers resented having to take part in the slaughter. The Head Stalker resigned and the Estate Manager protested against a culling policy that contradicted game management wisdom acquired over generations. Protesting cost him his job and a younger more ecologically focused manager came to the Estate to continue the regeneration program. Accessible to the centers of population, the Scottish government planned to re-wild the Cairngorms as an icon of national virtue. For hill walking politicians, inspired by John Muir and Yellowstone National Park, re-wilding the Cairngorms was long overdue. For the indigenous human community it felt like ethnic cleansing. The Monarch of the Glen was now considered vermin.

The shooting party had had a less than satisfactory corporate break. The Braemar hotel had been first class and, unexpected in the heart of the highlands, they found the Lithuanian staff provided exemplary service. The problem had been the lack of deer. Long days out on the hill with their allocated stalkers had proved fruitless. A few deer had been seen but, since the culling policy on the Estate began, the deer had become alert and stayed beyond range of their hunting rifles. One of the Guests, frustrated at the lack of result, wanted to chance a long shot but was dissuaded by the stalker whose professional ethics demanded certainty of a clean kill before the shot was taken. The City group were used to achieving results and were no strangers to hard work but days on the wintry hillside with nothing to show for it were beginning to feel like failure. Back at the hotel they drafted a complaint to the sporting tour company which had organized the trip.

After several heated telephone calls it was agreed that the group would be offered a complimentary sightseeing flight. The consensus was that after an unproductive week on unseasonably snowy hillsides the flight should take in a different aspect of what Scotland could offer. The tour company contacted the small charter plane operator they had used to fly the group to Aberdeen. The pilot suggested a trip out to the Hebrides and over to the St Kilda islands. The frustrated shooters grudgingly accepted the compromise of a flight out to the World Heritage Site before turning south for London. Time was going to be tight and the pilot insisted the group loaded all their luggage into the light aircraft before the flight. They could refuel at Benbecula and then just make it back to London in one stretch.

Early on Monday morning, a large taxi picked up the considerably hung-over party from their hotel in Braemar and dropped them off just over an hour later at Aberdeen airport. Suitcases, rucksacks and rifle cases were loaded into the twin engine Piper Chieftain. The aircraft could accommodate all nine of the group and their luggage and, with large passenger windows, it proved ideal for the sightseeing flight setting off that wintry morning.

The aircraft took off easily and turned west toward the Cairngorms, approaching the mountains shortly after leaving Aberdeen. Following Royal Deeside, the pilot pointed out Balmoral Castle the Queen's Scottish holiday home. Looking down the frustrated shooting party could see groups of stags and hinds on the slopes of Lochnagar. It seemed the neighboring estate had managed to keep its herds at home to prevent slaughter on neighboring land to the west of Braemar. The Piper continued along Glen Dee past the Victorian Hunting Lodge that had been their home for the past week. The visible absence of deer was remarked upon compared with Balmoral. As Glen Dee turned northward into the snowy heart of the mountains the aircraft continued straight on its westward course passing over more remote and deserted hunting lodges before the ground dropped toward Aviemore. The wintry scene below proved mesmerizing until the group were snapped out of their reverie by unexpected clear air turbulence. The Piper dropped three hundred feet before levelling out and climbing back to its intended flight path.

"Sorry about that folks," the pilot apologized. "We are on the edge of localized high pressure over the cold Cairngorms but the atmospheric pressure will be dropping as we head into the milder west. Just to let you know it will also be getting windier as we approach the Atlantic. Probably a good idea to make sure your seatbelts stay fastened. The north-westerlies can get pretty gusty over the hills."

The landscape began to change beneath them as the Piper headed toward Mallaig. Passing over Loch Lochy and Loch Arkaig their thoughts turned toward summer fishing holidays. Passing to the south of Skye the pilot pointed out the islands of Eigg, Rum and Canna. He was in his favorite flying area, the mix of sea and islands a welcome change from executive commuter flights to the south of England or across the North Sea to Norway.

"Canna's an interesting place. They were advertising for new families to move there. They wanted to re-kindle the dying community rather than the usual story of just funding nature conservation down there."

His comment brought murmurs of agreement from the party deprived of their sport by nature conservation in the Cairngorms.

"The only trouble was the people they reintroduced fell out with each other, cooped up on a small island like that. Then they voted with their feet and bloody left again. I did hear they are going to try something similar at St Kilda. As you will shortly see, that really is some remote place. Good luck to them is all I can say!"

Looking down they could see the Caledonian MacBraine car ferry crossing from Oban to Lochboisdale on South Uist. It was a signal for the pilot to turn the aircraft north-west toward Benbecula. The small aircraft was already being tracked by radar operators at the Hebrides Missile Range. The bored operators often broke their tedium by tracking small low flying planes as if they were actual targets for their missile testing program. After the embarrassing terrorist incident on St Kilda an airborne suicide attack had to be considered an actual possibility. The Piper pilot assumed they had already locked onto his aircraft and jokingly called them on VHF.

"OK guys, I've got my hands up! – over."

"Bang, bang, you're dead man!" came the Hebridean accented reply. "Where are you heading?"

"St Kilda. Just for a ride around the islands. What are the conditions like out there today? – over."

The Hebridean Range provided very detailed weather forecasts, ostensibly for missile testing. The last thing anyone wanted was a Sea Viper getting blown off course and scaring the living daylights out of a passing fishing boat or, worse still, hitting St Kilda. It had happened once before in the early days of military occupation when a small missile had hit the Base kitchens. Although the incident had occurred way back in the 1960s the Hebrides Range had never been able to live it down.

"Wind 335 degrees, 25 knots, gusting to 45 on the cliff tops, no significant cloud base to worry about – over."

"Thanks guys, might be a bit bumpy out there but catch you later when I refuel at Benbecula – Piper out."

The MOD meteorologists predicted fresh north-west winds gusting at the cliff edges. At least there would be no low cloud to worry about. St Kilda often generated long plumes of cloud when moist warm air lifted over the peaks of Conachair and Boreray. Under such conditions helicopter flights to the island were suspended until visibility improved. Even out over the Western Isles the unusually cold weather and northerly winds were keeping the air clear and the St Kilda archipelago could be clearly seen on the horizon. Beneath them the Monach islands lay deserted. No one bothered putting sheep there nowadays and the lighthouse keeper's cottage had stood empty since 1948 when automation made human presence redundant. In the 1990s a new lighthouse was erected but unable to withstand the Atlantic storms, so the pilot told his passengers, the modern light was transferred to the old Stevenson tower. Stevenson, he also told them, had built the Manse at St Kilda. That building too had stood the test of time while more modern structures failed out there.

As the plane approached St Kilda from the south-east the enormity of the rocky islands awed the party into silence. To the right the Stacs of Boreray were white with guano from the largest Gannet colony in the north Atlantic. The young Gannets had left by the start of October but the prevailing high pressure weather system had prevented autumnal storms from washing away evidence of their birthplace. Three hundred odd white sheep grazed the green south facing slope, descendants of a flock of Highland Blackface abandoned in 1930 when the elderly human residents evacuated their homes. For the sight-seeing party from southern England it seemed incredible that generations of St Kildans had actually farmed such a precipitous place.

Approaching Levenish, the small and barren island marking the entrance to Village Bay, the pilot turned south to begin a clockwise circuit of the main island of Hirta. "Afraid the rules say we have to keep two miles away from the island so we don't disturb the birds. There's none nesting here this time of year but I don't want a blot on my license." The pilot added, "But as the island is now empty since the military left we can get in a bit closer. We're not supposed to go below two thousand feet either. The guys on the Ranges will be tracking us but they won't mind. It's only the Western Isles Trust who would kick up a fuss and they've laid off their last Warden. Don't think there is anyone back on the island yet."

The Piper followed the cliffs of Dun about a thousand yards out from sea caverns running right under the headland. Skimming the waves, the party could see the waters of Village Bay reflecting through the tunnels. The motion of the swell clearly visible rising and falling against the pink algae encrusted rock walls. With the wind coming from the north-west the Piper could maintain lift at lower speeds. Looking up, the passengers saw the ruins of the radar installation on Mullach Sgar, the incredible boulder scree slopes of Carn Mór and the towering cliffs of Mullach Bi in near perfect conditions. Ahead was the island of Soay, the island of sheep so named by Norse Viking settlers twelve hundred years earlier. Between Hirta and Soay lay a narrow strait blocked by Stac Biorach and Stac Shoaigh, both capped with the droppings of seasonally departed Guillemots. Beneath they saw caves, homes to countless Atlantic Grey seals and safe refuges from Orca hunting packs. Killer whale pods were known to occasionally operate around St Kilda but the departing Base staff had reported seeing them more frequently that autumn, following shoals of fish in the colder waters driven down from the north. Just one of the party spotted the wreckage of a WWII Wellington bomber lying shattered on the scree slope on east side of Soay, facing Hirta. He thought it inappropriate to comment on it as the pilot struggled with strong gusts as the aircraft approached the gap between the two islands. The pilot opened the throttles and turned the Piper westwards to circuit Soay rather than risk flying through unpredictable turbulence in the canyon like gap.

Out to the north of Soay flying conditions became more predictable and the north-westerly wind gave the aircraft extra lift as they turned eastward to fly between Boreray and Hirta. They were going to fly past the highest sea cliff in Europe, so the pilot said. The shooter who spotted the wrecked Wellington on Soay mentioned what he had seen. The pilot had thought not to mention this aspect of St Kilda's history either but now it had been brought up he would explain the wreckage.

"There were a spate of air-wrecks here during the Second World War. No one really knows why but for a while the island effectively came under an air exclusion zone. Probably the most famous wreck is that of a Sunderland Flying Boat that came down in the valley you can see on your right." The Piper was passing Glen Bay, the northerly landing point taken advantage of by the terrorists earlier that year. They could see the long valley, Glen Mór reaching up to the damaged radomes on the spine of the island. Now, seventy years after the event, pieces of aluminum fuselage and other plane wreckage could still be seen strewn across the glen.

"It's a war grave," said the pilot. "Strangely, no one really knows what happened. As you can see there should be no real problem flying up that glen and over the top into Village Bay. Should be a piece of cake, the military tried to bury the remains of the plane so no one else would fly up there sight-seeing and come to a similar fate. No one can explain that crash, really strange."

The aircraft continued along the eastern cliffs of Hirta, hardly a bird to be seen at that time of year. As the pilot said, they were looking at the highest sea-cliffs in Europe rising almost sheer to nearly fifteen hundred feet above sea level. The lonely trig point at the island summit of Conachair marked the last point in the UK cartographic triangulation survey, now obsolete since the advent of GPS navigation. Hard to imagine that Ordnance Surveyors carried bags of concrete all the way up there just so they could build a fixed point on the planet to work from. Apparently they went up at night with a car battery and spot light to point at the next trig point on the Uists, That way they could plot their survey lines without heat haze causing refraction problems.

"You are a mine of information aren't you?" Jim Wilson was a London city banker and voiced his frustration to the pilot. "We came up here for a shooting holiday, for a bit of excitement and I suppose that's it now?"

The aircraft was approaching Levenish again and the pilot was turning to follow a bearing of 120 degrees for Benbecula airport where he would refuel for the journey south. Jim's words stung the pilot, after all it wasn't his fault the Estate had slaughtered most of the deer in the southern Cairngorms.

"OK, point taken. I'll take you around the island of Boreray before we head back." The group murmured assent but Jim had a further idea. "We came to Scotland for a bit of excitement and it looks like we have a chance out here. How about you flying us up the Glen, the one where the Sunderland crashed. That lumbering great thing never made it over the top but in this light and faster plane it should be great. It would be really cool if you'd fly as fast and low as you can up the valley and then rocket over the ridge into Village Bay. Better than Alton Towers, I reckon. Come on pilot what do think?"

"What I think is I would stand a good chance of losing my job. I also think, given the reputation this island has for flyers it would be a very foolish maneuver."

"Oh, come on man. Be the hero just for once, eh?"

"Well, I suppose it could be done. We'd have a strong tailwind with the north-westerly funneling up the glen today. It's just the last few hundred meters that I have heard can be so unpredictable. A mate of mine used to fly helicopters out here and he said if anyone asked you to fly up there to run as fast as possible in the opposite direction. Even landing at the helipad required nerves of steel as the wind can turn all points of the compass in the last moments of approach. It's the turbulence caused by this mountain suddenly jutting out of the sea into Atlantic airstreams, so the weathermen tell us."

"Yeah, right," said Jim. "Tell you what, why don't we have a whip round for you? Say we put in a tenner each for the ride of a lifetime. Then we can go back to Benbecula and fuel up for the trip home."

The rest of the group had mixed feelings about flying up the glen but not wanting to appear less than macho in the face of Jim's challenge they agreed. "OK, ninety quid says you can do it! That's straight in your pocket, mate. As you said earlier there's no on the island to report you, so come on, let's go for it!"

The pilot was beginning to get caught up in the bravado and he could certainly use the extra cash. Even as a well-paid charter pilot his work was drying up. The recession was worsening and the cash would pay for a good meal out with his wife. They had been having difficulties lately and he felt she would appreciate the gesture if nothing else.

"Well alright but be prepared for turbulence as we pass over the top. It's a clear day and I won't be able to see anything until it hits us. I am going to have to insist you all wear your seatbelts or I may be scraping you off the cabin ceiling after we drop. So first a circuit of Boreray then I'll open her up and give you the low-level ride of your life. Don't say I didn't warn you, though."

The pilot pocketed the ninety pounds cash and banked the aircraft to the left for the short crossing and anti-clockwise circuit of Boreray, St Kilda's second biggest island. "Widdershins, folks! Hope you're not superstitious about these things?" the pilot joked. This stunt was going to take a lot of fuel and they would definitely be going absolutely straight back to Benbecula afterwards. It did feel good though, just to let go of the reins for once. God knows what the Range radar operators would think as they tracked him from South Uist. Probably wouldn't see him until he came over the top anyway. That's if they were watching St Kilda at all, they rarely bothered unless the Range was active.

Passing round the north side of Boreray, the shooting party seemed barely interested in the spectacular scenery passing on their left. Not one of them mentioned the white sheep that had somehow survived for a hundred years since their last shepherd abandoned them. The aircraft turned at the guano whitened stacs and dropped height to begin its approach to Glen Bay. "Bit like beginning an attack run, eh lads?" The ex-RAF pilot was getting into this and dropped the aircraft as low as he dared, skimming the waves would have been out of the question at any other time of the year as a million seabirds would have risen in protest making bird-strike inevitable. As it was on that day only a few curious seals turned to watch as the twin engine Piper flew toward them with throttles wide open. The engine note in the cabin changed from a gentle purr to a full throated snarl. Outside, had there been anyone to hear it, the scream of the fast approaching plane would have suggested the drama of a full blown military exercise. That it was a civilian charter plane breaking every flying regulation in the St Kilda book, the flight path was not only irresponsible but had they made it back to Benbecula, would have been virtually unbelievable.

"OK folks, here we go! Hold on tight, don't say I didn't warn you!" The occupants of the Piper were glued to the windows as the ground-rush brought home just how low and fast they were actually flying. The first sudden gust lifted the plane over the low cliff at the foot of the glen. The small aircraft roared over the small lochan locally known as the Bonxie Pond and past the ruined homestead of the Amazon's House, built by an unknown community thousands of years earlier. The pilot had accepted the challenge and was now flying as fast and low as his nerves, and the aircraft, would permit. The weather was clear and he could see the concave slope ahead rising in front of them as they sped toward the ridge before dropping into Village Bay. At this speed and low altitude, they were committed.

"Look, fucking deer, boys!" Jim spotted the flock of dark brown Soay sheep scattering in front of them. Wreckage from the Sunderland lay all around as the Piper followed the line of cleits guiding the aircraft up the rising hillside. Twelve hundred of these small stone storehouses were dotted across the islands and were uniquely built to take advantage of local wind conditions, not stand against them. Swirling winds blew through gaps in the dry stone walls and capped with turf roofs these simple but effective stone built stores dehydrated hay, peat, and other heavy island products before being carried down to the village.

The pilot suddenly realized the implication of these structures. He had read avidly about St Kilda and remembered how the villagers took advantage of the swirling wind to dry their produce. They were heading at full power into an aviator's death trap. "Brace, brace!" he screamed to the passengers, all but one out of their seats to look out of the panoramic windows.

The brown sheep had stopped running and looked back impassively as the Piper roared up toward the ridge where generations of cleit builders had taken advantage of winds that would predictably blow hard from any and all directions. Pulling back hard on the joystick the pilot managed to lift the aircraft above the certain but unseen turbulence beneath them. Such was the forward speed of the plane that the Piper enabled a near vertical climb before its underside was hit by the blast of a near gale-force north westerly air current. With the underside of the fuselage and wings hit by the blast, the near vertical aircraft was picked up and thrown across the ridge like a dry leaf. The Piper hit the ground, cart-wheeled several times before coming to rest smashed against another group of cleits in the wind gap below Mullach Bi. The propellers had hit the ground at maximum revs and the starboard engine lay ripped from the airframe. Lying almost upside down, there had been no fire or explosion. Safety features in the fuel tanks had prevented spillage. The dying aircraft and its injured occupants shifted against the cleit supporting it, machined alloy panels scraped along the hand built granite wall. The gusts subsided leaving the breeze to sough gently through rough moorland grasses until the metallic chinking of the cooling port engine finally subsided.

At the back of the plane there was just one survivor. Phil Jones had been the only one to have heeded the pilot's advice to remain strapped in his seat. Blood and body fluids were splattered against the remaining cracked windows. Several panes had been knocked out as the aircraft flexed on impact and male bodies lay broken across the shattered remains of the inverted cabin interior. The luggage hold under the tail had burst open leaving rucksacks and suit cases scattered along the earth dyke built by the St Kildan women to indicate the limit of safe grazing for cattle, long departed, which had once supported island life. Many of the cases had burst open on impact with their contents swirling around the cleits before rising to be picked up and blown over the cliff edge by unseen gusts.

Phil Jones had managed to uncomfortably extricate himself from his four point harness, falling to the padded ceiling without further injury. The wind blew through glassless window frames as he crawled out on to the moor. Trying to stand, the urge to vomit brought him back down to his knees. It was an instinctive response to the overwhelming shock of the situation and only after a few minutes retching did he finally stand. When he turned round he realized he was the only member of the party to survive the crash.

The Piper's panels scraped noisily against granite as it slid down the cleit. The sound made him turn just in time to see the plane slip and tumble over the cliff edge before another sudden gust blew him to the ground. The sound of the plane bouncing off rocks below the Lover's Stone before disappearing into the Atlantic swell was barely audible above the wind which had seemingly reappeared out of nowhere. The small aircraft sank under the waves breaking up as it fell into incredibly bio-diverse submarine caverns, one of the reasons for St Kilda's world heritage status. The battered machine and its broken occupants slid gently down to decompose in unseen chasms below the island leaving hardly a trace of their passing. The small oil slick on the surface would be dispersed in minutes by the natural energy of the north Atlantic.

Phil picked himself up confused by the suddenness of the calm that had returned. The blast of wind that had nearly sent him, maybe even tried to send him, over the edge to follow the lifeless remains of the shooting party had dropped as quickly as it had come. Looking up to Mullach Mór a thin plume of mist was beginning to stretch out above the ridge dividing the island into its two distinct halves. He thought he heard the sound of dogs howling hundreds of feet below but put it down to imagination playing tricks on him. Seals, disturbed by the falling wreckage of the Piper, had temporarily ceased their mournful song but were now resuming their eerie calls. Phil instinctively followed the path along the ridge until he could look down on the village a thousand feet below. He had failed to notice the rusting rotary engine from the wrecked Sunderland Flying Boat close to where the still warm starboard engine of the Piper lay amongst a boggy clump of Mothan, where it had been ripped off in the crash.

The line of abandoned cottages and their allotted plots appeared peaceful, conserved in their state of arrested decline. At the end of the street six cottages looked habitable with tarred roofs but not a wisp of smoke from any chimney hinted at occupancy. Beyond the whiteness of the larger Factor's House the MOD base lay silent. Its 1970s infrastructure recently evacuated. The grey power station was still connected to green fuel storage tanks above the pristine sandy beach. Not a sound other than wind and sea. Phil saw no sign of life other than brown sheep grazing the rich south-facing pastures of the croft allotments. It was a long way down to the deserted Base where help could have been found just a few weeks before. The island now felt totally devoid of human life, layer upon layer of history evident in the landscape but not a living soul to be seen. Out in the Atlantic, at least fifty miles from the nearest working telephone, Phil sat down dejected in his isolation. As awful as it had been, the wreckage of the Piper would have provided some small comfort, the broken aircraft a connection with familiar reality.

The chill wind decided matters and he began to head down toward the village. He noted with surprise that on the ridge road was written in white paint *Welcome to St Kilda* – an improvised emergency landing strip where the wind blew consistently from the north-west. The MOD had obviously learned a trick from their island forebears. He entered the radome buildings left unlocked by departing technicians. No lights came on as he flicked the wall switch inside the door and all phones were dead. Tangled steel pylons still lay where they had been felled in the terrorist attack earlier that year. A few yards down the track toward the village the wind blew strongly again, but from the south this time. Five minutes later he came to a collection of cleits protected by a circular dry stone wall. The winds were swirling again, the vortex drawing particles of dried grasses upwards until they caught the prevailing current and disappeared. He stood puzzled at the anomaly and caught sight of the helipad a few hundred feet beneath him. No wonder pilots had trouble here, he thought.

It was then that he saw the wake of a small boat moving fast across the swell from the east. He could just make it out to be a large red and white cabin cruiser and now with the wind blowing up from the bay he could clearly hear the approach of powerful diesel engines. His exhausted mind wondered how rescue could be coming before he had even called for help, still more, how could he have called for help from this abandoned place? The thought reminded him to check his mobile phone. There was no signal, it being at least fifty five miles to the nearest cell phone mast. Even with a modern smart phone he quickly realized there was no chance. The GPS function told him where he was but it couldn't let anyone else know. So how did this fast moving boat know he was there?

As quickly as he could, he ran down the hill until the pain in his knees slowed him to a walk. A large rock on the left of the road caught his attention. It looked freshly damaged as if recently hit by a vehicle. The rock marked the entrance to an old quarry just below the cluster of cleits at the meeting of the winds. He had a bad feeling about the place and hurried on downhill to where a beaten path reached from the deteriorating concrete road toward the street of abandoned cottages. He could hear the note of the powerful launch clearly now as it approached the jetty. For some reason it made a sweep past the beach before turning back to the jetty. The skipper must have been checking something in the bay before deciding to tie up alongside the sea-weed encrusted steps against the sea-wall. He was later to learn that the Western Isles Trust had forbidden compartment boats to tie up at the jetty for fear of rats or other species alien to the island coming ashore. Now the warden service had been stood down and the MOD evacuated there was no-one to enforce the rules.

Following the path past the abandoned homes, several cottages had been restored as he came nearer to the empty Base. If he was to be a modern day Robinson Crusoe, at least he would have a ready-made roof over his head, and with all these sheep, no shortage of mutton. The end of the path brought him to a second single story white house besides a simple nineteenth century church building. Compared to the villagers, the ministers who lived in the low and solid Manse must have thought their residence palatial indeed. The well-built Manse was a small compensation for those on a mission to save Britain's remotest community from their home grown freedom of religious expression. For now, Phil Jones needed saving himself and made his way down to the jetty to find a small group of men and women landing from the twin hulled *Beluga*, the red and white launch he had seen and heard roaring into the bay. Boxes were being passed from the launch onto the concrete jetty and looking up the group seemed as surprised to see him as he was to find them arriving that afternoon to resettle Britain's remotest community.

6 ARRIVAL

The confirmation letter arrived on Monday morning. It listed their itinerary and essential things to take and asked that the family be ready to go as soon as possible. Erica was the only one required to give any formal notice to her employer. Dave would just have to let the Job Centre know he would be unable to sign every fortnight and Deborah, though theoretically required to give a term's notice was effectively firing herself. A brief note to the Principal would suffice as she had no intention of returning to what she now saw as the thankless teaching profession. Anne would soon be leaving high school, post-16 so no serious problem there. Going to St Kilda would be the opportunity of a lifetime for her and, with good grades already, she could pick up her higher education as soon as they returned to the mainland.

That same afternoon Deborah made an appointment with the local estate agent and arranged to let the house, fully furnished, on a short-hold tenancy. Due to the recession letting would be no problem, she was assured. There was the matter of the cat of course, she would have to go with them, regardless of Josephine, so on the way home Deborah visited the hardware store and bought a travelling basket for her beloved pet.

The car was going to pose a problem but Erica suggested they get Dan to meet them at Leverburgh and let him drive the estate car back to Edinburgh. In return he could have free loan of the Peugeot while they were away. At first neither Dave nor Deborah were keen on the idea. They didn't know Dan that well but Erica obviously thought highly enough of him so it was arranged. He would make his way to Leverburgh on Harris by bus, staying the night in Stornoway. When they left for St Kilda he would take the car back on the condition it was looked after and serviced regularly. After the Calton Hill debacle that contributed to him losing his job, Dave wasn't certain this deal would be honored. However he was always one for looking at the optimistic side of life, so trusted Dan to keep his part of the bargain.

The list of essentials was pretty obvious; warm, waterproof outdoor clothing, stout boots, rucksacks, personal medicines and so on. Absolutely no firearms were to be taken and no alien species to be introduced whatsoever. Even then no thought was given to the cat being alien, she was simply another member of the family. Rod and line fishing would be permitted as long as this activity was kept away from areas frequented by seals. There was no need to take fishing equipment as there would be plenty stored in the boathouse adjacent the jetty. Dave was quite looking forward to fishing, he had only ever dallied with the sport in the past.

The main thing to remember was that they had volunteered as Custodians, which meant they had been accepted as volunteers to represent and maintain the interests of the Western Isles Trust on the islands. It would be a responsible role and as with former paid positions subject to regular appraisal. Josephine added that she required certificates of good health from their doctor to keep on file in Edinburgh along with any other personal information they thought relevant. As they were to be with their next of kin they could ignore that part of the medical form, but she would need emergency contacts back on the mainland should anything go seriously awry. Sally would keep a file with all their medical details to aid her in case of problems while they were there.

They were to report to Don Macintyre on Leverburgh Pier at 0800 on January 15th. He would load their belongings into his fast launch and take them out to St Kilda. The winter crossing would take about three hours and likely to be fairly rough going, so anti-seasickness medication was advised.

Josephine's letter reminded them there was no mobile phone signal on the island but they would find a satellite phone hand set and spare, fully charged batteries in the former Warden's office in the Manse. The satellite phone would be their lifeline and was to be well looked after. There was a solar panel battery charger they could use to keep the batteries charged.

The list went into minor detail regarding housekeeping standards expected but the lack of mobile phone signal and poor radio and TV reception sounded a positive bonus after their busy lives in Edinburgh. Erica had doubts about lack of mobile phone signal, but apart from that all arrangements seemed fine. They were to ring Josephine on the satellite phone as soon as they had settled in.

Christmas and New Year festivities were almost ignored in the Williams household as they prepared themselves for the trip to St Kilda. Packing, unpacking and repacking was the theme for holidays. It was a bitterly cold period but the dominant high pressure kept snow laden winds away as they completed their preparations. The cat was restless sensing change in the air. On the Friday before the January 15th rendezvous on Leverburgh Pier they loaded their final essential belongings into Dave's Peugeot estate. The cat was in her basket protesting intermittently at the unaccustomed turn of events. Setting off, leaving suburban Edinburgh for the west coast was almost an anti-climax. The only one to see them off was Dan, giving Erica a final and appreciated hug. He promised to be at Leverburgh first thing on Monday morning to collect their car.

Leaving Edinburgh they travelled west along the M8 toward Glasgow. They were to pick up Sally on the way and finding her tenement proved the first challenge of the day. Feline protests accorded with the rise in human tension as they drove around housing blocks just off central Glasgow looking for her address. Although now well into the twenty-first century, neither Dave nor Deborah had thought to equip the

Peugeot with sat-nav. Deborah's Toyota had been written off by her insurance company after being joy-ridden by the boys who had stolen it from Castlemount High School. The re-saleable sat-nav no doubt removed before the car was torched. Eventually Sally's apartment was found and she loaded her, to the Williams, surprisingly minimal belongings into their car. Dave had thoughtfully fitted the roof rack to accommodate her luggage but it turned out not to be necessary. Sally, he reminded himself, was an old St Kilda hand. She knew just to take the minimum required from regular experience travelling on the small charter helicopter from Benbecula.

Passing the turning for Glasgow Airport they crossed the Erskine Bridge bidding the Central belt goodbye and headed north-west toward Crianlarich. Following the A82 and A87 the Peugeot reached Uig ferry terminal on Skye mid-afternoon just over five hours after collecting Sally. They were only just in time for the Calmac ferry taking vehicles to Tarbert on the Isle of Harris. To Dave, who had driven his passengers all the way, the one and three-quarter hour crossing felt like a well-earned break. He settled down in the café area of the boat with enthusiasm and ordered a full fry-up meal to the dismay of Deborah who, just for the moment, thought better than challenge the cholesterol loaded assault on her husband's metabolism. Anne, surprisingly joined him in bacon and eggs while the other three women chose allegedly healthier options. Whatever the outcome of the potentially rough crossing to St Kilda, they would at least have started the voyage well fed.

The ferry sailed into the gentle north-west breeze blowing across the Minches. The motion of the sturdy ferry proved not to be a problem and Dave was spared the indignity of his usual seasickness. The catering staff in the café remarked to them how calm it was compared to conditions the previous year when many sailings had been cancelled.

"Pretty good sailor, I am!" Dave quipped to his female co-travelers. "We'll see," provoked Erica. "Just wait till we set off from Leverburgh."

Sally was silent on the subject, feeling seasickness was not appropriate topic just as they were eating. Anne was transfixed, gazing out of the windows spotting the occasional Gannet dropping like a stone to catch fish just below the surface. Swallowed whole, the Gannets then took off in front of them, flying into the wind to gain the extra lift needed for a full stomach.

Docking at Tarbert, a handful of cars, three large refrigerated vans and their occupants disembarked. The Williams party pulled into the car park in the center of the small town to get their bearings. It was late afternoon and already getting dark as the last bus pulled in from Stornoway. There would be no onward connection to Leverburgh due to lack of passengers requiring the service that evening. The financial cut-backs had curtailed the connecting service for the Berneray ferry that winter unless specifically requested. Their sailing to St Kilda was a special charter, Donald Macintyre was bringing his boat out especially for them. Even his regular summer sailings were weather dependent and passengers often had to wait several days before sea conditions were suitable for the crossing. Delayed sailings meant extra business for local bed and breakfast establishments and Don was canny enough not to deprive guest houses of business for the sake of an unpopular rough crossing. The Hebridean economy depended on mutual support. Keep everyone happy was his motto when it came to St Kilda. The independent hostel at Leverburgh, just a short walk from the Pier, had also opened especially for them. They would be out of luck with the restaurant though they had been assured by the hostel owner that bar meals would still be available in the pub.

Taking the road from Tarbert to Leverburgh, a landscape of moorland, machair, dunes and abandoned crofts opened in front of them. This area had been depopulated by forced Clearances in the nineteenth century. Once a busy and populous area, the proliferation of clearly visible hand worked lazy-beds commemorated long departed tenants. Sheep now took the place of people in this landscape and the emptiness attracted visitors from the busy mainland in search of much needed solitude. Two weeks was usually enough before the uneasy truth behind this depopulated landscape began to make itself felt. The few families still living in the decimated crofting townships were isolated as never before. The blind young man taking the summer bus back from medical appointments in Stornoway would be guided more by sounds of nature than humanity as he felt his way along the rough path from the roadside bus-stop to his cottage.

Turning right at the red telephone box on the edge of Leverburgh, Dave slowed the Peugeot slowed down as they approached the Pier with its cluster of fish sheds, workshops and pub adjacent the empty car park. Lights were on in the pub and a couple of regulars were already sat at the bar. Deborah was keen to find their accommodation before anything else so Dave turned the car round and drove back up the short hill from the Pier. The hostel stood on an area of raised ground to their right, a hundred yards or so in front of the freshly whitewashed Free Church Kirk. They had missed it driving past from the other direction but the hostel looked welcoming. It had been freshly decorated in bright and cheery colors. No problem with parking outside the door at this time of year. There were no other occupants that week and the owner, Euan invited them in with genuine enthusiasm. His partner Liz was working away as journalist assigned to report on long term effects of the continuing riots in England. Edinburgh's riot seemed to have been a one-off but Deborah was particularly keen on avoiding getting caught up in any more. They were shown to their pine clad bed-rooms, Dave and Deborah shared one room and next door Erica and Anne settled in for the night. Sally was pleased to have a double room to herself. She preferred her own company at night, spending her days mentoring and advising others was fine but out of hours, personal space meant a lot to her. The Williams cat was not allowed indoors but was accommodated in the kennel at the back of the hostel reserved for summer visitors' dogs. Euan was easy going about most things, but not the risk of fleas getting into hostel bedding.

They all agreed to meet outside in half an hour and walk down to the Moorings for their last meal out and social occasion for the foreseeable future. Walking down they could see the three refrigerated vans parked up with small auxiliary engines running to cool their loads. It had only become necessary to run the coolers in January since climate change had warmed the winter nights. It was noticeably milder in the Western Isles than in frosty Edinburgh. They would be collecting frozen fish before returning to Skye via Tarbert and then onwards to supermarkets on the mainland. Data recorders in the vans certified their contents remained frozen before unloading at the supermarkets. Should the crates thaw, however briefly, the catch would be rejected, something the west-coast fishermen could ill afford. The last of the daylight was rapidly disappearing when they entered the warmth of the pub. Erica had already remarked that it seemed less cold here than it would have been in Edinburgh that night. Dave, as geographer, was about to enlighten her on the effect of the Gulf Stream on the Western Isles but thought better of it. He had had a long day, in fact it felt like considerably more than a day since they set out on the M8 that morning. It seemed time ran slower in the west. Sunset was certainly thirty minutes later than Edinburgh. Maybe I've got Peugeot estate lag, he mused to himself.

Gathering at the bar they studied the menu. There were no specials out of season so it was going to be micro-waved meals or nothing. Fresh salad was an unexpected surprise in January. The pub had links with the organic growers co-operative for Harris and Lewis. Idealistic incomers had arrived in the latter decade of the twentieth century and had now become established members of the community. Initially expected to fail, their endeavors had brought a new energy to the dying area south of Stornoway. Polytunnels could provide fresh produce at most times of the year, even in January. Wind energy supplied cheap electricity for the extra lighting needed to extend the short natural winter daylight. Polytunnel greenhouses were commonplace and should winter gales destroy the coverings they were easy and cheap to replace. With the price of sheep fluctuating year on year, many land owners had embraced wind-turbines to supplement their income. The big development on Harris had been controversial but for a while local builders found a new source of employment. The controversy was soon forgotten when the returns started to role in. Wind was free and available all year round to all in the Hebrides prepared to harness its natural energy.

Dave bought a round of dark local beer. He was hard up since losing his job but the occasion demanded the gesture. Anne asked for a soft drink and was satisfied with a cola. The others gratefully accepted the Hebridean beers. The food came within a few minutes, nothing that special but at the end of a long day the Moorings provided a good meal in the small dining room adjacent the bar. The five travelers were hungry and ate virtually in silence. As they finished their meals, Erica commented she had just seen a middle-aged man enter the bar with a guitar case. A few minutes later a woman carrying a fiddle came in followed by another younger man with a banjo. It seemed to Dave that the Moorings was hosting a music session. A final bonus before they set off for an unknown chapter of life in the morning.

The session proved to be a quieter affair than he had expected. After all it was only January and the three musicians from Leverburgh came to the Moorings to practice in the warmth of the pub as much as anything else. It also seemed a bit odd to Dave that the trio were playing country and western classics rather than so called Celtic music he had expected to hear in the Hebrides. It seemed the locals liked country and western and the band kept atmospheric ballads, jigs and reels for tourists in the summer months.

This time Deborah got up to buy the round. Dave felt uncomfortable but too tired to protest. With a sigh he sat back against the bench and turned to his daughters. "So, here we are. What do you expect the next few months are going to be like?"

Erica smiled and shrugged. "Don't really know, Dad. It is going to be interesting though. We will just have to wait and see what happens."

"Anne?" She looked up from studying a tourist brochure on Hebridean wildlife. "Sorry, Dad. What was that?"

"I was wondering how you expect to find life at St Kilda?"

"Oh, that's easy. I'll be studying the birds and any other wildlife. I am looking forward to recording it for the Western Isles Trust. My long term aim is to work for them out there, it would be just perfect. Realistically though, I doubt anyone will get employed solely as an ecologist in this recession. Yes, I am really looking forward to walking out each day with my binoculars and camera. It's a dream come true!"

Sally, though not directly involved in the conversation felt the need to comment. "What you will find is an end to social life as you know it. The island is effectively dead. It was problematic before, when the MOD guys were there, but we will be starting with a pretty clean sheet. I know the place but you are going to have to make your own lives and entertainment out there."

Erica remained silent but Anne was adamant. "I don't need a social life! I'd be quite happy without anyone out there at all. Anyway, people ruin things for me."

Returning with a tray of drinks, Deborah frowned as she caught Anne's last comment. Anne's self-isolation was the one thing that worried her about her younger daughter. As a teenager she had rarely joined in with the girlish escapades of her peers. She always seemed OK on the surface but it was hard to know what made her tick, how she really felt growing up in a world of uncertainty. Sometimes Deborah thought Anne was old beyond her teenage years, so unlike Erica who had blundered into just about every pitfall waiting for a growing young woman in the twenty-first century. At least Erica had survived and her new found worldly wisdom might yet prove an asset for them all.

Deborah passed the drinks around, Dave accepted his beer, noticing the inquisitive glance she gave him. There were odd occasions during their marriage when she had wondered about Dave too. With all his professed academic equality and diversity, from time to time she had caught glimpses of another side to him, a patriarchal yet also fragile side to his character, a male ego that was all too easily offended. Not a totally bad trait, it was nice to think that when it came to the crunch he might rise up and slay any dragon threatening the family. Completely unrealistic of course and where they were going she felt, though had yet to openly mention, they would need a strong maternal presence to hold the family together rather than male egoism. If she was completely honest she would have preferred not to have had Sally with them. Again that was an unrealistic ideal, Sally's skills would be needed should any medical emergency arise, but she was another mature woman. Could she turn out to be a potential rival?

"Mum! Where have you gone?" Erica had noticed Deborah's thoughts drifting away and perceived the passing shadow. "Sorry, Erica, I was miles away." She thought both her daughters' perception uncanny at times but Deborah quickly returned to the present as the trio of musicians struck up across the other side of the bar. The middle-aged guitarist was singing the old Eagles classic 'Take it Easy' and the lyrics struck a chord with her.

"I'm a running down the road trying to loosen my load. I got seven women on my mind." The guitarist was getting into his stride. Poor Dave, she thought. He's going to have all four of us women on his mind out there.

"Four that wanna own me, two that wanna stone me, one says she's just a friend of mine – take it easy, take it easy."

"Hey Dave, this must be our song, eh?" He pretended not to be impressed by his wife's tease. Bit too astute, he thought. "When are the other three arriving then? I'll have quite a harem by the sounds of it!"

Erica laughed, "In your dreams old man!"

"We'll see what we can do for the old man when we get to St Kilda!" Deborah was back into the family jokes. Sally, although feeling slightly excluded, managed a smile. The musicians stopped their song abruptly to take their drinks and chatted amongst themselves. Clapping didn't seem appropriate as the performance had seemed more of a rehearsal than anything else.

The evening in the pub continued. Dave got up to talk with the musicians, now seated at the bar, while the women chatted and laughed together round the table. Sally's yawn reminded them all that they had an early start, needing to be back at the pier for 07.30 to get their stuff loaded and hand the car over to Dan who was going to meet them there. They got up to go, somewhat reluctantly in Dave's case. He was beginning to feel at home in the bar chatting with the locals. Leverburgh was more sociable than he had expected and he would have been happy to have ended their westward trek there if he had the choice. Anne would have never forgiven him of course. Cheery goodbyes from the bar staff and drinkers sent them out into the blustery but dry darkness. The sparse street lighting made their route back to the hostel barely possible without resorting to a flashlight. Anne rummaged in her fleece pocket and produced a small head-torch. After city life the darkness came as a surprise. Goodness knows what it would be like on St Kilda with no outside light at all, thought Deborah. But still, there would be nobody else there to worry about and precious little need to go out after dark anyway.

"Fuck, shit!" Dave, slightly drunk had walked into an iron bollard just at the right height to hit him where it hurt most. "Excuse my French, ladies. I hadn't expected it to be this dark. There'll be no rioting in Leverburgh, that's for sure. You can't see enough to do anything out here!" None of them had noticed the *Beluga* slide up to the jetty as they left the pub. Donald Macintyre would be in the Moorings shortly when the real music session started finishing in the small hours of the morning, when in summer it would already be light. "Come on, Dad. Let's get you home." Erica put her arm through his and the group wound their way back up the hill to the hostel and waiting beds.

Euan was still up when they got back. He wanted to know what they would like for breakfast. Options ranged from a full fried breakfast to fruit and yoghurt. Coffee, tea or fruit juice for drinks. Dave, in his bruised and slightly drunken condition opted for the full fried breakfast with coffee while Deborah, Erica and Anne chose from muesli and fruit options. Sally asked for filled rolls to take with her. She didn't want to eat before the sea crossing to St Kilda.

Lying in bed next to Deborah, who by that time was fast asleep, Dave tried to imagine what it would be like. He compared their small group to pioneer families of the past led by their knowledgeable patriarch as they made their way into unknown territory. Yes, it was his manifold destiny to be doing this. With his family he would be resettling St Kilda. At last, after the rebuff from the female Head of Geography, he could regain his self-esteem in a man's world. Looking at his wife snoring gently beside him, he felt aroused by the warmth of her body. It felt reassuring that she had opted to come with them. He hadn't expected this adventure to have come about so easily. Perhaps, if he ever got the chance, he should thank the young carjackers who made all this possible.

The grey and windy dawn came all too soon. The northwesterly breeze was pushing the swell to the pier. Donald Macintyre was fueling the craft as the Williams sat down for their hostel breakfast. Sally had picked up her filled rolls and was walking down to the pier to chat with Don and Lachie, his young assistant, who was busy checking that all first aid supplies and other requirements for the journey were in place. The *Beluga* hadn't been out of Tarbert since the end of last season and this was not going to be an easy crossing. It rarely was, even in the summer months.

Dave was enthusiastically tucking into his fried breakfast. The black pudding, eggs and bacon were complimented by mushrooms, tomatoes and fried bread. He washed it all down with a pot of strong black coffee. "It doesn't get much better than this, does it?" The women looked somewhat appalled at his indulgence that morning. Erica and Anne picked at their own light breakfasts. Deborah downed her tea and toast noting that Sally kept to her planned abstinence that morning. Sally knew from previous experience not to eat before the three hour crossing.

Euan came over to them, looking at his watch, and suggested they had better get down to the pier promptly as Donald would be ready for them by now. Taking the hint they all got up and fetched their overnight bags to load the car for the three hundred yard journey to their future. The cat was retrieved from her night in the kennel and it took only a few moments to get her, again protesting loudly, back into the basket. After paying Euan they piled in and drove the car down the hill to where Donald and Lachie were waiting for them. They unloaded the baggage into the gently rocking red and white *Beluga* that was going to be their lifeline between Harris and St Kilda.

There was no sign that Dan had arrived to collect the car. It turned out he had missed the last bus from Stornoway so Donald advised Dave to leave the car in the Moorings car park. Lachie would drop the keys off at the hostel and Euan would sort things out when Dan turned up, there being no other accommodation he'd be likely to find open that time of the year. Dave was taken aback by the informality of the arrangement but it seemed to be the way things worked in Leverburgh. Everyone knew each other and most of each other's business in the small Hebridean community.

The boat was loaded by 08.15 and the group safely on board. In spite of the informality, Donald and Lachie were professional operators and insisted on giving a short health and safety presentation. They were surprised to see the cat basket and it was left to Sally to explain. "I did warn them about the no alien species rule, but there will be no-one there to complain. It might be nice to have a pet around anyway." Don laughed at the disregard for Trust rules even before they got there.

"One thing to remember folks, never, ever take off your life jackets on the crossing. We will be sailing west across a north-westerly wind today – so it's not going to be comfortable, I am afraid. I strongly advise you to stay in the cabin at all times and Lachie will do his best to keep you comfortable." Don's euphemism implies that seasickness is going to be almost inevitable, thought Deborah.

"In the unlikely event of emergency the life-rafts are stowed on deck. We have the latest communication technology so if the worst comes to the worst we won't be bobbing about for long – I hope!"

Don rarely wore his own life-jacket, it was a local joke that if you saw him actually wearing one you knew the crossing was going to be rough. He was wearing it that Tuesday morning and underneath it a warm fleece, on his head a matching woolen hat. Lachie, as was his norm, dressed casually in jeans, trainers and a nylon bomber jacket under the life-jacket Don insisted he wore. Throwing his cigarette into the water, Lachie untied the mooring ropes. Donald gently opened the throttles controlling the burbling diesel engines and the *Beluga* pulled gently away from the pier. Only when they were safely past the moored fishing boats did he open up the powerful twin diesels. Surging forward, the *Beluga* mounted each swell before twisting to the left and rising again. The group sat grim and silent in the cabin. Sally felt vindicated in her abstinence regarding breakfast. She had made this trip several times before when the helicopter had been cancelled due to adverse weather conditions.

Soon regretting the fried breakfast, Dave went to get up and go aft. Lachie gently but firmly placed one hand on his shoulder, implicitly advising him to stay seated as the boat rose, twisted and fell across the rising swell. He handed Dave a plastic pint glass to catch his regurgitated breakfast. With grim fascination, Anne began to think of several species of seabirds that regurgitate oily stomach contents to feed their young. The thought made her feel queasy too and Lachie must have noticed the signs and passed a pint glass to her as well. Dave filled three plastic pints over the next few minutes and Anne just one. Deborah lasted a few minutes longer and Erica just managed to keep her light breakfast down, though the ashen color of her face betrayed how she was feeling. Only Sally remained virtually untouched by the gastric protest around her. For her, the unhealthy smell of cat diarrhea tested her stomach to the limit and nearly proved the last straw.

By the time the boat passed the Monach lighthouse on the island of Shillay, the swell had risen considerably. White horses were breaking over the twin bows of the *Beluga*. The relentless corkscrew motion permitted only intermittent views of the one of the most isolated lighthouses in Europe. Dave was by this time past caring about anything other than getting this crossing over but shortly afterwards Anne caught sight of the island of Boreray away to the right. The iconic image of the second largest of the St Kilda islands appeared and disappeared as the boat lurched towards their destination. With minds concentrated on simply surviving the crossing intact, the unexpected arrival into calmer waters came as a complete surprise. Passing rocky Levenish, the island at the entrance to Village Bay, the *Beluga*'s engines slowed to a steady drone as the boat approached the St Kilda landing almost four hours after leaving Leverburgh. The trip could take an hour less in optimum conditions. Donald perceptibly relaxed and Lachie went aft to light another cigarette, looking around him at the islands he had not expected to see until Easter at the earliest. For him the most noticeable thing that morning was the almost total absence of seabirds. Apart from the drone of their engines and the slapping waves, the island was silent. There was no sign of life anywhere. No rumble from the power-station floated across the bay. No beep of the reversing Case loader greeted them as it usually did. The sounds of St Kilda were changed, and it wasn't just the lack of seabirds. The village seemed really dead this time. The only signs of life came from the slowly moving flock of brown Soay sheep calmly grazing the south facing village fields as usual.

Taking a last drag on his cigarette, Lachie spotted a solitary figure walking past the front of the power-station toward the jetty. The figure stopped briefly, looking out toward them as they slowed toward the landing. The tide was high and there would be no problem tying up the *Beluga* for a couple of hours. There would be no Warden to complain about it either. The idea that rats might come ashore from the *Beluga* had always seemed ridiculous to Don but he had to abide with the rules if he was to keep his business afloat. Lachie went back into the cabin and spoke quietly to him indicating that he had seen someone walking toward the jetty and it might be prudent to tie-up to the orange buoy marking the mooring they used in summer months. Don sounded surprised but sensing his passengers had had enough that morning, decided to tie up at the jetty anyway. Transferring by small open dingy was always risky for the passengers and the Williams party looked done in. The figure now walking down the old slipway toward them was a surprise though.

Phil Jones was feeling sick again with the shock of all that had happened to him that morning. They had left Aberdeen in high spirits for the trip of a lifetime and now he was the only survivor of a foolish, very foolish aircraft wreck. He had heeded all received advice regarding air travel. He had sat at the back of the plane, kept himself strapped in his seat and survived while the other eight now lay dead, somewhere under the waters of the north Atlantic. Whether they were dead or alive when the Piper went over the cliff he would have no way of knowing but they were certain to be dead now. He hoped that they were dead before the aircraft slipped under the waves into whatever watery grave awaited them. The thought of his companions trying to claw their way out as the water in the cabin rose to smother them proved too much and he staggered and fell retching on the slippery descent to the jetty. He picked himself up as the *Beluga* came alongside.

Don Macintyre looked at Lachie, "Who on earth could that be?" As far as everyone knew, the island was empty. By now the Williams party had noticed the man walking, painfully by appearances, toward them. While the others began unloading their belongings and equipment, Sally briskly walked over to him. She didn't have a chance to ask her first question. Phil virtually broke down as he tried to explain what had happened on the far side of the island.

"We crashed, we bloody crashed. They've gone over the cliff, they're all gone." He broke down sobbing as Sally placed a comforting arm around him and led him to sit down on the stepped jetty wall. "OK, can you tell me your name?" she asked.

"It's Phil, Phil Brown and I am from Banstead in Surrey."

"So Phil, can you tell me if you think you're hurt beyond the scratches I can see?" Sally thought she could assume that, although clearly in shock, there couldn't be too much physically wrong with him if he had, as he claimed, walked down from the top of the hill.

"I was in the back of the plane and I thought that low flying run pretty stupid so I stayed strapped into my seat just in case. Even the pilot advised it but no-one else seemed to take any notice. It saved my life but I think the rest are all dead. I tried to ring for help but all the phones are down."

Sally asked further, "Where is the wreck, Phil. We'll have to go up there and see if there is anyone else left alive." Phil explained that just after he had managed to get out of the aircraft, a strong gust of wind had blown him to the ground and sent the crashed plane sliding over the cliff edge. Sally walked back to the others. "Seems we have a serious incident to deal with, I am afraid."

In her previous experience the Base Supervisor would have taken charge in such a situation. Now it would be up to her. She explained the situation as related by Phil. Don shook his head, "They never learn, this is no place for aerobatics. However we'd better do something, I'll go out to the mouth of the bay and try calling out on VHF. Somebody ought to pick it up when I am past Oiseval and Dun." VHF radio transmission was always problematic due to signals being blocked by the topography of the islands. Village Bay was in a radio shadow.

As the youngest and fittest member of the party, Anne volunteered to walk up the hill to check if there were any survivors up there. Sally suggested she went with her knowing the terrain well.

The *Beluga* raced out beyond the entrance to the Bay. Donald switched his VHF radio to Channel 16 and made an emergency call. He tried several times before he got a crackly reply. Not from the closed coastguard station at Stornoway but from the Rangehead Offices on South Uist.

"Hi, Don – what's up?" The operator sounded quite jocular at first but her tone became serious as Don described what he believed to have happened to a small sight-seeing aircraft. "OK, I'll pass the message to the Range Supervisor and I expect we'll get a chopper out there shortly. I'll notify the Coastguard in Aberdeen as well, but I am sure we will get there first."

Anne and Sally made their way slowly up the twisting track to the top of the hill. Anne's lungs and legs were soon complaining at the sudden climb without relief from sea-level to over a thousand feet in less than a mile. They got their breath back at the T-junction where the track separated to service the radar installations at Mullach Mór and Mullach Sgar. Walking quickly along the earth dyke at the top of Glen Mór they soon saw the ripped turf where the Piper had come down. Various personal items lay scattered at the top of the glen but of the aircraft itself there was no sign. They walked over to the cleits near the Lover's Stone and saw that Phil's account had been accurate. One cleit showed damage from the plane's impact and there was a distinctive gouge in the turf where the inverted tail had dragged along the ground before sliding over the cliff and into the sea hundreds of feet below. Apart from gouged turf, a few oily smears on the granite were the only evidence the Piper had ever been there. Apart from the Pipers port engine, other rusting aircraft parts in the vicinity had been there since the Second World War.

It had taken them forty-five minutes to walk up from the jetty. Don had obviously got through to someone as a small helicopter could be seen approaching from the south-east. After slowly circuiting the area, so the pilot could check the direction of the wind from the way the ground vegetation was blowing, the helicopter finally settled on flat ground near the Mullach Sgar radome. Strong winds deflected from the cliff edge passed safely above the helicopter after it landed. The pilot and paramedic walked over slowly. They had seen no sign of the Piper and in their heavy immersion flying suits were not going to rush.

"Doesn't look like there's much we can do here. Just one survivor, Sally?"

"Yes, he's down at the jetty. Probably best if you take him back with you. It's been a real nightmare of a day for him by all accounts."

"Rightio, Sal. We'll flip down to the helipad and collect him. Is he hurt?"

"Don't think so. But he was in shock when he came down. I'll leave him to you. Can you contact the Coastguard and explain they might as well stand down for the time being. Nothing further anyone can do out here for now. They might send a salvage vessel out later, but I doubt they'll bother."

The small helicopter was buffeted by winds from all directions before settling again several hundred feet below them at the helipad not far from the Cailleach's Cave. The crew walked along the road to the jetty, past the deserted Base. In the past they would have been invited in for a mug of tea, maybe a dram, but not today. Phil Jones was still in shock but managed to walk back to the helipad unaided. He was seated in the back seat of the helicopter after assuring the crew he would be alright. The chopper was buffeted once again as it took off and followed the sheltering slope of Oiseval before turning into the tail wind back to South Uist. As the small helicopter disappeared over the horizon emptiness returned to St Kilda.

Don Macintyre had stacked all the boxes, cases and rucksacks at the landward end of the jetty, waiting for the short transit up the slope to the Manse. It was an old habit dating from when the military drivers obliged with Landrover transport to carry baggage up to the cottages. "Well that was an unexpected introduction for you out here. To be honest, just about anything can happen out here. If it's within the remit of the human condition, it'll happen out here I reckon. So that must be us just about done. Remember you can ring me when you get your phones up and running and I am generally available on VHF Channel 12, but of course you'll have to go up to the top of the hill if you want to transmit beyond the bay. I'll be coming out regularly after Easter but for the next three months you should have enough tinned stuff in the Base stores to be getting on with. I know I shouldn't say it but this island used to grow the best barley in the Hebrides. It's a shame these fields have been left untended after all the hard work the St Kildans put into them. Josephine would hate me for this but if I was living here, I'd be turning the ground right now. Sod the archaeology, it's the future that matters not the mess of the past."

Dave looked amazed at the archaeological heresy he was hearing. The women simply nodded their agreement, apart from Anne whose mind seemed to be elsewhere, gazing across the bay to the silent rocky peaks of Dun. She had noticed a spinning column of spray disappearing into one of the sea caverns running under the narrow, rock peaked island. "Come on, let's get our stuff up to the Manse."

Group activity would get them all focused, thought Dave. It hadn't been too good so far with a plane crash and Don's advice that the heritage organizations had been getting it all wrong. The last fifty yards up the flagstone slipway proved harder than he had expected. The former warden used to clean weed and algae off the stone path but now it was slippery as grease. They had all slipped and fallen a couple of times before everything was stacked up outside the Manse porch. The stone wall at the front of the house had been quickly thrown up after Manse had been renovated and the work of unskilled student labor was already beginning to tumble. Soay lambs thought of nothing better than running along the wall bleating to their dams. Ovine traffic was not what the wall had been intended for and instead of enhancing first impressions of the island the crumbling wall hinted at decay and impermanence. Even Dave had to admit that Josephine's instruction that they were not to change anything, not even make minor repairs to damaged walls was a bit ridiculous. Funding for the resettlement project could be withdrawn if they attempted any such thing.

Deborah had the keys and she went around the Manse opening front and back doors. She found the small diesel generator left for them in the low store room on the end of the building. It struck her that in an all-electric house they would have to start this machine every time they wanted to make a cup of tea. This was not going to be easy but at least the generator had a battery powered starter motor. They went inside, finding the Manse dry and clean if a little unaired. The building contractors had made a good job of renovating the house. Draught proofing around the doorways and double glazing was excellent and she would soon have the house cozy for the family. Sally walked around with her, marveling at the standard of the accommodation inside the Manse.

The warden's office was well equipped with modern computers and communication equipment, just a pity there was such a limited electrical supply. The shop held a good stock of books on the Island, so no shortage of background information there. Don had mentioned he liked to have the shop open for his passengers before they left the island. It did smell a little musty in the shop, probably a legacy of so many, often damp, human bodies crammed in there during the summer tourist season. At the end of the main corridor from the front porch was a living room complete with new looking three piece suite and to cap it all, mounted on the wall beside the window, a sizeable plasma television screen. That small generator was going to have its work cut out, Deborah thought. Past the small bedrooms they came to the all-electric kitchen. It was spotless, whoever had been here last had been obsessive about cleaning. Sally made the comment that such obsessive cleaning was often a compensation for deep seated unhappiness. Whoever had used this kitchen before them had not been happy, even with such panoramic views across the bay to the now darkening rocks of Dun as the early January evening drew in.

Erica shivered as they moved on down the corridor to the shower rooms and toilets. The new fittings were already looking rusty and blue green copper stains in the wash basins indicated acidic water was eating away at the copper pipes. Likely to be a few stomach upsets here before we get used to this, Sally thought. They had been assured the water was potable and the high acidity would no doubt help counteract the effect of bacteria from the frequent sheep corpses lying in the water catchment beneath Conachair. They were not even supposed to dispose of them but should leave them to rot where they fell so as not to affect the island ecology. The sheep population was to be left to rise and fall as nature dictated, according to the strict instructions given them by Josephine Miller.

In the back porch area there was a laundry room and additional toilet, apparently for visitor use. There was also a large upright freezer, clean and emptied now there was no mains electricity supply. The tour around the house brought home to Erica just how unsustainable life on St Kilda had become.

"Not just unsustainable with energy," Sally added, "but how could the community have sustained itself without family life. There were just not enough women here and those that were here generally beyond child bearing age. No wonder a few female conservation volunteers went home pregnant. The communal urge for procreation is a strong one, stronger still where there is so little outlet for its expression."

Outside, cleits stood timeless, scattered across the hill side like so many enormous barnacles. Sally pointed them out to Dave and Deborah. Just look at those cleits, the St Kildans got it right. You can store anything in those. The wind blows in through the dry stone walls and the turf capped roof keeps the rain out. They used to store everything in there from plucked Puffins to peat for their fires."

"Don't think I'd fancy going up and over the hill to get milk for my tea though." Anne made her first comment since they started the tour of the Manse.

"Ah, but youngsters like you held the community together. That's how it worked, Anne. The young supported the old and when they became too infirm to go up the hill a new generation of youngsters would support them. The change came at the end of the nineteenth century and beginning of the twentieth when young adults left for a better life on the mainland and as for the latter years of the twentieth century it was just ridiculous. No matter how pally the men got, there was no way they could produce kids to keep the place going, and none of them were fit enough to make it up the hill!"

The women had to laugh at Sally's wry observation. Meanwhile Dave was exploring too. He had found the office and shop and realizing everything was dependent on electricity determined that he would assume responsibility for getting the generator going. He left the women to their exploration of the domestic domain not realizing Deborah had already found the generator and fathomed how to use it. As Josephine had written down in the instruction folder, there was a key cabinet in the office and he quickly found the brass key marked 'Flare Store', a small dry store room which now housed the small generator they would all depend on. He had to stoop slightly to get in there and brushing cobwebs aside found the machine and its control panel mounted on the wall. There was a laminated instruction card hanging on the back of the door but of course as he couldn't flick on the light until the generator was running, he took it outside to read. It looked easy enough; make sure the fuel tank was topped up – it was. Make sure no heavy use appliance was switched on before starting up. He was sure the cooker and heaters in the Manse were all turned off. He checked the oil, it looked fresh and golden. This engine didn't look like it had ever been used. The key was in the ignition switch and it was just a simple matter of turning the key and off she'd go. That's what the instruction sheet implied but when he turned the key all he heard was a grating noise as the ratchet of the starter motor failed to engage fully with the gear ring on the flywheel. The battery was exhausted. He unscrewed the caps on the battery and peered into the cells which were grey and sulphated. Even with his limited mechanical knowledge he could tell this battery was scrap. Oh, well there was probably another battery in the Base somewhere and there was a manual method to start the engine with a cranking handle.

The rust was beginning to show through the galvanized coating on the starting handle clipped to the side of the generator. He inserted the handle onto the end of the engine crankshaft and turned it as hard as he could. As the engine came up to compression the handle stopped dead. There must be a knack to this, he thought. The same thing happened a second time, he was getting nowhere. Male pride was at stake and he wanted get the generator running to impress the women if nothing else. He stepped back from the small engine and invoked, half seriously, whoever or whatever was the patron saint of small engines. Trying a third time he put all his effort into turning the handle. It stopped dead again but this time the handle slipped on the crankshaft and came off in his hand. Having put so much energy into swinging the handle his head came down hard on top of the generator casing causing a deep cut and heavy bruise to his right eyebrow. Roaring with pain and frustration he rushed out of the Flare Store dripping blood onto the short cropped turf outside.

The blood flow quickly stemmed but the bruise had swelled impressively and was eyebrow was wobbling like jelly by the time Deborah ran round to see what on earth had happened. They had heard him bellow and Sally was fast behind her. Without asking for his OK, she turned his head and felt the injury. Dave winced but before he could say anything was told he would live but should be more careful in future. The resettlement wasn't going to work if they had wholly avoidable accidents like this. Sally went to the First Aid box in the office and came back with an anti-septic wipe and large adhesive plaster. "This really ought to have a stitch in it, Dave, but you'll have to live without for now until I find out how to get things sterilized with no electricity."

Her father's bellowing had snapped Anne out of her thoughts and, while his cut was being attended to, she went into the shed and brought the instruction card out into the daylight. "So for manual start, it says - first ensure the de-compressor lever is lifted - whatever that means?" Dave reached for the laminated card, taking it from Anne, and scrutinized the instructions.

"Hmm! I think I'll try again." His eyebrow was stinging badly and the bruise still wobbling as he turned the handle easily with the de-compressor lever lifted. Anne read out further instructions to him.

"When a vigorous momentum has been reached lower the de-compressor lever and the engine should start. Repeat procedure if engine does not start immediately."

Dave kept swinging as fast as he could with his right arm and lowered the de-compressor lever on top of the engine with his left. Immediately the small engine spluttered into life. A brief puff of black smoke issued from the exhaust pipe coming out of the side wall of the stone shed. The generator was running.

"Well done, Dad – when all else fails, read the instructions, eh?" Anne could be merciless but Deborah and Sally simply grinned at him, they were enjoying his humiliation. Feeling slightly foolish, Dave noticed that Erica was nowhere in sight.

"Has anyone seen Erica?" Anne called out for her sister several times before the nearby church door opened and Erica came back out into the daylight. "It's dark in there with the shutters up but I managed to see enough. God, this is sad place!" The group walked over to the Church building with its high Georgian window frames the only hint of ornamentation apart from an impressive wooden lectern. Out of regular use for years, damp and mold were taking their toll inside. Dry rot was evident in the wooden panels at floor level and iron gratings supposed to allow adequate ventilation were rusting unpainted in the salt laden atmosphere. Through the gloom, they saw just enough to enter the rear annex which housed a simple school room where, according to the display boards, scholars from age four to forty would receive education in the sight of the Lord. Some early photographs had been reproduced showing groups of children scowling at the camera while their teacher maintained strict control of what could and should have been a happy school group photo.

"You know, I couldn't help thinking that the photographer froze the life out of those children when he took the picture. No wonder they wanted to leave when they grew up."

"That's a bit hard, Erica. They must have had some fun out here." Deborah retorted.

"Yes, but looking at such photos perpetuates the misconception. They look miserable so it must be miserable here. It kind of feeds on itself. You know, in a way a bit like us coming here expecting to find just cottages and there's a bloody old army base here. They don't show that in the tourist brochures, do they, and the photographer here didn't show any happiness in the children either. It must have been different, but we don't see it. God, it makes me so mad!"

"Erica, I don't think you should be blaspheming in here." Dave surprised her by being half-serious. "We don't want any more bad luck, do we?"

The diesel generator, after charging its spare battery, had settled down to a steady putter and Sally, sensing the subject ought to be changed suggested they went into the kitchen and made their first cup of tea at St Kilda. There was plenty of tea and sugar left for them in tins and plastic boxes in the cupboards, only dried milk of course. Switching the electric kettle on raised the exhaust note of the generator from a gentle putter to a deeper pop, pop, pop sound reminiscent of an approaching fishing boat, joked Sally. "Well I'm glad I won't be sleeping beside this racket," she joked. Sally had yet to take her stuff up the path to the Factor's House. It wouldn't have changed much since her previous contract ended. Just a few mouse droppings to clear up, she assumed. The large St Kilda mice seemed to love that house. She suddenly remembered the Williams cat still in its basket in the Manse hallway. "Hey, what about the cat?" Sally was genuinely concerned.

"Flipping heck Sal, I'd forgotten about her with everything else going on. I'll go and get her." Deborah returned with the now purring cat in her arms. Its fur somewhat greasy after her travels but happy to be in human habitation and familiar company again. "You know we never gave her a proper name, did we?" This time Anne spoke for the cat. "'She can't just be called 'cat' now she's come out here with us. I'd like to call her something special."

"Like what?" queried her mother already pouring the tea into immaculately cleaned cups.

"Cailly! That would be brilliant, really cool in fact." Anne beamed at the name. "Cailly? You mean like Kylie, Kylie Minogue?" her mother was puzzled. "No Mum, Cailly after Cailleach the Gaelic word for wise old woman." Dave interrupted, "Shouldn't that be more like Kaya?" He had already done some background reading on Hebridean folklore area and thought Cailly too much of an Anglicization, even diminutive.

"Cailly sounds sweet though. I agree with Anne for once, let's call her just that. Cailly the sweet little wise cat of St Kilda." Deborah's maternal authority settled the matter. "Anyway now we have found out the hard way how to get electricity in this house I propose that, when we have finished our tea, we have a look round the rest of the village. We have enough food for tonight so we can leave exploring the Base till the morning."

Twenty minutes later the family, led by Sally, set out to explore the village. Turning left out of the front door the first building they encountered was the boat house. Opening the sliding door a quick peek inside revealed a dated RIB on its rusty trailer. The rigid hulled inflatable boat had been used to store various related clutter. Several lifejackets had been stowed but were showing signs of mouse damage. Somehow the rodents had managed to climb up and into the boat. Several fishing rods were stacked in a corner and a couple of lobster pots lay to the right of the door. There was an old metal cupboard in there and when opened revealed a collection of rusty tools and boxes of fishing accessories consisting hooks, line and various lures. "We'll be alright for some fish then," commented Dave. The women ignored him and turned to return outside.

The next building was a two story late eighteenth century house perched right at the sea's edge. Cliff erosion had eaten the ground away almost as far as its foundations. "This place," said Sally, "is the Feather Store. It was the best building on St Kilda and used as the warehouse the island produce before it was shipped away by the Factor to pay rent in kind. It's recently been brought into use as accommodation. There's a very basic apartment upstairs, though downstairs it is still storage space. It's full of ladders and building materials. It must be a wild place to stay when there's a storm raging. Don't know if I'd fancy it myself, though."

Erica was quietly thinking that the Feather Store flat might be just the place she would fancy living in, away from the clinical sterility of the refurbished Manse. Already she wasn't intending to stay in the Manse for any longer than was absolutely necessary. One of the shutters on an upstairs window had come loose and was swinging in the breeze. Dave went up the stone steps into the flat to secure it from inside. The rest of the group followed, including Cailly who was by now showing a keen interest in the smell of mice within the flat. Dave secured the shutter and they found themselves in semi-darkness and stumbled slightly making their way back to the door. The mouse smell was strongest in the kitchen area and had they opened the low cupboards they would have seen crockery and cutlery stained with droppings and mouse urine.

Out in the fresh air again, Sally led them to the straight path that ran gently uphill through the village. The first structure they encountered was a small well protected by stone walls and turf capped roof. Erica asked why the water looked stagnant and undrinkable in a supposedly pristine environment. Dave suggested it was because the well hadn't been used in years, not since the 1930 evacuation, probably. "Yes, it's a common problem with old wells. If you don't keep drawing water from them they stagnate and become breeding grounds for all sorts of pathogens," Sally informed them. Erica walked over to the lip of the well and began scraping away at the muddy surround with her boot to release the stagnant water.

"Erica! What are you doing?" Dave was aghast. After all they had been told about not touching the archaeology, his daughter was altering it within hours of arrival on St Kilda. "This water needs to flow! As Sally just said, the well will be no good unless we use it. It's as good as poison right now."

Sally protested, "Erica, I would strongly advise against drinking well water anywhere here. There are any number of rotting sheep beyond the head-dyke and you could catch just about anything drinking from this well. The water supply for the village is by no means perfect but is at least drawn from an underground source relatively uncontaminated. Two years ago the chlorination plant was closed due to health risks associated with the chemical and a new borehole was dug up in An Lag. Let's just drink tap-water, OK?"

The Williams were surprised to hear Sally being so forceful but accepted that on matters of health, she was to be respected. That is apart from Erica who had been stung by the unexpected rebuke at her effort to improve the well.

Moving up the path they passed between large, almost monumental, dry stone walls. Entrances in wall faces marked storage areas reminiscent of the cleits on the hillside above. Copious sheep droppings in the entrances indicated their adoption as shelters by the village sheep population. As soon as it rained, Sally said, the well fed village sheep made a bee-line for the Victorian cleits to shelter leaving their lush meadow grazing until the downpour ceased. It was the same with strong sunshine and high winds. They really had it made in the village, unlike the flocks away on the hill and far side of the island which had to fend for themselves in poor conditions. "Down here in the village, they are a bit wimpy," Sally added.

Cailly's tail went up as a brown Soay ewe and her yearling lamb came along the muddy path toward them. The lamb was fearless and the group watched with some amusement as the lamb went up to Cailly and touched noses with her. The lamb was much bigger than the cat and after a moment's hesitation, Cailly rubbed herself on the lambs shoulder. Introductions having been made, the lamb jumped up effortlessly onto the remains of a fallen cleit while its mother eyed Cailly with suspicion. The sheep were virtually fearless of humans who for years had studied them as part of a long-running Edinburgh University research project. Cats were an unknown quantity but finally assuming Cailly to be harmless the ewe joined its lamb on the ruined cleit, knocking a few more stones down as it clambered up.

"Look at that," pointed Erica, still smarting from her rebuke. It's OK for sheep to knock everything down but we have to just stand here and watch them do it!"

"'I am afraid so, Erica. It's just part of the deal of being here," said Sally. The sheep get everywhere and we have to let them do what they want. They've considerably altered the ground flora, cropping the turf much closer than it used to be when the villagers controlled their livestock. To Sally, Erica was showing signs of becoming trying. She hoped Erica would be able to cope with living here for the next year or two. If her behavior became too much, Josephine had advised that as Nurse, she could recommend removal of anyone she considered psychologically unsuited to custodianship at St Kilda.

"Come on, I'll show you where I'm staying." A few yards further up the path Sally stood before the first house in the village. Compared with the single story granite cottages further along the 'street', the white painted and rendered two floored Factor's House was impressive by contrast. The nineteenth century house had been used by more socially important visitors throughout its life. It had been the home of nurses in the past and was now being returned to this former function. Sally led them in through the front porch to show them around. Immediately in front of them was the bathroom. Sally was to have exclusive use of the village's one and only bathtub. Deborah was envious. Candle-wax marks were evident either side of the taps indicating someone had luxuriated here just a few months earlier. The house had been the privilege of the University sheep project leader when on island. Like so many of her colleagues she had been made redundant when funding for their research had been withdrawn. The sheep project had run almost uninterrupted since the first evacuation and the, now middle-aged, project leader had worked with the Soays since her graduation in the late nineteen-seventies. A collection of eco-philosophy magazines left in the porch for recycling attested to the previous occupant's sentiments.

Erica perked up at the sight of these magazines. Her sulk lifted as she thumbed the top copy. "Well, this is better. A kindred spirit at last, what a pity she's not here anymore."

"Yeah, on the whole the women here did get on well as a small outnumbered group. We used to meet at the first cottage up the street to get away from the male enclave in the Base. We had some good times in there, I'll show it to you in a minute." Sally was coming to life revisiting better memories from her past, when she was employed on the island.

The Williams were shown the two rooms downstairs in the Factor's House, the basic kitchen and living room which doubled as an office. Going out to the back they were shown external steps leading to the upper floor housing two bedrooms and a toilet. It was all basic, functional and tidy but although not as strong, here too there was a smell of mouse urine. Cailly had gone into the storage area behind the toilet following the enticing scent. The sudden commotion attracted their attention and a moment later the group watched stunned as the cat emerged proudly carrying a plump St Kilda mouse in her jaws. "What, with Erica and now the cat I don't know why I bother!" Dave's frustration was becoming evident. "We've only been here a few hours and already the archaeology and wild life are getting damaged. Can I remind you we are supposed to be looking after this place?"

Sally gave him an exasperated look and moved on. "OK, let's go and look at Cottage One where we all used to meet after work – and Dave, please lighten up." She led them around the back of the Factor's House back onto the grassy street reinforced with granite sets. "Mind your footing here, the tourists were always slipping over on this section of path."

They followed the path over a small clapper bridge made of granite slabs. The water of the 'dry burn' rushed beneath them. Cailly was a bit hesitant, still carrying her mouse. This stream used to supply the Base water before the borehole was drilled. It used to run dry most of the summer as the flow was diverted into nearby storage tanks. A short way up hill stood the concrete platform above the new borehole was already weathering to a dull grey matching granite walls nearby. It often overflowed and around the wellhead the saturated ground supported prolific growth of Butterwort, the 'Mothan' plant known throughout the Hebrides for its allegedly beneficial, if mildly psychotropic, properties. The sheep had grazed everything else to the ground but wisely left the Mothan untouched. "There's a local myth that drinking the milk of the cow that ate the Mothan brings unnatural good fortune to the drinker." Sally added that it was a bit unlikely cows would eat it, considering the sheep would not touch it.

There was however an anecdote about an island priest exiled for lascivious behavior on the island. He had been taken for trial at Dunvegan Castle to explain his unholy communion with the good wives of St Kilda but got off with a warning to mend his ways, allegedly, due to having eaten handfuls of Mothan before the hearing."

"Dan told me a tale like that about Fly Agaric mushrooms, Sally." Erica was interested in this subject. "Apparently, he said, Lapland Reindeer herders drink the urine of their animals to get a desirable psychotropic effect. If they ingested the mushrooms direct they could go mad or even die. Hope Mothan isn't as powerful as that?"

"Don't worry, Erica. The new well is covered with a concrete cap so no Mothan is going to fall in and even if it does, it will bring us unnatural good luck and maybe, along with the good luck, a bit of unholy communion too," she laughed. At this last comment, Erica looked slightly perplexed.

Approaching the first cottage, Cailly dropped her mouse and showed interest in the faint food smells coming from a drainpipe below the front window. Behind them a flash of brown feathers pounced on the dead mouse and flew away with it. Anne spotted the small fast flying bird and quickly identified it.

"Hey that was a Merlin! They must be here all year round. They're going to like you Cailly." Cailly was less than impressed and made a resentful chattering miaow as the small raptor departed with her precious catch.

Entering the cottage, the Williams were surprised to see a large and well equipped electric kitchen on one side and dining room tables and benches on the other. In the fireplace stood a Scandinavian wood-burning stove. Above, on the mantelpiece, various postcards had been placed having been sent from all over the world by past conservation volunteers, particularly those who had worked with the sheep project. There was a well-stocked bookshelf and boxes of board games and in the ceiling a loft hatch, behind which Sally advised them, 'Sheepie' stuff was stored. Another inviolate area beyond the prying eyes of men, she added without attempting to joke about it.

Deborah asked the obvious question. "St Kilda is treeless, right? We are not allowed to dig peat so what gets burned in that stove, Sally?"

"Thought you'd ask that. The Base used a hell of a lot of packing crates. Everything came containerized in some way or other so it could be handled by the mechanical loader, the one I remember that nearly got dropped in the sea when we left. The wood is stored in the open shed just over there." She pointed to the MOD workshop area about a hundred yards away from the picturesque cottages. "We can go and get firewood anytime we like though I suppose it will run out eventually now the Base is closed. We'll be back to digging peats then, Dave."

Dave felt a slight pang of concern. He hadn't reckoned on a women's meeting place like this. He could sense they were looking forward to private get-togethers organized by Sally, to which he would feel, if not actually be, excluded. Back on the street Sally pointed out Cottage Two, the female dormitory conveniently next door to their meeting place. They stopped and entered Cottage Three, the museum. It was difficult to read the faded display panels in the late winter light but they obviously told the story of past island life. Erica commented that they should go back there later when there was more daylight. Cottage Four, the male dormitory stood empty, its ex-army single beds pulled away from the wall to protect the mattresses from damp. Sally led them into Cottage Five, a well-equipped workshop and paint store. Deborah tripped on the step inside the front door and only just saved herself by grabbing hold of the work bench vice. Seeing her sucking a bruised finger, Sally was reminded of the island's primary health hazard.

"That reminds me, tomorrow I am going to have to double check your tetanus vaccination status. You will have read that this island had a big tetanus problem in the past. Tetanus is the last thing we want to catch while we are out here."

The last habitable cottage, number Six had been faithfully restored by the Western Isles Trust to its original 1860s design. Entering the small wood paneled lobby, doors to the left and right opened into the two rooms of a St Kildan 'White House'. Windows looked out across fields leading to the sea. Open fireplaces allowed adequate ventilation but the rooms still smelled of damp and it appeared water had been oozing between the single skin stone walls and concrete floor. "In spite of these being the most modern houses in the Hebrides when they were built, they soon became undesirable. Thin walls couldn't keep them warm. The tin roofs led to condensation problems and the open fireplaces were terribly inefficient compared with the cozy central hearths of the Blackhouses."

Sally was obviously very knowledgeable on St Kildan community health issues, thought Erica. Leaving Cottage Six, it was becoming noticeably gloomier outside. A few wet flakes of sleet were beginning to fall and the group were feeling eager to get back to the Manse. They had left the generator running and anticipated warmth and light ahead for a cozy first evening. Erica noticed an especially large cleit just off the street. Standing in a nearby field, the circular stone building had the usual turf capped roof but also a wooden door with rudimentary lock.

"Hey, Sally. What's that place over there?"

"That's Lady Grange's House, or where it used to be. Lady Grange was exiled here before the Jacobite Rebellion in the eighteenth century."

"Why?" asked Anne.

"Apparently she questioned her husband's politics and his Jacobite pals considered her a security risk. She was sent to Skye first but, still questioning her husband's authority, she was eventually sent out here where she wouldn't be heard by anyone with political influence." Sally laughed, "I read somewhere that she practically drove the St Kildans mad with her bossiness!"

"Fucking hell!" Erica was shocked that Sally thought this funny. "You know, I heard that this place was considered Utopia, a land of equality, an island republic even. It seems to me it's worse than the mainland ever was."

"That's just it, Erica. In its isolation, away from moderating influences, the St Kildan community actually exhibited more extreme versions of the cultural trends prevailing on the mainland. It was a case of cultural inbreeding and became just as unhealthy for the community as sexual inbreeding, which incidentally isn't recorded as being prevalent here. Sorry, I am going off on one of my pet subjects. Let's go back now."

There seemed to be something Sally had almost touched on but thought better of it, felt Deborah. She connected this to Josephine's aside that their experience was likely to prove 'interesting.' A shiver ran down her spine not just as a result of the squall of sleet that hurried them back down the path toward the Manse. Though neither had voiced it, Deborah was joining her husband in having doubts about this venture, even before their first day was over.

The electric space heaters had warmed the living room and kitchen areas. The bedrooms, though chilly were at least dry compared with the cottages. They gathered in the kitchen. Sally left them at the Factor's House to reclaim it as home after her short absence from the island. Deborah offered to prepare their first evening meal back at the Manse, suggesting it might be a good idea if they took turns in future, but somehow feeling this role would be hers whether she wanted it or not. Dave unpacked their bags in the double bedroom before wandering into the living room followed by Cailly who settled down to sleep on the settee, sated from two more St Kilda mice caught and eaten while the Williams explored the cottages. They had been easy prey compared with their sharper counterparts back in Edinburgh, and twice the size too. Erica helped her mother while Anne followed her father's example by unpacking her own bags in the front bedroom. Erica would leave her bags until later.

The generator suddenly increased its revs. Deborah also noticed the electric rings on the cooker dimmed slightly. "Dave!" she shouted down the hall. "Something's going on with the generator, can you check it out?" There was no answer but instead she heard the faint but familiar voice of a BBC newsreader.

"Dave? You are not doing what I think you are doing, are you?" She marched into the living room to find Dave on the settee with Cailly settled on his lap. He was watching the early evening BBC news on the plasma screen television set dominating the room. "Dave, we came here to get away from television and the mindless clutter we had to tolerate back in Edinburgh. Now you have brought it here to us." She frowned and added, "On a practical note, I am trying to cook dinner and you are hogging the power supply with that thing. Come on, husband dear, play fair if you want feeding tonight." Disgruntled, Dave shifted Cailly back onto the cushions and turned the TV set off. Immediately the generator settled down to a steady chug inside the Flare Store.

"There's a battery radio in my suitcase, give that a go if you want to hear the news." Reluctantly Dave followed Deborah's advice and returned with the small portable radio. Turning it on, all he could hear was hissing where his favorite BBC station should have been. The radio could pick up a few unintelligible north Atlantic stations. Faeroese or Icelandic, he thought, and a popular music station from the Irish Republic several hundred miles to the south. "Bloody typical!" he shouted to Deborah. "If we can't get Radio 4, we really are going to be disconnected out here." She smiled back, "Don't worry, Dave. Just let me finish cooking, OK?"

The meal was soon prepared, but before Erica went to call her sister and father, she mentioned they ought to check out what had been left for them in the base kitchen. Don wouldn't be coming out regularly until Easter and the fresh stuff they had brought with them wouldn't last for more than a few days. The fridge would warm up with the generator turned off. It wouldn't use a lot of power so they could leave it running in the background. Erica had always preferred wholefoods back in town and she didn't fancy living off tinned food for months on end. She fetched Anne and Dave and the family sat down to their first meal together at St Kilda. "Just one thing missing, Debs." His observation irritated her a little. "Wouldn't it be great if we had a bottle of wine or two right now to celebrate our freedom from Edinburgh?"

With the meal finished the washing up was left till the morning and they retired to their rooms for an early night. The Trust had certainly splashed out on refurbishment thought Deborah. There were small television sets in each bedroom and intermittent surges from the generator indicated when these smaller sets were being switched on and off. Erica remembered to switch off the room heaters. The small diesel engine surged again when Anne had a hot shower before turning in. Finally the generator settled down to tick-over supplying only the kitchen refrigerator and a low energy lightbulb in the corridor.

At some time in the small hours Erica woke up to a dark and silent house. The generator had stopped, having exhausted its fuel tank during the night. She reached for the small head-torch she had placed on her bedside cabinet, slipped on her jeans, jumper and heavy fleece jacket and walked outside to sit down on the wall above the jetty. The sea was swelling gently beneath her, it was high tide. No light could be seen anywhere on the island or in the bay. Reaching up to her forehead she switched off the torch and let her eyes become accustomed to the starlight. It was the time of the new moon, the dark moon as she preferred to call the intuitive few days when the moon lay in the Earth's shadow and gravitational energy pulled the oceans unseen through the period of darkness. Deep in thought, Erica suddenly realized her own period was starting. Good job she had brought some tampons with her. Bit unlikely there'd be many in the Base, she thought realizing the irony of the situation. Not to worry, it was a good sign and she supposed that living with the elements rather than forever trying to escape them would be bound to affect her in many ways. Relaxing, she pulled a woolen hat from her jacket pocket and pulled it over her short hair. It was cold out in the January night. She reached into her other pocket and pulled out a battered tobacco tin and rolled a cigarette, she had mixed herbal cannabis with light tobacco before they left Leverburgh. It had been a surprise to have been offered a bag of the stuff in the Moorings car-park when she went out for a smoke. Some things never change, even in the Hebrides.

Dragging deeply on the spliff, she took in just how many stars there were. Feeling alternately insignificant and empowered by the St Kildan night, she could see starlight reflecting off the waters of the bay framing the dark silhouette of Dun under a mile away. She could just make out more starlight through the gap between Dun and the headland of

Ruiaval on Hirta. This resettlement was going to be a challenge but it was going to be good, she decided. She barely noticed Anne sit down beside her, woken too by the unaccustomed silence around them.

"It would never have been like this when the Base was occupied." Anne as usual was straight to the point. She knew about Erica's cannabis habit. Through astute observation she had learned of virtually every secret in the Williams family. She knew about Deborah's brief affair with one of her teacher colleagues and had calculated, for the time being, not to divulge she knew. Her memory held a library of secrets, knowledge to be exposed only as necessary, necessary to furthering Anne's own plans.

The two sisters sat together looking out over the starlit bay. In the clean air she couldn't help notice the faint odor from her sister. The smell of cannabis quickly dispersed in the light breeze blowing off shore, but the subtle smell of her sister's menstruation heightened her aspiration for a fresh start, a new beginning for womanhood at St Kilda.

7 SETTLING IN

Dave woke before Deborah. He didn't take in the significance of the silence at first. It was beginning to feel chilly as the electric heaters had been turned off when they went to bed. Early morning sunshine through the kitchen window landed in the hallway illuminating his way to the bathroom. It was only after several minutes of waiting for the warm water to appear from the shower-head that he realized the generator had stopped sometime in the night.

"Shit! Now I'll have to fix that I suppose." Dave also thought it would be good to get the generator up and running away from the critical gaze of the women. He could retrieve his dignity after the previous afternoon's embarrassment with the machine. Realizing the silence was probably due to no more than a lack of fuel he went back to his room and studied Josephine's brief to them. Diesel fuel was to be drawn from the tap on the wall of the power station facing the sea. Jerry cans were to be found in the workshop area and were to be stood in the concrete bund to prevent spillage escaping.

Getting dressed, Dave went to the front porch and put on his heavy duty fleece jacket and rubber boots over thick socks. Latent warmth from the sea had prevented a hard frost in the night but on the slopes of the hill the close cropped heather looked crisp and white away from the bay. He imagined what it must have been like to have smelled peat smoke from their chimney on a crisp morning like this. Walking over to the workshop area to find a jerry can, he was glad of his rubber boots. The grass was littered with sheep droppings and at the front of the south facing wall, the turf was heavily eroded where several generations of sheep were resting, still expecting the comforting sound and warmth of the power-station. They would rest elsewhere soon, he thought, now the great engines had fallen silent.

Just a couple of months before, there would have been several men walking over with him to begin their day in the workshops. Dave felt slightly spooked at the thought. He was entering a place of ghosts to borrow tools from men who had occupied the island for almost ninety years before abandoning it in as many days. Five gallon metal jerry cans were stacked neatly at the back of one of the vehicle garages. He took one and also an orange plastic funnel hanging up nearby. Crossing the yard, he could see the empty office where the supervisor would have been organizing the day's work. At the bottom of the concrete slope leading from the workshop yard, Dave turned the corner and placed the can beneath the tap on the power station wall. Unclipping the locking handle, he flipped open the filler cap and placed the nozzle of a short black rubber hose into the neck of the can. He opened the valve and heard the steady flow of five gallons of diesel into the can. Filling the can took less time than he had expected and it was overflowing by the time he managed to turn the tap back off. The bund was stained black with the evidence of countless similar spillages and Dave was glad of his rubber boots when he stepped over the low concrete wall to retrieve his now heavy fuel can. Stepping back out of the bund his oily rubber boots lost their grip on the dew wet greasy concrete and he slipped. Diesel fuel slopped from the can as it lay on its side. He had fallen heavily and as he picked himself up his hip felt bruised. Cursing he up righted the can and secured the filler cap with the locking handle. A sizeable pool of fuel was now evident on the concrete standing. He knew this would have to be cleaned up and went to look for something suitable. Outside the office door he found a fire-bucket full of wet sand. Already algae was beginning to grow over cigarette butts stubbed out in the sand weeks earlier. He returned to the spilled diesel noticing a large blue beetle struggling through the liquid. He quickly trod on the insect to spare it a lingering oil soaked death and emptied the sand and cigarette butts on the spillage. He would return with a shovel to clear it up later and hopefully before his sharp eyed younger daughter spotted the sand and asked any awkward questions.

Approaching the door of the Flare Store with the heavy jerry can he had to kick away sheep droppings in front of the entrance. A nearby yearling watched with interest as he opened the door and went inside. Instinctively he flicked on the light switch. To be expected, nothing happened. Not wanting further embarrassment he read the instruction card outside in the light before attempting to refill the fuel tank. The flow chart indicated that in the event of non-start due to lack of fuel the tank was to be replenished and then the engine had to be bled. There was a diagram with arrows pointing to two screws, one on the fuel filter housing and another on the injector pump. He could feel a sick tension building up, realizing he hadn't a clue about this sort of thing. He was an academic, not a mechanic but the job was obviously going to need a large screwdriver, he could handle that at least. Retracing his steps he returned to the workshop and took a large plastic handled screwdriver from the tool rack beside the long workbench under the window.

Erica was waiting by the Flare Store when he got back. She had also wakened to find the generator dead and had gone to investigate. At least it wasn't Anne, Dave thought. He had a better rapport with his eldest stepdaughter and they could sort out this problem in an adult way. "It's run out of fuel. Trouble is the instructions say we have to bleed the engine and I haven't got a clue." He was always honest with Erica, a quality she appreciated after the insincerity of most male attention she had received back in Edinburgh.

"Let me see, Dad. I've done this once before when Dan's van ran out of fuel. I turned the ignition key and kept the engine cranking while he undid the bleed screws." Looking at the text beside the diagram on the instruction card, she read out, "When the fuel flows from around bleed-screw (A), on the filter canister, without bubbles close the screw tightly. Repeat with the bleed-screw (B) on the injector pump. I think we can handle this, don't you? If the engine fails to start, repeat the procedure as necessary."

Dave acquiesced to Erica's slight knowledge on the matter and offered to turn the starter handle while she carried out the technical part of the bleeding procedure. This time he remembered to lift the decompression lever and the engine turned easily. He had picked up the orange plastic funnel left lying in the bund when he went back to fetch the screwdriver and used it to fill the fuel tank beside the generator. It would have been easier had the tank been on top of the engine to let the fuel run through by gravity. Dave's mind was beginning to take a practical turn but such designs had long been considered a fire risk and the engine had to be cranked to raise fuel from floor level. He turned the handle slowly watching with interest as Erica undid the first screw until fuel spurted out following the rhythm of his arm movement. With Erica half bent over the engine, he couldn't but help notice how his step-daughter had grown into a shapely young woman. Quickly dismissing further thoughts in that direction he watched her undo and then close up the second screw. She reached into her jacket pocket and produced a tissue to wipe up the small spillage on the side of the engine. "Think that will do it, let's give it a go then." Dave swung the handle faster this time and Erica reached over and lowered the decompression lever. The engine started straight away and the handle automatically slid off the end of the crankshaft. Dave clipped it back in place on the side of the generator casing. The fuel can, funnel and screwdriver were left in the shed for future use, on Erica's advice.

"Time for a coffee after that, I reckon, Dave?" He readily agreed and they went back into the Manse. Dave left his diesel stained rubber boots in the porch and followed Erica to the kitchen. She attempted to wash the diesel off her hands but instead found she had effectively waterproofed her skin. Her fingers were beginning to itch and she held her fingers under running hot water for as long as she could bear to counteract the irritation from fuel oil. "I'm going to have to see Sally for some hand cream. She wants us for tetanus jabs today so I'll get some off her later." Dave commented, "She said she was going to come down around ten this morning, if I remember rightly. Give us all a chance to wake up before we have our shots, she said last night."

Sally actually appeared in the kitchen doorway around nine-thirty and joined Dave and Erica for coffee. There was no sign of Deborah or Anne yet, though sounds of movement from the bathroom suggested one of them was already up, Anne probably, if it involved showering. At times Dave had been concerned about her obsessive showering but Deborah had assured him it was simply a teenage girl thing and nothing to worry about. Good job they had got the generator going, he thought. Deborah had been wide awake since Dave got up. She had lain in their bed in the back bedroom taking stock of the new and unfamiliar situation she now found herself in. Her job had quickly been filled at the high school. With so many highly qualified young applicants there had been no problem filling the vacancy. She was on St Kilda now so there was little point in harboring the doubts that had kept her awake for much of the night. The failure of the electric supply had occurred after she had finally managed to drop off to sleep so when she joined the others in the kitchen, all seemed normal. There was just a faint odor of diesel fuel not entirely masked by the enticing aroma of the bacon Dave was cooking for them. Erica had brought several weeks supply of muesli and was already tucking into her own breakfast. Deborah noticed she put her spoon down to scratch her fingers from time to time.

Having shared breakfast with them, Sally asked if she could use their shower. The Factor's House had no electricity supply now the power station had been shut down. Cooking was going to be a problem but she had managed to light the woodstove next door in Cottage One and boiled a kettle. It wasn't going to be too bad once she got herself organized. When she had showered and returned to the kitchen, she explained her plan for their vaccinations. "Seeing as it's going to be dark and cold in the Base, I'll go and fetch the tetanus vaccine from the medical room and treat you in here, it will be much nicer."

Sally had been issued with a master key to the Base and leaving the Manse, she turned right and entered the deserted loading bay. It seemed very strange yet also very familiar walking the quiet corridor past empty offices and up the steps to the medical wing. She turned right and with her own separate key opened the Yale locked door into the MRS rooms. She had consulted with her senior medical officer back on South Uist about vaccine storage without electricity. She had been assured that as long as the vials were stored below 8.0C they would be fine for the duration of their shelf life. It had been thought highly unlikely that the temperature in the unheated buildings would rise above that figure before the summer months. All seemed uncannily in order, just as she had left it. She returned to the Manse with two vials of tetanus vaccine, a 5ml plastic syringe and a packet of disposable hypodermic needles. She also took a packet of individually wrapped anti-septic wipes.

With the family gathered in the kitchen, the good natural light made vaccination easy. Given St Kilda's history of tetanus deaths Sally made sure that the Williams were protected. She noticed the redness of Erica's fingers and the way she rubbed them together to counteract a skin irritation. Erica explained about bleeding the generator earlier that morning. Dave had hoped to have kept that secret between the two of them but now it was common knowledge. Deborah made the practical suggestion that they should keep two jerry cans full of fuel outside the Flare Store at all times and top up at least once a day. Anne was less sympathetic and was more concerned about localized effects of spillage to the island ecology.

"Come on, it's our first full day here and we must have better things to worry about than a little spilled diesel. First of all I am going to ring Josephine." Dave went back to the office and connected the batteries to the satellite phone. It took a few moments to connect to the national telephone network but the call to Inverness was made surprisingly easily. Josephine was pleased they had arrived safely but, other than wishing them well, she sounded preoccupied and cut the call short, saying she had a meeting to attend and needed to prepare for it. They were to contact her if they needed administrative back up, but Donald Macintyre should be able to deal with grocery supplies, etc.. She would be in touch again to advise when the first tourists were likely to arrive. Dave returned to the kitchen, "That was short and sweet. She doesn't sound too bothered. We are to liaise with Don for supplies and such like. She'll let us know when the tourists are likely to arrive."

"Hopefully never," Anne made no bones about wanting to be left alone in their new island home.

"I'm looking forward to Dan coming over." Erica was more positive about visitors.

"It will be good to have another man here too," Dave chipped in.

"I could second that!" Deborah teased.

"Now, now, people!" Sally went on to suggest they explored the Base and then she would take anyone who felt like some exercise for a walk round the island. Sally took them to the loading bay next door and led them into the long corridor she had entered earlier that morning. "On the right is the corridor to the kitchens, canteen, gym and VIP lounge.

Just up here, on the left, are the logistics offices where transport on and off the island used to be organized." The group were led along the corridor to the foot of a short flight of steps. "This is the Base Supervisor's Office. Poor devil was killed in a Landrover crash last October, same time as the terrorist attack you probably all heard about."

They climbed the short flight of steps at the end of the corridor. "On the right is my area, the medical wing. I keep the door locked but there are First Aid boxes in all the offices, just let me know if you take anything out of them. I used to keep a record when I worked here but it's still a good idea to keep them topped up. We've plenty of plasters and so on." She led the group through the double doors on their left. "Now here's the root of much past evil." Sally was only half jesting about the bar, quirkily named the 'Puff-Inn'. "It was never a pub in the true sense of the word, but a recreational facility for people working here."

They looked around in amazement. Flags from passing boats and T-shirts from transient servicemen decorated the walls. Mementos of everything from Special Forces to Greenpeace brought home just how many cherished memories had been embedded in that room. There was a dark side too, Sally pointed out. Alcohol dependency had become endemic and was one of the reasons the MOD decided to pull their civilian contractors out and close the Base. The regular military contingent had been removed several years earlier but the legacy of hard drinking had endured. In its heyday the bar staff had admitted passing yacht crews and fishermen and their generally harmless antics had been the talk of the Hebrides.

"Let's have a look in here," she took a key from her bunch and opened the door marked 'Cellar'. Erica, in particular, was surprised by the boxes and boxes of canned beer stacked from floor to ceiling in the storeroom. Well stacked wine racks occupied one wall and on the other dozens of full bottles of whisky and rum waited to be served to customers unlikely to ever return. "Wish I'd known about this last night, Sal." Deborah had missed being able to serve wine with their evening meal. "Technically, this stuff doesn't belong to us, does it, but I suppose if we keep a tally and offer to pay later we could have some of this, Sally?"

"Nothing to do with me, Deborah. You know my feelings on the drink history out here. Be it on your own head, but I'd advise caution. Alcohol has done enough damage to lives here already."

"Oh, Sally. You're being a bit hard aren't you? This must have been such a fun place, too." Deborah imagined the good times had in this bar rather than subsequent problems related to the Puff-Inn.

Erica thought about her times in the Fir Cone back in Edinburgh. "It's not all that different really, Sal."

"It is different, or was, I should say. There have been some awful stories relating to drink here. I hope you never have to find out for yourself, just believe me." Sally suggested they move on. Further up the corridor she pointed out the private quarters of the men who used to work there. Anne crinkled up her nose at the smell of male occupation still lingering in the empty rooms. "They weren't always too particular about where they dried their damp trainers," Sally joked, lightening up as they came to the exit door and led the group outside.

"Dave, I know you poked around here earlier, but for the rest of you this is the remains of the sports hall." The corrugated iron clad Romney Hut had all but collapsed from years of standing in damp salt laden winds blowing up from the bay. She then turned around and pointed to the quiet yet surprisingly modern looking power station building. "There you see the heart of the island. That place used to provide all the heat and power for the Base and the restored cottages in the village. Effectively St Kilda's mothership!"

The rest of the Base buildings looked tired. The supposedly temporary sprayed concrete and wire buildings were beginning to crumble but the power station stood proud as an icon of 1970s modernist design. A Porsche in a scrap yard, thought Dave. A man-made edifice set against the sublime back ground of St Kilda, it almost looked appropriate. There was something surreal about the great structure and he got a strange thrill imagining the great engines turning inside to keep the wilderness at bay.

"Now we have Red Square and the KGB offices." The Williams looked puzzled. "OK, I'll explain. This yard and workshop area was occupied by the maintenance crew whose primary purpose was to maintain the power station. They called themselves the Kilda Generating Board and with initials like that where better to be located than Red Square," she chuckled. "Appropriate for this place set up at the height of the Cold War."

"And cold it is too," shivered Deborah. "Think I've seen enough and I'd like to get back in the warm now."

"We can go back along the front so you get your bearings. Then, as I suggested, I'll take anyone who wants for a walk round the island. It's a good crisp day and the walk will certainly do me some good after yesterday and that rough crossing. I'd like to check out the crash site too, just in case there's anything left lying around up there. There'll doubtless be an air-crash investigation team here soon and I'd like to see if there's anything worth picking up before they get there."

Dave looked surprised at Sally's wrecker attitude to the crash site but on thinking about it realized she was right. "We might as well make use of what's left up there, if anything is of course. Once the investigators cordon off the area that will be that." They made their way back to the Manse along the sea-front road and after making sure they were adequately dressed, Sally led Erica and Anne back outside, Dave and Deborah having declined a potentially arduous guided walk for the time being.

"We'll walk back along the front to the helipad then head out toward the Mistress Stone on Ruiaval. We can have a good look at the old blackhouses later." The three women set off along the front pausing briefly to look down on the jetty. They stood on top of a high gabion sea defense wall. The wire baskets were rusting and quite a few had begun to sag and lose their stones to the relentless pressure of the waves below. Sally explained that in trying to protect the Base, all the MOD engineers had managed to do was deflect the sea's energy a few yards along the shore where it was now undermining the Feather Store which had stood safely for two hundred years until the military intervened.

"This is where that drunken idiot fell off the wall rushing out from the bar to see the students skinny-dipping." Sally recounted the story of the attractive young researcher who had allegedly 'enticed' men to the edge of the cliff. The Coastguard had been less than impressed with the explanation but the siren tale had already reached mythical proportion in Leverburgh. Sally went on to point out the jetty was one of the few places where rod and line fishing was feasible as the structure reached out beyond the kelp forest that surrounded all but the sandy beach.

"It was pretty daft really, the guys went fishing but they had no way of cooking their catch. They were all fed in the canteen. Even when fishing boats came in and offered fresh herring the cooks turned them away because they were not allowed to take anything that had not come through MOD supply chain. It was like a basic human instinct to provide for yourself being played out yet never coming to fruition. That's the story of this island since it became a world heritage asset rather than the sustainable community it once was."

As Sally led the two sisters further along the road, Erica enquired about the massive stone walls crossing the pasture that seemed to serve no logical purpose. The Soay sheep sunning themselves against it were in good condition and the ewes obviously in lamb. "These are the consumption walls, built simply to 'consume' the vast amount of stone that was removed to create this field system in the nineteenth century. Led by the Minister, the villagers cleared stones from the land and, with their copious composting, produced rich and fertile fields. I think I mentioned that these fields were reputed to have grown the best barley in the Hebrides. Looking at these sheep I'd say the ground was still pretty rich, wouldn't you?"

A few yards further they came to a series of green fuel tanks to the left of the road, half hidden behind a man-made bank and standing inside a concrete bund. "This is the fuel store for the power station," Sally explained. She pointed out large steel plates thrown up on rocks nearby. "They extended the slipway across the beach but the sea was always lifting them. It was an endless task keeping the landing-craft slipway operational. Being all electric we used a hell of a lot of fuel to keep the power station running, a thousand pounds a day I believe it cost and us being in the windiest place in the UK too. Why they didn't bring in wind turbines I'll never know. The landing craft used to bring the fuel and when it beached the warden had to stand and watch like a hawk to ensure no rat or other alien species came ashore. No cats, eh? The fuel landings were the weak point that could have burst the bubble of our island biosphere."

Immediately after the diesel tanks they came to the helipad with its hand written sign *International Airport Lounge*. Weeds were starting to grow in cracks in the concrete and the drains had long blocked up. This tiny airport would have had a distinctly run down third world feel to it, had it been big enough. A shredded orange wind sock moved gently in the breeze. It had never been put away after the last evacuation flight left. The chopper pilot from South Uist had been glad of it though when he picked up the one survivor of the Piper crash. Hard to believe that had been only the morning before, it felt like weeks ago, thought Erica, still struggling to take in everything that she was being shown.

"Here's the fire-pond. It supplies water to the hydrants around the Base. There's a big pump in that shed over there." Turning to Anne, "You see some great birds washing here in the summer. It's the only fresh water pond this side of the island. There's a lochan in Glen Mór but its full of Bonxies, no other bird dares go near it."

"Ever heard of Saint Columba?" Erica certainly new the connection with Iona and the speculative link with the Loch Ness Monster but according to Sally the Irish missionary had also landed at St Kilda. He certainly got around, she thought to herself. The remains of his early Christian chapel could just be made out beyond the twentieth century helipad. Sally led the group up a steep track not much more than a sheep path. After five minutes they stopped to get their breath back beneath the scree slope of Mullach Sgar.

Apart from the considerable numbers of cleits utilizing the ready supply of stone, Sally pointed out what looked like slit trenches dug out in the scree. "Those are the 'hidey-holes'", Sally continued. "The villagers used to hide there and keep a watch whenever pirates entered the bay. It was a regular occurrence in the Middle Ages, so I read. Barbary pirates from North Africa raided all up the west of the British Isles and took slaves away with them. The St Kildans wouldn't have stood a chance without having somewhere to hide out and wait till they had gone. The hidey-holes are ideal places where you can keep a watch on the bay yet not be seen by anyone looking up. They can only be seen by looking down from above."

"I'll make a mental note of that for the next time pirates turn up here, Sally." Erica was not convinced but was polite enough not to challenge Sally on a subject she knew even less about herself.

The group got their breath back and following the cliff path again they shortly came to another small settlement and some rusting remains of what, to Anne, looked like harbor lights. "What are these, Sally?"

"These are, as you rightly suspected, navigation lights. Any large ship, of which there were many, would sail slowly into the bay and when the captain saw these two lights align he knew he had reached the safe anchorage point. A simple but clever idea, Anne." Anne thought the explanation a bit too simple but wasn't going to let Sally see it.

"Now we are at another ecclesiastical settlement. This is the site of Saint Brendan's Chapel, another Irish missionary who came here to save the St Kildans from themselves. They must have been a bad lot in the Dark Ages!" Sally laughed at her own joke. "The reality would have most likely been a party of Celtic monks coming to settle closer to their God who could be found more readily in wild and lonely places away from human distraction on the mainland."

"Away from distracting womankind too." Erica could see a thread connecting centuries of male occupation at St Kilda. "You've got something there, Erica. Wealthy Victorians used to flock here to experience the Sublime. They'd look out in awe from their cruise boats and wax lyrically on the divine works of nature without engaging with anything, least of all the island's inhabitants who lived and worked here. The

Church was just as bad, flogging male fundamentalism out here without any one to challenge them. Nearer my God to thee, pah! Nearer their own empty male egos, more like. I bet it's no coincidence the Cailleach's Cave is just below us here. Brendan probably deliberately chose this place so he could build his chapel on top of her."

This time both Erica and Anne looked genuinely puzzled. "Wait a minute, we've named our cat Cailly, short for Cailleach, the wise woman. Do you mean a wise woman, maybe a Hebridean witch actually lived here?"

"Not a witch, Anne. You are just repeating accepted prejudice by using that term for a woman strong enough to resist male domination. Legend suggests there was a female deity resident on this island too. She is reported from all over the Western Isles but out here on the horizon, the edge of the known world to medieval Hebrideans, she had her home. Later on I'll show you the Amazon's House in Glen Mór, a later 'male' interpretation of the legend. The cave below us is named after the Cailleach and you are supposed to be able to keep a secret watch over the village from inside it too. There's a story of sea-borne raiders locking the chapel door after everyone had gone inside to seek sanctuary and then burning the place down. Just one sensible woman decided against the God's protection and hid in the Cailleach's Cave instead. Unseen amongst the Mothan plants that grow so well down there, she survived to tell the story. So Saint's Brendan and Columba, suck on that!"

She hadn't expected it, but Erica was really warming to Sally. Anne was not so sure but had listened intently to the legend of St Kilda's Amazon. "Enough of my ranting about male injustice on this island, come on I'll show you where we women had the upper hand. Let's see the Mistress Stone."

The three women made their way across the grassy slope toward the rocky hill of Ruiaval, the Viking Red Hill, towering above the narrow strait between Hirta and Dun. Anne noticed a subtle change in the springy turf. As they crossed the saddle of the headland, the grass beneath their feet changed to close cropped Thrift a pink flowering plant she knew tolerated salt spray in a way few other vascular plants could. Un-noticed by Erica, Anne realized this meant that at certain times sea-spray must wash over this pasture hundreds of feet above the now calm waters of the bay. The latent power of elemental forces waiting to be unleashed both disturbed and exited her. Sally led the sisters along a narrow path leading underneath a natural arch where a slab of granite had slipped from the Tor to form a bridge above the gullied path. They climbed underneath and then up above onto the slab with the exposed Atlantic surging far below.

"Yep, this place is one of ours, girls!" Sally explained how men wanting to impress their sweethearts would walk to the edge of this slab, stand on one leg and then touch their big-toe clinging to the edge. If they overbalanced that would be it. No woman would marry a man until he had performed the feat for her, cool or what? The reality was that a man had to have a good head for heights if he was going to provide for his family by collecting seabird eggs from the cliffs. This ritual ensured survival of the fittest. You were no good if you got scared on the cliff face. If you look further along you can see cleits built in the most ridiculous places. I reckon that was a test too. Extreme cleit building to prove you knew how to build a stone house on these slopes, as well as having a good head for heights. Just imagine coming out of your bothy first thing in the morning to find a five hundred foot drop right in front of you. OK, back to the present."

She led them down from the Mistress Stone and followed the cliff path on the Atlantic side of the headland toward the first of the twentieth century radomes. Here, on the side of the headland fully exposed to the Atlantic, the prevailing wind from the north-west was relentless. The women pulled back from the cliff path and opted for the crumbling metaled track servicing the damaged radome and ancillary buildings of Mullach Sgar. A heavy door was banging open and closed in the wind. "This must have been where that bloke tried to ring for help after the plane crash," suggested Anne. "I never came down this far yesterday. Hey look at that!"

They could just make out the words *Welcome to St Kilda* painted on the crumbling surface of the roadway as it levelled out toward the flat top ridge of Mullach Sgar. "Oh, yeah. Apparently, before the regular supply helicopter service, small planes would line up here to drop mail and lightweight supplies. Rather them than me is all I can say. If you look further along you'll see a zebra crossing and, so I have been told, there used to be red telephone box at the T-junction. That is just so bizarre but at least the guys did have a sense of humor when they first came here. I think I would have liked to have worked here then but it was all alcoholism and depression by the time I arrived."

Anne recognized the T-junction where she and Sally had gasped their way up the previous afternoon. The steep road back to the village dropped rapidly through a series of hair-pin bends. The grey granite cottages and blackhouses were catching the sunlight and contrasted with the surrounding unnaturally green village fields. They walked the few hundred yards or so over to the crash site and examined the damaged cleit where the light plane had gone over the edge.

The rusting remains of a Sunderland flying boat engine lay close by as a testimony to the perils of aviation in Glen Mór. "I do hope this is the last accident here but somehow I doubt it. Most men never escape their own testosterone poisoning. I just hope they were all dead before it went over," said Sally.

There was nothing to salvage seen lying on the ground around the cleit. Only the one wrecked Piper engine as evidence there had been a light plane there at all. It was of no interest to the women and neither, probably they thought, to any subsequent investigation team. The wind had quickly dispersed whatever could be blown away. The oil stained granite would quickly be blasted clean by the elements and gouge in the turf would eventually grow over. Maybe an interesting summer season as new plants colonize the bare soil, thought Anne. The wind was beginning to gust around the cleits and Sally suggested they kept moving before they got cold. Only Anne noticed the long green Cordura bag inside the damaged cleit, partially concealed by dislodged stones and turf. She decided not to mention it but come back on her own later so find out what it contained.

Sally led them on past the Sunderland engine, following the low boundary earth dyke, a bank that had demarcated the limit of centuries of safe grazing in Glen Mor. "Curious isn't it, how the cattle knew never to cross this barrier? Bit like a modern electric fence, cattle could easily push past but had been trained to experience pain if they tried. It must have been a similar thing but the St Kildan women trained their cattle to fear crossing this barrier, what do you think?" She left the question open for the sisters to ponder on as they walked toward the first steep climb for a while. The earth dyke terminated at a steep rocky incline just beyond a collection of cleits overlooking a steep grass slope beneath them leading to the sea. The slope covered several acres and once sliding there would be no stopping anyone foolish enough to venture there in wet conditions. Experienced mountaineers had suggested her taking an ice axe when she wanted to go there in the past. There was a relatively safe way down to Carn Mór, the interesting boulder field beneath the peak of Mullach Bi which she could show them later. In April, Puffins would return to nest among the rocks in their thousands. There were stories of some kind of tunnel down there, maybe an aborted attempt at mining had taken place in an age of eighteenth century entrepreneurship. Who knew? There were no records from an island that had no need for the written word almost into living memory. Sally had never actually explored Carn Mór thoroughly so couldn't enlighten them further. With knees aching they reached the top of Mullach Bi where the path levelled out. The cliff on the seaward side dropped shear for over a thousand feet and as the available flat land narrowed the path took them into a small pass where, below, the precipitous slope into Glen Mór was accessible by only the most agile of the island sheep. Many a day tripper had turned back at this point, not wanting to risk going further, Sally recounted. "Good for the soul and bad for the knees is what I say about this bit," she joked.

Having had aspirations for small-holding in the past, Erica was concerned at the poor condition of the wild sheep in this area and asked Sally about it. "The answer lies in the soil, Erica. Back on the village fields there's been years and years of intense fertilization. The St Kildans made compost from whatever was to hand, from seabird offal to their own body waste mixed with soot from the peat fires. They even composted sooty thatch when they re-roofed the blackhouses. Out here at the back of the island the land is much poorer though you'll see in a minute that any available flat area was utilized at some time or other. We'll come to the Cambir shortly and flat areas there have obviously been cultivated sometime in the past."

The Cambir peninsular reached out toward Soay, less than a mile north-west of the main island, Hirta. From here arguably the most dramatic views of the St Kilda archipelago could be seen, though few tourists had the fitness to venture that far from the village. Many would have been physically up to it but psychologically, it proved too much of a challenge to be really alone and unseen on the far side of the island. Sally made a very salient point about tourists not crossing to the far side of the island. "Men in particular have to run the gauntlet of Bonxie attack during summer months. The local name for the Great Skua comes from the Norse for grumpy old woman. For some reason or other the grumpy Skuas are less aggressive to female walkers."

"Getting back to the landscape, it wouldn't be true to say there are no signs of human habitation on the Cambir, just no recent signs. The ruins at the foot of Glen Mór are ancient, from a time neither the archaeologists nor modern visitors can connect with. Psychologically, Glen Mór is a very uneasy place for any man to be in. Not so difficult for women as we will shortly find out."

Apart from that, as Sally had said, it was proving very difficult going under foot. Easy to get down the slopes but quite another story climbing back up again.

The women came to the 'neck' of the Cambir where the sea was eroding from both sides. At this narrow point the St Kildans had built another low barrier to deter livestock from entering the cultivated area. Although more substantial than the earth barrier at the top of the glen, stones were crumbling into the sea at both ends of the old wall. A few hundred yards further the women climbed laboriously to the end point of the peninsular and looked in awe at the strait between Hirta and Soay. Seals could be heard calling from caves hidden beneath adding to their feeling of isolation.

Anne asked the question, "Soay Sheep, is that where they come from, then?"

"Yes," Sally replied. "*Soay* is Norse for sheep, the Vikings named the island apparently and after the 1930 evacuation a flock of one hundred was brought over to 'maintain the grazing'. In other words they were brought over as four-legged lawnmowers. If you look around the island they are doing a pretty good job. Doubt you could find anything long enough to thatch a blackhouse roof with today. If you look over there," she pointed to the island of Boreray four miles away to the north-east. "With binoculars you can see descendants of other sheep abandoned in 1930. Regular white Highland blackface types but in 1930 there was no-one able enough to go and get them. Their descendants live on as the most isolated flock in Britain."

"Hey, look at that, another plane wreck?" Erica had spotted metal wreckage across the strait on Soay. Near the top of a scree slope lay the weathered remains of another aircraft. "Yep, some other silly sods tried to fly gung-ho through the gap only to find themselves picked up by the wind and slammed into the side of Soay, ironically close to the site where Duggan, one of the pirate bastards who burnt the church down was exiled to die alone. Like the Sunderland wreck, that crash was during World War Two when this island was a flight training area. There's a small memorial plaque to them in the village Kirk."

"This place is like a male graveyard," said Anne, out loud this time. "You'd be surprised Anne. Over there on top of Soay is an altar erected by St Kildan men in the nineteenth century. The Free Church required they worshiped every day and when they went off bird nesting or sheep shearing away from Hirta they always took a minister with them, even on the Stacs out there."

"They would probably be too shit scared to be over here without their God to protect them," added Anne. "Well that's one way of looking at it, Anne," Sally added pointing to the towering rock stacs looming from the waters at the end of Boreray. "There's been some weird shit out here to put it mildly. Ever heard of the Great Auk?" The sisters shook their heads. "That's because it's fucking extinct! The Church really screwed up minds on this island. A party of men were out there and got marooned in bad weather and came across a Great Auk. With all the stories of fornication and sin they'd been hearing, those sad bastards got it into their heads that they had found a witch who was conjuring up a storm just to spite them. They stoned the poor bird to death. Great Auks were the northern penguin and this one was maybe the last one on the planet. It was stoned to death right here because local cultural practice conflicted with patriarchal Christianity to bring about a medieval mind-fuck here in 19th century St Kilda, and you wonder why I'm an eco-feminist. I love the natural world but these Church elders came here and screwed the place along with everything in it. Their sad legacy is embedded here, as you will surely find out sooner or later."

Erica and Anne stood stunned into silence by Sally's tearful outburst. It felt slightly uncomfortable to find themselves in this isolated spot with their guide in such a volatile psychological state. Anne switched off from it all and concentrated on spanning the far side of Glen Bay. Erica reached out and squeezed Sally's hand in a gesture of support.

"Sorry, I've gone and done it again, that tale about the last Great Auk really gets to me."

"Oh, Sally; this island must be an awful place for you?"

"No, Erica. I see St Kilda as a place of opportunity. There's a chance here to put things right. Rebuild a real community where everyone's effort is valued, not just male efforts to dominate everything. Just look over there." Erica pointed at the radomes and fallen mast clearly visible across the glen on the high ground of Mullach Mor. There could have been regular work here for several families. They could have carried on small scale farming and had a resident nurse cum teacher, just like in the old days when this island still worked. Now look at it, a place where men attack other men over their precious ideologies. When we go back, have a look in the museum. You see old photographs of the women who lived here, I just don't understand why they accepted domination by the Church. Do we ask to be dominated like that?"

Anne had been listening intently to this conversation and, though the youngest woman there, she made a knowing comment. "I think that in accepting male values, we are not being dominated. In their pathetic attempt to dominate lies our source of power. We should not consider ourselves dominated; in their attempts to control, men demean themselves and that should actually empower us."

Erica added, "I expect it was more a matter of being worn down by unremitting hard work trying to keep a community going here. I did a little reading before we came and by the time of the evacuation the community consisted mainly of ageing women. There was only so much they could do after the men and young adults left rather than stay and support elderly women. Maybe it's no wonder women turned to the ministers, male figures strong enough to actually stay on the island and try to help even if, in our eyes, they were seriously misguided?"

Through the discussion, Sally regained her composure and led the party down the steep slope to the ruins at the bottom of Glen Mór. "Mind your step here, it's very slippery," she warned as they slithered down to the remains of substantial stone rows and outline of a small megalithic stone circle.

"This area is a mystery. It's so old even the archaeologists can't agree on an age for it but the consensus says it's the remains of a settlement begun four thousand years ago. It's easy walking now we are down here and I'll try not to rant anymore. I shouldn't unburden myself on you like that."

"That's OK," said Erica. "Carry on with the tour, Leader!" With the mood lightened, the women quickly crossed the bottom of the glen taking care to avoid the slippery sloping rock shelf reaching to the sea.

"This, believe it or not is an alternative landing place and boats do occasionally anchor in Glen Bay to shelter from south-easterly winds. This must have been where the terrorists landed last year. The glen was full of Bonxies at that time and I doubt they'd have managed their attack in daylight. There's a supposedly holy well here too." Sally led the group to a small well covered with a dry stone shelter similar to the one Erica provocatively attempted to clear the previous evening back in the village. "Around the time Church influence began, the 'Apostle of the North', Dr John MacDonald landed here and blessed this well. It is lovely clean water and was probably a blessed well long before he arrived to claim it for his own God. We are only a few yards from the Amazon's House here."

She led them up the sloping path past the lochan where, each Spring, the islands Great Skua population would congregate. The Bonxies had a special attraction for this place though, she added, no-one had so far ascertained why. "A research job for you, Anne?" Sally quipped to the sisters.

The stone settlement of the Amazon's House was now clearly visible but unlike anything they had seen before. Erica had travelled in West Africa during her student days and thought they reminded her of family compounds. There were around a dozen of these compounds referred to by archaeologists simply as 'horned structures'. Three domed cells linked by a stone wall sat at the back of a horseshoe shaped corral, presumably for penning livestock, Sally surmised.

"Indeed," Sally continued. "St Kildan women made use of these structures as lambing sheds or as shielings when they had to spend the night away from home. It's a bit odd that they would spend the night out when home is just over the hill though. So much history here that we simply have no idea about. The later St Kildans didn't know what these buildings were for so named the biggest one the Amazon's House, connecting it with the Cailleach legend, perhaps? Pretty well every nook and cranny on this island is connected to some personal anecdote or other, I just love it!"

The women began the long climb up the glen following the line the doomed Piper had taken the day before. "Save your energy, folks. It gets steeper as we go up the glen. I always say it's easier getting down into this place than to get out again, bit like life ha, ha."

The climb proved harder than Erica or Anne had expected and even more unexpected was the sudden blast of wind that hit them as they reached the line of cleits leading to the ridge of Mullach Geal The three of them momentarily struggled to keep their feet and Erica's woolen hat span away, snatched from her by an unseen vortex.

"Bloody hell! Where did that come from?" Erica was annoyed at the loss of her hat and absolutely amazed that a wind like that had come out of nowhere on such a calm morning. It felt almost personal.

"That," said Sally, "is probably what caused the plane crash yesterday and also probably what downed the Sunderland all those years ago and threw the Wellington Bomber into the side of Soay. The two-thousand foot flying rule wasn't put in place just to stop birds getting scared."

The women struggled up to the ridge and found themselves on the military road above the T-junction. Here they could see faint signs of where the zebra crossing had been painted shortly after the army engineers finished Operation Hardrock. "We'll turn left here and walk up past the damaged masts and then onto Conachair before we go back down. Are you all up for another climb?" Anne looked at Erica who had just found her woolly hat lying beside the road. "Go for it! We have survived OK so far." Anne was keen to see as much of the island she could on this their first full day there.

They followed the metaled road uphill through a double hairpin bend and soon came to the fallen communication mast. It had simply been pushed to one side of the road by the Case loader and abandoned. It was if the men had simply given up. No attempt had been made to dismantle or salvage the structure and the damaged buildings stood as reminder of the night that served as a catalyst to bringing military occupation of St Kilda to an end. The women made their way around the fallen mast and onto the flat moorland beyond. The moor was eroded away to bedrock in places for this area had been the prime source of peat for St Kilda, informed Sally. They looked down a thousand feet drop to the sea on one side and on the other side of the moor saw an equal though slightly less precipitous drop back to the village.

"By the end of the nineteenth century, there were no pack animals left here and young adults were leaving the island. Can you imagine getting on in years and having to struggle up here to dig peat and carry it back down again? Yes, it would have been dried in cleits first but what an effort to be able to warm your cottage and cook your food down there. The old people began resorting to digging up pasture turf nearer home some years before they left. It really pissed off the landlord but keeping warm had taken priority over grazing by the time the evacuation came."

The ground started to rise steeply in front of them as they followed the cliff path to the summit of Conachair. A few minutes later they reached the stone cairn erected on the peak. Sally informed them they were now atop the highest sea cliff in Western Europe. The view across to Boreray and the stacks was stupendous. On top of Stac Armin the white gannets and their guano looked as dazzling as snow set against the dark rock and sea beneath.

"That, she pointed out, "is the biggest gannet colony in the world." Sally looked at Anne who nodded her head in confirmation. The women had been out for several hours and up here in the wind they quickly began to feel cold.

"Come on, time to go down out of the wind, I think." Sally was eager to get back though the sisters were still fascinated by the new world revealing itself to them. Not simply the land and seascapes but fascinated by a landscape so embedded with past failings and future hopes.

"That's odd," pointed out Erica. "Why isn't that trig point on top of the hill instead of below the summit?" She had spotted the Ordnance Survey triangulation point fifty feet and a hundred yards below the hill top. These cartographic survey points, obsolete since the advent of GPS technology, are found on summits across the British Isles. It was imperative one could be seen from the other to facilitate survey using optical equipment. "I've wondered about that, Erica. I reckon it must be that we are at the edge of the map here, the last trig point this side of the British Isles. Makes sense really as there's no more land to survey beyond here, is there?"

Satisfied with her explanation the sisters followed Sally on the steep descent to the corrie at the foot of the slope below the cliff edge known as the Gap. Between the two hills of Conachair and Oiseval, the Gap above An Lag to give the corrie its Gaelic name held the remains of many stone structures. Lines of cleits on the slopes terminated at a nineteenth century stone walled field system. These enclosures had previously been used for the annual sheep gathering and, so Sally explained, for growing crops in the one south facing area away from strong winds and salt spray. The first Church minister who organized their construction had had his head screwed on when it came to agriculture. Closer to the village cleits became numerous and other stone structures became evident. Sally pointed out what the archaeologists termed boat shaped settings. They weren't sure but it was considered feasible these were Viking graves. With no timber on the island and the impossibility of dragging a boat up there, the Norse settlers had built stone boats in which to sail their fallen dignitaries off to Nirvana. There was evidence of Viking burial on the island, later medieval and Victorian gravestones, but nothing from the Iron Age, which, Sally emphasized, continued at St Kilda while the mainland was in the medieval period. "They really were culturally isolated out here," she added.

"Bet they had sky-burials," quipped Anne. "That would account for the lack of funerary evidence from the Iron Age. The Bonxies would have liked sky burials had they been around at the time!"

From the head of the Gap, the women walked down into what one warden had jokingly named the Valley of Death, there being so many Skuas nesting there in the spring and summer months. Great Skuas nested on the flatter areas of Oiseval and the faster and meaner Arctic Skuas attacked anyone foolish enough to venture into their nesting ground beneath Conachair. The trick was to walk strictly up the center of the valley, between the two Skua territories, keeping the stone walled enclosures on your left. When the carrion feeding Bonxies came to dive-bomb human intruders, parasitic Arctic Skuas scrambled and attacked their encroaching neighbors with ferocious aerial agility. The walker could then continue on his or her way unmolested while the Skuas sparred in the air above them.

The women walked down past the enclosures and found

themselves at the head of the supposedly dry burn and remains of old water tanks. They were disconcerted to see so many sheep carcasses in the water catchment area. "You can see why we had that new borehole dug, can't you. Before, we had to heavily chlorinate all the drinking water out here. It wasn't reliable either, in summer we often had to go without showers and drink bottled water brought in on the landing craft." The new borehole stood out in the marshy ground though it was too early in the year for the Mothan that had colonized the disturbed damp soil to be much evident, other than a scattering of dead brown leaves lying around the concrete well head.

Cloud was forming over Dun and behind them the summit of Conachair was now hidden. Moist winds had lifted up over the cooling summits to condense into the long plumes of cloud the islands were famous for, adding to the sublime effect beloved by artists and photographers and detested by helicopter pilots. A flash of brown feathers diving behind a nearby cleit indicated time was getting on and the Merlin was hunting. A few steps more and the women came out on the street beside the Factor's House.

"One thing puzzles me Sally, I know you can cook on the woodstove in Cottage One but what are you doing about light in there?" The Factor's House looked gloomy in the lowering evening light. "I thought of that one, Erica. I brought some oil lamps over with me just before my contract ended and left them in the Sheepie store. They work a treat with diesel oil. They'd have used Fulmar oil in the past so not that different really, just a lot less smelly I expect."

Anne was eager to get back to the Manse, Erica said she would just walk back up the street and look at the old blackhouses before coming in.

Beyond Cottage Six, the roofless former homes and empty windows proved a poignant reminder of everything Sally had been talking about on their walk. The abandonment of this planned settlement must have been down to more than simply male religious intransigence. Blackhouses stood between the shells of bleak Victorian cottages facing the sea. It looked like there had been two distinct phases in the development of the village. Two mind-sets at work? The wind suddenly gusted from the bay nearly blowing her hat off for the second time that day. Odd, she thought the wind was from the north up on top of the hill, now it's gusting from the south. The blackhouses were end on to the gust and low doors and windows faced each other across narrow alleyways set ninety degrees to the linear street or Sea-View Terrace she was thinking to herself. She went up one of the alleys and entered a roofless, yet still surprisingly cozy blackhouse. The penny dropped, it must have been the wind that conspired against inappropriate Victorian planning to ruin this community as much as subservience to male dogma. The first phase in the development would have accepted local, indigenous wisdom to work with the elements rather than stand four square against them, unlike the second phase. Erica was slightly puzzled, the Manse was OK though. Facing the bay it had stood strong since the beginning of the nineteenth century. Designed by the lighthouse engineer Robert Stevenson, both the Manse and Kirk had been well located. Likewise the eighteenth century Feather Store protected by the great bulk of Oiseval. Further up in the village, away from the Kirk and on the edge of the wilderness, winds gusted unpredictably and with far greater ferocity. The ultimate folly had been to build the helipad in the worst possible position for safe landing. No wonder the pilots treated landings at St Kilda with the greatest of respect, as Sally had mentioned earlier.

Slowly walking back, deep in thought, Sally imagined what it would be like to restore one of those eminently practical blackhouses. She had visited the Earthship houses near Brighton in south-east England and could see distinct similarities in the way these structures worked with the elements and landscape around them. She dreamed of a Hebridean Blackhouse with efficient wood stove and solar panels. Well maybe a small wind generator would be a better idea given the persistent gusts out here, even a micro-hydro system as well to make use of the burns running down from Conachair. The prospect was exiting, so obvious in fact. Only the Western Isles Trust wouldn't entertain the idea of them changing anything, according to her father. Well she'd make plans to restore one of those black houses anyway.

First knocking on the door, she called into Cottage One where Sally had lit the woodstove and was boiling a Kettle. A reproduction Victorian oil lamp was burning brightly on the long wooden table contrasting with the dark stainless steel kitchen facility opposite.

"Hi Sally, would you mind if I had another look at your books?"

"They're not mine, they were left by behind by Trust volunteers over the years. Go ahead, borrow what you like."

Erica studied the bookshelves and settled on a volume by Andrew Fleming *St Kilda and the Wider World*. "I'll take this one and bring it back later, if that's OK?" Sally said she could keep it as long as she liked. It was one of the more popular books on St Kilda and there were plenty more in the shop. Erica felt slightly uncomfortable in Cottage One. Sally was using it as her personal space and Erica could sense she needed time to herself after the physically and, for her, emotionally draining tour of the island.

Evening was drawing in and Dave had topped up the generator fuel tank by the time Erica got back to the Manse. The diesel engine was beginning to sound comforting rather than irritating to her, a sign that there would be light and warmth inside. Blackhouses could be made light and warm again too, she thought, and without the need for importing fossil fuel. She was fired up by her idea and longed to have someone to share plans with.

Erica shared her dreams over their evening meal in the brightly lit kitchen. Dave was enthusiastic in principle. There would be nothing he would like better than restore a blackhouse and really live off grid using the plentiful natural energy sources around them. There was just one problem and that was they were on St Kilda as custodians for the Trust and had to keep things exactly as they were when they arrived. Yes, it felt nonsensical to him also to have to keep a generator running on imported diesel to be able to function in this house. It was alright for Sally, she had a wood stove handy and was used to the place. Deborah poured cold water on the whole prospect of restoring a blackhouse. She wanted home comforts and that included being able to flick a switch for light and warmth, especially as they didn't have to pay the bill for it.

"As long as I keep the generator topped up," added Dave somewhat irritated by his wife's seeming lack of adventurous spirit he admired in Erica. "Dave, I do actually have to stay on this God forsaken island with you, or had you forgotten that fact?"

Anne looked up from her bird identification book and added that as far as she was concerned, she wanted electricity from whatever source as long as it kept her room warm and powered her lap-top. Erica threw her hands up in resignation and continued eating though barely hid her underlying tension. Dave broke the ice forming around the dinner table by saying he had had a brief phone message from Dan. Due to the cost of ringing a satellite connection he had just let him know the car was safely back in Edinburgh and that he was looking forward to visiting at Easter. Erica looked up showing interest at the prospect. "At least he might be supportive of my sustainability ideas," she commented.

Deborah was looking out of the kitchen window and in the front porch light she could see snowflakes beginning to fall. "Brrr! Now it's beginning to snow. Speaking for myself I am very, very glad we have got this generator and a free supply of diesel."

Erica stood up abruptly and picking up her hooded coat by the door, put it on and walked down to the jetty for a smoke. The Atlantic Grey seal that popped up to watch her gave her fresh hope that her dream for living on St Kilda would be supported when Dan turned up. He had promised as much when they sat up late into the small hours at his flat, talking about the adventure she was about to undertake. He admitted that though 'obviously intelligent', he was no academic and doubted he would finish his course. If he had the opportunity she now had to live a sustainable life away from the chaos of the city, he would do exactly the same. His words hadn't quite rung true but they were good enough for her to feel very close to him and after they finally made love that night she lay awake imagining how it would be with him on the island.

The Williams family established a routine around fueling the generator that sustained late winter life for them. Sally busied herself with looking after their welfare. She not only administered first aid as necessary but kept notes on their psychological state, effectively she kept a diary on the mental health of her co-residents, though not one of the Williams family thought to keep a watch on her, apart from Anne who made it her business to miss nothing. Without electricity the bath in the Factor's House remained unused and Sally became a regular, if brief visitor, in the Manse to take her evening shower. Once washed, Sally kept to herself preferring to spend her evenings beside the woodstove in Cottage One. It didn't take Cailly long either to adopt the rug in front of Sally's stove as her main residence and with the ready supply of oversized mice the large sack of dried cat food brought for her from the mainland was little used.

There were some birds wintering on the island; Redwings, Pied Wagtails, Meadow Pipits, Wrens and Starlings to name some of them plus the occasional vagrant blown in from the north Atlantic. Cailly sensed there were no others of her kind on the island, the last cats having been shot in the 1930s. Cailly kept to the abandoned cottages and hunted along the stone walls rarely bothering the birds which would have involved leaving her cover. The flash of brown as the Merlin pounced on yet another Pipit unsettled her and there were days when she refused to leave Cottage One, making use of the sand tray placed inside for her by Sally who understood her predicament. The sheep which had previously gathered around the comforting rumble of the power station now spent their nights around the east end of the Manse drawn to the similar, if diminutive, sound and smell of the small generator maintained by the Williams family. Sheep folding in the former Manse walled garden would soon come to be a problem for Dave's plans to feed his family from the land.

The winter on St Kilda passed with more quiet frosty days than in previous years. The prolonged cold brought little snow. It seemed to Dave, with his geographers' understanding, that the north Atlantic must be cooling and less moisture than usual was lifting from waters that would have previously been warmed by the Gulf Stream. Caribbean warmth was failing to reach the north-east Atlantic and exceptional cold was being experienced along the west of Ireland, Norway and the western coastline of the British Isles. The climate was changing and the first yacht arrived in Village Bay in early March when in previous years Spring storm conditions would have precluded any small boat from venturing out in the Hebrides. An iceberg had been reported floating off the Faeroes according to the experienced yacht skipper who landed to make his acquaintance. He had heard that global warming was melting the Greenland ice-cap and icebergs were being calved into the north Atlantic at an unprecedented rate. The other side of the coin was that with less temperature differential between the tropics and the arctic the Gulf Stream was meandering, its current slowing down the flow of warm water to the Western Isles that kept them several degrees warmer than the Scottish mainland. The arctic might be warming but the Hebrides were getting colder. As if to compensate, in 2010 and 2011 Icelandic volcanoes had belched out thousands upon thousands of tons of cooling ash into the upper atmosphere, disrupting air travel. The climate of the North East Atlantic was definitely becoming more and more unpredictable.

8 BONXIES

The *Beluga* roared into Village Bay bringing the first tourists to St Kilda just before Easter. The unusually calm conditions created by high pressure centered over drifting pack ice south of Greenland had enabled an early start to the visitor season that year. The Williams were caught on the hop with Cottage Three, the museum still mothballed for the winter. Erica and Anne quickly placed the exhibits back on display and opened up for the public. Sally and Deborah got the shop ready for business while Dave went down to the jetty to greet the fare paying arrivals. Don apologized for not notifying them beforehand but he was taking advantage of the unexpected calm conditions. The weather was strange for the time of year and he didn't want to lose out if autumn storms brought an end to the season earlier than expected.

The visitors came ashore in good spirits. Don usually reckoned on one or two cases of seasickness on the best of crossings. With the sea so calm there were none. Fulmars whirled around the cliffs reclaiming their nesting places. The Puffins had yet to arrive from wintering out in the Atlantic. Similarly the Shearwaters and Petrels had yet to return nor the Great Skuas that predated on them. The arrival and departure of seabirds coincided with Spring and Autumn equinoxes, likewise human visitors. Breeding success for many of the seabirds had been poor in recent years with changing sea currents taking sand eels and other small fish out of range of Puffins and Kittiwakes reliant on them to feed their young. Few human visitors understood that seabirds could do everything but build a nest out on the ocean. If the small fish on which they relied to feed their young were carried beyond ecologic flying range the population was bound to crash. Fulmars and other far ranging birds converted their stomach contents to oil before returning to their young. A stomach full of oil contained far more calories than a beak full of small fish and Fulmars survived when Puffins failed. It was no wonder the Fulmar was such a mainstay of the former St Kilda economy. The exception on the island was the Great Skua which with size and aggression managed to feed its young by intimidating other birds into giving up their catch or simply predating on them. Screams of outrage, even from Greater Black-backed Gulls, announced the Spring arrival of the Skuas to the island. Away from the safe confines of village fields, new-born Soay lambs were decimated by these large brown seabirds. This year with fewer humans to contend with Skuas were beginning to predate closer to the abandoned village than ever before.

"Back on the jetty for three-thirty folks!" Don's cheery instruction to the visitors gave them about four and a half hours in which to explore the island. Not many made the long slog up the track to the island summit and those that did were becoming increasingly bothered by Skua attack. The Bonxies, Don warned them, were getting worse. While working for the Base, Sally frequently had had to apply anti-septic and dressings where heavy beaks and claws had torn at bald heads. Tall men were the most likely to be attacked. The trick, she always advised, was to hold a walking stick up over your shoulder like an aerial and the birds would attack the highest point. It worked for Great Skuas but not the Arctic Skuas which would fly straight for your eyes.

With advice from Don Macintyre, the Williams soon managed workable procedures for the museum and souvenir shop. Cruise ships were no longer coming to the island now that Base facilities had been closed down. After the Mediterranean sinking of the Costa Concordia in 2012, cruise ship operators steered well clear of rocky islands with few facilities. Daily visits from the *Beluga* brought new life to the Williams family and after several days of waiting, Erica was delighted to see Dan come up the jetty steps carrying a heavy rucksack and guitar case. Slipping on algal growth, his first comment had been to request a stiff broom and he'd scrub the weed off the steps before anyone else came a cropper.

Erica thought this a good sign of practical common sense and, putting her arm through his, led him up the slipway to the Manse. She took him inside past the shop and down the corridor to the kitchen. He had left his luggage in the hallway and sat down at the kitchen table as Erica made them both coffee. Since the *Beluga* was now making regular trips out there was no problem with fresh supplies. Don bought vegetables for them from the Harris Cooperative and anything else could be arranged given a few days' notice. Life was certainly going to get easier as Spring advanced into early Summer. Dan rolled a cigarette and went to light it. "Sorry Dan, you'll have to go outside for that." Erica was insistent, although an occasional smoker herself.

Noticing an empty lager can on the counter near the sink he asked, "Where does one get a drink round here?"

"Ah, you'd be surprised. The Base guys left a cellar full of booze here when they evacuated, the cause of their downfall I understand. We'd be doing well to get through that lot!"

"This is sounding good already, Erica," and lowering his voice Dan added, "I've brought you a fresh supply of weed, thinking you must be pretty low by now."

Erica had barely touched cannabis since their first night on the island. The reality of being there had fully occupied her and there had been no need for induced methods of relaxation after days spent walking on the hilly island. "Well, thank you

Dan. Actually I hardly touch the stuff now but since you're here I'll make an exception! Dave's not bothered but I'd rather keep the stuff away from Mum. We can have a smoke later. Now, when you've finished your coffee I'll show you around. You can leave your rucksack in the living room - where you'll be sleeping for now."

Anne was out looking for migratory bird arrivals and Dave and Deborah had gone out to the *Beluga* for a natter with Don and Lachie, his assistant again for the coming season. Sally had her feet up, reading in Cottage One. The thin plume of wood smoke from the chimney indicated she was in. Once the visitors had landed there was not a lot to do until the time came to open the souvenir shop just before departure. The toilet block near the Factor's House was Sally's responsibility but usually only needed a quick clean after they had left. It wasn't a bad deal in return for free accommodation, she thought. A whole house to herself was far better than the single room in the Base she had used before.

Erica thought Dan looked as good as ever. Tall with a muscular body and long dark hair tied back in a ponytail he looked the part in her eyes. If he shaved his short beard off he'd be perfect, she thought. Maybe she'd have to give up on that for, as Dave with his frequent stubble had said on more than one occasion, shaving was not, as in the past, going to be a priority for the men of St Kilda.

Whether it was the weeks away from normal social contact, she wasn't sure but she felt very warm toward Dan as she led him along the street. Showing him the main points of the village, they passed the Factor's House and saw smoke from the Cottage One chimney indicating Sally was in residence. Erica had the inexplicable urge to show off 'her man' to her friend and possible rival when it came to Dan's affections. Having only just landed, Dan's primary concern was simply taking in everything that was unfolding around him. He found himself in a deserted village on a remote island with his old friend Erica and who knew what lay ahead. He had decided to be open about possibilities St Kilda might offer now that the recession had made regular employment on the mainland unlikely.

Erica knocked on the door of Cottage One. Sally was particular about that, valuing her private space, even on the almost deserted island. She opened the door and was surprised to see Erica with Dan.

"Come in, won't you," she said hesitatingly taking in the new arrival.

"Dan will be staying for a few days with us. He's an old mate from Edinburgh. It will be good to have another man here, won't it Sally?"

Sally gave Erica a questioning look, not quite sure what she was implying. She thought he looked a good catch whatever his reason for being here. Strong as well by the look of it, Sally thought. Erica gestured around the cottage pointing out the good supply of books to Dan and the only wood stove on the island. She had expected to find Cailly curled up asleep on the rug in front of it, but she was out. "You've just missed Cailly, she went out a few minutes ago. She'll be back later, with a mouse no doubt," Sally laughed.

Erica and Dan shared a cup of tea with Sally before continuing their tour round the village. Erica talked about the ruined blackhouses and how she would love to restore one. She longed to get away from the pristine confines of the Manse and live in a sustainable way making full use of the natural resources the island had to offer. She looked to Dan whose nodded agreement didn't seem immediately convincing. Erica opened the wooden lattice gate into the graveyard and they looked at the gravestones surrounded by growing flag irises. The older ones showed no inscription, placed there by an oral culture having no need for the written word. The later nineteenth century monuments did bear inscriptions commemorating wealthier members of the community including the children of one of the Victorian Ministers. So many children had died of tetanus and it reminded Erica to ask Dan if his vaccinations were up to date. Sally would sort him out if not. There was an early twenty-first century grave stone marking the burial of ashes brought over from the mainland to St Kilda for interment. The graveyard rose several feet above the surrounding pasture, an indication of just how many St Kildans had been buried there over the centuries. Leaving the graveyard the pair walked a few yards uphill to the souterrain known by St Kildans as the Fairies' House. In Gaelic tradition, virtually every feature of the island landscape was associated with a human or supernatural story. The St Kildans could not explain this underground passage tomb and named it the Fairies House to account for the doorway and ceiling being just four feet high, or so the popular explanation went. With his tall stature, Dan had trouble shuffling inside and returning to the day light complained of a stiff back. "OK, I'll show you an even smaller house then, big man!" Erica joked.

She led him over to the nearby mound known as Calum Mór's House, again sensibly built with its entrance facing away from the bay.

"I've been doing some reading up on this and archaeologists suggest it is an Iron Age dwelling. According to St Kildan myth, it was erected in a day by Calum Mór, that's Big Calum by the way. He wanted to prove his worth after being told he wasn't man enough to go bird nesting on the cliffs. St Kilda is full of myths concerning male challenge. There's nothing new under the Sun, is there? You'd certainly have a bad back shifting stones like these." Erica pointed at the stone lintel over the entrance just three foot above ground level. It looked very damp inside so he decided against crawling in there. As they moved toward the village boundary wall, the Head Dyke as it was usually referred to, from amongst a nearby patch of Mothan two large brown seabirds lifted off and flew away lazily to perch and watch them from a nearby cleit. "Those are Bonxies, Dan."

"Bonxies?" he was puzzled by the name. "Great Skuas, mean bastards so I've read and they go for just about anything when they are defending their nests. That's what it said in the bird book lying on Sally's table when we were in her cottage." Dan began walking over to the spot the large birds had just vacated. There was something furry and obviously half devoured lying there. Erica followed him to see what it was they had left. "It looks like they have had a cat," Dan commented. Erica turned pale at his words.

"Oh, God! It's Cailly, those bastards have got her." Erica began to sob. "This fucking place, Dan. If it's not one thing, it's another. Poor Cailly, she seemed so happy out here. Look her eyes have gone, they must have pecked them out so she couldn't see to get away before they killed her. She would have had no idea of the danger she was in until it was too late."

Dan unconsciously disengaged from the cruel reality he was witnessing in front of his eyes. He had expected a light hearted time visiting an old girlfriend. He could now see himself getting drawn into a darker situation than he had ever expected.

The Bonxies were watching from the cleit roof fifty yards away, waiting for the pair to leave so they could resume their meal. "Hadn't we better pick her up? Those birds look like they will come back as soon as we are round the corner."

"You're right, Dan, they will for sure."

Dan pulled a plastic carrier bag from his jacket pocket. It was normally reserved for his plant foraging expeditions. Erica picked up Cailly by her eyeless head. Her rear legs were missing and dark entrails spilled from her ripped stomach as she was placed in the bag Dan held open for her. He involuntarily heaved at the sight of the feline remains deposited in his plant hunting bag.

"We'd better tell Mum and Dad, they would want to see her before we bury her." Erica and Dan carried the bag and its gruesome contents to the jetty and called to the *Beluga* for Dave or Deborah to come over.

Deborah heard the concern in Erica's voice and got up from the cabin bench. "OK, I'll go over, Dave. It's almost time for the shop anyway. I wonder what's so urgent that she wants us now. Hey, it's Dan by the looks of it. You've got a mate here now, Dave," she joked. The *Beluga* was alongside the jetty and it was Erica who spoke first. "Mum, it's Cailly, she's been killed."

Deborah looked stunned. "What do you mean killed? There's nothing here other than mice and sheep, is there?"

"Bonxies, Mum. They must have arrived in Glen Mór last night and come hunting around the village now there's hardly anyone here."

"Dave! Dave! You'd better come over here."

"Christ! Poor Cailly. She wouldn't have known what hit her. Hell, we can't even bury her in the village area. I suppose we will just have to put her in the sea."

"For fuck's sake, Dad. She's our pet! Why can't we bury her?"

"Erica, remember what we are supposed to be about here. We can't just go burying things willy-nilly and confusing future archaeologists. Look the tide is flowing out; just slip her remains discretely into the sea and let the crabs dispose of her. It doesn't sound too bad an end, does it?"

It was Dan who eventually took the plastic bag and emptied the remains of Cailly from the end of the jetty. The small mutilated body floated and drifted out a couple of hundred yards before being spotted by more Skuas circling high above the bay. Screaming in excitement the birds dived and within seconds half a dozen Bonxies were floating around her, squabbling over the meaty remains. Their brown heads bobbed up and down rhythmically, heavy hooked beaks ripping further chunks from the cat's body. The gruesome spectacle was over in minutes before the birds flapped away lazily catching a thermal lifting them high over the bay and then settling on Mullach Mór.

"Sorry, that wasn't the best of introductions to our island, Dan." Dave was genuinely pleased to have another man there. "We just need to get rid of this lot," he gestured to the dozen passengers making their way along the jetty toward the *Beluga* which had come alongside from its mooring a few yards out in the bay. "When they've gone we'll have a beer. Has Erica shown you to the spare bed in the living room?"

"Yes, thanks, it's all sorted," or soon would be when he found where Erica was sleeping, he thought. The unpleasant business with the cat still seemed too unreal to have actually registered with him, if it ever would.

The *Beluga* roared out of the bay. Rising on its hydrofoils, the powerful catamaran headed for Boreray and the Stacs before turning toward Leverburgh, fifty miles away to the east across the still unnaturally calm sea.

"That's some engine he's got in there, man."

Dave nodded but thought it better to show empathy with

his elder daughter and his wife over the loss of Cailly than enthuse over marine horsepower. Dan, sensing the sensitivity of the situation, walked over to Erica and squeezed her hand. Her lack of response surprised him. She seemed to have withdrawn from her pain inside a psychological shell. Deborah, having seen the tourists off was cleaning the shop ready for the next day's visitors. She would grieve for her cat later.

Anne came back from her bird-walk around the island to see Erica sitting smoking on the jetty wall. This was unlike her and Anne recognized the unhappiness in her sister's hunched posture. Seeing Anne walking down toward her, Erica stood up and threw her roll-up into the water. She didn't normally smoke during the day and it surprised Anne who realized something must be wrong. "The Bonxies are back, Erica. The tourists will get a run for their money up there now!"

Anne was usually sensitive to her sister's moods but Erica's sob came unexpectedly. Tears ran down her cheeks as she explained what had happened to Cailly. Out on the bay all was calm with no trace to indicate where the Skuas had devoured her floating remains. Anne reached out and took her sister's hand and this time Erica softened toward her.

"You know this island was full of cats and dogs, before the evacuation. There was an awful ending for them too. Rather than let government vets put them down, according to what I read, the St Kildans hung stones around their dog's necks and drowned them in the bay. The cats were abandoned and managed to live on for a couple of years before being finally shot out by visiting naturalists. I suppose the Bonxies just saw Cailly as food, maybe a threat, at least no one was trying to kill her simply for being unwelcome here."

Erica was touched and at the same time surprised at her sister's comment but felt better after crying and walked with Anne back up to the Manse. Dave and Dan were sitting at the kitchen table and had already consumed several cans of lager judging by the empties piling up. Deborah had finished making the shop ready for the following day's visitors and came into join them.

"Really sorry about the cat, Erica." Dan repeated his concern over what he had witnessed. Erica was still feeling numbed but managed curt thanks before disappearing into her room to lie down. Anne rarely drank alcohol but helped herself to an orange juice from the kitchen cupboard and joined her father and Dan round the table.

"I know it's a shame what happened but according to Sally we shouldn't have brought her here anyway. Josephine did say we were to ensure not to bring any alien species with us, alien to the island as it is now, she was only a cat," Anne qualified.

"I don't know how you can say that, Anne. She was your pet as much as anyone's."

Deborah was angry at Anne's matter of fact approach to Cailly's death. "You even named her! Christ, you girls are two complete opposites. One who couldn't keep her legs closed for longer than five minutes and you, hard as nails just to suit your own ends!" Deborah ran from the kitchen and down the corridor to the bathroom. Dave looked up when Deborah mentioned his elder daughter's past. He had to admit it would have been better had Erica behaved a little more responsibly when it came to her love life. The abortion, insisted on by her mother, should have drummed some sense into her when it came to men, he thought. For him it was all in the past now but obviously still a sore point with Deborah. Thankfully Anne was too young to really grasp what the family tension had been about at the time, or so he hoped.

Deborah could be heard vomiting in the bathroom, the tension over Cailly's death finally expressed itself. For her it felt as if the legally protected predators had just taken the one comfort from her that she had on the island. It had felt good to have a family to look after at first but staring out at the same view day after day was now beginning to get to her. She had hoped the women would have more of a meeting place in Cottage One but Sally seemed reluctant to share the space with anyone but Erica, who also shared her feminist outlook on life. Who was she to impose herself in their private space, a mere mother who had successfully raised two troublesome girls and supported a dreamer of a husband? What would these intellectual and child-free young women know about life anyway? Dave was like a pig in shit out here, she thought. Cock of his roost after the put downs at the university, and now he had Dan to side with him too. They were both arrogant and weak, their enthusiasm propped up by the bloody endless supply of booze left behind in the Base. To stop her thoughts from spiraling down further, Deborah took herself outside for a walk along the front.

There seemed to be more life out in the bay that evening. Apart from the usual Fulmars patrolling the cliff edges she could see other white birds briefly landing on ledges and taking off to pick something from the sea before returning. She had binoculars with her and, putting them to her eyes, could make out newly arrived Kittiwakes repairing their seaweed nests for the new season. The onomatopoeic 'kitt-i-wake' calls echoed around the cliffs as they squabbled for nesting space on the limited ledges. One would sometimes knock another off the ledge to fall fluttering to the sea during territorial squabbles. Nearby she could see Razorbills and Guillemots similarly intent on reclaiming space to rear the coming year's chicks. Greater Black Backed Gulls were already on the lookout for unattended eggs and would soon predate chicks whenever they had the opportunity. Skuas patrolled the skies overhead also on the lookout for whatever feeding opportunity presented itself. From eggs to lambs, and cats, nothing left unattended would be safe now the Bonxies had returned.

Deborah walked on to the helipad and followed the slipway down to the beach. Standing on the shore she noticed a small group of black specks floating a few hundred yards out in the bay. Focusing her binoculars she saw the first Puffins had arrived and were floating, waiting in rafts beneath the grassy slopes where they would soon begin to reclaim and refurbish their previous year's burrows. There had been much concern over poor breeding success in the Puffin population at St Kilda. It seemed they had to fly too far out to catch food for their chicks since global warming shifted the north Atlantic currents. Sand eels and other small fish followed the plankton which in turn were taken by the currents. As Anne had reminded her, Puffins could only carry a full beak of sand eels so far before, ecologically, the effort became counterproductive. An exhausted parent bird would have to consume the catch itself if it was going to sustain its energy over a long flight. Darkness was falling by the time Deborah left the beach and that evening noticed phosphorescence in the waves. Her footsteps also left brief glowing imprints in the sand. Though she was not aware of the significance at the time, the luminescence was the result of a spring plankton bloom and this year the small fish had returned to Village Bay to feed in their thousands, following the bounteous food source. The seabirds of St Kilda would benefit from the recent locally cold winter which had switched the surface sea currents yet again. The cold, calm conditions had brought plankton rich currents closer to the islands than for many years. It was going to be a fertile year at St Kilda on several counts.

The shock of Cailly's death, though not entirely forgotten, became less significant as the season progressed. Many smaller birds would definitely have suffered from her predation had she lived long enough to see their arrival. Fledgling Wrens struggled in the wind as they emerged from the security of their moss lined nests well protected inside stone walls around the village. Small animated balls of grey-brown fluff would have been tempting prey for the most docile of felines.

The Easter vacation came and went and with Dave's agreement Dan decided to remain on the island. His geography degree could wait for he reckoned an extended time on St Kilda was going to be the opportunity of a lifetime. They discussed accommodation and it was agreed that he could move, along with his few possessions, into the Feather Store and occupied the small basic apartment on the upper floor. Deborah had insisted he would have to vacate their living room if he was going to stay on the island. The Manse was accommodation for her family and she wanted to keep it that way. Although a relationship appeared to be developing between Dan and Erica, he certainly wasn't family yet and, if things developed between them, she didn't want another couple under her roof. There was no power supply to the Feather Store so the small electric cooker in there was useless. He had to fetch water from the tap outside the Manse so for all intents and purposes the Feather Store served merely as his sleeping quarters, and a place where he and Erica could spend time together in private.

Erica spent more and more time in the Feather Store or sitting on the shelving rocks outside as the summer evenings lengthened out. The light evenings saw Dave and Deborah take walks around the island at a more leisurely pace, often taking time out to watch the sunset over Soay, listening to the drumming of the Snipe and seals calling from caves below. Anne was busy with bird recording and to all outward intents and purposes was perfectly content on the island. Spending most of her daylight hours outside, she had become particularly drawn to the foot of Glen Mór. The long natural rock arch, known as 'The Tunnel' was a particular favorite of hers. The wild sounds of nesting Guillemots and the singing of seals echoing through the cavern expressed, to her, the soul of St Kilda. Anne privately associated herself with the Amazon's House and mythical female warrior said to reside in the glen. While her elder sister dreamed of restoring the village Blackhouses, Anne dreamed of the far side of the island and resettling the Amazon's compound with a family of her own. Dave Williams' dream was to be head of his family of pioneers, following their manifest destiny by leaving the chaos of Edinburgh and mainland Britain far behind them. Deborah Williams just needed a recuperative break away from the pressures of trying to teach young people too distracted by recent urban events, to achieve without the professional help she felt too exhausted to offer them. As for Dan, he didn't have any more than transient dreams to guide him. Living rent free with few responsibilities and good friends was enough. The facilities were a bit basic and lack of mobile signal tedious but all in all not a bad way to spend the summer, he considered.

Dan would wait until the Williams had finished their meals before he went into the Manse kitchen to cook and take his own meal back to the Feather Store. In spite of her outwardly feminist principles, Erica started to take meals over to Dan to save him from having to cross over to the Manse to cook. On windy days his food was more often than not cold by the time he got to eat it. Like her mother, in spite of feminist leanings, out on St Kilda she found herself starting to perform a supporting role for her man.

Nights in the Feather Store became more and more the norm for Erica. Two ex-Army single beds pushed together in the small bedroom overlooking the sea could only be described as a magical experience. Snuggled up on a stormy night, Erica felt at peace in a way she had not felt since childhood, before hormonal change and emotional trials of adolescence re-determined her life. Having Dan on the island, it seemed only natural to include him in her dreams for the future. She would spend hours discussing restoration of a blackhouse, poring over archaeological plans she found in the Manse office. One thing she was enthusiastic to try was installing a modern wood-burning stove, like the one in Cottage One. The idea of sitting around an open hearth and coming out kippered in the morning didn't appeal much. If ever she realized the dream, her blackhouse would be an evolution but based on past tradition.

Dan was enthusiastic about living in a traditional Hebridean cottage, more for reasons of self-image as it subsequently turned out. He could imagine himself sitting at the open half-door on a sunny day, playing his guitar and maybe singing a song or two. The hard work of climbing the hill to fetch peat and continuous repairs against the force of the elements never occurred to him. Life in the Feather Store with Erica was good and she allowed him time to dream too. Dan had built a good friendship with Lachie, and had arranged with him to bring the occasional bag of grass over on the *Beluga* from Leverburgh. He had also asked for some seeds so he could grow his own in a window box in the Feather Store away from the critical eye of Deborah. He rightly assumed Dave wouldn't object but he didn't want Deborah giving him a hard time over it, seeing how reliant he was on using her kitchen facilities. There was good fertile soil inside the cleits where generations of sheep had sheltered from bad weather. He quickly found a suitable plastic box and punched drainage holes in the bottom. The box was filled with rich compost, the seeds sown, and placed on the inside of the south facing window sill overlooking the bay. Lachie had brought him enough seeds for several sowings. Growing had become quite a cottage industry in the Uists, now the MOD was cutting back. Virtually every holding had a geodesic dome or polytunnel greenhouse. There was no shortage of seeds selected to thrive in the local conditions. No different to any other agriculture, Dan had explained to a slightly dubious Erica when she questioned the plants' ability to grow in the salt laden atmosphere at St Kilda. What neither of them had considered was the predilection the mice had for sprouting cannabis seeds. It seemed that no matter how they tried to prevent them, the resourceful Feather Store mice always managed to get inside the growing containers to dig up and consume the germinating seeds. Eventually Dan conceded defeat and the two of them constrained their consumption of intoxicants to those retrieved from the Puff-Inn cellar room. Over bottles of red wine, Erica explained to Dan how, in keeping with tradition, she would love to keep a house-cow in the lower side of her blackhouse. Dan felt that making his way over a dung heap to the living area extremely off-putting but kept the thought to himself. One early summer evening, as Erica quietly read one of the many histories of the island, she called Dan over as he played guitar on the Feather Store steps.

"Hey, Dan! This is interesting; the St Kildans used to rub a Mothan ointment on the cows udders to produce good milk. And there was also a belief that anyone who drank milk from the cow that ate the Mothan would be endowed with good fortune. Also any girl who placed Mothan under her pillow would have her future husband revealed in a dream; sounds a pretty cool plant!"

Dan normally listened impassively to Erica on the subject of St Kildan history but reference to a magical plant found on the island focused his attention. "I wonder what the Mothan is, Erica? Is there a picture of it in that book?"

"No I don't see one but it must be a local plant name. I'll

go back to the Manse and fetch the Gaelic dictionary from the office." She came back a few minutes later. "Here it is – Mothan, it's the Butterwort. Says it's an insectivorous plant found in acid boggy conditions and able to survive in the nutrient poor environment by absorbing insects trapped on its thick leaves. Oh, yes, that makes sense. The plant exudes a compound that both attracts and stupefies small insects. Apparently any girl who chewed the plant before kissing her man stupefied him and caught him for life. Better watch out there, Dan!" she joked.

"That makes more sense than you think. Last autumn your Dad gave me such a bollocking I thought I'd be asked to leave the University. I had made a hooch out of vodka and Fly Agaric mushroom. One of the students was sick after trying it. I wasn't doing anything illegal either, just wanted to share the power of the mushroom as a shamanic tool. We were on Calton Hill and I had read it is one of the mythical hollow hills where fairies are supposed to live. Who knows, we might have seen one after drinking that brew. What I am getting to is that Fly Agaric, associated with the Birch tree, contains a compound that attracts and stupefies insects too, hence its name. God, it was cold that day; one way or another we all had strange experiences doing our fieldwork. One girl even went back into St. Cuthbert's churchyard after dark and got herself raped."

"That's enough of that, Dan." Erica didn't want to hear about another young woman's misfortune or the precise reasons why her father had not been re-employed by the university that year. "There's no Birch here or any other tree for that matter, so get any ideas like those out of your head."

"I hadn't given her any of the brew. She was just headstrong and determined to get to the bottom of the spirit of place, as Dave had asked. She simply found out there's more to landscape than initially meets the eye. There can be so much hidden beneath the surface, things our so called inclusive society doesn't want us to find out about."

Erica was looking doubtful as Dan continued. "Who would have expected to find World Heritage Site St Kilda dominated by a run-down military base? Apart from those who used to work here, this is an imagined place. In the past, every nook and cranny had some supernatural association. We just don't know about real connections here as the St Kildans wrote nothing down, simply passed oral history, myths and legends down the generations before the Church landed and changed the story. Then, Poof! Everything was lost in favor of Scriptures determining another way of being, even more imaginary if you ask me."

"You could have something there, Dan. The story was changed and now we've lost connection to this place. I look out beyond the village and see bleak moorland, void of any story. Even the military had stories about their life out here. The echoes of their landscape are strong and we still depend on them for so much. Will anyone remember us from our landscape, I wonder?"

"We'll have to set about making our own impact first, our own landscape if we are ever allowed to." Dan commented.

"Well I want to make a start by restoring a blackhouse and bringing it into the 21st century, not taking it back into the 19th. I know Dad dreams of crofting here though I haven't a clue about Mum."

"What about Anne?" Dan asked.

"Ah, who knows what goes on inside the head of that sister of mine? I really don't know, she hides behind everything being ecological and I don't think she includes emotion in the equations she is so fond of quoting at me. One day she will learn that there is more to life than energy flows."

Dan was beginning to feel out of his depth and wanted to change the subject. "There haven't been many tourists this week, have there? It's been good weather too. Lachie was telling me Don is getting quite worried after investing so much in that new boat."

"Tourists, Dan. Sometimes I feel we are tourists in our own lives. So many of us never really get there, just see the bits of life we want to see. Never mind about looking under the skin of St. Cuthbert's kirkyard as that girl did, we rarely look underneath our own skins."

"Not sure I know what you mean there," Dan was puzzled.

"Do you know who you are, Dan? Who you really are? I see the happy go lucky boy, sometimes the big man. Yes, you are fit and strong, have a great body," she smiled. "But what makes you really tick? All I see is you dependent on borrowed dreams, especially for your self-image, to quote a cliché you are adorned with male dreams just like my Dad."

"Christ, Erica. You are getting heavy!"

"There you go again, Dan. Invoking Christ for fucks sake! Why can't you just be yourself and relate with me now rather than an imagined figure that you guys have kept alive for the last two thousand years. You men even make nonsense out of his mother only wanting to acknowledge her as a virgin. What complete and utter male drivel! Oh, fuck this I'm going to see if Sally's in. See you later, Dan."

"Don't forget your torch, Erica. It's the new moon tonight, you won't be able to see where you're going if you stay out late."

"Dark moon, Dan! It's the dark moon so stop your guitar twiddling and listen to what you feel for once rather than rehashing someone else's second hand emotions."

Erica walked up the street at a brisk pace leaving Dan to wonder what, if anything, he had done to upset her. A glance at the closed porch door told her Sally was not in the Factor's House, she rarely was until she felt it was time to sleep. Marching over the stone clapper bridge spanning the dry burn she slipped on the damp granite worn smooth by years of tourist footfall and cursed out loud. She was not in the best of moods when she opened the door to Cottage One. It was warm and inviting in there, the gentle music from Sally's battery powered CD player should have soothed her bad mood but Sally's unexpected rebuke shocked her.

"Bloody hell, Erica! Can't you first knock before barging in here like this?"

Stung by the reprimand, Erica found her own raging emotion too much and burst into tears in front of her friend. "Sally, I am so sorry. I really didn't mean to upset you. I just feel so tense and screwed up. I just fell out with Dan and felt the need to get away and came to find you. I never thought about whether you'd want to see me, and in this state, sorry I can be so selfish."

"It's OK, Erica, sit yourself down and we can talk about it. I'll make us a cuppa." Sally filled the kettle and put it to heat on top of the wood stove. It was soon singing and she poured the boiling water into two mugs of instant coffee. Erica took the mug offered and both women sipped at their hot drinks for a moment before Sally spoke.

"You know, Erica, I am a trained nurse and that makes me a Jack, or should I say Jill, of all medical trades out here. One thing I have noticed since working on this island is the effect of the sea and weather on the human psyche. The tides, phases of the moon, atmospheric pressure, wind speed and so on. Out here we cannot help but find ourselves living with natural rhythms most people run away from back in the cities. On this small island there is little in the way of architecture to shield us, distract us from the elements, the darkness and so on. No monuments to remind us who is in charge. The weather is the boss, eventually knocking down anything we put up to protect ourselves. We look at the ever moving sea, rising and falling with the tides and seasons. Temperatures rise and fall between day and night. There are no street lights here, we feel the effect of the rhythms of the natural world as much as the birds and fish, whether we try to deny it or not. On top of that we are women with our own cycles. Erica, you have only been here a few months and it will take a full year for your body and psyche to readjust. When that happens you will barely notice these mood swings. In fact I predict you will feel better than ever without the confusion of trying to manage your moods and emotions to fit male expectations. Yes, men do get affected out here but not in the same way. After centuries wanting to control the natural world, living this close to the ocean can often prove too much. Uncontrollable nature can pose a big psychological problem unless they learn to live with it, live with her so I should say. I predict your father, and Dan, will have crises before they come to terms with the reality of being out here and", she softly emphasized, "living with us."

Erica was fascinated by what she was hearing. Sally's explanations made so much sense. "I had a go at Dan and unkindly told him he was adorned with dreams but what I really wanted to tell him was he was full of shit! Why did I say that?"

"That's what many men do, especially when they find themselves out of their comfort zone. Rather than go with the changes they spin an ever stronger image around themselves, spin themselves an unassailable guise to protect their fragile ego from collapsing in the face of a stronger reality. When the last defense fails they either learn from the experience and grow, or crawl away defeated by life. Believe me I have seen both many times out here. I have had to arrange evacuation of cocky young servicemen reduced to tears and drunkenness after failing to come to terms with this place. Those that do come to terms with being here turn out to be a real asset and one or two became great friends."

Erica felt herself calming down and tried to place her current experience in the context of what Sally was saying. She also became uncomfortably aware her period was starting.

"So what you are saying is that I am adjusting to living here. My mind and body are returning to their natural state – and Dan with his guitar playing and cliché spouting is starting to defend himself against a natural force that in sustaining me will inevitably beat him?"

"Got it in one, Erica!"

"What about my Dad?" Erica understood what she was hearing though in an incredulous way.

"Well, he's been around considerably longer. He's also a very intelligent man and, I hope, he will learn and become a great asset to us. Don't get me wrong, Erica, we need strong male energy in our lives or we will become uncontrolled and a liability to ourselves. Ha, ha – we hens need our cock, don't we?"

Both women collapsed in a fit of giggles at Sally's joke. The serious conversation finished with a joke had been just what Erica needed.

"There's just one thing Sally. As an expert on the human species at St Kilda, what about my Mum? Sometimes she seems a real mess and at other times a real source of strength to us."

"That's a hard one to answer. It's hard for me to predict as there were never many middle-age women out here. I haven't been enrolled in the Grand Mother's Council yet! We can look at her motivation for coming here, didn't she give up a senior teaching position?"

"Yes, she got mugged in the school car park and lost her nerve afterwards." Erica explained about the carjacking and Deborah's loss of confidence in the face of Edinburgh's youth. "At first she was dead against coming here, thought it was a crazy idea. After the mugging she just gave up and followed Dad in his dream. I thought it was a great idea to get away from all that crap and start again but Mum didn't seem to have strong feelings about it either way, she just eventually agreed to come."

Sally thought for a moment. "Well, I reckon that given her age we could be in for some fireworks, her menopause must be just around the corner. I remember my Mum had an affair in her late forties. It was like a final fling before her fertility ended. My Dad understood about it, in the end. Now they have both retired, his ruffled feathers have settled. The rhythms of life affect us strongly enough," she emphasized, "and we have time left. Deborah must feel an urgent need out here, hope Dave's up to it!" The two women laughed again at the thought of Dave being pursued by an amorous Deborah. "Dan had better watch out too!"

Erica frowned at the thought of her mother chasing Dan. "Yep, all nature runs to the tidal clock here. You'd be amazed how it ticks. Fish lay their eggs at full moon, they hatch and swim away at the next, we are no exception, Erica. If you want to know more it's all in that marine ecology book over there." Sally pointed to the bookcase beside the window.

"Changing the subject Sally, we haven't had many tourists recently, have we?" Erica felt a need to steer the conversation away from personal matters. "No," Sally replied. "I suppose it must be a sign of the times. No one's got spare cash anymore. Don must be getting worried after spending so much on that new boat of his and to be honest this can't be the most attractive place to visit given the rough sea crossing and steep ground once you get here. Last year I had a fright when one of the tourists had an angina attack half way up Conachair. He had taken the route up from the Gap and since that incident I asked Don to advise the visitors to follow the road up the hill, then at least we can get to them easily, or could when we had vehicles here."

The short St Kilda summer season passed with tourists tailing off as the seabirds left with the approach of autumn. Advice to follow the road up the hill had kept Sally's first aid treatments to little more than pulled tendons and sprained ankles. Thankfully for her, most visitors kept to the relatively level ground of the village but even a few of those found themselves incapacitated for the day following three hours of seasickness. Don had hoped that by investing in his new twin hulled craft, the extra speed would have brought more business. The *Beluga,* supposedly more stable than the single hulled boat it replaced, came to be known as the vomit comet among the Leverburgh guest-houses. The reputation spread and with the recession there had been no increase in paying passengers. The downturn had become a real cause for concern. Without an upturn the following year, Don advised Josephine he was going to have to cut his losses and sell the boat. That would mean he would not be able to supply the Williams as often as she, or they, had hoped.

It was not only Don Mackintyre's business feeling the pinch by the end of the season. Josephine and Derek, the Islands Factor, sat down at the round table in the corner of the Western Ilse Trust office.

"It's not looking good, Josephine." Derek explained that funding for St Kilda was being pulled. They had always known European money for nature conservation was under threat but hadn't expected funding for archaeology to be cut too. "I tried the Scottish Government, explained we have the country's only dual world heritage site. Do you know the response I had from the minister? I was told that there would no likelihood of state support for a rocky island out in the Atlantic that no-one could get to. Public funding would only be given to mainland National Parks accessible to the majority population who could actually afford to get there and reap benefits publicly provided."

Derek was genuinely concerned. "We are going to have to think outside the box, Josephine. I know we have discussed this before but I think we now have to push forward the agricultural tenant idea. We have the Williams on the island as custodians, could you sound them out for the role? It would mean year round occupation of the island if we are going to be able to apply for CAP funding, of course. The latest amendment to the Common Agricultural Policy was insistent on that condition. I know we are not supposed to have anyone out there permanently but essential agricultural occupancy should swing that one."

"I think we ought to tap into the sustainable tourism option too, Derek." Josephine had done some research the day before. They could attract further funds by encouraging public access. Historic Scotland had not been keen on deliberately building up visitor numbers for fear of damaging the very resource they sought to preserve in its original condition. Now Historic Scotland would no longer fund the Trust to manage the island's archaeology, then they could surely be more entrepreneurial about their management. Josephine was eager to build an eco-tourism business based at St Kilda.

"Don Macintyre rang the other day and told me that unless he had more business next year he will have to sell the *Beluga*. The fuel costs are bankrupting him at present."

"I thought he would be blasting more passengers than ever out there in that new high speed boat of his?"

"That's what he had hoped! More horsepower equals more speed but the boat's got a bad reputation as a vomit comet."

"Please, Josephine, don't go there!" Derek hadn't been to St Kilda in years having been put off in the past by an experience of, what felt to him, a near fatal bout of seasickness. The small helicopter flight was even less appealing for very similar reasons. Having to choose between being thrown around by the sea or by gusting winds meant he tried to avoid going to the island altogether.

Josephine arrived with Don on the *Beluga* on his last scheduled trip of the season. She had convened the meeting in the Manse living room which doubled as the island conference venue now the Base was closed. Dave had got the generator going early that morning and the room was warmed by rarely used electric storage heaters in there. The room smelled of hot dust by the time the visitors arrived. Lachie had brought an offering of cakes from Leverburgh and the prevailing high pressure had, thankfully for Josephine, kept feelings of seasickness to a minimum. The *Beluga* had to slow through the mist hanging low across Village Bay but, after a smooth crossing, the meeting proceeded at eleven o'clock as scheduled with the sun breaking through on a perfect St Kilda autumn morning.

Josephine stood in front of the wall mounted screen TV unused for many months. Images of happenings in the wider world had begun to feel irrelevant to the Williams as they acclimatized to living on the island. She began her presentation by explaining the near impossible financial position the Trust found itself in regarding St Kilda. The Williams family listened intently to what she had to say concerning their future. Sally MacDonald was also present as whatever was coming up would inevitably affect her too. Don and Lachie stood at the back of the room by the picture window looking out onto the deteriorating church building, though listening intently to what was being said behind them.

"To put it bluntly, we cannot afford to financially support you here next year. We are a charity and people are no longer giving. We are losing our members in droves and external funding is becoming next to impossible to find. We have even approached a few American philanthropist foundations but we just don't seem to be able to obtain across the board funding any more. The national government refuses to support an island, however historically important, that few people will ever manage to visit and European money for conservation is virtually non-existent unless there is strong community involvement. It's not only us, the National Trust for Scotland, Historic Scotland and Scottish Natural Heritage have all lost their funding from Europe and St. Andrews House will only support projects they consider readily accessible to the general public. So as things stand we are facing a bleak prospect out here. However, we have looked into alternative options and it seems we could tap into the European Social Fund on the basis of resettling an agricultural community. Supporting small farmers has always been a cherished European aim since the Treaty of Rome and I am feel sure the St Kildans, had they remained on the island, would have been prime candidates for support. There is also more recent provision for eco-tourism business proposals." Josephine looked directly at Don, who had turned his gaze away from the deteriorating church and back toward Josephine. "So what we are suggesting is that next year you consider yourselves, if you chose to remain here and I include you in this Sally, as small farmers rather than custodians. Don, you should be able to find extra income bringing eco-tourists out here to a living museum, though I appreciate that could be considered a contradiction in terms."

Turning to Dave and Deborah she continued with

enthusiasm. "You will be free to manage the island sheep as you see fit and," she hesitated, "if you wish you can reinstate cultivation in the village fields for the first time since 1930. You will be nominally expected to try and make a living from small scale agriculture and tourism but you will at least receive some financial assistance for your effort. Without funding for conservation both Historic Scotland and SNH are de-listing St Kilda. To be honest, since the 1930 evacuation and supposed protection, the island has never seen so much damaging change. The Base and radar infrastructure changed things here more since 1957 than over the previous thousand years."

Don chose to mention the cost of running the boat service out to St Kilda regardless of European subsidy. The deciding factor would be fuel costs of the *Beluga*. It was a fast craft but that inevitably meant high fuel consumption. He was an astute businessman and knew the storage tanks near the helipad held many thousands of gallons of MOD diesel fuel. The William's small generator and handful of oil lamps were hardly likely to exhaust the reserve in several lifetimes. He wanted to know if an arrangement could be made to refuel the *Beluga* from island supplies. It would make all the difference between viability and running at a loss for his Leverburgh based operation. He was playing his trump card quite deliberately. Few other boat operators would make the risky crossing and without a guaranteed boat service, he knew there would be no ESF funding for any St Kilda eco-tourism project.

Josephine did not like being put on the spot like this but considered his argument valid. "I doubt there will be a problem with that Don. That diesel has been a concern of mine. Without regular maintenance of the storage tanks I am worried that one day we could have a leak and big pollution issue to deal with. What I can do is ask the MOD to empty their diesel storage tanks on pollution risk grounds. I am pretty sure they will throw their hands up and say the pumping operation would cost more than the diesel is worth to them. Using the fuel for the purpose intended, running diesel engines until it is exhausted would seem the logical solution."

Turning back to the Williams she continued, "So how do you feel about becoming small farmers and running an eco-tourism enterprise?" The Williams, though thoughtful, were basically enthusiastic. Erica noticed a knowing wink aimed at her from Don. He had obviously planned for this scenario already. A far as his business acumen was concerned this plan was going to work.

"There is one thing I ought to warn you about, though." Josephine addressed the whole group and spoke measuredly. "You are doubtless aware of the predictions for climate change. Generally speaking the planet is warming but here in the north Atlantic things are not so clear. The arctic ice is melting and the glacial cap on Greenland deteriorating. However there are certain sub-arctic localities predicted to become colder. What this means is that you could find St Kilda actually becomes colder as ice breaks away and begins to flow south carried on changing oceanic currents and the now prevailing north-westerly airflow. There is also the possibility of increasing volcanic activity in Iceland which could also affect St Kilda. What I am warning you about is that climatic events could make agricultural viability a bit of a challenge though, in terms of strict economics, European funding should keep you in the black. So, I will leave you all to think about it over the next few days. If you decide to call it a day and evacuate I will understand completely but if I was in your shoes I'd relish the challenge of bringing St Kilda back to life.

9 CHANGES

After all that Josephine had emphasized about not making changes on the island, her own enthusiasm for doing just that came as a surprise to them all. Even Don scratched his head in bemusement.

"Well, if you want to give me free diesel to keep coming out here, I am not going to argue!"

Josephine went on to explain that the constraints she had insisted on over the past season were due to funding conditions from Historic Scotland and Scottish Natural Heritage. If it been simply up to her, she would have encouraged an eco-museum approach where at least one blackhouse would have been restored and its allotted fields cultivated and grazed. The custodians would be encouraged to live as latter day St Kildans, before the village went into decline. Effectively, she would have liked the Trust to have built a small tourist business taking advantage of a century and a half's popular preconceptions of a sustainable island Utopia.

"But my hands were tied, you know," she apologized. "So feel free to make your plans for next season. Can I assume you do not have any great urge to evacuate right now?"

Deborah opened her mouth to speak but then, as the incident in the school car park flashed up in her mind, thought better of voicing her doubts. Dave was more than enthusiastic. "This is what I have been waiting for all my life. Christ, what an opportunity!"

Erica and Sally were chatting excitedly at the back of the room. Resettling the village looked like turning into reality, no longer just a female dream. Anne looked as if her mind was elsewhere than in the Manse living room at that moment, but a quiet satisfaction betrayed itself in the small smile that crossed her face.

Dan felt left out from this display of family enthusiasm and turned to Don and asked about opportunities to leave the island during the winter months. It occurred to him that he had two choices, either go back with Don and Lachie that evening or stay on at St Kilda for the next few months, maybe longer if the weather turned bad. "The deciding factor will be the sea conditions, Dan. What I intend to do is to bring out supplies to you, as much as the boat will take, during calm windows in the weather. As you must be aware by now, the island lies in the path of regular Atlantic depressions sweeping in from Labrador. You can come back with Josephine this evening or take a chance and stay longer which will most likely mean winter at St Kilda, I am afraid."

Dan felt Erica slide her arm through his. "We are going to need a strong young man about the place from now on," she teased. "St Kilda failed after strapping men like you left the women and oldies to fend for themselves."

The simple if cleverly timed gesture swung the argument for him. "OK, if you put it like that, Erica, how can I refuse?"

Dave was amused to see Dan decide so easily. It really was quite a commitment Dan was making as the only genuinely young man in the group.

"Thanks, Erica. It really is true that an inch of, ahem, can move mountains!"

"Dad! Don't you even go there," she warned him but all the same felt pleased her female powers of persuasion had been acknowledged. Deborah moved up to Dan and put her own arm through the crook of his free arm and purposefully pulled him away from her daughter. "So, if you are staying now, you had better pull your weight young man. Come and help me get the supper ready. Sure you can manage a can opener?" Deborah led Dan out of the living room and down the corridor to the kitchen. Erica gave her mother a quizzical look, her intuition recognizing her mother's gesture as possibly more than outwardly implied.

"So, if there is nothing else to discuss today I reckon it's time I got back to Leverburgh," commented Josephine.

Don nodded, "Aye, the weather doesn't look good for tomorrow and I'd rather not have to disinfect the cabin again, Josephine!" He grinned at her for she had acquired notoriety among the local boatmen for having poor sea-legs and on the new high speed craft she was even more susceptible to seasickness. Josephine picked up her coat and attaché case and left with Don and Lachie to walk down to the jetty. Lachie started the dinghy's small outboard engine and took them over to the *Beluga* rolling gently at its mooring a few yards off the jetty. Don had followed the biosecurity rules for once with Josephine on board. He fired up the twin diesel engines while Lachie hoisted the dingy up over the stern. The act symbolized the end of a season unusual in the number of calm crossings. Free diesel was going to make next year a lot better, he thought. Anne came outside to watch as the *Beluga* roared away from the village bouncing on heavier swell at the mouth of the bay. They wouldn't be seeing Josephine until next year, if at all should her own job fall through, as she had hinted could happen.

"Do you fancy eating with us tonight, Sally? It feels appropriate considering our new venture together. Spam sarnies and Tennent's OK with you?" Dave was in a jocular mood that evening. After towing the official line all summer he was now being encouraged to throw caution to the wind and turn his St Kilda dream into reality.

"My God, Dad!" Erica was momentarily appalled. "'Sally, I can assure you we will be having neither tonight."

"Please yourself girl, or should I say, hen!" he loved to tease his eldest. "More Tennent's for the lads, then." Dave was looking forward to having Dan around as another man to share the load with. With the potential of being cooped up with four strong minded women for the winter, he could do with some male support. Sally consciously decided not to rise to the bait. "I'll leave you with your Dad and go and help Debs and Dan in the kitchen."

Deborah was already preparing an impressive evening meal. Dan was sitting at the table chopping vegetables. He had already rigged up a small extension from the digital TV in Erica's bedroom. The generator was chugging away outside, accompanied by the reggae beat from the small speaker he had pillaged from the Puff-Inn the previous week. To her surprise Erica noticed Deborah and Dan had already opened a bottle of red wine similarly pillaged for the occasion. Erica realized she was witnessing a familiar domestic scene, though on this occasion Dan was occupying the subservient role formerly played by her step-father. They could have been back home in Edinburgh had it not been for the sound of the generator outside.

"Do you want any help, Mum?" she asked. "No thanks, Erica. We're just fine, aren't we Dan?" Dan nodded to the beat. "Mmm, mmm, have a glass, sister!" Erica could sense three would be a crowd so left Deborah and Dan to preparing the meal. "Later, Dan, thank you. Well if you don't need me I'll leave you to get on with it and go back to Dave and Sally."

"We'll give you a shout when it's ready!" Deborah called back without looking up from her preparations. Erica observed her mother invigorated in a way she hadn't seen since they first arrived on the island. Phase two of the resettlement was at least starting on a cheery note, she thought, but all the same she sensed rivalry from her mother concerning Dan or maybe, she reflected, was she just imagining things?

Dave and Sally were poring over an archaeological plan of the village. "I know you want to get cracking with cultivation, Dave. I agree winter is the right time to prepare for Spring sowing, but let's not try to reinvent the wheel. The St Kildans kept sheep and protected their gardens behind high dry stone walls. Here and here....." she pointed out the planticrubs, small stone-walled rings dotted around the planned settlement. "You can tell the difference between the handling pens and garden enclosures by the gateways or lack of them. The livestock enclosures have gateways but not the walled gardens. The sheep and cattle would not climb over six foot walls to get at the vegetables and there would probably have been a boy or girl employed to keep them out of cultivated areas within the head dyke. There would have been plenty of children to keep occupied until infantile tetanus took most of island babies. It is a good thing I jabbed you all when we first arrived. By the way, now the sheep are attracted to the generator noise at the back of the Manse, you'll have to make sure they don't get into your own veg garden. There'll be a bit of stone walling for you to do straight off!"

Dave agreed that it had been a sensible precaution to be vaccinated before they began working with the potentially infected soils of the village. The epidemic of infantile tetanus of the late nineteenth century had always been an unexplained phenomenon. The Free Church minister explained to the grieving parents that the deaths of their new-born was the will of God. There was nothing they could or should do about it. Dave had mentioned before they arrived how Reverend Mackay had been ridiculed by the islanders over his more extreme doctrinal interpretations. Reverend Mackenzie, his predecessor had taken a more pragmatic approach to island life. They should all seek penitence in the ever more arduous manual work not he, but God demanded of them. The divine request appealed to the egos of the men folk who rose to the challenge. With God's help the magnificent stone walls of their planned village would be the envy of the Hebrides. God would be pleased and they would prosper. The God fearing St Kildans would certainly show a thing or two to the decadent Catholics of South Uist and Barra, had said Reverend Mackay. Dave had been shocked by Anne's explanation for the infantile tetanus outbreaks. As an ecological phenomenon, she said, tetanus was simply keeping the size of the population within numbers the island could support, nothing to do with God or any such nonsense. However she did acknowledge the human, ecological, need for a spiritual dimension to life in such a bleak environment, starved of outside human contact.

"Dave.....are you still there?" Sally noticed Dave appeared vacant, lost in a private reverie of stone wall building. "I think we should just repair what's here already before thinking of anything grander, don't you?" His attention returned to what she was saying. "Oh, yes. Sorry Sally, I was miles away. You're right small is beautiful, as they say. I agree, we need to trial vegetable growing first as I am sure the weather will make things very different to growing on my allotment back in Edinburgh. I'll make sure enough of the planticrubs are in good shape by Spring to keep the sheep off our plants."

Sally continued at some length. "It will be milder, so less frost to worry about and from what I read the villagers over-fertilized their growing areas. Should be OK by now and if we can keep the salt spray off and sheep out we could be in for bumper crops. Again, according to Dunvegan Castle records, St Kilda produced the best barley in the Hebrides. They had to pay rent to Macleod of Dunvegan in kind and barley made this a wealthy village in the past. As you get to know the island better you will recognize many small cultivated areas and just past the Factor's House you can see the remains of a small threshing barn. There's even a small watermill further up the street where the burn crosses. I know Erica wants to add solar panels and micro-hydro energy in her blackhouse project but she's basically reinventing what's already gone before. They cultivated every corner possible, leaving Glen Mór as the only large open area free for quality grazing and milk production. That was probably because it was the only accessible pasture land then. The close cropped slopes you see on the steeper hillsides today wouldn't have existed. Livestock was kept away as they needed long heather for thatching black house roofs on an annual basis. The economy of the island was dependent on maximizing its natural resources. Whether it was seabird products, peat digging or cattle grazing, every square inch possible was put to good use. Plots were rotated so everyone had a fair crack of the whip, even the cliffs were rotated under Run-Rig. That shared way of life came to an end with the building of the new village. The bull even had his own little house in the nineteenth century, maybe the cows had to knock before going in for a service? You guys were well catered for when the new village got built!"

Dave was slightly confused and missed the joke. "But wasn't the enclosed village system meant to improve living standards and land husbandry? I thought that was the whole idea. Most of England's agriculture was improved that way, which is where the idea came from of course. Agreed, it wasn't universally popular with the peasants who had their centuries old common lifestyle disrupted. By parceling up the land into individual properties and allotments, the Enclosures enabled England to feed her growing industrial population. Wouldn't that principal have applied here too?"

"With fields fertilized almost to the point of toxicity and the island youngsters driven away by the unceasing labor demanded of them, it could hardly be considered an improvement, Dave. Then to cap it all, disturbing the ground like that allowed tetanus to run amok in the babies. You know, this community was killed off by male focused good intentions. From what I read," Sally continued, "I got the impression the Enclosures made white slaves of England's poor. Protest and you were driven from the land that ran through your blood. I once went down to Exmoor, that region is characterized by high hedges and banks. They must have built by gangs of workers pressed into wage slavery by the land owners. Now you are hard pressed to find anyone there other than visiting walkers and horse-riders. Where did all those people go? It was the same up here, maybe even worse. English landlords drove their tenants from the land to graze sheep. The so called 'peasants' were considered almost sub-human and ethnically cleansed in a way Nazis would have proud of."

He knew it wasn't so straightforward but Dave could appreciate the connection between the enclosure of south-west of England and the Highland Clearances. Highland shepherds had been employed to manage sheep on southern pastures. People of the hills and moors had been marginalized in the nineteenth century, right across the British Isles. As Sally continued her rant, Dave began to wish they had left the subject well alone.

"Read Neil Gunn's *Butcher's Broom* if you don't believe me. Even out in the Hebrides local landlords followed the example of English agri-barons. The difference was that our 'peasants' still accepted divine right long after the Battle of Culloden had been lost, especially out in the west away from Edinburgh's secular influence. We were subjugated by Queen Victoria but still believed she was one step removed from God and likewise the puppet Lairds and Church ministers appointed beneath them. St Kilda was not cleared for sheep production, probably too uneconomical to bother with. Out here, they must have heard of the Clearances and their clansmen and women sent into exile as penitents by the vengeful God imposed on them. The self-same Ministers came here and convinced the contented villagers of their sinful, immoral way of life. Ha! A way of life that had fucking sustained them since time immemorial. You know there was a nurse on the island in the late nineteenth century. She wanted to take practical measures to prevent tetanus killing the babies but, no she was told, it was God's way of punishing the sinful St Kildans. She was stopped from saving the future of the village by those stupid bastards. You know, Dave, if she had managed to stop Ministers from anointing new born umbilical cuts with Fulmar oil, and used iodine instead, we might have had a thriving community here today. Luckily, some women had the sense and will power to get away to give birth and bring back a few healthy babies, but not enough to keep the population viable. Then, of course, with limited genetic resources the risk of inbreeding reared its ugly head. Had nature been allowed to take its course, allowing in fresh blood from visiting seamen, and even frisky tourists, we could have kept the population healthy. But then the poor buggers would have been driven from the church, exiled for immoral behavior that could have saved them. Exiled to where? I could imagine two communities on this island, the righteous here in the sunshine of village bay with sinners banished to the northern gloom of Glen Mór. Oh, there is so much pain in this landscape! Those ministers really got things sewn up here, Dave – and I mean that in more ways than you probably imagine. We women were beaten down by male doctrine here and I am telling you, it's not going to happen again!"

Dave was left stunned by Sally's outburst. He had been tempted to challenge her extreme view of events leading to the decline of St Kilda. There was more to the story than simply patriarchal domination but he could sense tonight was not the time to argue with her. He could see Sally was close to tears and using his educator's skill managed to steer their discussion back to gardening and the delicious evening meal he could smell wafting from the kitchen.

"Sorry, Dave, I rather got ranting again but you have to agree nineteenth century 'improvements' paved the road to hell with their good intentions."

Dave made his cursory point. "I do think there was more to it, Sally, the tourism business and so on but can we leave it for tonight and let's enjoy the meal Deborah and Dan are making for us?"

Sally agreed, blew her nose and smiled at him. The redness of her eyes betrayed the pent up emotion released since she herself had been released from constraints of MOD employment. She was glad Dave had seemed genuinely interested in the way she felt. Dave had to admit he had enjoyed listening to Sally open up to him in a way that Deborah rarely did. The last time his wife dropped her professional façade had been when she broke down after being mugged in the school car park. Dave noticed she now appeared to be adopting a new professional role, as domestic matriarch and equally hard to influence.

Sitting round the supper table the group bounced their ideas around. "First and foremost we have to remember this venture has to be sustainable. We are not going to be able to sell island produce to pay our rent. We might make a bit selling odd bits and pieces – home spun socks maybe? The St Kildans did it."

Dave had appointed himself chair of the discussion and was not impressed by female grimaces at the thought of knitting socks for tourists. He continued, "Our income is going to come from milking the European Social Fund and eco-tourism. We are going to have to put on a good act for Don's passengers. With free diesel I reckon he will bring out as many as he can. The Trust still owns the place so we will still have to work with Josephine but at least our hands are no longer tied, that's if she keeps her job of course. So who's coming up with the first good idea?"

Erica and Sally were first to announce their plan to restore one of the village blackhouses. They would make it a perfect example of 21st century resettlement complete with woodstove, solar panels and micro-hydro. That way the cottage would remain clean inside. There could be quite a bit of heavy work involved so extended family help would be appreciated. Dave hadn't thought much further than vegetable gardens but could see the sense in working with Erica and Sally on a joint project. Together they would restore the first St Kildan farmstead in nearly a hundred years. Deborah said she wasn't much good with her hands outdoors but would happily provide domestic support for the rest of them. The thought of younger members of the family out working to build a future for them appealed to her and she could play a supporting role providing hot meals and home comforts to come back to at the end of the day.

"If Don doesn't use up the entire diesel supply first!" Anne, pragmatic as ever, thought about what she could offer. She didn't really fancy the hard labor of restoring a farmstead but suggested she could lead nature orientated guided walks. She would liaise with Don about that. She could lead visitors down to the seal caves below the Amazon's House, show them the remote seabird colonies. Don might even arrange outings to Boreray and Soay for them. She would never get to the outlying islands without his assistance and if there was money to be made so much the better. Getting away from the village was something that appealed to her more solitary ambitions.

"So, Dan? If you are going to be with us what can you offer St Kilda's resettlement project?" Dan was put on the spot – what could he offer. He was genuinely perplexed; he'd come out basically to have a good time with Erica but she seemed to have changed. Still the same Erica in many respects but St Kilda had given her a new sense of purpose and having teamed up with Sally, he could see himself being pushed aside. Edinburgh values didn't seem to fit here and it was confusing him. It was Deborah who suggested a role for him.

"Dan, this island has an amazing spiritual heritage. It's been neglected since the 1930 evacuation. The church has hardly been used since and the outlying chapels, St. Brendan's and St. Columba's, lie in ruins. Iona makes a living from spiritual guidance based on Celtic Christianity so why don't we do the same here? I can just see you walking around with staff and cloak leading your flock to the Promised Land!" Deborah laughed at the idea she had just suggested. "With your long hair and beard you could be Daniel Rasputin the mad monk of St Kilda. How does that grab you?"

"Ra–ra, Rasputin......lover of the Kilda Queen!" sang Dave, getting in on the joke but failing to notice the tell-tale sign of color rising beneath Deborah's open necked shirt. She turned her face away before the heat showed in her cheeks. "Roderick the Impostor, even!" Sally briefly mentioned the salacious tale of the renegade priest of St Kilda evicted by Church missionaries when they first arrived on the island.

"OK, you're on!" The idea appealed to the showman in Dan, "Just as long as I didn't have to adopt the puritan traditions of a Free Church elder!" The rest of the group laughed together at his concern. "Perish the thought, Dan. If there's one thing we could never imagine in a million years, it's you as Puritan!" Erica knew him a little bit too well but wasn't going to let on to the others. She didn't know her mother well enough though.

Deborah turned to Dave, "You're going to be our great leader, no doubt. With your passion for stone walling you're already beginning to sound a bit like old Minister Mackenzie out here. Just make sure, like him, you are not building edifices to your own ego." Dave was surprised to realize his wife must have researched the history of their island as much as any of them, in spite of her expressed desire to take only a domestic role. Reflecting on this, he considered whether his surprise said more about him than he cared to admit.

"To tell you the truth Dave, this adventure feels to me like the Old Testament story of Lot and his family escaping to the wilderness from God's destruction of Sodom and Gomorrah. He had two daughters with him as well, if I remember that story correctly?"

"No turning back then, Debs, or you'll become a pillar of salt! Mind you, as you spend so much time standing on that wave soaked jetty looking back to the Uists, it might just happen anyway!"

As the scientist of the family Anne had no idea about implications in the Lot reference, though Erica shifted uncomfortably in her chair. Anne decided she ought to find out what her sister's embarrassment had been about, she didn't like being in the dark about anything. Her mother took Dan to the counter near the stove and they brought the meal over to the table.

Dave added, "For even when we were with you, this we commanded you, that if any would not work, neither should he eat."

"Come on guys, dig in!" Deborah changed the subject quickly before conversation on religion turned to point scoring or argument. Sally, now silent after her earlier rant, considered the banter across the table. She had worked in the Western Isles as a student nurse and had heard such conversations before. On the islands many a true word had been spoken to her in jest and she hoped the Williams were not going to prove another example of ancient memories, real or imagined, reaching across time to connect with and determine their futures.

"This is lovely Deborah; how did you make the sauce?" The pasta bake certainly had something different about it and Sally reckoned Deborah could do with some backup in moving the subject away from Scriptures. "I found lots of unopened herbs and spices in the kitchen cupboards when we arrived and I saved the best of them. There's Star Anise in the tomato sauce which gives it the interesting flavor."

Deborah and Sally kept the conversation focused around creating interesting meals from the resources the island had to offer. While the dried food and cans lasted out there would be no trouble satisfying Erica and Sally's vegetarian preferences. Don, given a little notice could bring them anything they wanted during the visitor season. Should times get tough, as Dave often joked, there were plenty of fish in the sea and sheep on the land. "And eggs on the cliffs," added Anne provocatively.

"You're the expert there, Anne! We'll leave that highly illegal task up to you, I think. Thinking about it naturalists like you made the whole Kildan way of life unviable by making egg collection illegal…" Dave was preparing to challenge his younger daughter but Deborah gave him a meaningful look leaving him in no doubt the conversation should be moved on. "Well, anyway, one thing's for certain, we are going to have our work cut out to get things ready for next season." Dave voiced the one opinion they all agreed on. "But for tonight, let's just relax and enjoy ourselves. Thanks for the lovely meal, Deborah. How about some more wine seeing this bottle's finished?"

The meal proceeded amicably with no further point scoring and as the evening drew on Erica and Dan went outside to smoke and find privacy on the shore below the Feather Store. Anne returned to her room leaving Dave and Sally to clear the table and wash up. Deborah sat outside on the Manse step taking in the still mild evening air. For now sea was quiet but she knew it would soon turn wild as the north Atlantic winter approached.

Dave quickly realized that repairing the village's garden enclosures wasn't going to be as easy as he had anticipated. While Erica and Sally had taken on the more complex project of restoring a blackhouse the two women appeared to be making better progress. The walls of the garden enclosures or planticrubs were single skinned and generally took the shape of a circle or ellipse. The granite stones were also heavier than they looked and the rough surfaces soon wore through the work gloves he had found in the workshop. His only stone walling experience had been as a conservation volunteer while a student in Cumbria. The walls made of regular slabs of sedimentary sandstone had been straight forward to build but here irregular lumps of igneous granite needed a different and more individual approach.

It had been agreed to restore one of the cottage steadings at the far end of the village, near the burn running down from Mullach Mór. It needed to be close to running water for Erica had plans for a hydraulic ram pump and micro-hydro electricity generator. The far end of the village was also close to the track up to the top of the hill where there was still a decent and accessible peat deposit. The downside to that choice were the gusting winds which could come unexpectedly from any direction at the edge of the village, meaning they would have to place the solar panels with some ingenuity. Being south facing wasn't simply going to be enough. On a positive note they were close to the beach which could be idyllic on a summer evenings but would also make the garden vulnerable to the salt laden blasts from the south-east. Like the nearby graveyard, surrounding the garden with a continuous high stone wall was going to prove essential if Erica was going to grow anything worthwhile.

Behind the Manse, Dave accepted there was no point in trying to erect straight walls with squared corners. Gusting winds would make short work of demolishing any wall standing against it. He drew inspiration from the elliptical cleits dotted around the island, most quite deliberately placed in the windiest spots to dry and preserve island produce. End on into the wind, the fixed but un-pointed stonework allowed the wind to suffuse through rather than block its energy. It was a clever system he realized. Energy from the wind blowing through planticrub walls also maintained a frost-free environment inside ensuring winter vegetables to keep the St Kildan population supplied with essential produce outside the bird nesting season. The trick was to build up in a spiral pattern, making sure each stone was well locked into its neighbor. Dave felt an almost personal affinity with his handiwork once he had acquired the knack. The Western Isles Trust had already faithfully rebuilt several planticrubs in the village. The working holiday volunteers had an endless task repairing damaged walls where Soay sheep had jumped up and over to gain access to the sheltered grazing inside, lush even in the depths of winter. As he was building, it sometimes felt he was taking one step forward and two back as agile and curious yearlings climbed up on his new built walls. He realized the villagers' heavier commercial sheep, Cheviots probably, would not have jumped up like these feral Soays. He was experiencing a new problem for St Kilda, not insurmountable, but he had to take special care to lock each stone with the next. As he had been taught at Newton Rigg College, all those years ago, he would walk around the top of the wall himself, using his own weight to check for any weakness. He began to think some of the Soays regarded his work as a challenge and were making a game of scrambling up his newly restored walls to get at the sweet grass beginning to grow inside the shelter.

At the far end of the village, Erica and Sally worked tirelessly restoring 'their' blackhouse. The substantial double skinned walls had suffered less from scrambling sheep hooves. Built end on to the wind, the low doorway and windows of the cottage faced into a small alley between the restored home and the semi-ruin next door. Archaeological plans found in the Manse office showed some interesting features they could incorporate. Blackhouse walls, twin-skinned and over a meter thick were in-filled with smaller stones and rammed earth. In many instances they contained integral cupboards and bed spaces. Both women found the idea of secluded bed alcoves, either side of the central hearth, appealing and made a point of including these in their restoration project. The interior of the cottage was damp underfoot but once they had uncovered and cleared the floor drain in the lower half leading outside, the upper living quarters soon dried out. With the turf cleared from the floor they found stone slabs on which the central hearth had stood and could now support their wood burning stove. The rotted window frames were still in position and using fresh timber from the Base scrap wood store they replaced the original frames in situ. Don would bring them glass panes and there were still several tins of useable putty left in the workshop. Likewise there was plenty of timber to line the walls, make a new front door and make the home really cozy. As they finished rebuilding the low wall that divided human from animal occupation, Erica said she was really looking forward to ordering the new wood-burner and seeing the first smoke issuing from a stove-pipe chimney at St Kilda. Standing inside the restored shell of the cottage, hardly a breath of wind entered the building. Then Sally stated the now obvious flaw in their planning.

"We are going to have to put a roof on before we go any further, Erica. We will have to get Don to bring us a load of thatch. There's no heather, let alone reeds left on the island long enough with all the unmanaged sheep grazing. Dave is right, the St Kildans wouldn't have had to cope with this problem."

"God, it's going to cost a packet bringing thatch out here," Erica was concerned and then laughed. "I just can't see Don letting us use the *Beluga* as a hay cart, can you?" They made a satellite phone call to Don that evening and he said he would see what he could arrange for them. They agreed to have the phone switched on at the same time the next day and he hoped he would have come up with an answer for them. The thatch shouldn't be a problem, he had said, it was just getting it out there that would take some ingenuity.

Don rang back as arranged. He had come up with an answer but it wasn't going to be cheap. A military vehicle enthusiast he knew, named Garry, lived near Stornoway and he had a fully restored ex-Soviet PTS-M tracked amphibious transporter. It had a ten ton payload and was basically a barge on caterpillar tracks – were they interested?

"That tub will bring as much thatch as you need, Erica. We just need calm sea conditions and no wind or there'll be nothing left on board by the time it gets to you!" he joked. "I'll also need to come out with the *Beluga* just in case. Those amphibious landing craft can be a death trap if it turns rough. Now that it is so expensive, the promise of free diesel swung it and I suggested if he brought an extra few forty gallon drums out and you'd fill them for him. How does that sound as a deal to you?"

"Apart from the diesel, what's it going to cost us, Don?"

"Hard to say, Erica. If you used local water reed, local to Scotland that is, it shouldn't be too bad. Why not have a word with Josephine? She would know a good source from some loch side or other. Just get it delivered to Stornoway and we can take it from there." Erica rang Josephine and a price was arranged. The Trust had a reliable source at one of their larger island properties. Reed was regularly cut to save small lochs from succession to Alder Carr. It was standard wetland conservation management in winter and they would just need to collect at the loch-side, otherwise the cut reeds would be disposed of by burning.

Erica agreed the deal and asked Don to arrange collection of enough reed to re-thatch their blackhouse. He reckoned that she would need enough to fill the ten ton Russian amphibious transporter. It would never weigh that much but thatching reed was a bulky load. Best to hire a ten ton tipper then they shouldn't go far wrong if they filled the truck right up. "But Don, I'm out here and don't even know the first thing about hiring trucks and so on. Can you arrange all this for us?"

"That'll cost you another barrel of MOD diesel," he teased. "Sure, no bother Erica. It might be at short notice but the next period of calm weather we'll be there. Give me a ring every time it looks good and I'll tell you if we are on our way."

Erica reported back to the family at their evening meal. Dan took advantage of the impending delivery to borrow the phone and ring Lachie. He had run out of dope and it would be a few months until Mothan was in season. Even if it lived up to his expectations, which he wasn't sure about, he was most definitely going to try it out as a substitute. The deal was arranged and even if the *Beluga* couldn't come out just now, Don was cool about it, business was business after all.

Probably due to the seemingly interminable recession on the mainland, everyone involved jumped at the chance of supplying St Kilda with the thatch order. The Soviet PTM-S lumbered into Village Bay just two weeks later, accompanied by the *Beluga*. Don was known to be a good 'fixer' round the Hebrides and this job hadn't proved too difficult for Gary as the weather had been with him, not like the sheep he helped take off Eilean an Taighe a few weeks earlier. The wind and currents in the Minches combined to generate 'Blue Men', pillar like waves throwing the open craft around like a cork. It had been more by luck than judgment they had escaped the Sound of Shiant in one piece that day.

Don chatted over the VHF radio to Garry. Garry had brought his son along to help unload the thatch and the strange vessel used its variable speed twin screws to maneuver its line up with the beach slipway. Its arrival coincided with low tide and finally engaging its caterpillar tracks the hybrid ex-Soviet craft lumbered across the beach before climbing the concrete slipway to the helipad hard standing area. The whole Williams family were there with Sally and Dan to greet the strange vehicle piled high with thatching reed tied down under a heavy duty waterproof tarpaulin.

Garry parked the amphibious vehicle beside the fire pond pump house as the onlookers gathered around. He stepped down from the PTM-S and shook hands with all. Garry had been impressed by the performance of his treasured piece of Russian military surplus. Don arrived a few minutes later having walked along the front after tying his dinghy to the jetty. The tide was too low to bring the *Beluga* alongside that morning. Bio-security measures had last been observed when he brought Josephine out several weeks earlier. As far as the conservation bodies were concerned the big fear was the arrival of rats at St Kilda which would predate on the eggs and chicks of ground nesting sea birds. It had happened on many other islands around the British mainland and it had been not much short of a miracle that, so far, St Kilda had been spared. The arrival of the Soviet transporter, driven straight up into the village with its load of freshly cut thatching reed, was the greatest threat to St Kilda's bio-security since the Village Bay wreck of the fishing boat 'Spinningdale' in February 2008.

"So, where'd you like your thatch, folks?" Garry offered them a door to door delivery service.

"Well, if you are offering, maybe you could take it right up to the blackhouses. You'll easily see the one my daughter has been restoring."

"Hang on a minute, Dave." Sally was concerned. "There's always been a total ban on driving any kind of vehicle off road for fear of damaging the World Heritage Scheduled Monument area. Josephine would have a fit if she heard about this!" Sally was concerned that driving a large tracked vehicle across the village fields would completely sour relations with the Trust.

"What Josephine doesn't know about won't worry her, Garry. Go for it, that's what I say!" Don was enthusiastic to see the exotic vehicle put through its paces.

"You'll have to follow the road toward the power station, then turn left into Red Square, past the KGB offices, ha, ha!" The irony of modern Soviet military hardware maneuvering through the heart of a redundant Cold War UK military base did not escape him. "That way you can drive on concrete most of the way."

The Soviet vehicle, or should it be called a craft, no one could make up their minds, finally left the concrete standing near the scrap wood store and headed up the grassy slope toward the cottages. Surprised sheep scattered as Garry revved the machine's 350 horse power V-12 diesel engine causing a plume of black smoke to issue from its exhaust pipes. He was enjoying this, something very good about using a powerful machine in a wild environment. The load of thatch crossed the dry-burn with ease and in spite of its bulk the tracked transporter caused little damage to the ground. The underlying gravel soil proved surprisingly resilient to the vehicle's well spread 18 ton weight. Even so, this was the first time in Sally's memory that a vehicle of any type had been driven into the old village.

Pulling up outside Erica and Sally's blackhouse, Garry shut off the engine and stepped down with his son, Edward, to untie the tarpaulin sheet protecting the thatching reed. Anne came up the path from Cottage Five, the workshop, carrying four long-handled forks. Together with Dan, the three women unloaded the bundles of reed from the transporter within fifteen minutes. Unsurprisingly to Don, once the bundles of reed had been taken off, thirty empty oil drums could be seen stacked in the bottom of the hull. Garry was obviously going to take full advantage of the free MOD diesel offered as part of the deal. In their enthusiasm to get on with the task, no-one noticed the female brown rat and her three kits run out of one of the first bundles to be stacked on the ground. They quickly disappeared into a collapsed section of consumption wall adjacent to the Street.

Sally went into nearby Cottage One and brought out two six-packs of McEwan's Export, left over from the last sheep research volunteer party. All but Anne celebrated the arrival of the new thatch by downing a can of the popular Scottish beer.

"Can you show Garry where to fill up, Dave?" Don was keen to keep his part of the bargain. Garry had a handy piece of equipment and just the job for deliveries like this, even better for moving sheep around the remoter inner islands.

Dave climbed on board the PTS-M and guided Garry and Edward down to the delivery hose on the side of the power station building. With Dave out of earshot, Don took Dan to one side and gave him the large padded envelope he had placed inside his waterproof jacket for safe keeping. "This is from Lachie, Don. I'll leave it with you to sort things out with him later, OK?" Hebridean deals worked on the principle of trust. If trust was ever broken, there would be no future business, especially so when there was an element of illegality to be taken into consideration.

Parked beside the power station, Garry filled the fuel tank of the amphibious transporter and then filled each of the thirty oil drums he had brought with him. Considering the rapidly escalating cost of fuel this wasn't a bad deal for him and he had had a bit of fun playing with his big toy into the bargain. Filling the *Beluga* was going to be little more difficult but Garry had brought a small transfer pump to run off the craft's electrics. He would pull the Russian transporter alongside the moored *Beluga* and let Don pump out a couple of barrels for his return journey. They'd have to somehow manhandle full barrels down to the jetty when the tourist season began, easier said than done without a vehicle available. Don was keen to get going and be away from the rocks of St Kilda as soon as possible. The amphibious vehicle sailed like a bath tub and would struggle to negotiate the gusting winds close in to the island. The morning crossing had been smooth enough but the line of clouds on the horizon beyond Levenish indicated weather would be coming in from the south-east within a few hours. Village Bay could then be dangerous for the best of craft and skippers. Garry and his tracked barge were neither, Don thought.

The amphibious transporter trundled down to the beach slipway following the concrete road. The tide was high now and the machine was quickly in the sea, now within a few yards of the end of the concrete. Don winced hearing the gears grate as Garry changed the power transmission from tracks to the craft's twin propellers. The PTS-M was immediately underway toward the moored *Beluga*. Don walked down to the jetty and set off in his small dingy to re-join his boat. The two craft floated side by side for ten minutes as the diesel fuel was transferred to the *Beluga*. Don had thought to bring some large tires to use as fenders to protect his new red and white paintwork from the rugged olive green steel plate of Garry's Soviet vessel. With the transfer complete the two craft separated. Garry and Edward waved back to the residents gathered on the jetty to watch their departure. The PTS-M pulled away sounding more like a large and lumbering truck but the sound of the *Beluga*'s twin engines echoing off the cliffs as Don raced away again made the hairs rise on the back of Dave's neck. They had been very lucky with this delivery, it wouldn't always be this easy. Erica had already talked to Don about supplying a woodstove and flue pipe. He implied that should be easy to obtain on Harris and he'd bring them out with him next trip, though that might not be for a while should the winter weather deteriorate as he expected.

The high pressure system remained centered over the north of the British Isles ensuring good, if somewhat cold working conditions. Dave continued repairing garden walls around the village. Sheep still jumped up on his walls but by now he had mastered the technique well enough to prevent them collapsing. Erica and Sally progressed well with their blackhouse. Thatching the roof caused some discussion but the plentiful supply of scrap wood in the Red Square store enabled them to fabricate rafters and sways to suit. They found a good roll of galvanized soft wire in Cottage Five left by Trust volunteers who had used it to tie down the pitched roofs of the six restored white houses. This was perfect for wiring the sways to the rafters holding the thatch in place. Not exactly the traditional method of using tarred string but then what was tradition anyway? Dave agreed galvanized wire served the purpose well enough and that was all that really mattered. The original villagers utilized whatever they could get their hands on to make running repairs, considering the difficulty of getting building materials out to the island. They even used stone tools well into modern times. When they finally had regular access to iron and steel tools the old implements were recycled and used as fillers in stone walls. The two women were lucky to find spare glazing in the Base workshop and after some trial and error worked out how to cut the glass to fit their home made window frames. With winter ahead, they couldn't wait for Don to bring pre-cut glass panes out to them in the following Spring. Using the door on the Lady Grange cleit as a pattern they took scrap wood to make a weather tight door to protect their own entrance. Lady Grange, Rachel Chiesley, had been exiled to St Kilda in the eighteenth century after acrimonious separation from her husband who feared she would inform the Hanoverian government of his Jacobite sympathies. Sally had often referred to this lady's plight during her many rants on the injustices perpetrated through male dominance at St Kilda.

The outer shell of the blackhouse was complete just before the winter weather broke on the island. Bending double to avoid being blown over by gusting salt laden blasts from the bay, Erica and Sally turned into the narrow alley from the Street and entered their new home. With the roof newly thatched, nets formerly used to cover St Kilda's council skips were weighted with stones and thrown over to keep the reeds in place. With glass in the windows and a secure new door, it felt uncannily calm inside. All that was left was to panel the interior walls. Once again the piles of discarded pallets left behind in Red Square provided more than enough material for the job. Within a week they were ready to fit the woodstove but the weather made it impossible for Don to bring it out. A celebration was called for all the same so they decided to follow tradition and light an open wood fire in the center of the floor. It seemed they had made too good a job of the thatch. The non-traditional reeds they had used had been plentifully supplied and they had packed them too tight to let the tarry smoke out easily. The two women sat around the fire with a flask of tea and homemade biscuits until they could stand it no longer. With eyes streaming they spluttered their way outside to return to the relative civilization of the Manse for a shower. Dave was in the kitchen as they came in and made unappreciated comments about a pair of kippers having just entered, from the smell of things.

"Don't worry, girls. I've just been speaking to Don and he reckons he should be able to come out with your new stove next week. The high pressure is slipping south west so the winds will turn more northerly. It will be calm for a few days before the winds pick up again so he has a weather window to get here."

The woodstove and flue pipe was delivered the following week as promised. Erica and Sally took a hand cart, they had found in the Base workshop, down to the jetty. Don arrived on the high tide and tied up alongside and with Lachie they made relatively easy work of maneuvering the second hand Jotul into the cart. With Don and Lachie pulling and the two women pushing they hauled the cast iron stove and pipe up to the black house before walking it inside on its four sturdy legs. Rather than locate the stove in the middle of the floor, Erica had decided it would be far more space efficient to fit it at the upper end of the house with the chimney pipe sticking up through the thatch roughly where a fireplace and chimney would have been in a white house. Lachie left them planning how they would seal the thatch where the flue pipe went through the roof and went to find Dan who owed him a not inconsiderable sum for the herbal cannabis he had sent over previously with the thatching reed.

Dan hadn't been seen outside much during the wintry weather. He had preferred to stay inside the Feather Store 'planning', which was how he described his periods of absence from the daily grind that went on outside. Deborah had spent a fair amount of time in there with him 'advising' and role as family matriarch kept her more than occupied for the rest of the time. When Lachie went up the stone steps and opened the crude wooden door of the upper Featherstore the smell knocked him back. The smell of Dan's unwashed clothes mixed with stale red wine barely disguised the spicy smell lingering from the herbal cannabis he had all but finished smoking since Don supplied him shortly after his arrival. With red eyes and hoarse voice he greeted Lachie.

"Come in, man! Good to see you, Lachie." He moved to hug him but Lachie pulled back repulsed by Dan's unwashed odor. He could have sworn there were remnant vomit particles on his jumper making thoughts of a manly hug even more repulsive. "Never mind about all that, Dan. I believe you owe me a few quid, like."

"Hey, man. It's cool, it is really, but I just can't get to the bank here you know and I don't suppose you take Visa, eh?" Dan had not thought far enough ahead when he made the deal with Lachie. "A cheque will do, Dan – or we can go to the boat and Don has a Visa machine on board. He'll give you the cash so we can do it that way." Dan continued to be evasive, "Man, oh man! Just realized I left my card back in Edinburgh so no can do I am afraid."

Dan was used to blagging his way out of situations like this using boyish charm back in Edinburgh but quickly realized it wasn't going to work this time. "So Dan, you're telling me you can't pay, maybe won't pay even?"

"Come on, Lachie, it's not like that." Dan was starting to sweat. "Like fuck, it's not Dan! OK, let me make things quite clear; just remember where you are, dick-head. You're at St

Kilda and you are going to need us if you ever want to get off again. So, you are going to pay up pretty damn soon or start training to be a fucking long distance swimmer!" Lachie walked out slamming the door behind him and went to re-join Don who was arranging refueling with Dave.

"We can use that hand cart to move barrels down to the jetty then use your transfer pump to fill the boat. How does that sound, Don?" Dave had a plan. "OK by me, Dave. Lets' give it a go."

Don had brought four plastic twenty gallon barrels with him and the two men carried them up to the power station with ease. They placed them upright in the hand cart and filled them from the delivery hose. The weight of the eighty gallons of diesel was as much as the cart could carry. One pneumatic tire was underinflated and flattened under the load making pulling the cart along the level road difficult. When they came to the steep descent to the jetty, maneuvering the unstable and overloaded baggage cart became next to impossible. Don slipped and fell releasing his grip on the steering handle, leaving Dave to take the full weight of the cart and fuel barrels. Dave tried to hold the cart back but it was impossible. As the cart ran away out of control down the slope, the one flat tire caused it to turn violently throwing Dave to one side and tipping over. The full plastic barrels fell out and rolled down to splash heavily into the sea in front of the *Beluga*.

Don was rarely heard to swear but this time he made an exception. "Fuck it! Bloody, bloody fuck it!" The only good thing he could think of was that the tide was high and thankfully the barrels hadn't ruptured falling onto rocks. He picked himself up and went over to Dave lying at the bottom of the slope near the overturned hand cart. He went to help Dave to his feet but when Dave cried out in pain he realized he had been hurt.

"My back, Don, I can barely move. Christ what a balls

up! Where are the barrels now?" Don explained that the barrels were floating off the jetty, but they were intact and could easily be retrieved shortly. "They're in the water but they are OK for now. I'll send Lachie to find Sally, she will know what to do." Lachie had witnessed the commotion on his way back from the Feather Store and came straight down to the jetty. He ran up to the village and arrived at the restored blackhouse to find the two women deliberating over fitting the woodstove.

"Sally, can you come quickly! Dave's taken a bad fall on the jetty and hurt his back, we don't really know how to move him."

"Right, let's go to the medical wing and fetch the stretcher." This sort of incident had been common place during her Base employment. It could be a simple pulled muscle or at worst fractured vertebrae. She prayed it was simply a pulled muscle but she couldn't take any chances. They picked up the stretcher and some blankets to roll and place either side of Dave to stop him from turning. When they got to the jetty, Dave had managed to get himself up onto all fours but could stand no further, even with Don helping. It was a good sign, she thought. It was unlikely to be anything cracked or broken. She ran her fingers down his spine and when she gently pressed just above his sacroiliac joint, Dave winced with pain.

"You've got a compressed disc, Dave, a slipped disc to you. You're not going to die but it's going to be painful for a while. Let's see if we can get you on the stretcher and I'll get you to the medical wing." They strapped Dave into the stretcher after placing rolled blankets either side of him. Supported on the stretcher the pain was all but gone but as soon as he tried to move it came back with a vengeance. With Erica and Sally at the head of the stretcher and Don and

Lachie taking the weight at the bottom they carefully carried Dave up the slippery slope and in through the deserted loading bay, then up to the medical wing. They placed him, still strapped in the stretcher, on to Sally's examination couch. "You can leave him with me now, you had all better get down to the jetty and do something about those diesel barrels floating about before they get burst open on the rocks."

Don, Lachie and Erica walked quickly back to the jetty and stepped into the *Beluga*'s dinghy. Don kept a cargo net in one of the watertight bulkhead compartments of the boat and crossing over to the *Beluga* leaped agilely on board and threw the net down to Lachie and Erica. "Quick now! Get over there and throw the net over the barrels then tow them back here. We can pump them out as they are, floating will be OK as long as we don't let them roll about too much. Keep them tight in the net."

Don got the transfer pump set up and within a few minutes Lachie and Erica had the barrels netted and alongside. It still proved difficult to pump out barrels bobbing on the swell but was achieved without further accident. The *Beluga* was refueled and ready for the return trip. Lachie took Erica back to the jetty then turned around and went back to the *Beluga*. He climbed back aboard and winched the dingy onto the stern. Don fired up the engines and without waving they headed off at high speed in the direction of Harris. It had not been the best of days and now the adrenalin was wearing off Don was beginning to feel his own strained back.

"So how did you get on with that Danny boy, Lachie?" Don was curious.

"He never paid me, Don. I told him he better had if he ever wants to get off St Kilda again."

Don frowned, "OK, Lachie. We'll play it that way. I've seen his sort before and, believe me, they all pay in the end!"

10 RELATIONSHIPS

Deborah had heard none of the commotion on the jetty. Listening to afternoon radio, with the regular throb of the generator in the background, she had no knowledge of the refueling accident at the jetty. Her chores complete she decided it was about time she paid Dan a visit. Though he had spurned her initial advances a few days earlier, he had been receptive, appreciative even, of her innuendoes but for her it hadn't been a game. Like most young men, she thought, he had run a mile rather than get involved with a real woman and for some inexplicable reason she had been feeling very real over the past couple of weeks. Perhaps she had been too hard on him; it was time to make amends, try a more subtle approach.

She tentatively knocked on the Feather Store door. The wooden lock appeared damaged where Lachie had slammed it shut earlier without fully sliding the bolt back. She heard movement inside but there was no sound of footsteps approaching the door. The sound she heard was of Dan retreating to one of the inner bedrooms. After a minute or so she just opened the door and went in.

"Jesus Christ, Dan! What a mess in here. What on earth is the matter with you, living in squalor like this?" Then the smell hit her. He couldn't have changed or washed since they had the row, and that was over a week ago. Empty red wine bottles littered the room and an ashtray on the corner of the trestle table was overflowing with home rolled cigarette butts. There was another smell too, one she had recognized on the clothes of some of her more intelligent yet lethargic students back at the High School. Dirty crockery lay on the counter, the unwashed plates were speckled with droppings where mice had feasted overnight on scraps left and not cleaned up. Deborah heard a slight rustle of bedding from one of the inner rooms and opened the door to find Dan cowering on an old iron single bed beside the small window looking out onto the bay. He looked scared, even though the earlier threat had receded with the departure of the *Beluga*. On seeing Deborah he burst into tears.

"I'm fucked Deborah. I owe Don and Lachie shitloads of money for dope and I can't pay them. There's no way I can out here, is there? We are a bloody cashless society again," he added ruefully.

Deborah was less than impressed with what she found. "Dan, you are going to have to pull yourself together if you're going to stay here. We can't cope with you if you are going to fall to pieces when the going gets tough. I am sorry I gave you a hard time last week, but that is no excuse to wallow in self-pity. I'll ask Don to take you off next time he's in."

Dan burst into uncontrollable sobs, "That's just it Debs, they refuse to take me until I pay for my deal. Unless they take me I won't be able to get them the cash and I don't have cheque book or cards with me. My money is back in Edinburgh and I have no way of getting at it." He looked at her, his expression that of a small boy wanting her to take responsibility for his predicament. Deborah had known a few of her students break down like this at the college and referred them to the student councilor. She was going to have to deal with this, however clumsily, herself.

"Oh, dear, you are in a bad way, Dan," she teased. "You'd better come to Mummy then."

She sat down on the small bed next to him. The springs creaked with their combined weight as she put her arm around him. As he pressed his head to her bosom she actually found his unwashed condition arousing for reasons she couldn't quite fathom and taking a bold risk, slid her hand down inside the front of his jeans. With his face nuzzling into her left breast in an almost suckling position, she felt him stiffen immediately. She gently squeezed and stroked and felt him come surprisingly quickly. Amazed at herself for what she had just done, Deborah lifted his head from her chest and looked him straight in the eye. She felt the situation bizarre enough to continue the jocularity.

"You must have really needed that, Dan." She did feel genuine concern for him this time. In spite of his outward bravado he was obviously still a little boy underneath and in her albeit limited experience, most men were. Deborah wiped her fingers on Dan's shirt, it really couldn't have got much grubbier. Now visibly relaxed, he was actually beginning to return to an albeit unclean version of his old self.

"Tell you what Dan, come over to the house in a few minutes. Go and have a good shower first and then put on some clean clothes, if you have any. Then you join us for supper. Good food and company will do you the world of good, and for now at least please keep our little secret?"

He nodded and she left Dan to try and regain his usual extrovert composure. Deborah walked back over to the Manse and was surprised to see Dave moving stiffly toward her with the aid of a walking stick.

"What on earth have you done, love?" This was getting to be one of those days by the looks of it, she reflected.

Dave limped inside and sat down carefully on a high backed kitchen chair and related events leading to a stupid, very stupid accident. If only they had blown that flat tire up before trying to move the barrels or only tried to move one at a time. But then everything was clearer with hindsight. He explained how Sally had fixed him up, given him some gentle osteopathy to get everything back in place but he would have to be careful for a few days and not lift anything heavy.

Definitely no stone walling for a week or so until his inflamed lower back muscles settled down. He certainly wasn't going to tell her about the rest of his experience in the consulting room and had no inkling of what had just occurred in the Feather Store between Deborah and Dan.

After he had been left strapped in the stretcher on the examination couch, Dave expected Sally to have carefully released him, given him a thorough examination before manipulating his lower spine. A bit of massage, maybe a few chiropractic cricks and cracks and he'd be up and gone. He did think she was leaving him strapped down for longer than was really necessary and also had to admit that after a couple of cans of McEwan's with Don and Lachie earlier, he quite badly needed a pee. "No problem," she had said. Instead of allowing him to get up, as he had expected, she proceeded to fetch a cardboard urinal bottle, undid his zipper, pulled his penis out of his pants and held the bottle in place. He found it impossible to urinate with the erection that was rising in spite of his lower back discomfort. "Oh, dear David, what are we going to do? Looks like I am going to have to take care of that for you aren't I? If you can't pee normally I am going to have to catheterize you."

This really had been the furthest thought from Dave's mind when he was deposited in Sally's examination room for minor back injury treatment, but strapped up and almost pain free he was powerless to resist. He had to reluctantly admit to himself he was enjoying the experience. When Sally donned her white latex gloves and slid the smooth catheter tube into his urethra the sensation left him lost for words. All he could manage was a whimper and gasp as the tip of the tube pushed painlessly through the sphincter and entered his bladder. With his erection subsided the urine flowed freely and uncontrollably into the bottle she had placed at the other end of the tube. She gently withdrew the catheter when he finished urinating. Having relinquished all bodily control to Sally,

Dave felt she had made the first move in a game he would later find hard to resist.

"Better now, Dave?" He felt like putty in her hands as she un-strapped him from the stretcher and carefully turned him over to begin the manipulation. Not a word more was spoken about what had just happened but both acknowledged Sally as dominant in a game of power exchange. In spite of Dave's professed yearnings to lead his tribe to the Promised Land, she had skillfully led him into a world of submissive fantasy. For Sally, the self-professed radical feminist, previous opportunities to exert subtle sexual power over her male patients had been a perverse pleasure. She had enjoyed such moments before. While employed by the MOD, as one of the few women on the island, she had occasionally left her male patients to ponder over unexpected aspects of their treatment. It had been her way of putting a bit of color into a grey male world and at the same time feeding her own fantasy. There had been few protests, her white coat conveyed an authority her patients willingly accepted in their regimented lives. Now without the MOD structure in place social parameters were becoming blurred. For women of the new St Kilda, she realized, life could and often would become experimental as they worked out their new roles. St Kilda had been a balanced rather than patriarchal or matriarchal society before and if she had her way it soon would be again. For now, she needed to exercise feminine control until their time came. Sally had tried the traditional practice of leaving a sachet of Mothan under her pillow but dreams of a much wanted future family still eluded her.

Anne had been out walking the cliff paths at the time of her father's mishap with the handcart. Though having no knowledge of the personal events of that afternoon she was astutely aware of energies already at play in their nascent community. She had picked up on her mother's subtle flirtations with Dan, his weak attempts to resist and his pathetic escape attempts through alcohol and cannabis. Sally's desire to dominate had been pretty obvious from the start. Her experience of working on the island was proving useful but, Anne calculated, also made her vulnerable to the unexpected. Her father was OK but a remarkably easy man to predict. He had brought them out here to follow his dream of pioneer resettlement, albeit aided by the Trust and abandoned MOD food stores. She smiled at this; as a keen naturalist she had read the work of Henry David Thoreau, written in his cabin at Walden Pond. Like so many male authors on wilderness living he couldn't have done it without the support of women at home. Her mother seemed to have willingly accepted the role of the strong pioneer woman, looking after her men to ensure they were fit and strong enough to support the family. It was all so obvious, they were all working out their fantasies free from mainland constraints. Constraints here, she thought, were determined by the elements and rhythms of nature. Her scientific training told her there should be no other way but she found the draw to visit the ruins of the Amazon's House in Glen Mór, on an almost daily basis, hard to understand.

The Great Skuas nesting there during the summer had come to accept her as a familiar and trusted figure in their territory. The large and usually aggressive birds accepted her presence, almost befriending Anne as she sat for hours on end enjoying the spirit of the place. While idly chewing on Mothan leaves she felt an almost tangible presence around 'horned structures', the ageless horseshoe shaped stone compounds visiting archaeologists found so puzzling. Anne would have scoffed at meditation back in Edinburgh but out here she found herself doing just that. Her mind was beginning to relax and unquestioningly accept the spirit of the female deity she realized had long been suppressed on the island. Anne had read how, when sea levels were lower, St Kilda was the tip of a peninsula reaching out from Harris. St Kilda's mythical Amazon could have rode out to hunt across the Western Isles with her pack of hounds. Now as sea levels continued to rise Anne sensed the deity was trapped and, like any trapped wild creature, the Amazon or Cailleach needed to be treated with caution and respect. Anne had developed the ability to stand outside of herself and reflect on her place in this landscape. The Cailleach was embedded here, every rock and stream a portal to her energy, her life force. It dawned on Anne that it was no wonder there had been plane wrecks in this valley. Intrusive flying machines downed by inexplicable gusts on the clearest of days. Exiled to the cold north side of the island the Cailleach could not tolerate desecration of her home by men with their noisy polluting machines and macho lack of empathy for the world around them. The Cailleach had summoned aggressive Skuas in the 1960s to protect Glen Mór, after Operation Hardrock had blasted a huge chunk out of the southern slopes of Conachair. The revelation gave Anne goose pimples, the epiphany almost erotic in intensity. She suddenly realized why so many curious tourists had been driven back by Skua attack after venturing into the Cailleach's sanctuary. The Cailleach had summoned Skuas from the Arctic regions to protect her from male insensitivity and chewing another smoky Mothan leaf, Anne knew what she had to do redress the two hundred year old injustice.

Snapping out of her reverie, Anne remembered she had noticed some muddy green material poking out of the damaged cleit at the site of the small charter plane crash on the day of their arrival. As far as she knew, the deer hunters had all perished bar the one shocked survivor they had met on the jetty. In fact she was secretly pleased the remains, both mechanical and human, had tipped over the cliff and now lay hidden in submarine caves beneath the island. The aging but still visible remains of the Sunderland flying boat were bad enough. Another smashed plane would further deform the spirit of place she found so inspirational. She would pull up and throw the ugly piece of green canvas over the cliff to join the rest of the male rubbish hundreds of feet below. She pulled at the material and found it stronger than she had anticipated. It seemed to be the same material used in her climbing rucksack. After a struggle she pulled the Cordura bag out from under muddy turf and fallen stones inside the cleit. The bag was roughly five feet long and broader at one end, which seemed to be where most of the weight was located. It had a shoulder strap running from end to end and a heavy duty zip fastener running the whole length of one side. The fastener was seized with corrosion but she decided to take the long bag and its contents down to the village and free the zip at the workshop inside Cottage Five.

Walking back down the steep track the heavy shoulder bag annoyed her. Bumping against the outside of her thigh she had to change the bag from shoulder to shoulder to stay comfortable. She continued past the Operation Hardrock quarry and the Milking Stone, carefully replaced by the military blasters. It occurred to her surprising that the military had managed to retain a modicum of respect for the spirit of this island. Turning left from the track she crossed the burn nearly losing her footing when the bag slipped from her shoulder and knocked her ankle. Quietly cursing, she slung the bag back on her shoulder and made her way along the grass strewn Street to Cottage Five. She went inside but found the light inside too poor to see well enough to free the zip. She placed the long bag on the low wall outside and fetched a can of WD40 from the steel flammable liquids cupboard. Anne sprayed the thin penetrating oil along the length of the corroded brass zip and waited a few minutes for the lubricant to take effect.

Erica came out of the alleyway beside her newly thatched blackhouse having waited long enough for Sally to return and help with the woodstove logistics. Looking up the Street, instead of Sally, she saw her younger sister apparently struggling to open a long green bag. To her irritation, Anne spotted her sister walking toward her; she had hoped to discover the contents of the bag for herself. Now Erica was going to get in on the act. "What have you got there? Bloody hell Anne, that looks like a gun-slip! Where did you find it?"

Erica had briefly been in a relationship with a forester who she soon discovered to be an unstable gun enthusiast. A survivalist, he described himself, a 'Prepper' prepared for the breakdown of society and he was preparing to defend his woman and family living in the wilds of Assynt when the collapse assuredly came. In Erica's opinion, rather than being the deep ecologist she had hoped for, her forester boyfriend revealed himself as a rabid eco-fascist and she quickly ended the relationship hoping she wasn't going to attract a stalker who wanted to control her as much as the Highland deer population.

"'Here Anne, I'll hold the bag while you work the zip." Anne worked the zip back and forward until it eventually freed and the bag opened along its full length. She reached inside and, quickly realizing what the bag contained, pulled out a hunting rifle. It was well wrapped in a protective and lightly oiled cloth. The telescopic sight lenses were protected by plastic caps. Erica was amazed, "That's a Tikka T3 Lite Stainless! One of the best hunting rifles you can get. It's light as well as weather resistant. Do you remember Derek? That mad forester I went out with for a few weeks once? He had one of these and took me target shooting. There was no way I was going to shoot deer but target shooting was really cool. I amazed myself, never thought I would enjoy guns but I loved using one of these. My shoulder aches thinking about it! Hey, is there any ammo in there for it?" Anne rummaged further into the bag and discovered ten small plastic boxes each containing 20 rounds of 100 grain ammunition. "This must have been heavy to carry, Sis. Let's try it out! The magazine holds 3 rounds. We'll soon find out if it works OK."

Erica had been given basic firearms safety instruction by Derek before he let her try out his rifle so she knew to set up the target well away from the Base and any other of the buildings. Most importantly the bullet should land safely away from causing any harm. She walked across the field and placed a spare plywood window shutter on top of the remains of the village boundary wall above the shore. Erica considered this to be safe for if she missed the target, the bullet would fall harmlessly into the sea. The breeze proved a problem setting up the target so she propped it up with some large stones. A white spot where the green topcoat had flaked off the plywood made for a suitable bulls-eye. Walking back she estimated the range to be about two hundred and fifty yards and adjusted the telescopic sight accordingly, placed one round into the magazine and worked the bolt to load the round. Lying across the path, she rested the rifle on top of the low turf capped wall, took aim at the green board, breathed out, as Derek had told her to, released the safety catch and squeezed the trigger. The rifle cracked and a small neat hole appeared in the white patch on the green board which subsequently slid to the ground after the stone propping it up dislodged. The bullet had faultlessly punched through the target but then ricocheted off a beach stone. Rather than falling harmlessly into the sea, the spinning bullet whined across the foreshore to hit the steel door of the jetty store room with a resounding metallic bang.

"What the fucking hell!" he screamed out. Dan's nerves had already been strained to breaking point that afternoon and he had gone down to the jetty to contemplate over, what he considered, a well-deserved spliff. Dope psychosis was making him paranoid about the return of the *Beluga*. He was preparing himself for a beating unless he paid up, that is what would have happened in Edinburgh, but out here he was getting shot at. Deborah had reduced to him to a quivering boy and now he was being targeted by her daughters.

"Shit!" Erica realized what had happened, put the rifle down on the gun-slip to prevent it getting damaged on the stone wall and ran down to the road. She could see Dan pacing up and down on the jetty shaking his head in disbelief. "Dan, I am so sorry!" she shouted. "Are you OK?"

"For God's sake, Erica!" he yelled back. "What were you thinking of, and where the fuck did you get that gun from?"

Deborah had heard the shot from the Manse kitchen where she and Dave had been sitting sharing a pot of tea before she prepared the evening meal. Both had been quietly and separately contemplating the strange events of the afternoon but had been snapped into the present by the loud crack of the rifle, immediately followed by a loud clang and angry screams from the jetty.

"You stay there, Dave. I'll go out and see what that was all about." Dave hobbled to the window to watch his wife march out toward the top of the jetty. He saw her scratch her head as Erica explained what had happened. "No one has been hurt, that was the main thing," she assured her mother. Deborah was furious. "You'd better bring that thing down to the Manse and we'll keep it safely under lock and key." She thought a firearms incident was just typical of Erica, she would always be the wild child no matter what and she was certainly old enough to know better than play with guns.

Deborah unexpectedly recalled Erica had played with men, loaded guns in their own right, often enough back in Edinburgh and when she became pregnant she hadn't even been able to tell Deborah who the father was. An abortion seemed the only sensible option but when she collected Erica from Spire Murrayfield Hospital, she knew it had been a big mistake. Had she let Erica have the baby she would have no doubt settled into single motherhood in Edinburgh instead of playing with guns out here. Deborah would have been a grandmother by now had she not insisted on Erica's termination. She had wanted to do the best thing for her daughter but had so much looked forward to becoming a grandmother before she felt too old to be appreciated. Being a mother was the hardest job in the world and no matter how old, these girls would always be her babies. She also wondered if the tense relationship between her and Dave around that time made Erica more promiscuous to compensate for passive aggression in the home. They just hadn't been getting on during periods when Dave was at home, unemployed, while she was going from strength to strength in her teaching career. At least now Dave seemed fulfilled and happy out on St Kilda.

Anne joined them, she had already put the rifle back in its slip and slung it over her shoulder. "Who's going to steal it out here, Mum?"

"OK, clever clogs, we do at least need to keep it safely away from your crazy sister before there really is an accident!" Deborah was not amused by her younger daughter's nonchalance. The three walked back to the Manse and Deborah pulled the loft ladder down from the hatch in the hallway ceiling. "Pass that thing to me and I'll put it up in the loft for now. If anyone has any better ideas, keep them to yourself!" Deborah climbed up and placed the rifle, back in its slip, in the loft storeroom on a shelf alongside unsold books and postcards. She came back down to the hallway to find Dave had made his way from the kitchen to find out what was going on. Deborah explained that Anne had found a hunting rifle in a cleit near where the Piper crashed on the day they arrived. There was also some ammunition and their crazy eldest daughter had decided to try it out, nearly shooting Dan in the process. Dave tried very hard to suppress a smile but in doing so spluttered into a full throated laugh at the absurdity of his afternoon. "Oh Erica, you really are a piece of work sometimes."

By this time Sally, having also heard the shot, appeared to ask if everyone was alright. Erica was by now wishing the ground would open up and swallow her. Anne was standing beside her, passive and smug as usual whenever emotional tension was in the atmosphere. Deborah assured Sally that everyone was just fine while wishing she could simply tell her to piss off and keep her nose out of family business. This was her house and she was going to stay in charge, especially of the two men on the island.

"OK, that gun stays up in the loft unless I say otherwise. Is that clear girls? The sisters nodded to Dave acknowledging that his instruction was perfectly clear and left no room for argument. It suited Erica to play her father's game for the time being, at least until the embarrassing incident was forgotten. Anne shrugged her shoulders and went to her room while Erica went outside to talk with Dan, still nervous from his afternoon's experiences.

Don had been right about the deteriorating weather conditions. Atmospheric pressure was dropping rapidly to the south. As the unusually deep and intense depression span toward Skye, severe south-easterly gale force winds and an accompanying storm surge headed toward St Kilda. It was going to be a wild night. Erica helped Dan clear up the mess in the Feather Store, never very inviting at the best of times. Rather than let him spend the evening alone in his small flat, she decided to invite Dan up to Cottage One to share the planning of his so called spiritual tours of the island. He readily agreed, looking forward to her company and an evening beside the only functioning wood stove in the village. The sudden blast of wind slammed the window shutter with such force the glass cracked across two panes. "Fuck Shit!" Dan's nerves were still on edge in spite of Erica's attempts to calm him down. She was attracted to Dan's idea of resurrecting the islands spiritual significance rather than concentrating solely on the more quantifiable archaeological and natural history aspects of St Kilda. However, since the Western Isles Trust had pulled the plug, they were going to have to make their resettlement financially sustainable as much as anything else.

Shutting the wooden lock to the Feather Store door with some difficulty, they realized the wind speed outside was picking up rapidly. They both stood and watched the movement of the sea with amazement. The waters of Village Bay were palpably rising. The eastern horizon, instead of being flat was visibly rippling even at a distance of several miles. The sea level, still far from rough, rose and poured over the jetty in a steady torrent before hitting the beach and rising up to lap at the doors of the helipad waiting room. St Kilda's humorously named International Airport Lounge was in danger of inundation. Sally watched from the Factor's House amazed at the storm surge pouring into the bay. Even as an old hand she had never seen the sea level rise like this. Within moments the south-easterly gale hit the village, rattling the slates and lifting the roof lights to fall with a crash audible throughout the house. She could feel the force of the wind palpably shaking her home. No wonder, she thought, that the long abandoned Victorian cottages failed to withstand onslaughts like this. Sally opened the porch door and struggled into the wind, forcing her way round to the outside back steps up to the bedrooms. The back door was almost ripped out of her hands when she opened it and it took most of her strength to close it behind her as she entered the upper level of the house. Though a tempest raged outside it was warm inside. She was relieved to find the iron framed roof lights unbroken and secured them with their substantial nineteenth century latches. The noise of the wind blowing through the slates was incredible. How they didn't just blow away when such a wind arose, she would never understand. Opening the back door just enough to squeeze through and back out into the wind, she made her way with difficulty into the wind, turning the corner to be bodily thrown against her own front door. Sally had just managed to get back inside when, through the kitchen window, she saw Erica and Dan being pushed along by the wind on their way to Cottage One. Dan's long hair was lashing out in front of him, Erica's long coat flapping wildly around her knees as the pair made their way along the uneven granite pavement of the Street.

Erica almost had to drag Dan up from the Featherstore. Bad weather wasn't his thing as he had kept trying to explain but she insisted they left the squalor of his Featherstore apartment and began their planning in relative comfort where the flat surfaces were not covered in droppings or stained with mouse urine. There was also the woodstove to look forward to. The effort of going out into the gale made Dan cough, with his sore throat and smoker's lungs unaccustomed to clean air being forced into them. The wind sucked his breath away each time he turned his head sideways to take in the rapidly changing sea conditions in the bay. A huge swell had begun to crash along the slopes of Dun and vortices of winds, water devils, drove spinning columns of spray up onto the seafront roadway. For once he was glad of being led by Erica toward the promised shelter of Cottage One. He had enjoyed watching wild weather through the now cracked and draughty Featherstore window but, for him, being caught outside in it was another matter altogether.

Dave and Deborah had seen the storm surge enter the bay from the Manse windows. Deborah had run to the porch in time to see Anne struggling down the slipway with her camera to photograph the drama of the rising sea pouring over the jetty wall. She tried to call her daughter back but her shouts were ineffectual against the howling wind. When the first large wave exploded over the wall behind her Anne scurried back along the jetty to safer levels at the top of the slipway. Deborah ran outside and grabbed hold of Anne's arm and literally pulled her back into the house. Mother and daughter were both panting with the effort, both fighting the pull of the wind and Anne fighting the pull of her mother.

"What the hell are you playing at, Mum?" Anne was enraged that her mother should pull her like that. "I was perfectly OK out there. I love it and I was going to film the sea. We don't see something like this every day!"

"Anne, you are my daughter and you can do what you like out of my sight over in Glen Bay but I'm not going to watch you drown in front of my very eyes, right outside our front door!"

"Jesus Christ", Anne swore under her breath. "Mum. All I got was a little wet from a wave I didn't see coming."

"Well I did see it coming, my girl. Look Anne, I am sorry if you think my reaction was over the top but you just wait until you have children of your own. You'll think differently then. I just don't want to lose you, OK?"

The wind gusted violently and the generator in the Flare Store spluttered before picking up again. "That's all we need, the generator packing up too!" Anne sought to calm the situation with her mother. "Don't worry Mum, it was probably just the wind backing up the exhaust, it has done it before." Deborah was still angry. "So now you're the expert mechanic as well as ecologist? What do you know about engines then, or much else for that matter out here?"

"You'd be surprised about what I know around this place, mother." Anne growled back. Deborah felt the color rise to her throat; if only it wasn't so obvious she thought to herself. How much did her deep and apparently devious younger daughter really know?

Dave came to the hallway after hearing voices raised above the general clamor of the wind. He saw his wife's flushed features concluding it to be the result of tension between the two. Anne turned and marched to her room leaving Deborah standing, her evident flush subsiding, inside the hallway.

"What was that all about?" He questioned. Deborah thought she picked up an authoritarian rather than caring tone in his voice. To her embarrassment the obvious blush rose once more. "Our beloved youngest was only trying to drown herself to get a good photo from the jetty, Dave. Maybe I was being over protective but now she'll drive me nuts by walking round for days with that supercilious face she puts on every time she thinks she has got one over me."

"Got one what over you?" Dave was mildly amused but also feeling slightly anxious concerning the secret he shared with Sally. "Never you mind, Dave. Women's business - if you must know."

Sally settled down in her front room in the Factor's House. She had reopened the old fireplace but during winds like this all sorts of debris blew down the chimney, from dried moss to desiccated mice. When she lit the peat fire for the first time in nearly a century she had inadvertently asphyxiated several of St Kilda's oversized mice nesting in the chimney. She had got into the habit of digging a little peat and stacking it to dry in a convenient cleit each time she went for a walk on the hill. Bringing down a rucksack full of dried peat each time had proved worthwhile and setting a cheery fire on a wild evening like this made it well worth the effort. Going for a walk was all very well, she had often thought, but going for a walk with a purpose so much better. As every visitor remarked, the island was littered with these small stone structures. There were over a thousand stone cleits, many still capped with turf roofs and ideal for keeping anything dry, including one's self when caught out in bad weather. Since the Soay sheep had been given free access everywhere, they clambered up and damaged the cleits in a way fatter commercial sheep would never have done. Sally thought the Soays little more than vermin and with their incessant grazing damaging the island ecology. The Trust archaeologists had been for ever trying to find a way of stopping them climbing on cleits while the Soay Sheep Project continued to insist they were to be treated as unmanaged wild animals. The St Kildans would soon have sorted this out had they not evacuated leaving scientists to mismanage the islands. She had not been surprised to read that 100 of them had been brought over from Soay to 'maintain the grazing' and bred, well like wild sheep. Four legged lawn-mowers even able to graze cleit roofs until the turf capping disintegrated. Aggressive Skuas occupied the flatter ground and kept the sheep away from their nests allowing the vegetation to seasonally recover and were wary of her while digging peat. She did think that the Skuas could prove to be a keystone species in restoring the ecology of St Kilda. Not only did they deter human presence away from the village but they kept the sheep on the move and predated on their lambs. It was just a pity that the Skuas also predated on anything else they could get their beaks into, including the Puffins and Storm Petrels she loved to watch on her days off. Not even Gannets were safe. The large and graceful seabirds were picked off and harried by packs of Skuas until the exhausted and bloodied Gannet flopped into the sea to be ripped to pieces. What kind of nature conservation was this? The St Kildans would have kept the balance by driving these vicious killers away from the smaller birds that underpinned their livelihoods.

She stopped there, knowing her thoughts were about to spiral down until she found herself in a self-induced bad temper.

"Come on, Sal! Get that fire going and think about what you're going to eat tonight, girl." At St Kilda, she reckoned, talking to yourself was much healthier than not talking at all. Sally often talked to herself, a consequence of living alone she had realized and accepted long ago. Her meal wasn't going to take too much thinking about, something out of a tin and a dried staple to go with it. Sally was looking forward to the fresh vegetables Dave had promised her for next Spring, but she thought he might have underestimated the sheep problem somewhat.

Dan and Erica had managed to get the Cottage One woodstove lit though the gusting wind caused back-draughts of smoke to puff out into the living area. They both thought that the smell of stove smoke wasn't actually that unpleasant, certainly an improvement on the smell of mouse urine in the Featherstore. There was no way to light a fire in the Featherstore as the only fireplace was in the cluttered and unlivable store room downstairs. Built into the slope, the damp lower story had been used as a builder's store since the Trust restored the building back in the 1980s.

Erica placed two mugs of tea on the table. "Sorry there's no milk, Dan. I've got some dried stuff if you're desperate, otherwise you'll have to wait till I get my house cow over here!" They sipped at their sweet black tea and Erica decided to get the ball rolling. "Now then Dan, you are going to lead spiritual tours of the island, right? So we need to do some planning. Like where to go, what to see and so on. First of all let's throw some ideas in the pot. I know you have been doing some reading so you first, then."

Dan thought for a bit before picking up a nearby pencil and sheet of paper from the windowsill. He began to jot down ideas as they came to him, drew circles around the words the paper and began to link them with thin lines. Mind-mapping, he had been told at University, was the way to get a plan like this off the ground. Edinburgh University seemed a long way off in time and space from where the two of them now sat but the principle remained sound. The circles he drew on the paper contained the words 'Kirk', 'Graveyard', 'Christchurch', 'St, Columba', 'St. Briannan', 'Altars' and 'Sabbath'. The graveyard seemed central on the paper with the names of chapels and outlying altars around the edges of the sheet. The Kirk seemed to make the plan look a little asymmetrical, which he considered might not be so surprising, since its building in the 1820s had been designed to throw almost every other spiritual aspect of the archipelago off kilter. True, the new church had re-consecrated earlier altars erected on the outlying islands of Dun, Boreray and Soay. The Church of Scotland had considered them Pagan even though there were historical associations with the Irish missionary saints. After the Disruption of 1843, the Free Church had encouraged acts of worship that engaged with natural elements. In trying to replace the bland and emotionless national Church of Scotland, the radical Protestants acknowledged the island's wilder energies as much as their semi-pagan forbears had done in the Middle Ages. St Kilda's medieval period extended well into the eighteenth century due to the islands' cultural isolation. Away from the spiritually stifling city of Edinburgh, Free Church elders encouraged worship amongst rather than against these elements. "The wilder location the better to commune with God rather than Mammon," he told her.

Erica looked at Dan's mind-map and thought for a moment. "Just one thing, Dan. Haven't you mapped out a very male spiritual landscape here? These centers of ritual, it does look like a predominantly paternal structure to me. I'd like us to include female spirituality in the tours too."

"I'm not quite sure what you mean there, Erica." Dan was puzzled because he instinctively knew there was something really important missing from his plan.

Erica explained, "I'd like to see you include places of natural reverence. I don't mean huge vistas to Boreray but maybe some small secluded spots where flowers grow free from sheep grazing, where we can hear the seals singing to their pups and importantly where the Cailleach can be found, and her cave. Even the Amazon's House could be included though I do think that story a bit of a male fantasy!"

"Sorry, Erica, I hadn't thought of it from that angle." Erica had made a valid point he realized.

'No, you men rarely do," she replied. "But let's not get bogged down with it for now. Can you draw a plan to include the places I have just mentioned and we'll try and work it all together?"

Dan drew his second mind-map to include the Cailleach's Cave, the Tunnel where seals sing to their pups and the Well of Virtues. The fount at the foot of Glen Mór had been renamed from Tobar Brighid, Brid's Well after the Apostle of the North banished the Spring Maiden Brighid from the island. St Brighid of Kildare had been appropriated by the Catholic Church, but the Protestant Free Church had tried to banish her girlish spirit from the island all together. Now she remained as the angry Cailleach, still smarting from the injustices imposed on the mind and landscape of St Kilda in the early nineteenth century. Brighid, associated with the south had been dominated by male activity in Village Bay. Morrigan, the Cailleach lived on resentful in the north, he told Erica. There were just one or two places where as Brighid she remained, mainly in flower rich rocky verges of the deep burn running down from Mullach Mór. The Soays seemed to have a natural aversion to getting wet. They sheltered in cleits from the rain and wouldn't graze at the water's edge unless there was no drier alternative. Facing south, these sunny clefts were Brighid's last refuge. "Yeah, right! I'm with you, Erica. We need to include the Milking Stone and the Plain of Spells."

"That's better, Dan. The new St Kilda is going to need all these spiritual resources if we are going to survive as a community. Hey, what about Shoney the sea goddess. You'll like this one, Dan. The islanders used to throw a big party and go down to the sea and offer homemade beer to the sea in return for Shoney delivering seaweed as fertilizer for them. Candles would be lit and floated on the water and then it was party time. Not much likelihood of inbreeding in those families if you get my meaning!"

"This gets better and better, Erica. You get on with your blackhouse and leave this project to me." The plan was hatched and consummated by Erica's production of a partly emptied bottle of single-malt. "There's a few drams left here, let's celebrate our spiritual tour business beginning next year. I bet Don will be all for this, it'll mean extra punters for him. You know Dan, I am getting really excited about this!" She crossed the table and hugged Dan, still seated, from behind giving the top of his head a light kiss. "Who knows where this is going to end, Dan?"

11 MOTHAN

Dan and Erica met up the following afternoon to continue planning their spiritual tours after relative normality had returned to the Manse following the passing of the storm. Dave took the day off to nurse his bad back, Sally and Anne took a walk across the island bird watching and Deborah kept busy inside the Featherstore intending to restore at least some sense of order and cleanliness in there.

Dan suggested starting at the nineteenth century Kirk would be appropriate. Erica was initially hesitant but had to agree getting their visitors together under one roof would be a good way to start, especially if the weather was against them. Dan also thought perhaps an act of communion would be a good way to start. Erica was against this too until Dan explained he meant an act of communion with the island not communion with an imagined God justifying domination by the British Empire, the map of which still hung fading on the wall of the schoolroom annex. "Can you imagine, Erica, St Kildan children being taught about South Africa and Canada and their tiny, almost insignificant, place in Queen Victoria's Empire pretty well ignored? That must have felt unreal considering their parent's whole world would have revolved round the Hebrides."

"Yes," she replied, "and don't forget how unreal it must have been for their parents moving into a new structured settlement where equally structured religious practice bound their changed society in servitude to patriarchy. You must have heard Sally go on about the killing of the last Great Auk. Stoned as witch, I tell you! The last northern penguin was murdered out on Boreray where chains of Christian bondage weren't quite strong enough to suppress older fears. If they hadn't had to go out to earn cash to survive, they would have waited until better weather. They thought the harmless Great Auk was conjuring up the storm to spite them. Now we have to put up with the spite of Great Skuas. The road taken was certainly paved with good intentions but the change from shared run-rig to enclosed plots must have been complicated enough without the Minister trying to enclose mind and soul as well."

"Well, Erica I propose a toast to the loosening of ecclesiastical ties as well as minds. I have prepared a new communion wine just for this occasion." Dan reached inside his jacket and produced his silver hip flask.

"Try a drop of my special communion wine............" Dan passed the small silver hip-flask to Erica. She unscrewed the cap and sniffed the contents. "OK Dan....what have you actually got in this?"

"'Erica...it's OK, really it is. I picked some fresh Mothan growing near the bore-hole and let the leaves steep in vodka for a few weeks. I have been taking it for a couple of days now. Hardly notice any effect other than the vodka but the herb has a magical reputation."

"Oh yeah, are you going to enlighten me before I drink it Dan?"

"Well to start with it is anti-biotic." Erica looked quizzically at him. "Go on, tell me more then." Dan continued, "OK, the leaves are slimy, right? Insects get trapped in the slime and are absorbed over several days. It's a tactic used by certain plants growing in bog conditions where it's too acid for them to absorb enough nutrient from the soil." He noticed the moldy fly dead on the schoolroom window sill. "And the slime being anti-biotic keeps the insects from going moldy. If I was an insectivorous plant I'd want to keep my flies fresh, wouldn't you? It's the same with the tiny Sundew that grows here too."

Dan was on his pet subject now. "There's lots of folk lore about this plant. It was used for curdling milk and used as a poultice against infection on cattle. It was also rubbed into cows' udders to stop fairies from stealing the milk. If anyone had unnatural good fortune they were said to have drunk milk from a cow that had eaten Mothan. The best story of all concerns women and the effects of Mothan."

Erica frowned and waited for some chauvinistic comment but he proceeded to tell her how Mothan was a dreaming herb. It could be put in pillows to induce pleasant dreams for the sleeper, foretelling of the man she would marry and could be used by a woman to entrap a man. "And just how is a woman supposed to use Mothan to entrap a man, then?" Dan explained. "All you have to do is to chew leaves of Mothan before kissing the man you fancy. When your saliva mixes he is trapped as completely as any insect gently landing on the Mothan. In a state of blissful dreaming he is oblivious of her ulterior motive." Erica teased him, "And what might that ulterior motive be, Dan?" He laughed, "You tell me, Erica!"

Erica cautiously put the flask to her lips. She hadn't forgotten the furor over Dan's mixing Fly Agaric mushrooms in vodka back in Edinburgh, but Mothan didn't sound too bad. She took a sip and found it hardly tasted of anything other than the spirit. "How would you describe the taste, Dan? There's something there but I can't quite put my finger on it"

"How about love juice?" he quipped. Erica blushed, he was dead right. That was what it tasted like. Regaining her composure she repeated his words. "If I was to kiss a man then he'd be mine, forever, right?"

"That's about the deal, Erica." Dan approached her and pursing his lips teased her to kiss him. Entering the spirit of the occasion Erica reached out taking his tousled head in both hands and pulled him to her. Not only did she kiss him but provocatively slid her tongue into his mouth to make sure he received her saliva. "Blimey, Erica. In the house of God too! You've got me now." Now it was Dan's turn to blush. "And about time too, Dan. Now let's get on with our planning." She took another swig from the flask and sat down back to front on the teacher's high chair resting her chin on the top rail of the back rest. Dan took the flask back, had another swig himself before putting it away in his pocket. Like the good pupil Dan sat at the long school desk while Erica retained her dominant position astride the teacher's chair.

"Here's my idea, Dan. We start off in the Kirk as agreed then take in the Christ Church graveyard, the Fairies House, St. Columba's Chapel site, St. Brendan's Well, Cailleach's cave, Plain of Spells, Milking Stone then into Glen Mór for the Amazon's House, Stone Circle, Well of Virtues and finish at the Tunnel. How does that sound?"

"It's a lot to take in, a full day even. They could bring packed lunches as no one is going to fancy walking back to the village for lunch then back over the hill to finish off. Especially if they have got to run the gauntlet of Bonxies a second time." Erica thought for a moment. "You've got a point there, Dan. I have another idea. How about restoring the Amazon's House a bit. It can't be too bad as Anne often sleeps the night in there."

"Plenty of Mothan grows around there – we could open a tea house!" Dan was clearly on form, she thought. "Yeah, we'd have ourselves a right little love nest, wouldn't we? God, the tourists would be having orgies down there if we did that!" Erica was getting back to her old flirtatious self. Whether it was the vodka or the Mothan she couldn't be sure, but something was making her feel good that afternoon. "Tell you what, it's not a bad afternoon. Why don't we go to the top of Conachair and look out across the islands. We might get more inspiration up there drinking your New Communion wine'"

The pair made their way up through the village and past the Factor's House where they turned and walked up the slope into An Lag. Dan was out of breath and sweating heavily by the time they reached the cliff edge. Erica was in her stride and pointed out the white peaks of Boreray and the Stacs. Even at a distance of four miles you could see thousands of Gannets swirling around the rocky peaks whitened by years of guano dropping. Turning left and up the steepening path to Conachair, the island summit, Dan was lagging well behind. "Come on, slow coach. It's not that bad" She felt so good, so energized. Dan, by way of comparison felt weak and exhausted. "Going to have to stop smoking," he whispered barely able to speak as he followed her up the rough grass slope. Though a smoker he wasn't usually this fatigued. Erica got to the top and stood by the small cairn looking out over the rest of the island and the wide Atlantic horizon. Behind her lay the hills of North and South Uist, some fifty miles distance. She could just see the white statue of the Catholic Lady of the Isles standing against a backdrop of military radio masts that characterized much of the South Uist horizon. Erica could never accept the virgin birth as more than another piece of male bullshit.

Dan finally made it to the summit and collapsed at the foot of the cairn. Erica was already surveying the distant summits of Soay, Boreray and Dun. Levenish was too small and inaccessible so she had no plans for that island. Even before he had recovered from the climb, Erica was asking Dan what he thought of extended tours taking in the altars on Soay and Boreray. There probably would have been one on Dun so no problem getting there either if they got Don to run them over. "Just think, Dan. We could build Beltane fires for the Spring, Samhain fires for the Autumn Celtic New Year and ..." Dan cut back in, "Yeah, and a fucking great Wicker Man on the beach! Get real Erica, I am knackered just getting up here so how is the average tourist going to feel. We want them to pay for a good time not to end up half dead!"

Erica felt hurt by the put down but could see his point. She was a young woman and in her prime. Dan had enough sensitivity to tread carefully with her. Not to tread on her dreams as his favorite poet, W.B. Yeats, would have said.

"That Amazon's House idea sounded like a good one. We could make it habitable in a bunk house sort of way and, you know, it could be a winner all round. We would charge extra for the accommodation down there. It would pay for itself soon enough and Don would be happy as he used to charge double price for campers when the Trust ran this place. Seats have to be paid for both ways, even empty ones. Thinking laterally, if I put extra business his way he might even let me off the dope debt. Realistically though, we are going to have to keep our tour plan to Hirta, Erica. Do you have any more thoughts?"

Hardly had the words left his mouth when a Great Skua swooped past cuffing his head with an extended webbed foot. "Oh fuck off, you bastard shite-hawk!" The large brown sea bird turned to make another attack run. Dan was ready for it and waved his arms as it came close. Making its "ack, ack, ack" staccato alarm call the Skua turned and crossed An Lag gliding its way back along the cliff edge to Oiseval. "Cool down, Dan. It's only defending its nesting ground."

Like Sally, Erica hated to see male aggression directed toward the island's wildlife no matter how annoying these large birds could be. Seizing the moment, Erica mentioned a discussion she had had with Anne a few days earlier. "You know, Anne reckons the Bonxies were summoned here by the Cailleach to drive off insensitive men like you. What do you make of that?" Dan was incredulous. "Well that sounds even crazier than Beltane fires on Soay. They're just large birds and bloody annoying ones too."

Erica left it at that not wanting to challenge him further and risk spoiling the late afternoon sunshine on Conachair. They sat down together with their backs to the cairn and looked out across the deserted radar installations on Mullach Mór two hundred feet below them. "Any more of your brew, Dan? I fancy sharing a bit more communion while we are up here." He passed her the flask from his hip pocket. The subtle flavor seemed enhanced by the warmth of his body and she drank deeply. She passed the flask back to him and he finished the last few drops before screwing the cap tight and replacing it in his pocket. Erica snuggled up next to him happy to be there with a man she felt a growing respect for. There weren't many young men she respected but Dan was growing on her.

"Hey, what's that?" Dan had spotted a large white bird glide across the top of Glen Mór to land softly on a large cleit in the distance. As it turned its head virtually one hundred and eighty degrees to see where the human voice had come from, they could see, unmistakably, that it was a large white owl.

"What on Earth?" Dan, an amateur birder himself, was genuinely surprised to see this Arctic visitor. The solitary Snowy Owl had been recorded before on the island but this was the first time either Erica or Dan had ever seen one. It settled down to tear at something held in its talons. "Probably a St Kilda mouse," said Erica. "Those owls usually hunt Lemmings but our mice are just as big. Anyway we are honored to see it. I bet Anne knows about it being here but has, as usual, kept it to herself." Dan was bemused, "So much for global warming if Snowy Owls are taking up residence in the Western Isles. I wonder what's going to turn up next?"

"Hey Dan! Look out there. Can't you see the Viking long-ship rounding Boreray, and yeah, just look at those monks landing on the beach. Must be Saints Brendan and Columba if I'm not mistaken." She knew Dan was interested in archaeology and knew a fair bit of history relating to St Kilda.

"Stop taking the piss, Erica." He loved reading old stories embedded in the landscape and, like Anne, spent many hours dreaming life into the myths and legends surrounding him. He had especially spent many hours researching myths and legends associated with Mothan. Hebridean lore claimed it was the first plant to be trodden by Christ so, he considered, if the Christians appropriated it, it must be a scary herb. Mothan grows well in damp acid ground and he thought with so much of it growing around the military borehole the unique chemistry of this herb must have percolated into the island's main water supply. It was no wonder, he thought, that the MOD guys lost their work ethic, unwittingly taking Mothan in water drunk with subsidized whisky.

Returning by the most direct route, it didn't take long before the two were at the foot of Conachair standing on the raised glacial mounds looking across the village. There was so much to see, even for the untrained eye, something new became apparent on a daily basis. Having read so much about St Kildan domestic arrangements Erica could now see the Norse water mill, the threshing house, the corn drying kilns. Everything had been laid out so well by the Victorian architect of the new village. Seeing the several small burns channeled toward the Norse mill reminded Erica she must order a micro-hydro generator for her soon to be completed blackhouse. The combination of water, wind and solar energy would make their own new settlement the envy of the Hebrides once again, if she had anything to do with it. Those nineteenth century innovations were crude but they were in sympathy with their environment, acknowledged the spirit of place, unlike the diesel fired power station thankfully now standing quiet as a monument to twentieth century social failure and near nuclear Armageddon. There was so much potential here, she reminded

Dan. They were all going to play their part now there were women as well as men involved in the planning process. She was happy to leave Dan to plan the spiritual tours though, for after all she thought, in most traditional societies women had more practical things to be getting on with.

Dan had done his research on the islands folklore from the fantastic to the mundane. He thought he had been pretty thorough but the Cailleach was stretching things a bit, a female deity roaming the winter landscape or as an Amazon riding out across the Hebrides with her pack of hounds. But then, the Hounds of the Morrigan – he had heard of that myth elsewhere, so maybe not quite so fantastical after all. In defending Ulster, hero Cucuhlainn had been offered assistance from Morrigan, the Phantom Queen. She could shape shift into the form of an eel, a wolf or a cow. He rejected her offer of help but not to be so easily dismissed, she assisted by stampeding cattle onto the battlefield. Cucuhlainn injured one of the cattle, a red and white heifer leading the charge which turned out to be the shape-changing Phantom Queen herself. Her wounds were only healed when the hero accepted her offer of drinking milk from her teats. A classic Gaelic myth concerning masculine rejection of female assistance. The wounded and angry Queen Morrigan was only healed once the hero submitted and accepted her as an equal.

Glen Mór was, according to Erica and Sally, historically the female zone where cattle were tended and, of course, the Amazon's House was in that northern valley. It was also where most of the trouble occurred, from plane wrecks to Bonxie attack. All in all it was a very unfriendly place for any male bold enough to venture down there. Each evening when the women returned from milking they poured a libation on the Milking Stone, situated at the edge of the male zone. Failure to do so brought bad luck to the whole community. With cattle long gone from the island, the practice had been overlooked for years. Come to think of it, there had been few women here for years either. Dan was astounded at where his research was leading him. Glen Mór, now empty of cattle was a hostile place for men as he had quickly realized after being sent packing himself by Skua attacks. There was an angry, likely wounded, female spirit down there. Peace would only come to St Kilda once she was accepted, when male and female interests were reconciled. Instead of being trapped, miserable in a male dominated landscape, she should be free to ride out, with her hounds too, if she wanted to. First of all, cattle should be returned to Glen Mór. Fucking hell, the story of this island is beginning to come together, Dan thought. As the enormity of the revelation sunk in, Dan felt the need of drink. Taking a long swig from his recharged hip flask, the Mothan laced vodka calmed his racing thoughts.

During his research he had also come across the tale of Roderick the Imposter, a charismatic preacher on St Kilda before the Church of Scotland took charge of the congregation. He remembered how the Williams family had teased him about his superficial resemblance to this character. Modelling himself on St John the Baptist, Roderick had appointed himself spiritual leader of the islands though generally working toward his own material gain. Dan read with interest how he offered salvation to the women of St Kilda in return for a night in his bed and consecrated a Holy Bush. Should any person's sheep eat as much as one leaf of this bush, then the owner would forfeit the sheep to Roderick. Apparently the islanders built a high stone wall around this bush to prevent such an occurrence. Looking around the village, Dan could readily see small circular stone enclosures lending credence to the story. The part of the tale that Dan really appreciated came at the end when the disgraced Roderick was sent for trial at Dunvegan on various charges ranging from immorality to blasphemy. The story told of his deliberately eating Mothan for good luck before the hearing. Roderick, although banished from St Kilda, got off with nothing more serious than a public warning to mend his ways and refrain from communion with other men's wives, especially in the name of God. Cunning or what! Dan was impressed, if it was alright with God, then with a bit of Mothan involved, you could get away with just about anything out here. Dan returned to his freshly cleaned and uncluttered apartment with some trepidation but he was actually glad Deborah had sorted it all for him. Now inspired by Erica's enthusiasm for Green Tourism he settled down for the evening making further rough notes before getting down to draft a schedule for the morning.

Dan busied himself with the finer details of the St Kilda spiritual tour. A bit of a mouthful though. Maybe 'Spiritual St Kilda', 'Magical Island Tour', 'Holy Trails'? Whatever, he wasn't going to bother with a title just yet. Inspiration would no doubt hit him while out walking the route his pilgrims would take. Leading his flock through the wilderness really appealed to Dan and over the next few days he spent most of his daylight hours outdoors working out the route. He became a familiar figure to the thousand or so feral sheep on the island, striding the ground like the new prophet he was already imagining himself to be. Stopping at every well and natural spring he was amazed at the luxuriance of Mothan growing in damp places wherever potable water collected. Obviously the sheep had no taste for the herb, he mused. They didn't know what they were missing. He would make sure his followers received his specially prepared St Kilda

Communion Wine before following him on the little trod path to salvation.

Erica had left Dan to his dreaming, feeling she had sown seed in fertile ground. He was a dreamer but could get it together when the need arose. She could forgive occasional self-pity if he played his part well in the resettlement project. He always landed on his feet and would make a good man to have around soon enough. For now she had her own house plans to work on.

The blackhouse restoration was coming on well. The roof had been thatched and door and windows replaced. It really was quite snug inside the shell even though the tarry smell of burnt pallet wood still lingered from the central fire lit when they celebrated the new roof. Erica would get the woodstove fitted promptly and, with smoke piped outside the cottage, she would bring blackhouse living into the twenty-first century. On Don's advice she had taken the very sensible precaution of ordering a twin wall insulated flue pipe with high temperature rubber roof flashing. She neither wanted to set the thatch on fire nor have to deal with copious rainwater leaks in her beautiful new home. She had to admit though, it seemed incongruous to make a hole in new thatch but a modern woodstove had to be an improvement over a smoky open hearth. Her blackhouse was not going to be black on the inside if she could help it.

Fitting the stove and flue proved easier than she had expected. The insulated flue pipe was simply pushed up through the thatch with no need to cut the long reed stems. Once the high temperature rubber flashing was in place it could rain as much as it liked. At St Kilda it normally did rain a lot and the next part of the project was to rig up a micro-hydro generator in the burn beside the cottage. Technically a bit more challenging than the woodstove but having already consulted off-grid living suppliers before moving to the island she knew it could be done. She would just have to wait now until Don and Lachie returned to place her order. Sally suggested it would be a good idea to employ one of the newly redundant radar technicians to attend to the electrical side of things. She knew of former electrician who had taken retirement when the MOD left and had often enthused over renewable energy solutions for the village. He had openly criticized MOD reliance on imported diesel fuel while surrounded by inexhaustible sun and wind energy. Jeff, she knew, would be happy to help and could fix up her wind generator and solar panels while he was at it.

Erica was pleased with her newly fitted woodstove. She just couldn't understand why the St Kildans hadn't used free standing stoves before, even the army had used them in their early occupation of the island. But then this had been an island with cultural idiosyncrasies an outsider wouldn't understand. She had quickly tested the stove, burning some old papers and scraps of wood to check for smoke leaks. There were none and the interior of her blackhouse would definitely remain soot free. The next part of the project would be a low energy lighting system. Not knowing much about the technicalities involved, Erica had always been attracted to off-grid living and had read various magazines extolling this way of life. Now here was the chance to turn her dream into reality. Sally had also recommended she contact Jeff, the retired electrician who would do the necessary wiring. In hindsight it was a pity none of the new settlers had much in the way of electrical skills. There was endless diesel fuel still in the storage tanks and as long as the generator behaved itself the Manse would have electricity to spare. Here at the far western extremity of the village running an extension lead for half a mile wouldn't be an option. She couldn't wait and determined to contact Jeff as soon as possible, sooner if an out of season yacht sought anchorage in the bay. This was how it had been before the military came to the island, she had once read. Post was taken to the mainland by passing fishing boats. St Kilda also had a tradition of launching their very own mail-boats, small model boats holding a sealed letter container. Attached to a float of some sort they drifted with winds and currents until reaching land anywhere between Lewis and the coast of Norway. A bit too hit and miss, she would wait until some kind of full size boat came in. For now the hurricane lamps worked fine on diesel oil and the burn would still be running when her micro-hydro generator eventually turned up. The cow, of course, would not be living under the same roof as her. A divergence from blackhouse tradition she accepted on hygiene grounds. The animal could be housed next door in her own cow-house. The St Kildans had done just that when they moved into their new but ill-fated white-houses. From occupying just the lower end, the house cow was afforded the whole of the now redundant blackhouse next door. Erica was already dreaming of her clean, modernized blackhouse with woodstove and 12 volt lighting. The cow could have occupied the lower end but the thought of dung on the floor of her new cottage was too much. The warm milky smell of clean cow would be wonderful. The reality, she knew, would be the smell of shit and piss. She would make sure things moved forward for twenty-first century St Kilda living.

Rebuilding the stone wall enclosures was proving more of a task than Dave had anticipated. The slipped disc he suffered in the accident on the jetty had left him with a vulnerable lower back. Working with coarse stones in the damp and cold of approaching winter at St Kilda split the skin of his fingertips making each day rebuilding the small walled garden plots an endurance test. The stiffness of his back and pain from his cracked finger tips became, in his mind, a kind of penury for sins past. Maybe a payment required of him for those months he spent idling at home after losing his lectureship at the university. He had basically lived off the earnings of his wife and now it was his turn to support the family even if it did mean breaking his back out in all weathers on the island. The walls would get built in time for spring sowing and he could already picture the orderly rows of vegetables growing strong in the sun inside sheltering stone walls on the south slopes of Conachair. The enclosed fields of

An Lag were still in good shape after conservation volunteers had spent so much time and energy rebuilding the walls. They had actually paid to come out here and labor. Dave had given that concept plenty of thought while toiling alone on the hillside behind the cottages. He was working to rebuild these walls for a reason – to feed his family. The volunteers had done more than that, they had come here to pay for the privilege of engaging with hard manual labor under open skies and in all weathers as an archaeological exercise. Thankfully though, he hadn't had to pay out several hundred pounds for a fortnight of toil. Maybe it was something to do with an urban need to reconnect with a lost part of oneself, a reconnection only attainable through the physicality of reworking the land. The Western Isles Trust had been pretty canny, he had to admit. Selling people their dreams back to them and getting a whole load of hard labor done for free in the process.

Deborah hardly left the Manse during the short winter days. Not that it was particularly cold, the dampness and mist lowering from the hills held no attraction for her to venture outside. She made the occasional foray over to the Featherstore when Dan was available for her. It was understandable, she thought, that with Dave working himself into the ground repairing stone walls he had no energy for love making. Dan certainly made up for him in that respect and, if she was honest with herself, he was helping her become a better wife for Dave, now her physical needs were regularly satisfied. Life was certainly strange and out on the island away from social constraints in Edinburgh they could, at last, be themselves. Water would find its own level, as she was fond of saying when they discussed their feelings around the meal table. Away from the pressures of teaching she was actually enjoying her matriarchal role. Erica and Anne would no doubt come round to accepting her authority in due course, but for now with Erica setting up home at the far end of the village and Anne spending most of her waking hours in Glen Mór there was little challenge to her domestic authority. Anne was the one to watch out for, she realized. Creeping around with binoculars in hand, Deborah couldn't be sure she hadn't already been spotted making her regular visits to the Featherstore. Anne was an astute young woman and would quickly deduce what was going on. Dave was a good man but life out here demanded more than just his goodness. She might be turning into some sort of Magdalene, Deborah realized, but she had only one demon to cast not the seven she had heard Dave refer to after bringing that old family Bible back from the church. She had to agree with him it would be a shame to watch the ornate leather bound Bible deteriorate further in the cold and damp the Atlantic was continually throwing at them all.

The winter weather was becoming quite an issue. It was just so damn windy. Deborah hadn't really appreciated what it would be like to spend day after day struggling against gale force winds. The noise was something else, she had never experienced such a constant roar and buffeting. Slates rattling on the roofs and the infernal clanging and banging of the corrugated steel sheeting that clad the power station. It wouldn't take long before the wind got behind one of those sheets and sent it spinning away to join the remains of 19th century zinc roofs littering sheltered spots around the village. The remains of the crashed Sunderland had been blown far and wide since the original crash some eighty years earlier. It had been no wonder the recent wreck of the small Piper had been so quickly picked up and blown over the cliff. Rain had been less of a problem than she had expected though. On the rare calm days it could actually feel quite warm. Sally had related times when there had been water shortages on the island, hence the new deeper borehole tapping into artesian supplies originating goodness knows where. Obviously somewhere with currently higher rainfall than St Kilda judging by the proliferation of Mothan at the overflowing well-head. The plant took sustenance from swarms of midges trapped on its mucous covered leaves. Pretty good plant all round, Deborah considered. Then there was the added bonus of its power of entrapment when it came to virile young men. Poor Dan, she really didn't think it quite fair to have used it on him. His energies might have better suited to helping Dave rebuild garden walls rather than leaving him enslaved to her needs. She hadn't known that, in jest, Erica had done the same.

South easterly gales brought the sea thundering over the jetty wall again and again. Overnight the sandy beach would disappear, only to mysteriously reappear a few days later. The constant noise of the wind, sea and shifting boulders became normal and only noticeable by its absence. Watching from the kitchen window, Deborah noticed the change coming. Though still troubled, the sea was no longer crashing over the jetty and the swell running along the cliffs of Dun had definitely lessened as the gales turned to blow from the west. The ruined castle on the seaward tip of Dun gave the narrow island its name and according to Dan, had been a stronghold for the Fomorians, whoever they might be, before the Gaels took possession of the islands. A few acres of ancient ridge and furrow cultivation could be still be seen on Dun when the light was low and the villagers had obviously been able to get over in the past. Not so simple today though. Deborah had spotted a rusting chain hanging in the gap between Dun and Hirta. Sally had explained that it was possible to wade across the gap at extreme low tide and haul oneself up that chain to access Dun, but it had been many years since anyone had done it. Deborah certainly would want any of her family putting the rusted links to the test.

Though becoming calmer in Village Bay, Deborah could see the sea raging as wild as ever through the Dun gap. The waters boiled beyond the two islands with salt spray billowing through the southerly cleft to virtually pressure wash adjacent slopes. As the gale turned more into the west, she noticed flecks of spume blowing over the ridge between Ruiaval and Mullach Sgar. The occasional flecks became a blizzard as the wind turned, soaking the leeward slopes with sea-spray. Anne had commented on the way the grass suddenly ended over there. The consistency of the turf changed suddenly from hardy grasses to close cropped Thrift. This salt tolerant Thrift turf grew where grass could not due to the rain of salt spray blown over the ridge in westerly gales. During the day the wind turned into the north placing Village Bay in the lee of the storm. Deborah had thought the hills would shelter the bay with the wind coming from the north. To an extent this was true but with the fifteen hundred foot peak rising almost vertically into the wind, Conachair directed turbulent blasts that spun down from the heights to spin across the bay like Atlantic djinns. The spinning columns of sea spray were amazing to watch and God help, she thought, any small yacht caught by one. She had heard from Sally that no MOD helicopter would venture near the place in conditions like this and it had been these water-devils that had plagued the MOD evacuation before they arrived. Even on calmer days, with wind in the north, the helicopter pilot would fly close to the cliffs of Oiseval to avoid the aircraft being caught in turbulence over the bay.

Dave had been out repairing stone walls all day. If anything the unpredictable gusts were worse for his temper than the constant gale. They could come without warning and from any direction. One minute he could be working under a calm and clearing sky and the next find himself, seemingly under attack, blown off his feet. He had lost count of the times he had to retrieve his woolen hat or gloves momentarily put down. Deborah, at least, had seemed calm enough in the Manse lately. She must be settling in and it pleased him that, in the domestic sphere at least, things were working out well. Erica had made a brilliant job of her blackhouse and in spite of troubled times in Edinburgh she really was turning out to be her father's daughter. Her blackhouse walls were solid and the new thatch barely ruffled by the gale. According to Erica the strong winds did cause the woodstove to smoke a bit. A blackhouse should at least have some smoke stain inside, he reminded her. While out working, Dave had found time to reflect on their previous existence in Edinburgh. Existence it was and not much more, now out here they could find themselves, grow into the family he had always wanted them to be.

Dave always tested the stability of his restored walls by standing on top to feel if any stone dislodged. He had become adept at dry stone walling and generally nothing moved but he hadn't anticipated the sudden collapse of his last few hours work. In hindsight, the unpredictable blasts of icy wind had sapped his concentration and when the wall fell it took him with it. The turf was soft after years of past cultivation but he fell awkwardly and twisted his lower back. The damaged lumbar disc prolapsed again leaving him in excruciating pain. He could do no more than lie face down in the mossy turf until the agony subsided. Then, he knew, getting to his feet and taking the weight of his upper-body on his sacroiliac joint would be another story. Crying with pain and frustration, Dave remembered his namesake's plea from Psalm 22 in the old family bible he had been reading, rescued from decay in the damp Church.

"My God, my God, why hast thou forsaken me? Why art thou so far from helping me, and from the words of my roaring?" He couldn't remember the whole Psalm word for word but lying there on the wet ground biblical David's self-pitying lament became his own. He was the worm and his darling to be saved from the power of the dog, not that there were any on the island. Erica had mentioned she would like one but he knew what the words of the psalm implied. "But be not though far from me, O Lord: O my strength, haste thee to help me."

After maybe thirty minutes of lying there, David gingerly tried to lift himself to his feet using his spade as a crutch. The pain only became unbearable if he tried to straighten up so he kept to a stooped position and made his way laboriously down to the cottages. The spade, at least, did not let him down and once on the level street his movement, though stooped became less painful. Sally saw him pass the Factor's House and came out to offer help. "Hey Dave! What have you done this time?" Grimacing he replied that his back had gone again and he was going back to the Manse to lie down for a while. He would be OK in the morning, he assured her. "Why not come down to the MRS and I'll massage it again for you, Dave. It's what I am here for, isn't it?' Unaware of Dave's epiphany an hour earlier she wasn't prepared for what he growled back to her.

"Proverbs 7: 25-27, Sally! Let not thine heart decline to her ways, go not astray in her paths. For she hath cast down many wounded: yea, many strong men have been slain by her. Her house is the way to hell, going down to the chambers of death."

Sally was taken aback. "Whatever, Dave. I was just offering to help not send you to hell!" She suddenly realized what he was inferring to. "Oh, for God's sake, that was just a bit of fun. Wasn't it? You didn't seem to complain at the time. OK, go and lie down on your own and if you find you do actually want a purely professional massage, I'll come down to the Manse, alright? And another thing, find something better to read at night."

Sally turned back to the shelter of the thick walled Factor's House. Making his painful and stooped way to the

Manse, Dave never raised his eyes high enough to see brash ice flowing round the Point of Col. Deborah watched in amazement from the kitchen window as broken sea ice flowed into Village Bay below Oiseval, driven by freshening wind from the north.

12 CLIMATE CHANGE

Dave and Erica, while not exactly engaging in regular Bible studies, found the dog eared family Bible interesting reading. Friendly banter between father and daughter extended to quoting scriptures over breakfast that morning.

"Neither did we eat any man's bread for naught; but wrought with labor and travail night and day, that we might not be chargeable to any of you. Second Epistle of Paul The Apostle to the Thessalonians (3.8)"

"Right then, Dad. You asked for it! - And unto Adam he said, Because thou hast harkened unto the voice of thy wife, and hast eaten of the tree, of which I commanded thee, saying, Thou shalt not eat of it: cursed is the ground for thy sake: in sorrow shalt though eat of it all the days of thy life. Genesis 3.17."

Briefly taken aback by Erica's unexpected knowledge of key scriptures, Dave had struggled for a reply, flicking through the pages. "Aha……Let the woman learn in silence with all subjection. But I suffer not a woman to teach, nor to usurp authority over the man, but to be in silence. 1 Timothy 2:11, 12."

"Come off it Dave, don't take things too far!" Deborah considered this quote was going too far, quite a lot too far considering her teaching background. In her opinion Dave, with his university background, should also have known better than to rake up this outdated patriarchal crap, in her opinion. Her husband continued to quote from the First Epistle of Paul the Apostle to Timothy.

"1 Timothy 2:13, 14 and 15! For Adam was first formed,

then Eve. And Adam was not deceived, but the woman being deceived was in the transgression. Notwithstanding she shall be saved in childbearing if they continue in faith and charity and holiness with sobriety."

"What utter bollocks, Dad!" Anne made it clear she was not impressed by his, or anyone else's Bible quotes. "I'm going to my room and, if the satellite internet is not on the blink again, I am going to research the causes for sea ice around our island that is supposedly warmed by the Gulf Stream. Please don't try and tell me that's any kind of message from God!"

Philosophical writings of man (or woman) had little place in Anne's scientific world. Biblical reference to childbearing did, however, remind her that as a young woman she could and maybe should be doing just that. Having babies, but as for saving herself – from just what, she'd like to know. Unlike her sister she had very little sexual experience. Just brief teenage flings back in Edinburgh that had left her more frustrated than satisfied. Ecology was what turned her on, pressed her buttons and if she could meet a young man who thought the same way childbearing could be a distinct possibility. The only young men out here were Dan and Lachie. Dan absolutely wasn't her type. Lachie who came out with Don on the *Beluga* was good looking enough, carried some excellent genes, but with a world view limited to wheeling and dealing around the Hebrides, he wasn't going to come to much.

Anne could sense something in the air though. Something, some energy, was stirring around her. In her ecologists' opinion, even her pre-menopausal mother was showing signs of late fertility. She of course knew, that when cooped up together, women's menstruation tended to synchronize. She knew subtle signals from one woman could stimulate ovulation in the others. All fascinating stuff, but she wished she could be immune herself. She could not, and felt that living this close to open skies and ocean tides, the phases of the moon would inevitably affect her here more than on the mainland. Men had been out of their depth on this island. The military guys turned to drink for escape from the relentless energy washing over St Kilda. Sally had recounted how there had been more drink related accidents on nights of the full moon and on brief summer nights, drinking would often continue until after dawn at this northern, yet temperate, latitude. Dan was fast going the same way and as for her father, well it seemed that rather than drink, he was turning to God! Another angle on humans in the island's ecosystem, Anne thought. Humans, particularly male humans she considered, retreat to an imagined dimension when faced with an environment beyond their control. When the going got tough out here, female sheep survived and weaker males died before Spring renewed the grazing. That's after the males had beaten each other senseless during the autumn rut and the grass ran out. Why the hell did they do that if not to ensure survival of the fittest? It seemed obvious to her, females were definitely fitter, better adapted for life at St Kilda. Though without male insemination, there could be no females born to carry life, or genes she reminded herself, forward into the next generation. It was basically a very practical matter. She would think on it next time she was in Glen Mór. The Amazon, Morrigan she preferred to call her, wouldn't have bothered with romantic twaddle before reproducing herself. She would have just seduced the bravest warrior, had her way with him then sent him on his way. When her time came, that was exactly what Anne decided she would do. Walking to her room she felt erotically charged, thinking about seducing a hero before sending him on his way. But as for finding a hero at St Kilda? That would have to wait.

Anne's online research continued late into the evening. Making copious notes, she would have a quote or two of her own by the morning. She first looked at the Met Office Surface Pressure charts. Unusually, the Azores high had extended into the north-west Atlantic connecting with high pressure over Greenland. Warm moist air from the Caribbean was being drawn up the eastern seaboard of North America before circulating over the Greenland icecap and back down towards Iceland, the Faeroes and the British Isles. The moisture laden air cooled as it touched the wintry landmass of the United States generating the heaviest snowfall within living memory. It took a lot for snow to make headlines in Iceland but the winter storms flowed out from Labrador relentlessly. Deflected northwards by high pressure over Greenland the storms were picking up yet more moisture from the melting icecap. Looking further east, Anne could see low pressure over Scandinavia and the Baltic Sea where it was relatively warmer than over the north Atlantic. Air currents in high pressure zones circulated clockwise and in low pressure regions anti-clockwise and she saw that the north of Scotland and the Western Isles were caught between these two counter rotating weather systems. Winter storms were going to be drawn down between the teeth of two great cogs in the weather machine. The isobars looked pretty close and moisture laden air was being drawn directly from the Arctic Ocean and funneled clockwise into even colder air flowing anti-clockwise from Spitzbergen and the north of Siberia. No wonder it was bloody freezing, she thought, but looking closer at the surface pressure chart, Anne saw that St Kilda lay under the eastern edge of the extended Greenland high pressure dome. The blizzards were going to be deflected by high pressure away from the archipelago to hit the Highlands and Eilean Siar, the Western Isles, with a vengeance. At St Kilda, they were going to be cold for sure but not snowed in. The fast approaching arctic tempest was going to further disrupt troubled socio-economic conditions on the British mainland and in Western Europe. Out here, it looked like they were going to be on their own for a while, at least until either the mainland weather or the national economy improved.

Another bell rang for her. It had been a while but she remembered at high school having to discuss a documentary by US environmentalist Al Gore. *An Inconvenient Truth*, that's what it was called. She remembered the importance of the Gulf Stream, otherwise known as the Atlantic Conveyor current bringing warm water from the Caribbean to the arctic. It warmed the north-east Atlantic seaboard and made Spitzbergen the most amazingly bio-diverse of all the northern islands. The Atlantic Conveyor depended on a temperature gradient between the Caribbean tropics and the Atlantic arctic. Cold waters sinking displaced lower, warmer nutrient rich waters to the surface feeding the phytoplankton that underpin marine food chains. The greater the temperature difference between the tropics and the arctic, the stronger flowed the Gulf Stream. Looking at the Met Office chart it was pretty obvious that over the north Atlantic the sea temperature gradient must be lessening, as Al Gore had suggested would surely happen, as humans continued pumping greenhouse gasses into the atmosphere. So the north east Atlantic was getting colder. As far as she knew, seabird populations were recovering after a disastrous few years. The nutrient flush would feed phytoplankton, small marine organisms and so on up the food-chain. She thought it interesting that distant 19th Century industrial emissions might have had a part in historic climate change helping to bring about the collapse of the seabird dependent St Kildan economy. There were so many angles to this fascinating place. No wonder it was a major World Heritage Site.

The surface pressure charts forecasted imminent meteorological conditions but sea ice did not form overnight. There had to be more to the phenomenon. Another search engine referred her to solar cycles. She discovered there were *grand maximum* and *grand minimum* periods for levels of solar energy reaching Earth. The effects were all very subtle but amplified through oscillations of the Gulf Stream could have a major influence on local weather conditions, particularly in Europe and Eurasia. It seemed the twentieth century had been dominated by *grand maximum* solar activity and now, the BBC website suggested, the twenty-first century was entering into a *grand minimum* period. To put it bluntly, in the twenty-first century the British Isles were predicted to experience similar conditions to the Maunder Minimum of the late 17th and early 18th centuries known as the Little Ice Age. Paradoxically, Greenland and the Arctic regions could be a lot warmer.

The likelihood of Iceland becoming warmer led Anne down another route. She had heard all about the Eyjafjallajökull eruption in 2010 and subsequent chaotic effects for air travel in Western Europe. Apparently, the website suggested, this eruption was just the start of a dramatic increase in volcanic activity. Another article she came across suggested that in response to global warming, volcanic activity increases, spewing ash and dust particles into the atmosphere to reflect away excessive solar radiation. As a living entity, the Earth could cool herself. Anne had to think about it for a minute but the conclusion she drew from her research made her gasp. Everything pointed to St Kilda and the north-east Atlantic becoming much, much colder and it was happening right now. Greenland was warming and driving a persistent, moist north-west air current toward them from the melting ice-caps. Scandinavia was warming and arctic pack ice was flowing toward them from the north-east. Moist air from the north-west and icy currents from the north-east could mean months of fog and, if that wasn't enough, increasing volcanic activity in Iceland would send ash clouds over north-west Europe in a repeat of 2010. Maybe a lot worse if predictions of an imminent eruption of Iceland's Katia caldera proved correct. The 1783-84 eruption from, Grímsvötn, had spewed out 15 cubic kilometers of ash into the atmosphere compared to the fraction of a cubic kilometer ejected by Eyjafjallajökul in 2010. Grímsvötn had had a huge impact on the northern hemisphere, reducing temperatures by up to 3°C. Catastrophic effects extended far beyond the shores of Iceland (where at least a fifth of the population died), with thousands of deaths recorded in Britain due to poisoning and extreme cold, and there was record low rainfall in North Africa. Sod the Bible, just wait till she told them about this!

Anne found it hard to sleep that night. Her imagination was making oscillations of its own between erotic fantasy and volcanic eruption. It all boiled down to energy flows and as an ecologist she was fine with that. When at last she did sleep, it was deep and sound. For once she lay in and only emerged to join the others for breakfast. Still in her pajamas, she had abandoned her usual morning routine of walking the village for sightings of migrant birds. The heavy Bible was on the table in front of Dave as he exalted those present to give thanks for their meal.

"Whether therefore ye eat, or drink, or whatsoever ye do, do all to the glory of God. 1 Corinthians 10:31."

"Amen, Dad. But just listen to what I have found out about the ice!" Dave thought to cut Anne short to allow time for the meaning of his quote to sink in but genuinely interested in what she had been researching, he allowed her to continue. Anne could barely contain herself as just for once she had her father's undivided attention.

"What we could be experiencing is a solar grand minimum. That's when solar energy reaching the planet reduces. The last time this happened was in the late eighteenth and early nineteenth centuries. That was when the Thames regularly froze over and I bet there was sea-ice here then too. Not quite sure if it was connected but there were massive volcanic eruptions in Iceland during that period as well. Putting two and two together, the eruptions that shut down European air travel a few years ago and this sea-ice appearing would suggest to me that we are heading for challenging times. Not so for the birds though. They flourished after the cold event and just think, the feather trade and this village might not have been possible if it hadn't been for past climate change. It looks like it is happening again, Dad."

Anne's mother added, "And think of social conditions at that time too. All that upheaval led to over a century of European expansion, colonization and conflict. White slaves of England supported by the black slaves of Empire, not that dissimilar to what we came here to get away from!" Deborah was becoming actively interested in Anne's hypothesis.

Leaving Biblical scriptures aside, Dave too joined in the discussion, raising more on the cultural angle. "When you come to think of it, so much of our cultural landscape comes from that period. Those Christmas cards picturing snowy Georgian houses – why are they so appealing? That period of cold must be embedded itself in the national psyche. Our old home in Edinburgh New Town, the Athens of the north, suggested cultural values recognizable throughout the western world and its former colonies. It's like the Georgian spirit of place, for better and for worse, transfers across continents through reproduction of its architecture, including snowy postcards. Likewise the mind-set, as I used to tell my students. All that carefully contrived classical reproduction, what an incredible piece of social engineering. Walk around New Town and, just imagine, the work of long dead architects still influencing lives and minds today – just as they must be doing out here too."

Erica added to the discussion. "Yeah, I've been here before I do realize but those late eighteenth and early nineteenth century town planners did exert a controlling effect through symbolic architecture and landscaping. Keep women in their place, no blacks, slavery to pay for it all and all sorts of overseas cruelty out of sight of good townsfolk, like we used to be, Dad. Also you had to be able to see the damn architecture and if it stood out white on a prominent hill top the effect carried for miles. Take Calton Hill for example. The Beltane fun there could never happen in full daylight. Remember when we had TV? The US Whitehouse beamed its subliminal message across the airways every night through news broadcasts. The presenter boosts his or her own message by associating with the ultimate neo-classical power statement seen right behind them. The Soviets weren't any better and what did the Nazis do? Couldn't wait two hundred years to do exert control slowly and subtly, they made concrete casts of the wretched designs and threw them up in twenty years. Jazz that challenged classical music convention was made illegal and God help any poor sod who challenged what the authorities were doing. Getting back to Edinburgh New Town they actually fashioned women to support the obscenity. Jobson's department store actually has acquiescent women molded into its façade to support male neo-classical views of family life. Nazi women bought into the deal as well, encouraged to be not only national socialists but national mothers too. Some things just never change."

Deborah was looking puzzled, "What do you mean?" Deborah explained that she actually used to enjoy going into Jobson's. Its predictable familiarity was a pleasant and stable escape from the multi-cultural chaos outside in Princes Street or so she had always thought.

"Look further than the end of your nose next time you are there, Mum, and you will see the female figures in stone supporting the façade. The Caryatids are supposed to represent

Jobson's acknowledgement that women support society. If those women sprang to life and walked away, the whole damn edifice would come crashing down." Erica was on her pet subject and knew her mother resented challenge when it came to social status. In spite of her profession, Deborah had instinctively felt that as a middle class mother she had social capital. Jobson's department store recognized and made good use of that capital. Unlike other classes, those in the middle socio-economic bands could go either way and by shopping in Jobson's, to the outside world you were not going down.

"Those stone women have been supporting Jobson's patriarchy getting on for two hundred years, Mum. Been standing there all this time, mute, enslaved, colonized and subjugated. Turned to stone, frozen by the architecture of Enlightenment. Edinburgh women have been blinkered by the desire to conform to demands of male architecture. What an irony that the only sizeable group to actually see the light and get away were the Free Church male bible bashers!"

As if seeking approval from her father, Erica gave Dave a sideways glance before continuing. "At the 1843 Disruption the breakaway group pointedly walked out from neo-classical St. Andrews in George Street to worship well away from the all seeing eye of its portico. No wonder they came all the way out here to evangelize free from the constraints of malignant architecture. You know, it wasn't just buildings either. The clever bastards planted hill top groves that look like the Acropolis if you take a second look at them. With a bit of luck climate change will blow the fucking lot down. Too windy out here anyway, so no neo-classical columns and no trees either. No wonder the Wee Frees were so keen to come."

Anne added, "I did once read an article about the Forestry Commission and that it wasn't until the 1970s that they had a woman landscape architect in charge of things. Only then did they stop planting formal regiments of conifers. She changed things to make plantations fit with the landscape and be pleasing to the eye. Apparently the way trees are managed reflects on the society that manages them. Just think about it, when the St Kildans evacuated those able were sent to work for the Forestry Commission. The plantations and the control they represented won out in the end."

"Right, we'll be OK then. There are no fucking trees here so we can do what we like then, eh?" Erica winked at Anne, though the sisterly banter was noticeably not extended to Deborah who shrugged and turned away.

"Do what you like girls, but don't come running to me when you foul up. Society has its rules for a reason and trees or no trees we are still connected to it, even if you are starting to think otherwise."

Dave returned to the cultural angle. "Those Georgians, for all their faults, did bring structure and order. Apart from enduring architecture they introduced accurate artillery and properly surveyed maps. Quite basically, we wouldn't be here now if it wasn't for Georgian telemetry. In the twentieth century, the military employed most of the population of South Uist to test missiles using Georgian telemetry."

"Georgian teleonomy, long distance control more like!" Erica was back on her pet subject. "Without the military heritage we might have had families living here, a viable community with an equal balance of women and men. There could have been children too. Just look at this crazy place. Or should I say look back at the last unsustainable century of this crazy place. We are going to have to sort this one out, sister," looking at Anne, "are we not, girl?"

Anne blushed. She hadn't forgotten her previous night's fantasy. That elusive hero was ever going to be a problem, she thought. As the scientist in the family she was an Enlightenment woman through and through, but when the sun went down she had to acknowledge darker energies were drawing her away from the scientific career path she had planned for herself. After overhearing Dan one evening, she had experimented with placing dried Mothan under her pillow.

Dave continued, "I don't reckon it was all bad, girls. The Georgians introduced civic virtues, and yes they did express those values through the architecture of the period. Suppose that's where the term 'Period' design comes from? Neo-classical designs represented civic freedom, emancipation from servility and dependence on others. When that architecture crumbles we get the scenario for many a horror film, do we not?"

"Yeah, emancipation from sexual desire and feminine distraction. Manly 'virtues' were not to be diluted by female influence, or by engagement with common people. A discourse of patriarchy, Dad, it was nothing less. The Nazis coined an honest term for this dishonest crap. They offered 'freedom from freedom', freedom from freedom to engage with the fullness and diversity of human life. I used to wonder why those lonely sods hang out at the back of St Cuthbert's after dark. They are Edinburgh's 'Period' undesirables and they know it. The authorities still move them on if they appear in broad daylight."

Erica's rant was silenced by a loud boom followed by several sharp cracks which brought them all back to their immediate reality. The song of the ice building between the islands echoed around the bay. Larger blocks of ice, broken away by the intense pressures could be seen passing the Dun gap though none of significant size had yet entered Village Bay. The wind and currents were taking the ice past the entrance to the bay, which was fast becoming a refuge for the remaining winter seabirds. Gannets were diving to feed away from the moving ice pack. The far ranging birds needed to feed in open waters and avoided frozen conditions in the far north but now arctic ice had appeared around their home islands. Anne noted that even St Kilda's winter resident birds, the Meadow Pipits and Starlings seemed to have migrated this year. They must have known what was coming. Colder waters favored the fish, the plankton flush was revitalizing the food chain and the Gannets would do well in Village Bay if it remained ice free. So would the returning Puffins and everything else that relied on accessible fish stocks to feed their young next Spring. Unusual numbers of seals were hauling out on the beach to make use of what little warmth the wintry sun offered. At the edge of the high pressure dome, St Kilda was enjoying far more sunshine than the rest of the Western Isles, let alone the mainland.

Returning to historical events, Dave explained how the old St Kildans had planned their working lives by watching the movements of birds crossing the bay. What would they have made of this event? Probably some folk memory from the eighteenth century Little Ice Age would have been related by the female *Sennachie*, the Story-teller. She gave explanations the villagers could relate to and through myth and story understand natural events unfolding around them. Under Church of Scotland and Free Church tenures, interpretation of natural events continued but the male ministers quoted from carefully selected scriptures to forewarn their congregation of spiritual rather than practical consequences should they not heed the words of God, authorized for them in the King James' Bible of 1769. Half a century later the authorized Scriptures justified the suppression of indigenous wisdom in favor of British national standards. Uncontrollable natural events, such as those appearing before their eyes that day would simply be explained as the punitive will of God.

13 BLACKHOUSE

As Anne had predicted, the winter was proving unusually cold for the Western Isles and outlying St Kilda proved no exception. Erica tried to spend as much time as possible in her restored blackhouse but even with thick walls and new thatch the cold had beaten her. Retreating to the diesel powered electrical warmth of the Manse she concluded that having a couple of cows would be a priority before the next winter. Unhygienic as it sounded, Erica realized the previous occupants kept their cattle indoors for human warmth as much as for the animals' shelter. Her crib bed built into the thick wall of the cottage was too far away from the small woodstove to benefit from its warmth. Sally had also thought that, in ecological terms, collecting scrap wood and bringing it back from the old military buildings used up more precious calories than she received back from burning it in her grate. The cold kept Sally inside the thick-walled Factor's House though, when sick of her own company, she would occasionally join the Williams family in the Manse. Sally would sit by the open hearth built into the gable end of her house designed by a 19th century architect more used to the coalfields of Lanarkshire than the windswept Hebrides. She collected bags of peat on her island walks and combined this with scrap wood to try and keep herself warm. On the occasions she accepted her need for company, Sally would appear at the Manse door flushed and smelling of alcohol from self-medication to drive away her feelings of isolation. Even though well insulated, the Featherstore apartment was no place for Dan to fret away such winter months worrying about how he was going to pay Don and Lachie and get off the island. Of all the re-settlers, Dan felt trapped the most. His daily intake of alcohol, more often than not laced with dried Mothan, simply added to his sense of doom.

Dave's patriarchal vision was often at odds with Deborah's view of family life that winter. Both saw themselves leading their tribe in the wilderness, they just approached the challenge in different ways. As a professional educator Deborah allowed intuition to be her guide, sensing when and where to focus her attention and leadership. While she sought control through subtlety, Dave detached himself from personal engagement to deliver guidance and inspiration from his daily Bible study. He had not intended to go down this route to start with, choosing to read the scriptures out of academic interest, but as winter at St Kilda became ever more challenging for him, the Bible became his source of personal inspiration. For all but Anne, one way or another they had needed to suspend their disbelief to get through the months of hardship.

Erica's project had intrigued Don and Lachie as it had Jeff, the former St Kilda electrician brought out to join the re-settlers on a fine but cold day in February. The pack ice had dispersed enough to allow a relatively clear passage form Harris. It took a lot to impress Don, with his lifetime's experience of sailing Hebridean waters, but he was amazed at the sheer numbers and variety of cetaceans encountered on passage to St Kilda. He was beaming as he pulled the *Beluga* alongside the jetty, never had he seen so many whales and dolphins on the crossing. The three men soon set about unloading Erica's small wind turbine, micro-hydro unit and solar panels. The large ex-submarine deep cycle batteries proved troublesome to unload and proved even more troublesome to carry in wheelbarrows up the steep slipway to the Manse. Several adolescent seal pups lying on the slipway grumbled as they hauled themselves away, getting under the feet of the straining men.

"For fuck's sake, you wee bastards!" Don saw no cuteness in these animals, just potential fish thieves. Don had many income streams which included salmon farming and lobster fishing. In his opinion, seals were not good news. Now retired, Jeff was happy to tolerate most of God's creatures but drew the line at Bonxies which, for him, were thankfully away from the island in February. By April they would return to nest on the rough moorland to plague both man and beast. He remembered how aggressive Skuas had only appeared in the 1960s, just after military arrived at St Kilda. Ground nesting predators were never tolerated by the villagers but since nature conservation and non-intervention had taken precedence many protected species had been slaughtered by these birds. Jeff had been attacked and treated for head cuts and scratches from Skua attack on many occasions and their legal protection seemed a bad joke. Anne, however had spent much of her summer in their nesting territory but after only a few investigative forays the highly intelligent Skua packs left her alone. Packs were an appropriate description of the way flocks of Skuas co-operated to bring down their prey or hamstring and blind young lambs before disemboweling their victims alive, as Jeff said he had witnessed many times.

Anne had also been amazed at the sheer numbers of whales and dolphins feeding in the ice free bay that winter. Seals had long ceased to be a source of excitement for her but coming back from the farthest point of the island, at the Cambir peninsular, she claimed to have seen a group of Orcas, killer whales, hunting through the drift ice piling up in Glen Bay. Atlantic Seals, having difficulty escaping in the water, were climbing up on to the packed ice and the Orcas were using their tails co-operatively to create waves and wash their prey back into the sea. In a matter of fact way Anne related how the waters of Glen Bay had turned red with seal blood.

"Oh God, Anne. Do you have to tell us everything you

see?" Erica, though far from squeamish, hated to hear of deliberate animal cruelty even, as in this case, the perpetrators were animal themselves.

Anne's winter had simply required her to dress up warmer for her regular walks around the island observing seasonal progressions of the natural world. The Skuas had migrated back out to sea by late autumn and Glen Mór felt an empty place without their presence. The dry cold of the anticyclone over the North Atlantic had even suppressed the uncanny blasts of wind that traversed the glen unpredictably at any other time of the year. Apart from the arrival of Orcas in Glen Bay all seemed quiet. Across the narrow strait the sheep on Soay kept their activity to a minimum, conserving energy by sheltering in cleits and other ruins on this long uninhabited island. It hadn't always been that way. Small bothies and the storage cleits could still be seen perilously close to the head of a recent landslip. Anne was intrigued by the isolated structure not dissimilar to the three chambered Amazon's House in the glen. Through her binoculars, she could clearly see signs of another ancient settlement on Soay. Legend had it, she remembered, this had been the home of a certain Duggan who, having contravened medieval St Kilda's strict social codes, was banished to Soay for eternity. Near to Taigh Duggan lay the remains of the WW2 Wellington bomber caught by one of the inexplicable wind blasts and thrown against the near vertical hillside above Duggan's house. The surviving crew members had crawled from the wreckage only to find the route to help blocked by unexpectedly strong tidal currents surging through the deep strait between Soay and Hirta. It would take an expert archaeologist to distinguish between the medieval and twentieth century human remains scattered amongst the rocks in the vicinity. At the summit of Soay, Anne had also spotted the stone altar built at some indeterminable time in the islands past. There was so much still to learn but she could well imagine anyone left on Soay would try and do anything to escape their open air prison.

Standing on the point of the Cambir and looking across the wild narrow strait, Anne imagined Duggan, out of his mind with loneliness, sacrificing one of the small brown Soay lambs on the altar across the water from Morrigan's House in Glen Mór. Trapped by his androcentric beliefs as much as the island exile, sacrificing an innocent lamb, thought Anne, would have been an extremely bad move. Had he partaken of the abundant Mothan growing in the deep gullies over there, he might have been allowed to swim across to the safety of human company he desperately craved.

Through the eyes of Morrigan, Anne watched the whales feeding unmolested in Village Bay that winter. With strong winter sunshine filtering down through the clear waters, phytoplankton bloomed at the base of the marine food chain. No wonder the fish population in the Bay was good, she thought. Everything from microscopic zooplankton through krill to sand eels were benefiting from the winter abundance and right up the food chain to the Williams family themselves. Rod and line fishing from the jetty was providing welcome fresh food for them all. The calm conditions also benefited the kelp forest skirting the rocky shores allowing it to grow into an underwater jungle of marine diversity. While the rest of the group struggled through the winter, Anne's activities had remained relatively unaffected apart from her sensibly avoiding the steeper frozen slopes. She had badly bruised herself that autumn taking a painful tumble on the rocky slopes of Carn Mór and had no desire to repeat the performance. She enjoyed exploring the island but access to Carn Mór was always a challenge. This was no doubt why thousands of Puffins landed amongst the scree each April to raise their young in safety. Even the Skuas would think twice before commencing a low-level attack run through such rocky terrain.

The off-grid equipment arrived at Erica's blackhouse intact and the calm conditions made erecting her wind turbine a straightforward job. Four stainless steel cables were used to guy the upright pole in position. Once the pole was in the ground Jeff realized it would have been much easier to have fitted the generator on the pole before placing it in its upright position. Anne noticed this with smug satisfaction but did acknowledge that with the heavy generator on top, the pole would have been much harder to lift. With the pole securely guyed in position, Jeff found one of his old three section aluminum ladders still inside the power station building where he had left it the year before. With Don and Lachie holding everything steady he climbed up to fit the generator and its blades. With the blades in position, even on this calmest of days, a sudden gust hit the turbine causing the blades to spin and almost knocking him from the ladder.

"Watch out, Jeff!" Don had been casually chatting with Lachie, joking about when they'd be likely to see Dan's dope money when a large wrench fell and just missed them. "Aye, it will be hard hats you'll be needing next, lads!" After years of working on the Base infrastructure, Jeff had become accustomed to unexpected assaults from invisible and inexplicable gusts of wind.

Erica's solar panels were more of an issue for him. With their large surface area he reckoned she was asking for trouble. They would be likely to blow away as had the 19th century pitched roofs and zinc sheeting. He certainly wasn't going to fit solar panels on a pole for her but advised a frame at ground level to support the panels at forty-five degrees or thereabouts to the south. How these would stand up against one of the south-easterlies that so easily blew roofs off the cottages would be anyone's guess.

The third approach to Erica's electrical self-sufficiency

plan would be the small hydro-electric generator to be fitted in the burn at the side of her cottage. She had rightly considered it highly unlikely there would ever be a time on St Kilda without either sunshine, rain or wind to provide her with energy. She knew there had been a watermill in the village before. Not a conventional water wheel mechanism common in much of lowland Britain, but a Norse mill making use of a paddle wheel set horizontal to the stream. The grindstones were driven on a vertical shaft. The difference was in the water supply. The Norse mill ran from a controlled water supply while Erica's micro-hydro generator would run fast or slow according to the amount of water flowing down the burn from Mullach Mór. The three men worked over the weekend to install Erica's equipment. Don had long since given up Sabbath observance at St Kilda though he kept up the semblance back home on Harris. Not to have done so could well have left him with social consequences among his adherent neighbors. Jeff connected the wiring to the control panel and regulator as light faded late on Sunday afternoon. Erica had already lit the woodstove and running the cables along the rafters had proved a hot and dusty job. As a recent non-drinker, Jeff declined the offer of beer she produced for the three of them. No such restraint from Don or Lachie and the two boatmen were already in a jovial mood by the time Jeff packed up his tools.

"Well, is it going to work then, Jeff?" Lachie could be a tease at times, especially when it came to 'old' Jeff. "There's a fair chance, my lad, aye, there's a fair chance," he replied. "Let's just look at the control panel now." Gauges indicated how the three devices were performing. The micro-hydro was showing a steady current flowing into the battery, while to be expected very little was being delivered from the solar panels so late on a winter afternoon. The wind turbine gauge indicated it was fluctuating wildly, delivering full charge one minute and almost nothing the next. The needle of the voltmeter appeared to vibrating too. Jeff went out of the door of the blackhouse to see what was happening and was perturbed to see the wind turbine turning and spinning erratically on such a calm frosty evening. He went back inside to report to the others.

"It's bloody queer but your generator seems to have a mind of its own, Erica. You'd better take a look." Erica went outside and could see her new wind turbine shaking violently at the top of its pole. Cursing she ran to the pole, "Don't you play such fucking nonsense with me, you bloody machine. Work properly Goddamit!" To her surprise, the wind generator turned slowly into the correct position to take advantage of the evening breeze flowing down the glen from the Mullach Mór. Back inside the blackhouse the gauge settled down to read a steady 12.5 volts.

"Perfect!" said Jeff to Don and Lachie as Erica ducked her head and came back inside. "What did you do to fix it, Erica?" She was grinning, "I don't really know. As you said it was shaking and turning wildly. I just swore and blasphemed at it and the next thing it was working perfectly." Erica could hardly believe it herself but Jeff seemed to confirm things for her. "Well you must have the magic touch, girl!" Erica forgave Jeff his near chauvinist comment. Don and Lachie waited for the retort but none came. She was simply pleased to have the job done.

"Reckon we could turn the light on now, Jeff?" Don was as eager as anyone to see if it all worked. Jeff suggested Erica should flick the switch as by his reckoning the batteries should have charged up enough to run a twelve volt fluorescent strip light. She flicked the switch and for the first time in its two hundred year history, electric light filled the interior of the blackhouse. They all cheered at the success of the weekend's work. "This calls for a celebration, boys!" Sally emphasized the gender specific mainly for Jeff's benefit giving him a provocative wink. Lachie put more wood in the stove and Erica produced the bottle of malt she had ordered from Don for just this occasion. The celebrations continued into the late evening. Erica put her vegetarian principles to one side and provided skewers of tasty lamb for the men even indulging in some of the meat herself as the whisky took effect. Jeff surprised the others by accepting a small glass.

'We'll make a good carnivore of you yet, Erica." Lachie joked. Erica had to accept that by eating lamb she had crossed one of her own boundaries toward sustainable living on this island, as she had imagined it would be. There was certainly no shortage of the animals and cute as they looked these agile sheep were causing a lot of trouble. They hadn't been hard to catch trapped inside the shells of empty cottages and with Sally's help they had recently caught and slaughtered a yearling ram. Sally reckoned they would be even easier to catch on rainy days when they took shelter inside the cleits. That, apparently, had been how the sheep researchers had done it in the past. Dave was despairing over the damage they were doing to his newly repaired stone walls and she couldn't imagine how he would protect their vegetables in An Lag once the growing season started. Sheep eat vegetables so if that happened she would eat sheep, simple as that. With the 12volt lights burning bright and the whisky and meat finished, Don and Lachie bade her goodnight to make their way back to the *Beluga* tied up at the jetty. Jeff had brought a spare camp bed up from the Manse and with some borrowed bedding was making himself comfortable near the stove in the blackhouse. In planning her own home, Erica had omitted to think of more than one crib bed built into the thick walls of her cottage.

"Can't see a bloody thing, Lachie!" Don had lost his night vision after getting used to Erica's new electric lighting and nearly fell into the burn at the front of the derelict military buildings. Looking up at the small glow from an oil light in the Featherstore window he was reminded of the other matter they needed to deal with at St Kilda. "Just that fucker in there to sort out now, Lachie." The *Beluga* left at first light heading back to Leverburgh. For the first time in many weeks they didn't have to avoid drifting pack ice and a noticeable swell was rising as the twin hulled cabin boat rose and fell across the troughs. Don was feeling good, pushing the throttles forward the *Beluga* scattered countless Gannets feeding off Boreray as they headed for home.

It hadn't been a totally peaceful night in Erica's blackhouse. Jeff had woken with a start and rushed to open the door and small windows. "What's up, Jeff?' Erica was sleepy from the large meal and whisky and almost fell from her crib trying to get out. Wrapping a dressing gown around her pajamas she went over to Jeff standing staring at the control panel. "I am going to have to sort this out for you tomorrow, Erica. The batteries are over charging. I could smell the fumes. This could be bloody dangerous if we don't sort it."

"What should we do?" she asked. "Well, for now I have disconnected the leads from the regulator so the batteries won't charge any more tonight. The system is just too efficient with wind, water and solar energy so freely available. You need a dump load for occasions like this. Best would be storing the energy as hot water. Leave it with me, Erica. I'll get an old hot water cylinder and immersion heater form the base tomorrow and there's sure to be a 240 volt inverter knocking about in the workshops. They never took the cheap stuff away when the military moved out. I'll set everything up so that when the batteries reach capacity the excess current will automatically flow to the immersion heater and you'll have free hot water as well as lighting. The plumbing will be simple. We can collect water from a little higher up the burn and run it down through some Alkathene pipe."

"OK, Jeff. I trust in your abilities but if it's all safe for tonight I am going back to bed. See you in the morning." They both retired to their respective beds, though Jeff could barely sleep thinking about the strange behavior of the wind generator the previous evening. As an electrician, he did not like inexplicable events such as that one. Jeff was up bright and early and by the time Erica emerged, somewhat hung over, he had salvaged a copper hot water cylinder and a roll of blue plastic water pipe was stacked outside her door. Erica rubbed her eyes looking at it, taking in the fact that someone else was about to make a fairly large impact in her living space.

"We need the cylinder higher than your sink. Could be tricky so I thought of an easier way of doing this. I'll put the cylinder outside, it's well insulated with plastic foam coating. It will be above your sink and running the pipework through the walls will be a piece of cake. I've found a nice new tap in the old stores so all you will have to do is build small cleit around it to protect it from the elements, and the bloody sheep. The sods will be getting next to it to keep warm if we let them so don't leave a doorway. But still that will be your job, I am the technical man round here!" Erica again withheld from giving him a mouthful. She accepted the wisdom of what he was saying and wanted the job done. The tank, plumbing and wiring was completed the same day for which she was very grateful.

"You'll just be needing a tin bath now, Erica. One big enough for two?" Erica reached for the heather besom she had just recently finished making. "OK, only joking Erica, but I get the message!"

Rightly sensing that Erica might like the space to herself, Jeff moved his camp bed down to the Featherstore and slept with Dan that night. He would be eating in the Manse and leaving the island next time the *Beluga* came in, probably in a couple of days, weather permitting. Dan had made the

Featherstore bedroom facing the sea his own. Jeff moved into the room at the rear with the plainer view to the barren hillside a hundred yards or so behind the building. Erica had paid Jeff in cash for the off-grid electrical equipment and Dan noticed him place a sizeable bundle of notes into a secure pocket inside his rucksack.

"Hey, Jeff – I wonder if I could ask you a favor?" Dan was slightly sheepish about asking. "What is it, Dan?" Jeff was always eager to help but he was no fool and could sense the anxiety in Dan's voice. "Well you know Don and Lachie, the boat guys? I owe them a few quid like and there's no way I can get to the bank here. I don't have my cheque book either, I left it in Edinburgh. Could you possibly lend me fifty quid till I can get to the bank when I next get off the island?" Jeff was taken back a little at the directness of Dan's approach but could see the problem. There was no way anyone could get cash here, even if they had anywhere to spend it. When Jeff worked on St Kilda the men always ran up a bar tab and settled it with a cheque at the end of the month when their salary reached the bank. St Kilda was still a basically cashless community even though Erica had brought her savings with her for just such an occasion and for Dan, any cash was a welcome sight.

"Tell you what, Dan. Why don't I lend you a straight two hundred pounds then you'll have a little to spare for the next time you owe anyone anything." Jeff had correctly intuited Dan probably owed considerably more than fifty pounds but wasn't going to enquire just how much. Dan thought that making at least a down payment on his dope bill would take the pressure off and get him on the right side of the boatmen. "Thanks, Jeff. You're a pal!" Feeling more relaxed and sociable, Dan produced a bottle of *Glenmorangie* from under his bed. "Do fancy a dram, Jeff?"

"No thanks, Dan. It really doesn't agree with me nowadays." He had taken a big risk drinking at Erica's the previous evening. He wasn't going to push his luck in this tenser atmosphere. Just for once, Dan also decided not to drink alone.

Jeff hadn't really participated in Erica's blackhouse celebration, feeling uneasy at the proceedings. He had just been doing what he enjoyed doing, creative electrical engineering and he'd felt a little uncomfortable working alongside a young woman with considerable feminine presence like Erica. It had also been hard to resist drinking with the others after months of abstinence following treatment for alcohol related health problems. He would never have been able to keep off the drink had he still been working at the Base. Like many of the men on the remote Base he had never married or maintained more than passing relationships. A lot of them were more comfortable sharing their time with other men. Not that any of them were misogynist in any way, it just seemed easier somehow. The few women on the island, like Sally the nurse, he considered were dark horses and goodness knows what went on in their heads. Men were generally straight forward and predictable. Although Jeff was over twice Dan's age, he could surmise what made him tick. Dan hadn't however reckoned on Jeff's depth of perception from living and working predominantly alongside other men for most of his adult life.

Dan had been entranced listening to Jeff's tales of life at St Kilda. He hadn't heard much first-hand of social life on the Base, especially the Friday nights in the Puff-Inn which would commonly run on into Sunday morning, Saturdays being not much more than a hazy recollection. In their own way the Base guys had, like Jeff, been keen to observe a quiet Sabbath. Early Sunday morning tourists were particularly unwelcome, particularly those from the Scottish mainland who not infrequently hired a piper to play them ashore. After several incidences of abuse shouted from the Base accommodation block the tour operators got the message and had directed the pipers away from the jetty to the far end of the village. Apparently the good times had come to an end after the skinny-dipping incident in 2011. So the tale was true, when word got back to the bar that there was an actual naked woman swimming off the jetty, one of the voyeurs had fallen off the harbor wall onto rocks below. Suffering multiple injuries he was lucky to have lived. After the incident was investigated the then civilian management had closed the bar as a punitive measure. Over the following year a performance audit was carried out and the workforce found to be woefully inefficient. Millions of pounds worth of military assets were tied up while the Hebrides Missile Range was closed down until the radar technicians got their act together.

"What do you mean, Jeff?" Dan was looking puzzled.

"What I mean is because they were so bloody hung over most of the time, their performance was shambolic. Nothing ever got done on time and when it did it was rarely right first time. We were testing state of the art missile technology and it was all those prats could do to get up for work in the morning. Then the terrorists got wind of the situation out here and we were a sitting target. The only one half capable of finding out what had happened that night was the Supervisor and generally he wasn't much better himself, but he was on duty that night and had taken it easy. It was a shame it had to end for him like that though."

Jeff related to an incredulous Dan how, during a drunken night in the bar, terrorists had struck on the island laying charges that had demolished the communications mast sending it crashing onto the radomes below. The damage was never repaired and the terrorists, to his knowledge, never caught. They had landed in Glen Bay and no one knew a thing about it until it was too late. Only poor Derek had heard the explosion over the howl of the south easterly winds that night. He had driven up to the top of the hill to find a scene of chaos with the mast toppled and a tangle of steel hawsers and high voltage cables that had to be seen to be believed. It had taken months to clear it all up and by that time the Ministry of Defense had had enough. "Again, it all boiled down to excessive alcohol consumption away from the checks and balances of normal society."

Dan was curious about the women. "Well there were always one or two women here but they tended to get together as a clique and to be honest, I reckon they would plot mischief against us men. Things would regularly go missing, important things like a bunch of keys which would always turn up in unexpected places. Rumors would start setting one man against another and I reckon it was all women's work. Men rarely have the capability for serious scheming. And as for 'Aunt' Sally, there's another story, Dan."

"Go on, Jeff." Dan was intrigued. "Well your Sally out here now has quite a history. As you know she was the main nurse which included being personal councilor and agony aunt – hence her nickname. Quite a few of the men went to her feeling anxious and complaining of feeling trapped on this island. Usually after some tea and sympathy they went away satisfied but then our Sally began to have ideas. I only heard this from some of the other guys, but apparently one or two of them went to her to talk over some personal problem or get treated for a sore back and she'd have them on the massage couch strapped down before you could say hey presto. I am sure I can leave the rest to your imagination Dan, but it wasn't the type of massage that would do your bad back any good, I can tell you. No-one ever complained though, you could say she was dishing out a social service!"

Jeff chuckled at his own joke, leaving Dan wide eyed with amazement. It seemed his wilder student days had been nothing compared with what had been going on out here. "But anyway, now everything's operated from South Uist the management can keep a tight eye on things from Range Head.

It always makes me smile to see 'Our Lady of the Isles', the Virgin Mary on her pedestal just below the hill top control center. Actually you can see that from here on a clear day, Dan. Sally wouldn't have been allowed to model for that statue, I can tell you. Aye, that would have been the other Mary more like!"

Now it was Dan's turn to chuckle. He was aware that simple manly banter was just what he had been missing on this island again being affected by women's scheming. Jeff enjoyed Dan's student stories but did hold back from letting Jeff know about his growing affair with Deborah, even though rightly it should have been her affair with him, not the other way round. The tales continued until both headed for their respective beds satisfied from a good evening's story telling. Dan had raked up a few good anecdotes of his own, especially the one about getting into trouble for supplying other students with vodka laced with Fly Agaric mushrooms. Jeff had looked slightly shocked at this revelation. "You want to be careful, Dan. There have been a few strange events on this island and I don't mean just falling off high walls trying to look at naked women. There was a lad here once who had read about the Butterwort plant that grows in wet places here. The Gaelic name for it is Mothan and there's a lot of folklore attached to the plant. It was said to keep the faeries away from the milk but it was also used by Hebridean women to entrap men of their fancy. They would chew leaves of the plant before kissing their intended and that was it, he was ensnared and wrapped around their little fingers before you could say hey presto!" The bottom line is he lost his life trying to fly from the Gap.

"It is supposed to be a dreaming herb so think twice before you get any ideas to try it. Anyway, Mothan or no Mothan, I am going to sleep well tonight." Jeff got up to go to his bed. "See you in the morning, Dan."

The tinned and dried food in the base kitchens, as Deborah had reminded Dave on many occasions, was not inexhaustible. The tastiest items were already getting low and they had made serious inroads into the alcohol supply once destined for customers of the Puff-Inn. All good things would come to an end and it looked like that moment would come before too long. As long as the *Beluga* kept arriving, they would be alright, but they needed a contingency supply in case of prolonged bad weather. Islanders had run out of food in the past and sure as eggs were eggs it could happen again now there was no longer a helicopter service from the mainland. As for eggs Deborah, did not want to return to the old St Kildan seabird diet.

"Dave," she questioned over their evening meal. "How are the kale yards, you know, the gardens, coming on?"

"Well, I have repaired quite a few now. It will just be a question of digging them over, raking and sowing the seed. We should have great fresh vegetables this Summer at least. Don is going to bring me out plenty of seed, the stuff that grows well on Harris should be fine here. Thank God there are no rabbits. He told me he has a terrible time with them back home and has to shoot them on an almost daily basis. No amount of wire netting deters the little sods for long."

Dave had tried fishing from the jetty during times when his back pain stopped him from working. It wasn't the same as tilling the land for him but he felt he was providing something, at least. Coming back to the Manse with armfuls of fresh vegetables would soon become reality, especially if he could get them all outside, working as a team to dig ridge and furrow lazy-beds inside his repaired stone enclosures. The Hebrides were covered with ridge and furrow remnants of past agriculture when human muscle and hand tools prevailed to cultivate steep and inaccessible ground. Locally produced compost included all manner of organic waste and was used to build up raised beds flowing down the hillsides. St Kilda became a different place after the mid nineteenth century when Enclosure changed island life forever. Enclosure improved agricultural production across the whole of Britain including at St Kilda. For a few years, their rich seabird waste compost produced Barley crops the envy of the Western Isles. The warm and enclosed south facing fields, well-watered and cleared of stones produced heavy yields in the long summer days of intense sunshine. The level ground was perfect for agricultural production. High stone walls deflected the worst of the winds and for a while the villagers could not have improved further. Stones not used in building the protective Head Dyke were used to build the larger nineteenth century storage cleits. These large cleits mimicked the field barns of other upland areas of Britain cleared for Enclosure. Much has been written about changes to community life brought about by lowland Enclosure. St Kilda, at the extremity of the Western isles must have changed more than most, Dave reminded them all. Atlantic storms brought inevitable failure to the agricultural project in spite of romantic tourists in search of an island Utopia. The reality of never ending hard work and an ageing population was consciously ignored by the majority of visitors. As Dave was already beginning to realize, his middle aged body, unaccustomed to physical work on this scale, was not going to be strong enough on its own. He needed spiritual support to see the project through to completion. Not just Dave Williams, but each one of the new settlers was, in their own way, becoming more and more reliant on their personal gods and demons to guide them in the resettlement of St Kilda.

14 SHEEP

Dave had worked hard that winter repairing stone walls around the Manse. He was particularly proud of the six foot high wall around the Glebe plot originally set aside for the Minister's vegetable garden. Digging the soil had proved surprisingly easy. Not only had nearly a century of Soay sheep grazing kept deep rooted weeds away but several archaeological digs on the plot had left the ground friable and easy to rework for family vegetables. The free ranging Soay sheep were proving to be another matter. Brought over to Hirta in 1932, they showed no respect for the stone walls or cleit roofs. Western Isles Trust archaeologists had repeatedly complained about the damage these introduced feral sheep were doing to the island's architectural heritage. Nothing was ever done to mitigate their damage as the unmanaged flocks represented a unique research opportunity into the ecology of a closed population of large mammals. Zoologists considered the research opportunity unparalleled worldwide. The population rose and fell according to natural conditions and as grazing became sparse no blade of grass was spared, nor any blade of anything else edible for that matter. Dave compared them to John Muir's 'hoofed locusts' relentlessly devouring the native grasslands of North America. As the sheep population rose, no accessible part of the island would be left ungrazed. Only on the steepest rock faces could plants flower and set seed where even the agile brown sheep feared to tread. The population had risen exponentially to nearly two thousand animals before the Williams arrival and Dave's attempts at cultivation begun. In an ordinary year the Spring grass would have sustained the Soay flock but this year, with winter lingering much longer than usual, the sheep, especially the pregnant ewes, struggled to find sustenance.

Dave had already noticed how lush the vegetation grew inside the stone walled enclosures compared to that growing out in the open. Anne had explained to him, in ecological terms of course, how wind chill prevented plants from fully developing on this exposed island. She had described St Kildan vegetation as a plagio-climax community stunted by wind chill and heavy grazing. Behind protective dry-stone walls plants could grow un-checked and reach their full potential, especially on south facing sunny slopes. The St Kildans had been well aware of this and took great pains to keep both strong winds and livestock out of their southerly orientated enclosures. Only with the harvest over were the island's heavy Cheviot sheep allowed in to add their copious droppings to the soil of the enclosures. Ever since they had been introduced to maintain the grazing for future settlement, the agile brown sheep had become accustomed to free range in the name of zoological research, but to the detriment of just about everything else. He had also noticed how larger enclosures and been worked in ridge and furrow lazy-bed fashion and Dave was eager to try out horticultural methods known to have succeeded in the past.

Dave ridged the cultivated soil inside the Glebe garden. Not only would this increase the surface area for cultivation but would also allow drainage during the periods of heavy rainfall. He envisioned his vegetables growing strong in the sun, thriving in still rich soils behind the shelter of restored stone walls. The physical act of cultivating the soil and sowing heritage seeds sourced from the mainland proved inspirational and, for a while, Dave forgot his daily Bible readings. He had begun to draw solace from working with rather than against nature. It then came as a surprise to Deborah to hear her husband voluble abuse from inside their kitchen garden where recently sown seeds had germinated and begun to grow.

"Get out of here, you fucking bastard cunts!" he

screamed at them.

Dave had really lost it, she thought. The clatter of falling rocks was audible as three small brown sheep scrambled over the wall away from the rain of small stones Dave was hurling at them.

"Jesus, God almighty! What have I bloody done to deserve this?" Dave fell to his knees beside the Church wall and beat the freshly turned soil with his fists. His carefully tended young Kale plants had been defoliated by the opportunist yearlings.

"Dave, calm down. They will grow again quick enough. The roots are established and they'll just be bushier plants, that's all. Come on, all is not lost!"

Deborah tried to make light of the incident but knew her husband well enough to understand the pain he felt finding so much of his winter efforts undone in an unguarded moment. "The problem, as you know Dave, is the St Kildans never had to put up with this breed of sheep. Their heavier Cheviots and Closewools were selected because they didn't do this kind of damage, didn't climb over the walls. Any that did would soon end up in the pot, I can tell you."

Dave took himself for a walk and, this time in earnest, began searching his mind for Biblical explanations for his defeat in the face of three hungry Soays. His walk took him up into the corrie of An Lag where sturdy 19th century stone enclosures stood years after the last crops had been harvested. With wooden gates long since rotted, contented Soays ruminated inside the warm, sunny enclosures, chewing cud away from the biting wind. The walls here were taller than those around the Manse garden, maybe eight feet high, but Dave quickly realized the open gateways eliminated the risk of sheep scrambling over and damaging the loosely built stonework. He remembered reading that these arable enclosures had also served as sheep fanks during the annual round up or any other time the St Kildans needed to catch their sheep. Thinking about 19th century agricultural methods he continued to work his way upwards to the top of this formerly cultivated and sheltered corrie between Oiseval and the slopes of Conachair. Cresting the rise, Dave could see the dramatic peaks of Boreray and the Stacs four miles distant and he could just make out the 500 odd feral white sheep, descendants of the Boreray flock, living unmanaged on St Kilda's second largest island and left to their own devices in 1930. It simply hadn't been economically viable to remove them one by one down the precipitous paths for manhandling into a waiting vessel. The St Kildans, he had read, used to truss the sheep's legs before throwing them into the sea to be plucked from drowning by waiting boatmen.

Dave turned left and began to climb the steep path toward the summit of Conachair. At the highest point on the island he stood facing northward toward the dramatic land and seascapes where jagged white capped Stacs rose from the submerged volcanic rim of the archipelago. The power of the view was palpable and standing there exposed to the sea and sky with seabirds swirling around him, he heard God speak to him from afar, as if from Boreray. Determined to understand he quickly made his way back down to the village to consult the old family Bible for the first time in many weeks. Taking the fastest route back from the summit, skirting the one thousand foot sea-cliff, he regarded the gated walls of An Lag with fresh inspiration. On reaching the Manse he went straight to the battered Bible and began looking for the words he needed. Almost at random he flicked the pages of the Old Testament, looking for references to human trial and tribulation in the wilderness. After a few minutes searching he came across exactly what he needed. Dave had noticed before that when a word was on his mind, it seemed to jump out at him when scanning the pages. It had been a skill he acquired from marking hundreds of undergraduate assignments where no matter what waffle had been written around them, repetition of keywords and references were all he needed to see. His keyword that afternoon was *walls* and the words of Isaiah 62: 6-12 jumped out at him.

I have set watchmen upon thy walls, O Jerusalem, which shall never hold their peace day nor night: ye that make mention of the Lord, keep not silence all the day and all the night they shall never be silent. And give him no rest until he establish, and till he make Jerusalem a praise in the earth. The Lord has sworn by his right hand and by the arm of his strength, "Surely I will no more give thy corn to be meat for thine enemies; and the sons of the stranger shalt not drink thy wine for the which thou hast labored: But they that have gathered it shall eat it and praise the Lord, and they that have brought it together shall drink it in the courts of my holiness". Go through, go through the gates; prepare ye the way of the people; cast up, cast up the highway; gather out the stones; lift up a standard for the people.

In other words, if he returned to the ways of the Lord he would no more give Kale to be meat for Soay sheep, now his sworn enemies. That evening Dave returned to his former pattern of Bible reading before they ate.

"Don't let the food go cold, Dave!" Deborah tolerated her husband's idiosyncrasy but wasn't going to encourage it. As woman of the house she had more important things to worry about. Even with, sheep willing, a potential supply of fresh vegetables in the coming year it was going to be tight feeding them all. Dave briefly paused, glanced at Anne, before concluding his reading by quoting lines selected from Proverbs 31.

"Favor is deceitful, and beauty is vain: but a woman that

feareth the Lord, shall be praised. Give her of the fruit of her hands; and let her own works praise her in the gates."

"Whatever, Dad; can we eat now?" Anne was unmoved by her father's return to Bible reading before their evening meal. "So does that mean we all have to work in the garden now?"

"Well, it wouldn't be a bad idea Anne. Everyone else seems to have a job round here, even Dan has his guided walks to get organized. You wander off into Glen Mór most days of the week leaving the rest of us to labor on the land. It is a wonder you don't set up home over there. What I am going to do tomorrow is build a gate in the garden wall. That way the sheep won't need to climb over and when the ground is clear I can let them in and they can dung the ground - great idea, eh. Just like the old fold system. For now I am going to follow the Lord's advice and raise a great standard over the garden, the flapping flag will scare the sheep away - and we are all going to keep a regular watch to prevent the little devils getting in again."

It did not take Dave long to build a gateway into the garden enclosure and throw together a temporary gate made from a couple of old pallets he found in the deserted workshops of Red Square. The flag pole was more of a challenge but he remembered an old yacht mast lying behind the shingle beach. With the help of Dan, the mast was dragged back to the Manse and erected in the garden. Visiting ships had previously adorned the walls of the old Puff-Inn with donated flags and very soon a somewhat battered and nicotine stained Royal Ensign was flying over Dave's garden. Beyond the wall the sheep watched impassively, unmoved by either the flag or Dave's latest efforts to keep them away from his vegetable patch.

At the far end of the village, Sally had joined Erica, both

women were sitting on the low wall outside her restored blackhouse. Sally pointed out the small brown sheep again clambering on top of the garden wall behind the Manse. "Look at that, Erica. Those sheep just get everywhere. That flag Dave put up to deter them is useless, there's no stopping them." Erica looked up just in time to see one of the sheep jump high in the air and fall, legs thrashing, to the ground at the foot of the wall. Both women heard the crack of the rifle shot followed almost simultaneously by the thud of a hollow point slug smashing into the sheep's skull.

"What the fuck?" Erica was incredulous. She had just witnessed a perfect head shot, better than anything her deer stalker ex-boyfriend had ever managed. "Looks like your Dad's got the gun out that he wouldn't let you kids play with. Well that's one way of dealing with the problem but those sheep will keep coming back. There's plenty of them and nothing much to eat right now."

Sally and Erica quickly walked down the path toward the Manse in time to see Deborah and Anne racing out after hearing the shot. Deborah was flabbergasted. "Dave, I thought we had all agreed, that bloody gun was staying in the loft. You are surely not getting it out again!" Anne was equally horrified but more at the release of male violence against the island's sheep population. "Dad, what are you doing? Couldn't you have just shooed them off like last time?"

With the freshly cleaned and oiled Tikka T3 cradled in his arms, Dave's repost came immediately.

"The Lord has sworn by his right hand and by the arm of his strength, 'Surely I will no more give thy corn to be meat for thine enemies; and the sons of the stranger shalt not drink thy wine for which thou hast labored!'"

He was defiant, "I said we would stand guard and that's just what I have been doing!" The small brown ewe lay dead at their feet, a small drop of pre-natal milk leaking from one teat. Already a sharp eyed Skua circled overhead waiting to drop and feed on the carcass. Sally stood incredulous at the scene. She considered there was no need for a family argument over one dead sheep. Erica agreed and voiced her opinion that using the rifle certainly beat her plan to trap sheep in cleits when they sheltered from driving rain or strong sunshine.

"Look guys, I don't know about you but I reckon we should be grateful for small mercies, like some free mutton. Yeah, I know we are not supposed to touch these sheep but leaving it for the Bonxies seems a right waste to me."

Ever the pragmatist, Erica offered to skin and butcher the ewe, a proposal Deborah was ready to accept in light of their dwindling rations. Throughout the discussion over the dead sheep, Dan had been noticeable by his absence. From inside the Featherstore, the survivalist scenario unfolding not one hundred meters away was just too real. As usual, Dan would rather distance himself from the more visceral aspects of reality.

Picking up the spent cartridge case, Dave took the rifle back inside the Manse securing it in the hallway cupboard rather than back up in the loft. It could, he reckoned, be needed again at short notice. The matter of sheep in the vegetable garden was brought up by Anne over their evening meal. She reminded them all that before any more sheep were killed they ought to contact the Trust for advice.

"I agree that this island cannot ecologically support all these introduced sheep and in the absence of a terrestrial predator, we could fill that niche. Technically what Dad has just done is to deliberately kill a legally protected species and it is asking for trouble without at least having applied for the appropriate license, let alone holding a fire-arms permit." She also made it clear that she didn't like the way it had been done in anger. If culling was to be carried out, which she had no practical objection to, it should be done by professionals. Not by a deranged old man with an unlicensed hunting rifle.

Deborah agreed to contact the Western Isles Trust as soon as possible. The satellite internet system still worked and she sent an email to Josephine Miller, who as luck would have it, was still in post after her redundancy threat had been withdrawn. The problem was explained, there were simply too many sheep and they hadn't a hope in hell of growing vegetables unless they were culled professionally. Deborah carefully avoided any reference to the unprofessional culling that had already taken place. Josephine's reply came quicker than she had expected. It seemed the Trust had long been concerned over physical damage the Soay sheep were doing to St Kilda's archaeology and, by overgrazing, stunting the island's ecological potential. She quickly arranged for two deer stalkers to be sent over. The professional marksmen would be over as soon as possible, before Spring lambing made the cull ethically unacceptable.

As manager for the islands, Josephine had often remarked how ironic it was that, having been spared the 19th century Clearances, St Kilda had still ended up overrun with sheep and its human population evacuated, albeit at their own request. She hadn't really accepted the myth of the earlier medieval evacuation from Glen Mór after the northern settlement found it impossible to live and work there following the appearance of the 'Amazon'.

Initially thought to be another of St Kilda's wonder tales, archaeologists had recently confirmed there had been a small flock of deer on the island in the medieval period. Taking one or two of the animals for subsistence had been traditional over the centuries. Agricultural improvement techniques had been adopted and, against the women's intuitive advice, the men of Glen Mór learned to drive deer into the netted stone corrals outside their corbelled huts, catching several at a time.

Screams of deer being slaughtered with stone axes echoed around the glen at the autumn catch. The practice ceased after hunters connected the deer's screams with the sudden and inexplicably violent gusts of wind that ripped their valuable fishing nets from atop the stone corrals. It seemed the glen would tolerate a foot hunt taking one deer at a time but not organized slaughter, however primitive, which presaged modern agricultural practices on the island. The superstitious St Kildans heeded the warning and henceforth considered Glen Mór no place for human habitation. What became of the deer was never known. It was possible, that a primitive strain of sheep, pre-dating the Soays had been mistaken for small deer. The wide glen became demarked by a turf dyke along the high ridge separating it from the village. Crossing the ridge daily, the women of the village tended to and milked the grazing cattle below without incident. Men venturing amongst the cattle would find themselves blown off their feet by inexplicable gusts while the animals grazed unaffected just a few yards away. The message was portentous but even the women felt compelled to make libation at the Milking Stone before returning to the village.

It had been several days before sea conditions were suitable for the *Beluga* to come out again from Leverburgh. The Argocat had been driven across sturdy planks from the pier onto the aft deck of the boat without too much difficulty and the two stalkers were in high spirits as Don pushed the throttle levers forward to begin their crossing to St Kilda. The small eight wheeled all-terrain vehicle had been well lashed down and stayed secure throughout the crossing. The Highland stalkers however had felt increasingly uncomfortable with the motion as the boat gathered speed heading for open waters. Gavin was the first to give in to sea-sickness and throw up into the plastic pint glass Lachie had tactfully supplied as they set off. Sean followed suit soon after and three hours later, entering the calmer waters of Village Bay, the two stalkers were decidedly the worse for the experience. Still managing a grin, Sean cracked a joke about feeling better than this after a heavy Friday night with the ghillies in Braemar. Grey faced, Gavin could only silently nod his agreement.

"Here we are then lads!" Ever cheerful, Don had explained that getting the Argocat on board at Leverburgh had been the easy bit. Now they would have to find a way of getting it ashore as they had arrived at low tide and the *Beluga* could not pull up alongside the jetty. He would have to charge them six hours waiting time to make an easy job of it.

"Don, do you think your crane would take the Argocat? It's about one and a half tons deadweight." Sean was eager to get ashore without waiting for high tide, he couldn't face the thought of spending another six hours on board. "Should be OK, though if it ends up sinking don't blame me!"

Don had doubts about the manufacturers claim that this eight wheel drive 'golf buggy', as he saw it, was fully amphibious. Don also reckoned an extra six hours payment for sharing a dram or two with these lads sounded fair enough. Sean knew the Western Isles Trust had given them a tight budget and decided to risk the Argocat crossing the gentle swell of Village Bay. Don and Sean untied the lashings holding the Argocat to the deck and fixed them to the lugs on each corner of the amphibious vehicle. Don swung the rear mounted crane around and Sean bunched the straps to the hook on the end of the stainless steel cable. Lifting the Argocat a foot off the deck immediately made the *Beluga* feel less stable. Gavin groaned but gave a feeble thumbs up as Don swung the amphibious vehicle over the stern of the boat. The *Beluga*'s bow rose up in the water and Don quickly lowered the Argocat into the water fearing a scene of chaos in his galley as crockery slid along shelves as the boat reared up. Neither did he want the rear of the *Beluga* getting knocked about, let alone swamped. To his amazement, the Argocat floated perfectly, in fact it seemed more stable than their Zodiac tender which bobbed around like a cork when empty. Sean, now pretty well recovered, jumped down into the Argocat and started the engine. Don knew the principle but again was dubious about the spinning wheels driving the vehicle through the water but the heavily treaded tires worked like high speed paddle wheels. Casting off the loading straps, Sean grinned as he maneuvered the Argocat left and right, evidently beginning to enjoy himself. Lachie appeared with their various boxes of provisions, two stalking rifles and a pump-action shotgun. There were also eight jerry-cans of diesel for the machine. They hadn't been told there were still thousands of gallons of fuel in the power station storage tanks. Lachie then dragged up four heavy boxes of ammunition before Don suggested they might be pushing their luck loading the Argocat with those as well.

"It will take a thousand pounds on water, Don." Sean's professional pride was at stake. Don was still dubious, "Yeah, and I'll bet you a thousand pounds they meant in a test tank, not crossing Atlantic swell. You just drive that thing across to the beach and we'll bring the rest in the Zodiac." Don hadn't built up his charter business by taking unnecessary risks and wasn't going to start now. The small slipway on the beach had last been used by the ex-Russian Army transporter arriving with thatch for Erica's blackhouse project. Now that had been an amphibious vehicle alright, he thought, not like this jumped up golf cart.

In spite of his misgivings, the Argocat landed safely on the beach and Sean skidded it round a couple of times on the sand before driving it up the slipway onto the weed strewn concrete helipad. The Zodiac was lowered from the *Beluga* and loaded with the stalkers supplies. It took two trips to the jetty to get everything ashore. Gavin, now recovered, helped carry their provisions and equipment up the jetty steps. Sean had already driven the Argocat off the beach and onto the fields at the edge of the village. Scattering hundreds of small waders, the birds protested noisily at the disturbance. A sudden gust of wind took his deerstalker hat and hurled it far out into the bay as he drove the machine along the road toward the jetty, further disturbing a young Harbor Seals snoozing above the high water line.

Gavin was already introducing himself to the Williams when Sean arrived to load up their supplies stacked on the jetty. Maneuvering up and down the steep slope to the jetty was no problem for the Argocat and a whole lot easier than using wheelbarrows. "Only just bought that hat! That's a fucking good start, Gavin." Deborah joked with the two new male arrivals, "Don't worry, we can find you another one. We can't let our heroes go around with cold heads, can we?" A minor flirtation which didn't go unnoticed by Dave.

Apart from Erica, who was nowhere to be seen, the Williams family came out to greet the new arrivals. Even Dan overcame his insecurities, appearing sheepishly to hand over his outstanding debt to Lachie when the two boatmen came up the slope from the jetty. Dave formally welcomed them, "OK boys, you can stay up in the cottages. Number one has a good kitchen though there's no electric now. Do you think you can cope with oil lamps and cooking on a woodstove?"

"'Can't be any worse than the bothies we have to use back home. Nae bother, we'll be just fine. Just show us where these sheep are you want getting rid of." Dave's cynical reply was barely audible, "Where are they not?"

Once the stalkers had settled in, they walked up the Street toward the sound of scratchy fiddle music. Erica had long fancied herself as a traditional musician and, with a poor quality instrument she had found in the storeroom behind the

Puff-Inn, she practiced by ear when she thought no-one else was around to hear her. She stopped abruptly when Gavin and Sean entered her blackhouse.

"Jesus fucking wept! Where did you boys come from?" Erica felt outraged at the unexpected and uninvited intrusion into her private world. "We came to see a man about culling a few sheep for you, hen." Erica ignored the slight. "OK, right you must be the stalkers Dad was talking about, but you could have just knocked before bursting in like that!"

"Guilty conscience have we?" Sean winked at Gavin. "Right den of iniquity out here so I was told back at Braemar. Sex, drugs and rock n' roll is what we heard, eh Gavin." His reply was pretty accurate if outdated, Erica felt. "Reckon that was before the military left, Sean. Just some frustrated women now and a sharpshooter with religious mania." Erica thought the stalkers had a pretty astute first impression but didn't like the way they made it seem so obvious. Where Dan fitted into their picture wasn't entirely clear. She decided to make a friendly gesture and invite them to a cup of tea while they were in her house. The men gladly accepted and listened to Erica talk enthusiastically about how she had renovated the blackhouse. Even installed a wood stove so the house couldn't technically be called black anymore.

"Yeah, there's plenty of ruined blackhouse townships in the Highlands," commented Gavin. "The Clearances did for them. My granddad told me that the thatched roofs were lucky to last two years once the fires went out. Seemed the smoke kept the insects away but once they got in birds pulled the thatch to pieces to get at them."

Looking up at the pristine thatched ceiling he added, "Maybe you will be needing to spray a bit of DDT up there just in case, Erica? You can't get it nowadays but we've got a bit back in the yard. That'd sort out the birds too, I reckon, Sean." The jest was interrupted by a scurrying in the thatch and for a brief moment a naked rodent tail could be seen twitching hanging from under the thatch and a few hardened black droppings fell onto the table below. "St Kilda mouse!" Erica described the island's endemic and oversized field mice to the two unconvinced stalkers. "Fucking rat more like! Deer, sheep, rats, whatever. We'll clear the lot as long as you pay us. Reckon we could be here for a while."

15 STALKERS

It had been Deborah's idea to throw a party to honor the stalkers arrival. Both daughters raised their eyebrows at the unexpected gesture. Edinburgh parties were remembered as if from another planet, but the women agreed it would make a welcome break from hard work and Dave's fundamentalism. Dan perked up at the prospect of the first party St Kilda had seen for a long time. Cottage One had seen plenty of parties in the past, but none recently. It had been the social venue for visiting conservation groups and Christmas get-togethers for military staff away from the austere surroundings of their quarters and the open ditch of the nearby dry burn had caught out many inebriated revelers returning to their rooms after a good night in the village.

Dave had been predictably disapproving as Deborah began preparations for the party. Erica joined in to help Anne fastidiously wiping dust from the kitchen surfaces. As the afternoon began to fade, Deborah automatically flicked the switch near the door which would have turned on the fluorescent ceiling lights.

"Shit! I had forgotten about that." The small power station two hundred yards away remained silent, a monument to way of life long passed in experience if not years at St Kilda.

Sally paid little attention to the party preparations. She had seen plenty of parties in Cottage One and had first-hand experience of the medical consequences. Perhaps it had been the remoteness, or being away from constraints of Hebridean family life, but many men and quite a few of the women had indulged in behavior the memories of which could be revisited to impress or embarrass in equal measure. One thing there was no shortage of was drink. The two stalkers had brought a case of Speyside malt with them and the contents of store room of the old Puff-Inn would go a long way toward a good evening or two. The lack of electricity was an inconvenience but not one to stop the party happening. The diesel filled kerosene lamps gave passable illumination and the flickering light from the glass fronted wood stove would just add to the ambience of the evening. They all mucked in to prepare food in the Manse and carry it up to the Cottage.

"Just keep it out of reach of the mice," warned Erica. "Rats don't you mean", quipped Gavin. Erica reminded the stalkers that there were no rats at St Kilda, the Trust having enforced stringent bio-security measures to prevent vermin of any sort coming ashore. The Russian amphibious vehicle bringing Erica's thatching straw had been the first of such craft to land unsupervised in many years. The *Beluga,* now tied up at the jetty would have had to moor in the bay in the past for even the cleanest of vessels could not be guaranteed rat free. Anne had explained many times how ground nesting seabirds would be decimated by rats taking their eggs and chicks. Not even the nests of fearsome Great Skuas would be exempt from rodent predation although the adults would make short work of consuming any rat they actually came across. Anne had heard of Greater Black-backed Gulls catching rabbits on the island of Lundy so for the larger Great Skua, catching a rat or two would not be a problem. As for Don and Lachie, they joked that no sea-rats would be coming to the party. They were tired after a long day bringing the stalkers over. They had also been hard at it preparing the boat two hours before Sean and Gavin turned up that morning. If it was alright with everyone they would have an early night, sleeping on board. Deborah and Erica worked hard to get everything ready in Cottage One. By the time evening had fallen, Hurricane lamps had been lit and the woodstove was burning cheerily in the hearth. Candles had been arranged on the trestle tables and a few old Christmas tinsel decorations had been brought down from a box found in the cottage loft. Sally remarked that apart from the smell of diesel it was just like the old days of conservation work parties. By the time the rest of the family and the two stalkers arrived two large pots simmered on top of the woodstove. It had been Dave's suggestion to put the freshly shot Soay to good use and the mutton stew smelt delicious. Sean had professionally skinned and butchered the carcass, putting his deer larder skills to good use on this considerably smaller beast. He thought it a pity there was no dog around to take care of the offal. If he lived there, a good dog would be priority number one.

As he approached the cottages, Dave savored the smell of wood smoke in the air. Just seeing the blue-grey smoke issuing from one chimney gave the village a sign of life, a promise for the future. Ducking his head as he entered the cottage, he was struck how homely it appeared. The women had made a real effort. Erica was in a good mood and welcomed her father. "Hi, Dad! Your Soay proved useful in the end. May it be the first of many to end up in the pot, eh?" Dave felt prompted for a biblical reference. "Well if Job had fourteen thousand sheep to contend with, I am sure I can manage the two thousand plaguing these islands. Just think, Job 42:12, he considered himself blessed to have that huge flock. I would consider myself cursed!" Winking at his daughters he continued, "Perhaps I should let them have free reign to reproduce and also claim my six thousand camels, one thousand oxen and a thousand she asses – not just the paltry few I see before me!"

"Moving swiftly on, Dave……" Deborah was pleased to see that despite biblical referencing, her dour husband seemed to be getting into party mood. Music was going to be a problem though. The old Sony ghetto-blaster Sally used still stood on a corner shelf where it had been abandoned by its previous owner. Heavy items often got left behind, considered more trouble than they were worth to pack into limited rucksack space. Rummaging in nearby drawers produced a treasure trove of assorted batteries. Many were useless, well past their expiry date but as luck would have it, eight useable size 'D' batteries were put into service and the old Sony came to life. CDs were going to be a problem but Dan came to the rescue. He spent much of his time on the island in a world of his own. Through his earphones digital music stored on his phone generated a filter through which the reality of life could be toned-down. Dan offered to connect his phone to the Sony MD socket in return for taking charge of the play list. Dave sat by the woodstove occupying himself with keeping the open room warm and stirring the mutton stew simmering on top. Across the room Deborah and Erica finalized the food preparations. Sally entered the cottage and produced an unopened bottle of Botanical Gin produced by a small Hebridean distillery, so she claimed.

"I've been waiting for an occasion to get this bottle out. Why don't you join me, Dave?" Sitting down next to him she produced a couple of shot glasses from her bag and offered one to him. Dave studied her warily.

"And be not drunk with wine, wherein is excess; but be filled with the Spirit, (Ephesians 5: 18)"

Sally was momentarily surprised that her small gesture would provoke a biblical response. "Dave – I am sure a little of my spirit would do you the world of good. Might even make you see this island in a lighter vein rather than a source of torment for you!" With a little trepidation Dave accepted a shot of gin and Sally passed two more filled glasses to Deborah and Erica. "Cheers, all – here's to a new and better life for us all out here, *Slàinte mhath!*"

"*Dheagh shlàinte*! We've arrived at the right time, I see." Sally spun round to see Sean and Gavin ducking through the doorway, both carrying bottles of Speyside Malt. Anne came in with them and, if Sally's medical observation was correct, appeared slightly tipsy already. Dan looked up from his phone where he was putting the final touches to the party playlist. "Anne? Don't tell me you've finally become human at last!" Gavin assured the others that Anne was absolutely fine. "Don't worry, she took some water with it." He went on to explain Anne had been explaining the layout of the island to them before they set off in the morning. Anne collapsed in a fit of giggles, sitting down heavily on the trestle bench beside the table. Brushing her thick loose hair back away from her face she retorted, "Well, if Jesus could turn water to wine, that's just fine by me..." No more giggles this time but a glance at her father cautioned him against any rebuke. Dave recognized the challenge but decided not to rise to it, considering he was beginning to enjoy the effect of the botanical gin himself.

"Ecclesiastes 9: 7 – *Go thy way, eat thy bread with joy, and drink thy wine with a merry heart; for God now accepteth thy works.*"

Erica considered Dave's biblical justification sealed the matter.

"Amen, Dad. Now can we get on with the party? Tonight we are going to enjoy ourselves."

Her experience working at the Fir Cone back in Edinburgh's Old Town reminded her, "I had better put a jug of water on the table too considering all the booze we seem to have acquired tonight." Erica took a jug over to the tap above the sink and turned it on. Water gushed out into the jug only for the flow to suddenly slow to a trickle as small pieces of skin and fur, followed by mouse bones, dropped into the container. "Yuk! That's really gross. Hey, Anne! Be an angel and take this jug out to the well and get us some clean water, please."

Anne took the jug outside and walked to village well a short distance behind the cottages. There was just enough light to see by if she took full advantage of her peripheral vision. Looking straight in front wasn't the best strategy in such low light, she remembered that from her Outward Bound training as a teenager, and took pride in rarely using a flashlight unless it was pitch black. Approaching the well she slipped and fell heavily among the Mothan plants growing around the stone rim. Luckily the catering grade glass jug survived the impact with the damp ground but Anne was not so lucky and would have a serious bruise on her thigh to show where she fell against protruding granite stonework. Wincing she lowered the jug into the overflowing well. Carrying the heavy, filled water jug back to the cottage she took great care not to slip again and was feeling slightly nauseous with shock by the time she was back inside the warm kitchen.

Deborah noticed how pale Anne was looking. "Goodness, girl. You look like you've seen a ghost. Whatever happened out there?" Crushed small purple flowers stuck to the right leg of her jeans where Anne rubbed her bruise. "Leave it alone, Mum. I just slipped and fell heavily. I'm OK, honest." Anne had taken a number of falls lately as a result of her insistence on exploring the more inaccessible parts of the island. She had taken care not to let anyone see the bruises or how she had treated them with a Mothan poultice.

The two stalkers accepted glasses of Sally's gin and took the places offered at the long table. Erica and Anne joined Sally on the bench against the wall opposite the stalkers. Dan had finished setting up the playlist and his musical choice made a positive contribution to the atmosphere as Dave placed two large pans of stew and rice on the table. "Fresh vegetables are in short supply I'm afraid but if these two gentlemen do their job properly we should be in luck next year."

There was no wine at the meal but gin and well water made a palatable alternative. GNT Sally called it. "Gin and non-tonic water! I see we have Water of Life, *Uisge Beatha* for later." Sally's taste for alcohol was no secret at all that night. With the meal consumed plates and pans were put to one side as Sean produced his malt. Gavin had brought a second bottle from a different small distillery and Dan joined in the occasion by producing a flask of his 'special brew' concocted weeks earlier for 'communion' purposes. He had thought the evening an apt moment to test its efficacy. The fumes from the diesel fueled oil lamps were not adding to the occasion so Sean suggested they might prefer a better smell in the cottage. From the inside pocket of his wax jacket he produced a plastic bag. "Best grass in the Hebrides, so Dan and Lachie tell me. I got it off them on the way over. They swear by it as a preventative against sea-sickness and they should know. Strong stuff, mind, Gavin." It became clear that Gavin's queasiness on landing at St Kilda had been more than straight forward sea-sickness. "You don't mind, do you?" Sean enquired. Dave held his hands up in supplication, he has already feeling mellow from Sally's gin. Sharing a spliff and a dram of malt wouldn't make him worse in the eyes of God or anyone else for that matter and it was reputed to be good for back troubles, which he certainly knew much about at the moment. "Bring it on, boys!"

Deborah wasn't sure what to make of Dave's unexpected change to student party mode but it would be a damn sight easier to cope with his hangovers than his evangelizing. Erica was relaxing into the evening taking long tokes on the spliff as it passed round the table. Only Anne abstained, explaining that having to walk over the hill most days of the week, she needed to keep her lungs in good order. She would stick with whisky and water. Dan had never seen the Williams let their hair down like this and was interested to see how the evening would pan out. The spliff was passed round the table a couple of more times, the laughter increasing as it went, it seemed months of tension was being released that evening. They should have visitors like this more often, thought Deborah when a series of piercing bleeps shattered the ambience.

"What the fuck!" The shriek of a battery powered smoke detector drowned out Dan's carefully selected playlist. "Jesus fucking Christ, let me get the battery out of that thing!" Dan rose unsteadily to his feet to stand on his chair before unscrewing the cover of the smoke detector. It was stiff and when the cover finally shifted Dan slipped and fell from the chair striking his head on the corner of the table, upsetting glasses and ashtrays. Luckily Anne was sober enough to catch the whisky bottle as it rolled towards her. "You've saved the day, girl. Well caught!" Sean had sobered enough to show his appreciation though Gavin was by now pretty stoned and could only grunt his thanks for saving the bottle. Dan dragged himself painfully to his feet and sat down again. Shards of glass littered the floor where his glass had smashed. The cover of the smoke detector lay among the debris and, as if to make a point, the ceiling alarm emitted another series of loud bleeps.

"I'll deal with that, being as you lot are so incapable." Anne set the chair back upright and stood on it to successfully remove the battery. There was a fair bruise building on Dan's left temple. "Could you have a look at that for Dan, Sally?" Deborah turned to Sally who hesitated before replying. "Sorry, Debs, but I can't see too clearly at the moment. Bit too much self–medication tonight already and I wouldn't want to make a mistake." Sally at least had the professionalism to admit she was in no fit state to treat anyone that night. Deborah decided she needed to take charge of the situation.

"Anne – I've watched you treating the bruises on your arm where you fell. Seemed to have healed pretty quickly. Could you give me some of that ointment and I'll attend to Dan." Anne was annoyed that her mother had noticed the homemade poultice she used on her bruises. There wasn't much either women didn't notice about each other. "OK, I'll go and get it and be back in a few minutes." Anne returned shortly afterwards with a small plastic soap bag containing raw sheep wool soaked in the mix she had prepared to treat her own bruises. Deborah dabbed the poultice of lanolin and Mothan onto Dan's temples. He began to snivel like a small boy. "Come on Dan, I am," she hissed with emphasis, "not your bloody mother!" Dan clung to Deborah for a moment longer than necessary before she extricated herself, silently scorning his weakness.

"Now can we have some livelier music please, Dan....and let's get on with the party."

Dave had noticed the way Dan had clung to Deborah, it hadn't seemed appropriate. After all Dan had only banged his head, it wasn't that much of a big deal. Sally and Erica were relaxing again. They had found some fresh glasses and Sean poured the two women another dram while Gavin cleared up the broken glass and spilt ashtrays. The party atmosphere returned but Dave sat quietly next to the wood stove, lost in thought after seeing Dan's pathetic behavior with his wife. What was going on? His train of thought was interrupted by Anne reminding him the fire had nearly gone out. Focusing on the imminent matter of the woodstove, he forgot about the Dan incident and placed more broken pallet wood in the stove and waited for it to catch. The fire in the stove quickly flared again and with lively music from the old Sony, Erica suggested they got up and danced. Dan groaned but with encouragement from Anne, agreed to join in. Tables and chairs were pushed to one side to make space for dancing. "This sounds interesting Erica, what had you in mind?"

Deborah was intrigued while Dave excused himself citing his bad back as an excuse not to dance. "Back I Edinburgh, I was taught the Black-House Reel. A bit like set dancing but it is really just one tight set in a close star formation. It's great fun, I'll teach you! Apparently designed for dancing in the confined space of a blackhouse, or so I was told."

With Dave siting by the wood stove watching the proceedings, Erica led the dance. The five women and three men turned eight steps to the left, eight steps to the right turning and whirling till they were all giddy with laughter. Deborah was practically carrying Dan through the dance and Anne couldn't help but notice how close Sean and Gavin held Erica and Sally when the music stopped. Being the odd number, Anne sat down beside her father to wait out the next dance, some kind of techno-waltz from Dan's phone issued through the old Sony's speakers. "Yeah, let's get down to it…" there was no mistaking Erica's uninhibited intention toward Sean. Sally meanwhile was leading Gavin to the far side of the room, hanging onto his shoulder and audibly whispering into his ear.

"No need for either of us to be alone tonight, is there?" Though embarrassed, Gavin had to agree that a night with Sally, however drunk they both were, was a better prospect than listing to Sean snoring from the next bed in the cottage next door. Sean and Erica were going through some serious grooves while Deborah clapped encouragement to the beat of the music. As a mother she was more than pleased to see her family enjoying themselves like this for the first time since they had left Edinburgh. As a woman though, seeing Erica flirting outrageously with Sean and Sally practically devouring Gavin, she was beginning to feel very jealous. There was no way she could let on there had been anything between her and Dan in the present company, though Dan didn't look like he would be capable of anything tonight, stoned out of his skull with a lump on his forehead the size of a hen's egg. As for her husband, she just wasn't interested.

Anne did feel empathy with her father regardless. He had

come through so much only have his dreams dashed by a bad back and hungry sheep when his dogged attempts to feed his family from the land should have worked out. Lost in thought and rubbing her bruised leg she was unprepared for her father's outburst.

"1 Corinthians 7:9, 10 *Know ye not that the unrighteous shall not inherit the kingdom of God? Be not deceived: neither fornicators, nor idolaters, nor adulterers, nor effeminate, nor abusers of themselves with mankind,*

Nor thieves, nor covetous, nor drunkards, nor revilers, nor extortioners, shall inherit the kingdom of God!'

"Dave, for God's sake that's enough. If you don't like this party then go home. We'll speak about this tomorrow when you are sober!" Deborah's temper was up. She was simply not prepared to let her husband's religious mania ruin what had been, until that moment, a pretty good evening. Dave felt ashamed of his words but even through his inebriation recognized an internal battle was taking place. He had tried to relax and enjoy the evening but the combination of alcohol and cannabis had unleashed conflicting demons in him. Knowing the best thing for all would be for him to leave, he drank a glass of water before making his way back to the Manse and his bed alternately trying to dispel and accept his drunkenness.

Back in Cottage One, Deborah apologized for her husband's outburst. "Don't worry, let him be. He'll be full of remorse after he's slept it off." Sally was pragmatic; she had witnessed alcohol induced outbursts many times before. She began recounting tales of St Kilda during military occupation. Great times when the Puff-Inn would serve until dawn on summer nights, and sometimes beyond. With such short summer nights the parties would easily run over into the following day.

Under privatization, the ex-military drinking culture of St Kilda was not condoned and the early morning swimming accident had rung the changes. With hindsight she admitted, the accident could have initiated the process leading to the military's evacuation of the island. It was shortly after the new borehole had been dug in An Lag to improve water supplies for the new accommodation block that the accident had happened. She once again recounted the accident when a young serviceman had fallen from the sea-defense wall onto rocks 30 feet below. Many had blamed the young student girls swimming naked for luring him to the edge and he had been very lucky to have survived the fall. Multiple injuries had made it unlikely he would work again, certainly not at St Kilda. "Alcohol was investigated as the possible cause of the accident but when his blood sample was analyzed, it was found to contain high levels of Phenylpropanoid glycosides."

Her listeners had no idea of the medical implication so Sally continued the modern St Kilda tale. "His blood contained high levels of, a plant derived, water soluble bactericide. He certainly wouldn't have become infected from his wounds that was for certain. It was a real mystery but I came to realize I had treated no-one for bacterial infections since that new borehole had been operational. So I went up to An Lag to have a look and see if there was anything unusual going on. With the old well lower down the slope, there was always the risk of dead sheep or their remains getting into the water supply. It was treated, of course, but far from ideal. Now it seemed the water from the new borehole was dosed with a naturally occurring anti-biotic, but from where? It was a while before the penny dropped, all around the new borehole, the damp ground was covered in blue flowered Butterwort, the Gaelic Mothan plant used for all manner of Hebridean cures. I think Dan has already mentioned this but Mothan was also used to induce visions when placed under your pillow before sleeping. It transpires the active glycoside ingredient is readily absorbed by alcohol. So drinking St Kilda water with your whisky would prevent all manner of bacterial disease as well as reducing your likelihood of hangover. You could argue it was actually good for you! So when a couple of girls go skinny-dipping and a voyeur gets so exited he walks off the top of a wall I was curious. He hadn't even taken his shoes off, just stepped out into thin air above the beach, expecting to walk on water I suppose! He must have been hallucinating. The mystery is the reaction between anti-biotic Mothan and alcohol. The glycoside mixes readily but does it enhance or reduce the effect of alcohol, or *vice versa*?"

At this point, Dan who had been listening intently, offered his opinion. "Based on my recent experience, the effects of alcohol on the human mind is much enhanced by a Mothan mixer. You could be right that it is the other way round though. Try a swig of this and you'll understand!" Dan passed round his hip flask containing vodka infused with fresh leaves of Mothan. "Picked myself just a couple of days ago from the very spot Sally was talking about." Sean was not entirely convinced. "So what you're saying is that if we drink some of your hooch, it's going to blow our minds then Dan!" Sean laughed and took a deep swig from the flask. "Here, try some of this Gavin. It'll make a man of you, my boy." Gavin declined, saying he had plenty enough whisky already on top of the smoke. Spinning beds later on wasn't his idea of fun anymore. Especially as at the end of this evening he felt it was highly likely he would be in Sally's bed and didn't want to embarrass himself more than was inevitable under the circumstances. "Ach well. All the more for us then, eh Danny boy."

Dan wasn't too keen on the boy epithet, but grinned sheepishly at the attention he was pleased to receive from the stalkers. Dan wasn't the only one at the table pleased to receive attention from Sean and Gavin. Deborah had positioned herself on the bench close to Sean and across from Dan. It was as if she wanted Dan to play with the idea that she thought Sean was more of a man than he ever could be. Nothing was said but the body language was fully understood and did nothing to help Dan's feelings of low self-esteem. Sean however seemed to have fixed his attention on Erica who having declined the Mothan laced flask was now sitting looking pretty stoned in the corner at the far side of the woodstove. "You know something, Erica? You'd be quite passable with a bit of makeup, not too much mind. Not like my missus who slaps it on with a trowel!" Erica collected her thoughts before responding. "Does it ever occur to you to ask yourself why she slaps it on with a trowel, Sean? Could it be that living with you is just a little bit too much? Could it be that she slaps makeup on, with a trowel, to avoid facing up to the mistake of having married a prat like you?" Erica's words were measured to hit home. Though stoned her caustic response was drawn from experience of dealing with sexist remarks in the bars of Edinburgh. Not visibly chastened, Sean continued. Hitting back he remarked on the primitive facilities of her cherished blackhouse. "Jesus, Erica. How can you live in that place? Even this cottage is better than your blackhouse. It has a decent roof for a start, a proper kitchen and fridge and so on, if the electric worked I will admit. Ha, you'll never get a man if he hasn't got a fridge to keep his beer in, eh Gavin?" Gavin squirmed uncomfortably at being dragged into this conversation which he could sense was straying beyond banter and into the danger zone. "Dunno Sean, mate. Why don't we change the subject?" Sean was beginning to feel annoyed at Gavin's lack of support. "No, why should I? Our Erica here thinks she's lady muck in her little place up the end of the village. In fact she's putting the clock back, blocking progress is what I say. She's even got rats in there, disgusting! If she had her way, we would all go back to run-rig."

Erica looked puzzled at the remark but Anne enlightened the group around the table. "We are not talking about a Skye rock band, Erica. Run-rig was a feudal system of highland agriculture, a system of living really. Each family would be allocated a patch of land to husband for three years before moving onto another patch. That way the good was shared with the bad. Three years you'd have good land while your neighbor farmed a rough patch. Then you'd all move on to the next plot. Same thing happened here at St Kilda where run-rig included the bird cliffs. It was a way the landlord made sure his tenants had an equal share of the land and produce." Now Gavin was happier to join the banter. "Sounds like musical chairs. When the piper stops you move to a different field or something like that?" He would stay away from sexist comments he could tell the four women around the table were beginning to resent. Not so Sean.

"Run-rig should be brought up to date, I reckon. Out here at St Kilda, it's just what we need. Don't think Dave's up to it. Not tonight anyway and Dan, I don't reckon you are either with the amount of weed you've smoked." Deborah could sense something provocative was coming. "Come to the point, Sean." She wanted to tease it out of him rather than let Sean claim all the credit for risqué entertainment that evening.

Sean drank some water before, as Deborah had asked, making his point "As I see it, there are two functional men in this room and four of you ladies in need of a bit of husbanding. It wouldn't be fair not to share our affections while we are here, would it Gavin? We should reinstate run-rig while we are here and husband you four one night at a time. Not a bad idea if you ask me?" He then drank from his whisky glass. Deborah couldn't suppress her smirk but dare not show it in front of her daughters. "So it's St Kilda for swingers now, is it?" Sally saw the funny side but when Sean said he would start by sleeping with Erica that night, she exploded. "Just who the fucking hell do you think you are, coming here with your guns and arrogance. Thought you get an easy shag did you, well think again. Why don't you just get on that Argocat of yours and piss off back where you came from!" Erica got up and stomped out of the cottage and back to her blackhouse where she locked the door and lay on her futon crib crying tears of anger. Outside the wind rose and swirled around her home, blowing back down the stove pipe reigniting embers and sending puffs of smoke into the open space of her blackhouse.

Back in Cottage One, Sean had had enough. "Oh, to hell with this. Sorry if I caused offence but think I need to get out for some fresh air. Must be that bloody Mothan vodka of Dan's." Sean went outside and a few minutes later, those remaining at the table heard the engine of the Argocat start up and head away from the village. Sally knew the only route he could take was up the hill toward the top of the island. She said the steep hairpin bends were no place for drunk driving. It hadn't been that long ago, after the terrorist attack she reminded them, when a fatal Landrover accident claimed the life of the heavy drinking Base Supervisor. Gavin too was concerned about Sean taking the Argocat out so late. "What was that about a fatal accident, Sally?" She recounted the tale of the night of the accident, she loved telling tales to anyone who would listen and Gavin wanted to know more, having no detailed knowledge of events leading up to the departure of the military. "Well, about a year before the military left we had a terrorist attack. Yes even here at St Kilda we were not immune from world events. A bunch of self-styled jihadists from the mainland thought, quite rightly, our radar installations were an easy target, though in strategic terms it was nothing more than a nuisance attack. They chose a Saturday night when everyone would be in the Puff-Inn and they landed in Glen Bay, walked up to the top of the hill, laid their charges, and before you could say A*llah hu akbar* all our radar and comms equipment was lying in a tangled heap. No one was hurt in the attack but as far as the MOD was concerned it was the last straw. They would invest no more money in St Kilda if we were so lax about our own security. There was one later casualty of the attack though. The Base Supervisor heard the explosions from his room. Though having consumed best part of a bottle of whisky that evening, he was on duty and felt he ought to go and find out what was going on. He drove up the hill, saw the carnage and drove down, forgetting to put the Landrover back into low ratio. He lost control at the bend just above the quarry and rolled it over the edge. He was found in the morning and the Bonxies had already started on him. Apparently his face was not a pretty sight when he was dragged from the overturned vehicle." Gavin looked pale. "Well, all I can say is Sean is the best off-road driver I have worked with yet. Fingers crossed he'll be OK."

"Moving away from terrorism," Gavin changed the subject. "One thing that does concern me is the way these sheep are allowed to overpopulate and then die off without any management." Gavin was a part-time sheep farmer. His wife looked after their small flock while he was away but they would never be allowed to starve as these Soays were. If he couldn't feed his sheep for whatever reason, they would be slaughtered and put in the freezer. As far as he was concerned it was the only right thing to do. Anne, who up to that point had been thinking of calling it a night, looked almost as incensed as her sister had been over the sexist remarks from Sean. "You don't know what you are talking about, Gavin. Let me fill you in so you get the facts straight! Firstly, the Soays here are wild animals. They are not livestock and the only time we intervene is if we see one seriously injured and put it down, humanely. The sheep are part of the island ecosystem and the carcasses are a valuable nutrient source for scavenging sea birds, the St Kilda Field Mouse and a host of interesting detritivores. The situation here is virtually unique in the world – where else could students come and study a totally closed flock ecosystem like we have here? They are not farm animals, Gavin. They are a wild population and a valuable scientific study resource. Secondly, overriding any criticism aimed at us, we have a Government license to use these wild sheep for research and education purposes. Is that enough for you?" Gavin considered his reply carefully. "That's all very well, Anne, but don't you feel any concern when you see them dying before your eyes after they run out of winter grazing? There isn't a predator here for God's sake. A wolf or two would at least bring them a quick death rather than lingering suffering for the old and sick ones." Anne tried to convince him, "But Gavin, can't you understand? The pathogens and parasites are predators, even the island weather systems. When the winter gales blow, it's another form of predation." He could not accept her argument. "Anne, all I can say is that whether scientific study objects or farm animals, these sheep are sentient beings and need to be treated with respect." Anne could barely hide her contempt. "Hmmph! So you treat the Red deer in the Cairngorms with respect do you? Drive them from the shelter of the forest into the open snow where you shoot them down. Even allow wealthy gun-nuts to make a botch of the job too, so I heard from Sean."

Gavin realized that, with Anne, he never going to make a convincing argument. He had to accept they were both right and they were both wrong and was relieved to hear the Argocat coming back. The sound of the Kohler diesel motor could be heard approaching down the street, technically off-road. Anne was preparing to give Sean a piece of mind about ground damage to the fragile island soil ecology but changed her mind when she saw the color of his face. Deborah had known better than to intervene when Anne was lecturing Gavin on the Soay sheep. Sally was sleepy and was quietly waiting for the evening to come to a natural close but the women were all startled by Sean's appearance as he came through the door. "Sean, what's happened? Is everything alright?'

Deborah was genuinely concerned. His face the color of ash, Sean turned to Gavin. "I have never been so scared, Gavin. You know man, I went for a blast on the Cat to clear my head. There's something about this place. It's doing my head in. I gunned it up to the top of the hill, stayed on the road all the way, then switched the motor off and just listened to the silence. Not a gust of wind anywhere. I could hear the munching of sheep from a hundred yards, it was that quiet. I had a smoke before deciding to come back and not be such a party pooper. It was on the way down that it happened. The hairpins on that road are awesome, bloody awesome. Thankfully there are crash barriers or I wouldn't be here now. I'm not kidding you but as I approached the first hairpin, a fucking huge white owl flew up out of the rocks and then a blast of wind hit me out of nowhere and if it hadn't been for the barriers I'd have gone over the edge. I tell you, there wasn't a breath of wind up there. The owl must have known what was coming. That crash barrier is battered, man. I'm certainly not the first one to have been blown against it, that's for sure." Sally spoke for the first time since listening to Anne rebuking Gavin. "Sean, that spot on Mullach Geal is infamous. If you had been there in the daylight you'd have seen the deep wheel ruts in the moor where even the heaviest of vehicles have been forced off road. We had a mobile crane up there to help clear up the mess from the terrorist attack. Fourteen tons it weighed, even that machine was nearly blown over on the way back down. It took a large tractor and a bulldozer to pull it back onto the road. It was a really close thing, I can tell you. You probably heard about the light plane crash recently? That was hit by a blast of wind over the same part of the saddle at Mullach Geal."

Sally recounted some history of the flat peatland above Glen Mór. "As I expect you know, St Kildans were a superstitious lot and while nominally Christian, like many

Hebridean communities they held to pagan practices where it suited them. The winds at the top of Glen Mór are infamous and they built a small temple to the seasons to appease whatever deity it was that manifested through these inexplicable blasts of wind. When the Army built the road in the late 1950s they just bulldozed the remains of the small temple out of the way without realizing its significance. The women of St Kilda passed it every day to tend the cattle in Glen Mór as the menfolk had so many bad experiences down there. The old settlement near the foot of the glen is known as the Amazon's House. Named after a mythical female warrior who would ride out with her hounds across the Hebrides, a Phantom Queen, so the story goes. It has to a very ancient tale as there hasn't been a land bridge between St Kilda and the Long Island since the last ice-age, 10,000 years ago." Sean was impatient, "Yes, but what's that got to do with me nearly being blown off the road and all the dents in the crash barrier?" he asked. "The dents are where the mobile crane was blown against the barrier, it was put there for a reason, you know. Must have been some wind to blow fourteen tons off the road. When it's light tomorrow, you two will be out planning the cull but while you are up there take a look across to the southern side of Glen Mór, it looks like a scrap yard in places. It's where a Sunderland Flying Boat came down on a training flight in WW2. Apparently they were on a low flying training mission and the lumbering old plane came up the glen and suddenly got slammed into the ground. The crew were all killed. It was a queer thing but you can still find any number of spent machine gun cartridges lying in a rough line along the burn running down the glen. It makes you think the rear gunner was firing at something as they flew by." Listening to Sally's account, Sean was regaining his composure. "Culling bloody sheep, I expect!" he gratefully accepted the large malt Gavin poured for him. "There really was no explanation for that plane crash, or the other two out here that we know about."

Sally continued to explain about the mysterious plane wrecks at St Kilda. During the war a Bristol Beaufighter had hit the slopes of Conachair. Just its propellers remained stuck in the moor as a reminder of the awful event. The main body of the aircraft disappeared over the cliff to lie submerged beneath the highest sea cliff in the British Isles. The third crash was thought to be of a Wellington Bomber on the slopes of Soay, opposite the mouth of Glen Bay and just a stone's throw, or a wind blast, from the Amazon's House. "I say thought to be a Wellington, because no-one really knows. You can see some airframe and a propeller near Taigh Duggan, itself a haunted enough spot on the island of Soay. Nobody has done any serious research but a Wellington did go missing on a training flight around about the time. The land is slipping just below the wreckage and it won't be long before that too is lost under the waters of the Atlantic. After the accident, the MOD tried to break up and bury the Sunderland to prevent sight-seeing planes coming to the same fate. The military took the threat from these inexplicable gusts of wind very seriously. They didn't want any more servicemen lost this way." Sean was thoughtful, "But the wreckage is still in the Glen though?" Sally continued, "Yes, Sean, but it's being gradually blown piece by piece down toward Glen Bay and the heavier bits washed down by the burn in spate. Sooner or later it will all be out of sight beneath the water and no trace of servicemen left in Glen Mór, or on Soay for that matter." Anne was interested in the light plane crash just as they arrived at St Kilda.

"Yes Anne, that crash fits the picture too. A group of men on a hunting trip were flying low up the glen when the wind knocked their plane into the ground. Just one survivor and the wreck of the small aircraft was quickly blown over the cliff. Creepy really how these accidents all fit a similar pattern. Male casualties and their machines blown into the sea or soon after ending up there."

"One last question, Sally." Deborah was curious about the reference to Taigh Duggan, near the site of the Wellington bomber crash. "It's another St Kilda story from the medieval period. Two robbers were caught thieving from the village after setting the Church on fire with most of the population sheltering inside. One was named Duggan and the other Stallar and as punishment the pair were banished to the outlying islands. Their simple bothies remain to this day. Taigh Duggan, or Duggan's House, on Soay and Taigh Stallar on Boreray. They were exiled from friends and family and would have slowly gone mad with loneliness in clear sight of their former homes." Anne was curious about anything to do with Glen Mór, feeling more at home there than anywhere else on the island. "So the Amazon's House would be Taigh Amazon?" Sally thought about the question. "No, I don't think so. Amazon's House is a name imposed by Victorian tourists on an obviously ancient site. The dwellings down there are from a much earlier period than even the medieval blackhouse above this village. If it is to be properly named, I would call it Taigh Cailleach, the home of the Gaelic female deity who ages with the seasons to be reborn each Spring as Brighid or Bridie to anglicize her. The patriarchs could only deal with her as the old crone for they knew they could have no power over the lusty Brighid. She symbolizes the cycles of annual renewal and decay in the Gaelic year. It is interesting that the survivors of the Church fire were female and had hidden in the Cailleach's Cave below Ruaival when the trouble started. Only the men were daft enough to place their trust in God!"

Sally thought it apt to take the legend forward and into uncharted territory. "I have a personal theory about this event. At least those women had minds of their own and survived but there must have been more to it. The Temple of the Seasons that used to stand at the top of Glen Mór. That must have been built there in reverence to the Cailleach. No wonder she is pissed off with men and their infernal machines! There is another possibility concerning the Phantom Queen. Ever heard of The Hounds of the Morrigan?"

Deborah spoke, "What, Kate Bush? I have always liked that song."

Sally continued, "No, Deborah. There is a mythical Gaelic female warrior Morrigan who could take the shape of a cow, a wolf or an eel. Kind of a Hebridean Valkyrie by all accounts." Deborah was beginning to think she had heard enough. "Oh, come now, Sally. You'll be giving us all nightmares. Let's just be thankful Sean wasn't hurt tonight and bring the evening to an end. Don't know about you, but I need my bed." Deborah was tired and as host took responsibility for drawing things to a close. She said she would tidy up in the morning and got up to close down the woodstove for the night. Dan was snoring lightly in the chair beside it. "Come on sleepy head, time for bed."

Dan awoke blearily before staggering to his feet to walk back to the Featherstore. "It's in a straight line, he'll be OK," quipped Anne. Sean and Gavin made their way next door to Cottage 2 one of the dormitories used by conservation volunteers in the past. Deborah and Anne blew out the oil lamps, closed the door behind them and made their way back to the Manse. Sally followed close behind glancing back toward Cottage 2. She would sleep alone as usual that night. She wished the other two goodnight as they passed the Factor's House.

"That Sally can sure tell a yarn, can't she?" Deborah turned to her youngest daughter. "Yes, she certainly can, Mom." Deborah never noticed the glint in Anne's eyes as she thought about all that Sally had related about Glen Mór that evening.

The following morning, Sean and Gavin were up early to begin their recce of the island. They needed to watch the habits of the sheep before deciding on the safest places to use as killing ground. They wanted to make sure that when the shooting began, there would be no stray bullet or ricochet endangering the village. Deborah looked out from the kitchen window across the bay toward Ruiaval. The morning light highlighted not only the old lazy-bed cultivation lines on Dun but also picked out relief on the headland. It came as a surprise to her to see the outline of an old woman reclining, gazing out to sea. Gazing out to the south, the Cailleach of Ruiaval appeared to be waiting for Spring to return and invigorate her youth. Deborah wondered why on earth she had never noticed the figure in the landscape before, it or she was certainly big enough.

There was no sign of Dan, nor would there likely to be until early afternoon. He was never an early riser and after a heavy night any appearance before mid-afternoon would be surprising. Anne had taken herself off with binoculars and notebook as usual and smoke could be seen coming from Erica's blackhouse stove-pipe. Sally would no doubt be busying herself in the Factor's House, she always had something to do when Deborah wanted a woman to woman conversation about some personal matter. Dave was her worry that morning. He had been fast asleep in bed when Deborah returned after the party but now was nowhere to be seen. She hadn't even noticed him get up, being sound asleep herself. Dave had got up early, still full of remorse for his outburst the previous evening and walked up to the Gap to watch the sun rise over Boreray. He hadn't exactly got a hangover, he had made sure of drinking plenty of water before going to sleep, but everything around him felt unreal as if he wasn't really there. Though he knew Boreray was four miles away to the northeast, the Gannets swirling around the Stacs looked almost close enough to touch. Angels he thought, like Angels, and reached out toward them. It was only the imperious bleating of a lamb trying to summon its unconcerned mother that broke his vision before it could fully develop. The ripples of his hallucination spread to dissipate on the jagged rocks over 300 feet below him. Dave quickly stepped back from the cliff edge and retched. Had he really been thinking of walking over to join Angels on Boreray? He remembered reading of the nine men and boys marooned there on a fowling expedition. They had encountered the last Great Auk in the British Isles, possibly the world. Convinced that the penguin sized bird was a witch they had stoned her to death. He began to cry, "What is wrong with this place? Why such morbid visions, is it heaven or hell I see around me?" He heard another voice behind him. "Dave! There you are. I've been looking for you everywhere."

Deborah had been concerned enough to start looking for her husband. Luckily she hadn't got much further than the Factor's House when, through her binoculars, she could see him standing at the Gap. Standing on the cliff edge above An Lag, she thought him reminiscent of Casper David Friedrich's painting of the Monk by the Sea. The lonely figure, standing diminutive before the power of nature. She quickly made her way up to join him. "Come on, Mr. Monk. Time for breakfast!" Linking her arm through his, she felt a tender warmth toward him. Something neither had expressed for each other in many weeks. A few minutes later they were back in the village. Erica and Sally stood chatting over a cup of coffee outside the Factor's House, discussing the previous evening's events.

"Did you just hear the sexist remarks, Sally? It's a wonder I stayed in that room as long as I did." She nodded, "I did, Erica, and that wasn't the end of it. Anne had a spat with Gavin over the sheep later on. They really had their horns locked. Animal welfare versus ecology. Gavin reckoned it was a kindness to shoot them when the grazing got low while Anne was adamant they should be left to die and rot in the interests of the mice and beetles. Well I guess there will be a lot dying over the next few days so they'll all be happy, including the mice and beetles." Erica shook her head. "Not me, Sally. I won't be happy till those sexist bastards leave our island." Gavin, Erica stated, was as much a sexist as Sean in spite of his protesting animal welfare. They were two male imposters come to disrupt their renascent island community. Her father was OK, if getting more eccentric by the day and Dan really didn't count. He would be off at the earliest opportunity, back to Edinburgh where his bullshit would see him through. There was, she added, simply no room for male bullshit at St Kilda. Dave, who had until that moment been lost in his thoughts, commented on what he had just heard.

"Don't be too harsh on them, Erica. You know it's really hard to resist the landscape. Hard to buck the patterns laid down by those who have gone before you." Erica wanted to know more. "What do you mean, Dad?"

"If you remember, back in our former lives, I was a Geography lecturer. Landscape was my thing and you must have heard of spirit of place, *genius loci* or whatever you want to call it. Think about it, those two stalkers spend all their lives working and living in a field sports landscape evolved out of 19th century patriarchy. The landscape rubs off on you, there's no evading it. Yes, you can rebel but then even rebellion gets appropriated. You might briefly succeed with a protest but it will always be a pyrrhic victory. They really would find it next to impossible to give up their way of life, it's all encompassing for them. Hunting, shooting, fishing, to quote a cliché, their landscape was made for such male sport and entertainment. Then, as they are, you become a servant to that landscape and there really is no escape. You brand them as trigger happy sexists which reinforces their self-image, reinforces their landscape. Why don't you try and imagine them as kind, caring intelligent human beings who could support our way of life?" She did not agree. "Fucking hell, Dad. You really ask too much this time." Dave wanted to bridge the growing gap between them but then was not the right moment. "I am sorry, Erica, but that makes you as much a bigot as them in my eyes. You are as much a subject of Utopian feminist landscapes as the stalkers subjects of Highland patriarchy. Surely we can all find some common ground on this sheep problem somewhere?" Deborah was getting hungry and could sense a long drawn out argument over gender pros and cons of sheep culling.

"Here endeth the lesson folks! Don't know about you, Dave, but I need my breakfast. Let's go!" Thinking about what had just been said, Dave spoke the truth of their own situation over breakfast. "You know Debs, the longer we stay here, the more we will be affected and become a part of what is embedded in the St Kilda landscape. No wonder the military guys only stayed here a month at a time and while they were here recreated through alcohol and that huge flat screen TV on the wall of the old Puff-Inn. They didn't want to participate in the living landscape around them." Deborah thought of what Sally had said about the water supply. There was the additional factor of Mothan influencing how they perceived their surroundings. Working as hard as he did, Dave drank copiously from the island's water supply. Was it any wonder he was becoming eccentric?

"You know, Dave. I don't really buy into this landscape stuff where you say our surroundings rub off on us, sounds like some kind of long distance social control. I feel a free agent and can wander here mistress of my own destiny. Maybe it's you men who need a structured existence. I wouldn't want to feel like a pawn in some historical power game. I know that the Bible has become important to you, but at the end of the day it was written by men and gives a primarily male perspective on the human condition, doesn't it? What was it, not even 2% of biblical tales are narrated by women? Your faith does seem a little too blind at times. Do you ever think how we women feel about being out here? Male dominance is no longer relevant and St Kilda is rebalancing away from the structured, dare I say proscribed ways of thinking that dominated the late 19th and 20th centuries. There will be initial upheaval but water will find its own level. I am feeling quite at home here now, I didn't think I would but I came out to support you and the girls. Not much option considering our dire prospects back in Edinburgh. You're becoming a strange man, Dave. Working your body into the ground while you escape family reality by disappearing into your private imagined world. How can I give you the courage to come through this change we have embarked on without recourse to biblical scriptures?"

Challenged, Dave appeared silent, unresponsive even, but his mind was racing looking for a way to answer Deborah's well-meant challenge. Reaching inside his inner jacket pocket, Dave produced his pocket Bible. "I'll have to look this up as I can't remember it off by heart yet – so here we are. 2 Corinthians, 5 verses 6-9.

Therefore we are always confident, knowing that, whilst we are at home in the body, we are absent from the Lord. For we walk by faith, not by sight: We are confident, I say, and willing rather to be absent from the body, and to be present with the Lord. Wherefore we labor, that, whether present or absent, we may be accepted of him."

"I am sorry Dave, but you are being evasive as ever. I want you to get real and live among us, not among ancient misogynists! Get real if you want to be accepted by this place!"

Deborah's scorn silenced Dave and left him feeling distanced from his wife after what had seemed a promising start that morning. She just didn't understand and he was tired of trying to get her to see and follow the words of the Lord that would carry them through challenges yet to be faced. It was Deborah who broke the silence. "As I am unable to get through to my dear husband, I will go and check on a man who, after last night's indulgences might actually need, or at least appreciate my help!" Deborah walked out of the Manse kitchen, slamming the doors behind her and headed for the Featherstore.

16 TSUNAMI

Sean and Gavin had loaded the Argocat and fueled the vehicle before breakfast. They sat together in Cottage 1 cleaning and checking their rifles ready for the day's preliminary cull to begin. Left-overs from the previous evening still littered the room and a residual warmth lingered from the woodstove. In spite of the whisky and smoking the night before, they both had relatively clear heads having drunk plenty of water during the night. Gavin did remark on the sense of unreality he felt waking up that morning. Lying in bed in Cottage 2, he had heard the scurrying of mice through the backdrop sounds of the sea and bird calls. It was the time of year when most of the smaller seabirds left the island, migrating out to sea now the business of raising chicks was done with. The small balls of fluff matured at an amazing rate, Anne had told them, fed from rich pickings around this North Atlantic island. Young Puffins and Petrels left in their thousands when the moon was full. They always left at night to escape predation from Great Skuas. Anne had already reminded Sean and Gavin to take care to extinguish all lights before they retired for the night. Should the moon be hidden by clouds or fog, inexperienced young birds would head for the nearest light and find themselves in great danger when dawn broke. Should a Skua attack at sea they instinctively dived to safety, on land this was not possible. Anne had picked up many a fledgling and kept it safe until dusk when it could be released hungry but eager to resume its journey to the open sea. So much marine activity was associated with phases of the moon, she explained. "A bit like us females," she quipped that morning. "Our energies flow with the tides too, especially out here surrounded by the ocean. We could use the Tide tables for family planning, I reckon!"

Anne had walked up to Cottage 1 to ask the stalkers if they would mind her observing how they planned and executed the cull. They were engaging in a bit of mutual banter before setting off but this was going to be serious business. "That's fine by us, Anne. But there a couple of practical issues to consider. Firstly and most obviously we are using high powered rifles fitted with sound moderators so we need you to keep well out of the way. You really ought to wear a high visibility jacket, but on second thoughts forget that as it could spook the sheep. You should just keep well away so as not to distract the sheep while we are trying to drive them into killing ground. I do wish we had a couple of dogs, it would make life so much easier."

Anne reminded them how impracticable an idea that would be. "The sheep have never known dogs and would probably just scatter anyway. You need to quietly encourage them to go where you want them." Anne had experience of handling these feral Soays and knew what she was talking about. If you wanted to catch one, then you had to encourage it into a confined space such as a derelict cottage or a cleit. There were over a thousand of these simple stone storage structures on the island.

"Tell you what boys. I'll hide in a cleit then I can watch what is going on through the ventilation gaps and the sheep won't see me either. Then if you make a bad shot and the bullet comes my way I'll be safely inside, behind stone walls." Sean agreed her plan, "That's it then, sorted! Get your lunch and jump in the Argocat with us, Anne. Don't waste your tidal energies walking up the hill now." Sean joked with her. He was starting to warm to Dave's youngest daughter after the hostile run in he had with Erica the night before.

Dave had made no attempt to follow Deborah to the Featherstore. He felt past caring. After a few months at St Kilda, his wife was no longer the woman he knew and loved back in Edinburgh. She had changed in this very different place. He was no fool and considered how the ordered landscape of Edinburgh had, maybe, actually held their family together. Out here, in this abandoned settlement, fragmented cultural remains of the past failed to influence their lives in any positive way. He had to admit, as his wife repeatedly pointed out to him, the past was dead. As he had so often quoted to his students, the past was also a foreign country and with the future withheld, the present was just beginning. He had his Bible to guide him through the turmoil, but these women didn't take him seriously. How could he guide them if they increasingly refused to listen? If Erica was to be believed, they didn't need guidance in rebuilding a workable community on the island. They needed families and children, he agreed, but she had openly hoped that when the new tourist season began they could convince, seduce even, a few able bodied men to stay with them and help in the procreative process. The women needed a new Genesis, a neo-Genesis she had teased. Dave felt an arousing mix of emotional pain and pleasure at the thought of his daughters conceiving children for the new St Kilda. Thank goodness, he thought, Deborah was past all that now with her fiftieth birthday on the horizon. It would be good to have a look at the Book of Genesis, to throw a bit of light into his darkness after Deborah stormed out on him earlier that morning.

He went into the Kirk and opened the large English language Bible. He had put it back there after realizing the rest of the family were not taking Bible reading seriously enough. Dave had always been attracted to the story of Joseph and his coat of many colors. As a child it had fascinated him. He quickly found the relevant passages in Genesis 37 but then noticed a seemingly lascivious text in the next chapter which rekindled his bitter-sweet arousal over Erica's fecund ambitions. Genesis 38: 2-10, it all seemed to be about the pleasures of sexual infidelity and subsequent angst. Just for good measure the Lord slew you for it afterwards! The tension inherent in the passages he had just read triggered a lower back spasm forcing him to lie on the Kirk floor in front of the Pulpit. Staring up at the damp stained ceiling, patterns of light flickered through the south facing window. It was interesting, he thought, that this Kirk was laid out lengthways south to north, but then Dave remembered that was the orientation of all the older buildings and cleits of the village. They had been built at a time when the population respected and lived with the forces of nature with just a nodding deference to their remote God. No builder in their right mind would have orientated the Kirk east to west at St Kilda as was the usual Christian tradition. Unopposed gales blew in from the southeast, through the open mouth of the bay, and all but the modern buildings respected their destructive energy. Robert Stephenson, of light-house fame had built this Kirk taking the power of nature into account, also giving usable daylight as much credence as the rising light of God in his design. The Kirk had withstood the elements for over two hundred years while the neighboring military complex was crumbling after just fifty. He turned over to get more comfortable, reaching for a kneeling cushion from the adjacent pew to put under his chest.

"Dave! What on earth are you doing on the floor?" Sally stood in the Kirk doorway looking down at the prostrate man in front of her. "It's my back again, Sal. It just went on me and I'm better lying down for a few minutes until things click back into place." He was finally taking his condition seriously, Sally thought.

"Tell you what, Dave. I think you should come back to the Factor's House with me and I'll give you a cup of tea and a massage in which ever order you prefer – just like last time, if you like." He turned and looked at her, grateful for a gesture of kindness after Deborah's tantrum earlier. Sally's enigmatic smile took his thoughts back to what he had just read about Onan sleeping with his brother's wife. Dave carefully got to his feet. Sally reached down for him and replaced the kneeling cushion on the back of the pew. She linked her arm through his and led him out of the Kirk, closing the heavy black door behind them. "Better keep the Lamb of God out of the House of God, Dave!" The pair made their way slowly across the rough pasture toward the Street and the Factor's House. Going inside, Sally sat Dave down at the kitchen table while she set up her massage bench in the living room across the hallway. She then went back to the kitchen to make them both a cup of tea. It was good the clean rain kept her water-butt topped. Going to the old well near the Kirk would be no fun even though the water there was untainted by nothing but the grass growing around it.

"So, Dave. Tell me about it, what happened this morning. When I came into the Kirk you had a face like a ruptured crab." Dave managed a grin in spite of the combination of lower back pain and anxiety. "It's Deborah, we had a blazing row this morning and she stormed off on me. I think we should follow the words of the Lord to get us through our time in the wilderness, but she just doesn't understand. He speaks to me, gives me advice. I have worked so hard, rebuilding walls, tilling the land till my back is breaking, literally it seems today. She used to support me, bring me food when I was hungry, water when I was thirsty. We would sit and share a glass of water together while I rested from my labors. We'd talk about rebuilding a community here. Not for us being somewhat past it, but my daughters were talking about encouraging young men to the island to get something going. Talk about having a couple of Sirens on board!"

Sally was expert at teasing out the anxieties of her patients, but listening to Dave it wasn't easy to keep a professional distance. As the island nurse, on this trip as on all others she had tried to remain objective so that anyone could feel safe to confide in her if they so wished but she had her own feelings and needs to consider too. Tea and sympathy was often all they both needed as most of the problems she encountered derived from relationship issues. The developing situation out here was no different.

Sally went outside with her kettle, heading for the water butt. Dave was curious as to why she didn't fill her kettle from the kitchen tap. When she came back he asked her why. "It's the water here, Dave. I personally am not keen on drinking it. You'll see black staining in your kettle no doubt. The water supply is rich in some mineral or other. I'm no expert but it is very soft, quite acidic. I always collect rain water while I'm out here. I think it is much healthier than water from the ground, however much it is treated. Anyway, what makes you think you are past it, Dave? How old are you, actually?" Sally knew of course. Dave was fifty two and his wife forty eight. They should have been in their prime out here at St Kilda, away from the stress of struggling to make a living in Edinburgh, but once again she was having to minister to psychological problems on the island. Dave's and Deborah's drinking was very modest, not like in the old days when she had to scrape men up off the Puff-Inn floor on many an occasion. When she had first met her, Deborah had seemed a broken woman after losing her senior teaching position. Now after a few months out here she was looking revitalized. Many a forty eight year old on the mainland would give their right arm to look as vibrant as she did right now. It was really not surprising she was becoming frustrated over her husband's obsession with the Bible. However, it was not for her to become personally involved in the Williams' family affairs any more than be a good councilor and listen without criticizing either way. However, the thought of Erica randomly seducing young male tourists hit her in the stomach.

As Deborah approached the Featherstore she noticed the waves lapping at the turf above the low cliff edge outside the front of the building. It had been New Moon the night before and it hadn't been easy finding her way back to the Manse in near total darkness. This Spring tide was the highest she had ever seen, or maybe she had never noticed how close it reached to the Featherstore before. Dan's upper story accommodation had probably the best sea views in the Village but was also in the most precarious position when south-east gales blew. Surely, it wouldn't be long before storm driven waves undermined the building and brought an end to the late eighteenth century warehouse standing Canute like, four-square against the elements. Banging on the backdoor, Deborah heard Dan's footsteps approaching more confidently now he had paid his debt to Don and Lachie. He was surprisingly buoyant considering the state his head should have been in after the party. Plenty of water had always been his panacea at such times, and he had known many.

"Hi Debs, what brings you here so early?" Dan invited her in and, to her surprise, the flat seemed in reasonable order. There was an odor of cannabis as usual, but she had to admit she now quite liked the smell. "Are you going to make a girl a coffee then, Dan?"

Dan made them both a cup of coffee and they sat in the low settees by the window looking out across the bay. Deborah was entranced by the unusually gentle waves lapping almost at the lower front door of the building. She felt restless and kept shifting her position in the armchair in front of him. "What's the matter, Debs? Got ants in your pants or something?" Dan joked. "Yeah, something like that – oh, put that coffee down and come here." Dan got up from his old, battered but comfy armchair, and went over to Deborah. The coffee Dan had made for her was strong and without milk she needed a glass of water with it. "Before you sit with me, could I have a glass of water?" She certainly wanted to clear her head. "Sure – how do you take it?" Impatiently she replied, "In a glass, smart-arse!" Dan returned with water in a somewhat dull glass. He had yet to be domesticated to wash glasses before greasy plates, she realized. Deborah patted the tattered cushion beside her on the old two seat settee and he sat down beside her. In spite of making efforts to tidy the flat, he hadn't gone as far as showering that morning. Featherstore showers were in reality a stand up wash and Dan would go outside and pour water over himself from a large plastic bowl. The lack of hot water meant it didn't happen very often. Once Deborah would have been repulsed by the scent of an unwashed male body but was again surprised that she found it, not to put a too fine a word on it, quite arousing.

Sat on the small two seat settee, their thighs pressed together as he sat down next to her. Dan thought, mischievously, that she would be uncomfortable feeling him so close. But he liked the thought that she had come to see him, rarely had anyone else taken the trouble since he had been there. Away from the village, the Featherstore was out on a limb as far as social activity was concerned. Cottage 1 had been where it all happened, until now. He wriggled his hips against Deborah's. "Come on, budge up, my lady!" He expected her to at least try to move, even get up and cross to the other chair, but she made no attempt to pull away from him. Instead she rested her head on his shoulder. He could smell as much as feel her warmth and instinctively kissed the parting in her thick hair which she had let down while he got her the glass of water. To his surprise, he could see tears welling in her eyes. "Sorry about this, Dan. But I need someone to talk to right now." He felt unsure about where this might be leading. "Don't know if I'm really the right person for this – wouldn't Sally be better?" Deborah was emphatic that he was the one she needed right then.

"No Dan! Sally is not who I need right now. I am absolutely sick and tired of being the wife and mother who holds everything together for the family. What about me?" Dan felt in a position for which he had no past experience to guide him. He had known plenty of women, girls really, who could match him at his own games but now he was faced with an older woman telling him her problems and he realized he was well out of his depth.

"I have just had a blazing row with Dave. I can't stand his quoting the Bible on just about everything we do and talk about. The Bible is so male orientated, a one sided justification for what men want to do! Worst of all he avoids our own reality by disappearing into the world of Moses and the Promised Land or some other such fucking nonsense. I didn't come to St Kilda to be ignored, Dan." Not knowing quite what to do he put his arm around her, prompting sobbing and more tears. "Just let me get this out, Dan. I need to cry and I'll be OK in a minute, honest." She looked him in the eyes and he found Deborah's warmth and emotional release aroused him too. "Dan, it's been so long. I really would like some closeness, is there anywhere we could lie down?" He was back in known territory. "Well you are straight to the point, Debs! I'll say that for you."

Outside the high water lapped the steps of the Featherstore. The Moon was at its closest point to the earth for centuries. Had they known, this perigee brought the Moon, a super-Moon, to just 330,000 kilometers from the Earth and being so close, its gravitational effects were bound to influence more than just tidal ranges.

In the Factor's House, Sally led Dave into the living room and was helping him get undressed for the massage. The last thing he wanted was to have another back spasm while trying to take his socks off. She very professionally stripped him down to his underpants and helped him climb up onto the massage bench. "That's it Dave, lie face down and get comfy. Then I can get to work on you. Are you warm enough?" Dave nodded and then shivered from the chill of the room. Sally noticed and pulled a spread off her fireside chair and put it over him. "Just a minute, I'll get the fire going. That will warm us up." She put a match to the split pallet wood in the grate which caught at once. Putting a fire guard in front of the spitting blaze she went to the wall cupboard for her massage oil. "Think I had better warm my hands a little before we get going!"

Sally laughed and in spite of shivering, Dave laughed too. "That's better, Dave. When was the last time you had a really good laugh? Bet you haven't laughed in months. It's no wonder you're so tense." Rubbing her hands together in front of the spitting fire, it wasn't long before the room warmed up. Standing outside her blackhouse, Erica noticed the smoke from the Factor's House chimney and put two and two together after watching Sally help Dave into her porch. Erica hoped the massage would help her troubled father. Sally's massages were the best at St Kilda, she smirked to herself, remembering her own experiences under Sally's most capable hands.

Although her hands were warm, the cool fragrant oil took a bit of getting used to. For a brief moment the coldness made his skin pucker as Sally's hands took over, smoothing and caressing his cares away. Dave began to cry, inaudibly at first, then in wracking sobs. "I am so sorry, Sally. I can't help myself." She smiled down at him, "Dave, that's fine. Just let it out, you'll be all the better for it. Let go, relax. It's what I am here for. You're not the first and you certainly won't be the last one of your family I will be seeing on this bench." Dave never thought to ask who the first one was and Sally wasn't going to tell him. The massage lasted for some ten minutes by which time Dave was as relaxed as he was ever going to be. He climbed off the massage bench unaided with Sally beaming at him. "There, that's you set up for the day. Here put your T-shirt back on before you freeze. The brief flare from the pallet wood had all but died away and the room would soon chill. In his T-shirt and pants, Dave walked over to Sally and hugged her. She could feel his erection pressing against her belly. This she tolerated, it was a common enough reaction from male massage patients, but when he tried to kiss her she pushed him away. "Dave, stop that, please! We are friends, but I don't want to encourage anything further. Get dressed now and we'll forget about this." Dave turned, his erection still visible and quickly dressed himself. Boundaries had been crossed, he did realize, but why did this woman reject him?

"Sally, who was the first member of my family to lie on your massage bench?" She hesitated before cautiously replying. "Well, if you must know, it was Erica. She came to me complaining of tension last week and we had a good girl to girl chat before I offered her a massage. She was tense and concerned as to where your family is heading. She was afraid for what the future holds, especially for you Dave unless you drop your, how else can I say it, religious mania."

Dave looked thunderstruck. These women were discussing him behind his back, after all he had done for them. Did all his hard work and sacrifice mean nothing? The effect of Sally's soothing massage was lost in an instant.

"Jezebels! Jezebels the lot of you. Plotting against me, ridiculing me in the eyes of the Lord and now you say you have massaged Erica before me. You make me feel sick!" Sally was shocked at Dave's reaction to her having given Erica a massage.

"Dave, for God's sake!" This enraged him further, "How dare you blaspheme in my presence, Sally?" Dave spoke quiet words of condemnation regarding his daughter's massage. That Dave thought she was lesbian frightened Sally in a way she could not have anticipated. Dave asked Sally directly if she was corrupting Erica behind his back. She had just suggested recruiting young men to help rebuild the community, and she didn't just mean wall building. Was this female intrigue to make a fool of him? Sally ran from Dave's darkening anger toward sanctuary with Erica in her blackhouse at the end of the village.

Dave needed advice and resorted once more to the large Bible in the Kirk. He found Leviticus 18 advised on sexual mores. In particular should there be male homosexuality or female bestiality the land would be defiled, and in Verse 25, he read that in such situations *the land itself vomiteth out her inhabitants.* In Genesis 19, there was condemnation of male homosexuality in the cities of Sodom and Gomorrah and in 1 Corinthians 6: 9 condemnation of male effeminacy and self-abuse. It was hard to find scriptural advice regarding female homosexuality. Deborah's earlier scolding had sunk in and he was determined he would be able find advice for women somewhere in the Bible. The advice of Paul the Apostle to the Romans cleared things up for him. In Romans 1: 22-32 he read that those who saw God in nature, served creatures rather than their Creator which led to homosexuality in both sexes. He let that sink in. Should abandoned and lustful behavior become acceptable norms, even murder could be acceptable in the service of nature. If they only worshipped the Lord, he would protect them from all this confusion. Erica and Sally were breaking God's divine rules if, as he now suspected they were lying with each other. Anne, in the service of nature rather than God was making herself unforgiveable and 'worthy of death.' It was, he felt sure, only a matter of time before this island vomited out its vile inhabitants. The Bible said so.

The sudden pain in his lower back made him cry out and grip the pulpit for support. In his pain, Dave saw the cold, damp and the empty Kirk for what it was. Simply a tourist attraction, the collection boxes had funded nature conservation, rather than God's work. It seemed that on St Kilda the Lord had left, washed his hands of the community. Nature conservation had turned the island, their new home in fact, into a Godless void but he had seen Angels across the water, circling around the Stacs. The Lord was still to be found across the water at Boreray and was waiting to welcome Dave Williams, his faithful servant.

In the Featherstore, Dan was enjoying entertaining Deborah. Having finished her coffee, they shared a glass of his Mothan laced special brew. While not exactly drunk she remembered Sally's comments from the night before, but she certainly felt slightly intoxicated. Whether it was the freedom to express herself as a woman or the effects of the drink, one way or the other she didn't care. She would release herself from the shackles of male dominance and Dave could go hang. She would take what Dan had to offer. She hadn't made love with her husband more than a couple of times since arriving at St Kilda and last time he took her like he owned her. Make love? It was more like he was claiming her territory and it had done nothing but make her more resentful. She followed Dan into the small bedroom overlooking the sea. The waves lapped the steps below. By this time Dan had noticed how high the tide was. "I hope this doesn't happen too often or my place is going to get very damp." Deborah considered making a double entendre relating to her own dampness but thought better of it. "Let's not worry about that Dan. The tide will fall soon enough." They sat down on his single bed and Deborah pulled Dan down to lie beside her and in spite of his accepting the likelihood of the two of them getting into bed together earlier, she could read his concern. "Debs, I am not sure about this. What if Dave finds…"

She smothered his words with a passionate kiss, her tongue quickly seeking and finding his. Her hand was already on his strong erection and working to make it stronger. "I haven't even got a condom, Debs. This is madness."

Deborah kept her voice to a husky whisper even though

the Featherstore was a good hundred yards from the Manse. "Dave won't ever know, Dan, and I don't really care. I just want you, now!" She was strong woman and heavier built than the youthful bodied Dan. He didn't object as she took control by pulling down his jeans and underpants. Quickly stepping out of her own jeans and knickers she left her own upper garments on, the warm jumper a protection against the chill of the sea air as much as anything. She returned to the bed and straddled him. Seeing Deborah naked from the waist down, Dan knew as had Dave a few hundred yards away, that boundaries were again being crossed and it scared him. There could be no going back and they were both running with wetness as she lowered herself on to him. "Be careful Deborah. Remember I have no condom. I don't want to come." She looked down to him and smiled. "If Dave was here, he would tell you to be like Onan and spill your seed on the ground, he is fond of that passage the dirty old man! Don't you worry, just relax and let me do the work and anyway I am forty-eight. You're not going to make me pregnant."

Deborah began to ride him, gently at first. His hands on her buttocks following rather than guiding her movements. She felt him stiffen and swell as he neared climax. Taking his arms from her buttocks she held them down against the bed cover and sat down on him hard, all the way. Dan could feel her rhythmically gripping him inside her. He was powerless to stop what was happening. He wanted to pull out and put an end to this madness but she was heavier and stronger than him, and she was in control. He had never known an orgasm like it. The spasms seemed to go on forever but when he finally subsided she lay down beside him, her wetness against his thigh. She pulled the bed cover over them both and snuggled up to him. "My man, my man...."

Deborah murmured something about finding her man at last before closing her eyes and letting out a short snore. Dan took his chance and quickly got off the bed and pulled his jeans and pants up from around his ankles. He was soaking wet and worryingly he noticed his groin area was not only wet but colored slightly by Deborah's menstruation. She was still fertile in spite of her suggesting otherwise. "Bloody hell, Deborah! You've used me, you wanted to get pregnant didn't you. What am I to you, just a sperm bank" She woke contentedly and looked him square in the eyes. "Something like that my love, something like that. Don't worry about it, consider it an honor that I chose you. You have just fathered the first child to be born at St Kilda in a hundred years."

A tremor went through the building, rattling Dan's crockery and empty bottles. Outside the calm waters of the Village Bay shivered. A few loose rocks clattered down from the scree slope as Anne lowered the binoculars she had trained on the Featherstore window. She had seen everything from the Hidey-Hole in the rocks beneath Mullach Sgar. Anne was however more intrigued to see the tide retreating faster than normal exposing the rocks below the Featherstore quicker than the Turnstones could follow in their quest for food pickings. The volcanic archipelago of St Kilda sits at the very edge of the European continental shelf and, off the island Soay, nearly a million tons of sea bed had detached and slid into the abyss. Just half a mile from the foot of Glen Bay the sea is 900 feet deep and, as Anne had reminded, was a prime setting for earthquake and tsunami. This perigee super-moon was exerting a strong tectonic effect, pulling at continental plates as well as the ocean.

Erica burst into Sally's blackhouse, startling her as she sat by her stove with a mug of tea. "Sally, whatever is up with you? Maybe it was small earthquake." Erica was concerned, she had never seen Sally lose her composure like this. Normally a very private woman, this time it was Sally who needed to talk.

"I am not here about the earth tremor, which happens from time to time. It's your Dad, Erica. I know it's not a professional thing to say, but I think he's losing it. He was as jealous as hell when I told him I'd given you a massage last week. He's got it into his head there's something going on between us." Erica managed tried to hide her blush by pulling up her collar, but not before Sally noticed the reaction. She quickly dismissed Erica's blush but had to admit to herself that massaging Erica had been a far more pleasing task than soothing her father.

"I found him in the Kirk, poring over that old Bible again. His back is in a terrible state, he's working himself into the ground and becoming embittered at his physical limitations. You know, when I had finished the massage, he made a pass at me. I ask you…?"

Erica couldn't suppress her laughter at the thought. "My Dad, making a pass at you? I don't believe it! What about Mum?" Sally was perplexed. "From what I am picking up, I don't things have been too good between them lately. Not since Dave started his Bible-bashing." Erica poured Sally a coffee from the pot on the stove which was gratefully received. She dragged over the old milking stool Erica had found in the Trust workshop and sat down near her friend. Feeling better, she apologized for bursting in. "Sorry about rushing in without knocking, Erica. I know you don't like it, but I was scared. Dave had such a look in his eyes, he looked like a man prepared to kill me. I have picked up the pieces after many a bar brawl out here, but never seen a look like his before. If I had seen such a thing in the old days, I would have recommended removal from the island as a matter of urgency. Don and Lachie are leaving tonight – do you think he would go with them?" Erica doubted her father would leave the island. It was his dream project and he would not and probably could not, she thought, walk away from it now.

Dave had found a broom behind the Kirk door and used it as a makeshift crutch to ease the pressure on his lower back. He carefully limped back to the Manse where he thought he had some anti-inflammatory pain killers left. Slowly crossing in front of the derelict Base he noticed Deborah in conversation with Don and Lachie at the top of the old slipway leading down to the jetty. He thought they were probably talking about him too but it was another man they were discussing.

"I've been talking with Dan and he'd like to get off the island when you leave. Is there some way we can arrange this between us." Dan was desperate to leave after his experience with Deborah that morning. He didn't trust Deborah not to tell Dave about it in a fit of anger, even as a calculated snub to her husband. Quite simply he did not want to be around when Dave found out. Neither Dan nor Deborah could have guessed the informant would actually be Anne who had been watching them from the Hidey-Hole hundreds of yards away. The deep trench in the scree had hidden St Kildans from Barbary pirate attack in the 17th and 18th centuries when North African slavers roamed as far as Iceland. It was still a great place for Anne to keep a discrete watch on what was going on around the village below.

Deborah would also be glad to have Dan out of the way now he had fulfilled what she required of him. She felt certain she had conceived as the tide turned that morning and didn't want any emotional attachment from him as her pregnancy developed. "Tell you what, Debs. We'll take him back for £100 and we'll even give him a lift to Stornoway and put him on the ferry to the mainland. How about that?" Dan was a keen businessman but he would always help out where he could. We are not in a rush so I don't mind tying up here another night. Then we can set off in the morning. If anyone else wants to leave I can take them too. The stalkers reckon a week to complete the cull so we won't be gone for long. Any fresh supplies you need, just let us know before we sail and we'll bring them when we come back."

"'We don't want you back, you pair of sodomites!" Dave limped across to join the three of them chatting at the slipway. "Excuse me, Dave. What are you on about?" Lachie wasn't quite sure if Dave was joking or not, but he sounded serious enough. "You two, didn't want to come to the party, didn't want to sleep in the cottages but wanted to sleep together in that boat of yours didn't you? Leviticus 18: 22 *Though shalt not lie with mankind, as with womankind: it is an abomination.*"

Lachie had a quick temper unlike Don who was simply rendered speechless. "Dave, I hope your joking because if not you had better explain yourself!" Don quickly realized that Dave was being deadly serious. He thought that because they slept together in bunks on board they must be homosexual. "Dave, I carry and will carry all sorts on my boat be they gay, straight, pink, black or white and any combination of the same. Money needs no categorization. What I don't and will not carry is bigotry. Now I am a Sabbatarian and a follower of the Free Church and don't work on Sundays. That's as far as it goes. So I respect the words of the Lord and I'll pretend I didn't hear the disrespectful words you just spoke. For the record Lachie, with all his youthful good lucks, reserves himself for the girls of Stornoway, not middle aged men like you and me."

Feeling sorry for him, Don reached out and put his arm around Dave's shoulder. "Come on Dave, lighten up. It's not easy being out here and you have done better than most would have under the circumstances." Dave slowly and deliberately removed Don's arm from his shoulder in time to see Erica approaching. She was walking toward him and it was obvious she wanted to speak to him. "Dad, can you come over here a minute? I have something to talk about with you, in private." The relationship between Erica and her father had always been one of mutual respect and if anyone could convince him to take a break from the island, she could.

"Dad, Sally came to me and told me what happened. We both care about you and think your religion is getting the better of you. We know you mean well but wouldn't it be better if you left the island for a short while. Just a week until Dan and Lachie come back for the stalkers. It will help you get things in perspective and we'll all be a lot better for it. Right now you frighten us." Dave responded sarcastically, "What, leave the island so you can get on with your Godless nature conservation and debauchery without me?" Erica was becoming exasperated, "Well, Dad, debauchery would be a fine thing. But we will get on with nature conservation by culling the sheep while you rest up in Stornoway. You'll come back a new man with a manageable sized flock. Best of all you will be able to work your garden in peace."

Dave was barely listening to her. "Romans 1: 30-32 *Backbiters, haters of God, despiteful, proud, boasters, inventors of evil things, disobedient to parents.* That's what my family have come to. To think I brought you here to save you from, what can I say? Hell, yes the hell that is now Edinburgh. There are Angels here if you would only see them. Open your eyes before it is too late. Remember what Luke said about the prodigal son, Erica. Return to the ways of the Lord and you will be forgiven."

Deborah overheard the end of the conversation and hissed at him. "Always the Lord, the sons, isn't it? Why not tell us a story about the Lady, the daughters instead of being so fucking androcentric. We don't need you anymore. Just get on that boat with Dan in the morning. Do us all a favor and fuck off, will you!" Erica cut her short. "Mum! You are not helping, what's got in to you?" She turned on her daughter. "I'll tell you what's got into me, Erica. I have had enough of my life being dominated by men. At school I worked for a man who fired me when I had problems and out here I work for a man who doesn't give a damn about anything except his precious Lord. Men are only any good for one thing in my opinion and as Anne is so fond of reminding us, for the rest we women can do it ourselves!" Deborah pushed Dave away from her and he slipped at the top of the uneven stone path and fell heavily. The improvised crutch snapping under his weight. Deborah turned away from him, not offering to help. "You make me sick, Dave. Bloody, fucking sick!"

Crying with pain he looked pleadingly up at Erica. Don and Lachie stood appalled at the domestic violence they had just witnessed. Don helped Dave to his feet. "Best keep away from her for a while, I reckon, Dave. Come and join us on the boat until Dan sorts himself out and we'll put you in the Featherstore till Debs cools off. Don't know what on Earth has made her like this."

Don and Lachie helped Dave down to the *Beluga*. The tide had fallen far lower than normal and it was with some difficulty that they got him off the end of the iron ladder onto the grounded boat. The three men went inside the well apportioned interior. Dave was immediately fascinated by the high-tech navigation equipment and frankly amazed at how comfortable it was on board. The twin hulls ensured it sat level on the exposed sandy seabed until the tide returned. The hardships of St Kilda were going to be left behind for a few hours. Don and Lachie had forgiven Dave for his earlier outburst, they weren't the type to hold grudges, except when it came to unpaid debts as Dan had found out. As soon as the debt was paid the grudge was forgotten. They were like that. It was warm inside the *Beluga* and Dave felt at home with a mug of tea in his hands. Biscuits were passed around and the radio played softly in the background. Some kind of Gaelic country and western by the sound of it. He couldn't understand a word but the music was good after the hostile silences he had endured in the Manse lately. Lachie produced a bottle of whisky usually reserved as a treat for the passengers. It wasn't for nothing they won awards for their Hebridean hospitality. We've got water here if you want it, all the way from the Co-op. You don't want to be spoiling your whisky with the tainted stuff from this island!"

Anne had also been watching the goings on at the jetty slipway. She had seen her mother push her father and his subsequent fall. Now he was on board with Don and Lachie he would be OK for a while. Unlike Erica, she didn't wear her heart on her sleeve, but when it came to their father she didn't like to see him hurt and humiliated like this. Now it was time she joined Sean and Gavin for a ride up the hill in the Argocat and get the sheep cull underway.

17 SLAUGHTER

Gavin and Anne climbed aboard and Sean drove the loaded Argocat uphill to the T-junction on the ridge above the village. Beyond, the ground dropped steeply into Glen Mór. The air was as calm as the sea that morning, there was barely a breath of wind and it looked like it was going to be one of the rare St Kilda days when midges could be a nuisance. Sean selected lower gears and maneuvered the machine across the two hundred yards of moor before coming to the worn down turf dyke delineating the boundary of the former cattle grazing area. He switched the engine off and all three stood for a moment taking in the view and the silence. Beyond Glen Bay, they could see the cliffs of Soay, beneath which they could hear seals' mournful calling. On such a day as this sound would carry for miles. About two thirds down the glen, to the left and slightly raised in the moorland they could see the lochan at Arigh Mór. This small body of water was the only natural freshwater pool on the island and, in recent years, completely taken over by Great Skuas for bathing and socializing. Those who worked on the island had nick-named it the Bonxie Pond. Woe betide any other seabird having the audacity to alight on this pool. The burn running down the center of glen was littered with aluminum wreckage from the WW2 Sunderland flying-boat. The trail of spent cartridges had mostly disappeared into the boggy ground alongside the stream, though from time to time a few would wash up after a wet spell. To their right, Gavin could see the line of cleits ending abruptly before the ground dropped into the glen. He was curious.

"Cleits were generally built by the men of the island. They didn't want to build any further, but if you look down into the glen you can see remains of older structures." Anne pointed out the enigmatic dwellings that the archaeologists couldn't properly explain. They described these ruins as horned structures. Three stone beehive cells enclosed within a horseshoe shaped wall. The horns of the wall extended out from the two outer beehive cells with a narrow entrance where they almost met. Sean reckoned he had seen similar structures before while he was in the Special Forces serving in central Africa. "No, Sean. They are unique to St Kilda, it's one of the reasons we are designated a World Heritage Site." Anne was adamant but Sean was not convinced of their uniqueness. "Ah, but you haven't been where I have. We were trying, somewhat unsuccessfully, to control Islamist insurgents in the north of Cameroon, near the Chad border, and we raided compounds just like these. The villagers knew trouble was coming and while they lay hidden in the small conical huts their sheep and goats were corralled within the horseshoe shaped walls. Just a narrow gateway between the horns of the wall, as you can see here." Anne closed the argument, realizing it wasn't worth pursuing further. "Well I won't argue with you, Sean. I've never been there myself, so I'll take your word for it."

Gavin had been studying the glen below them through his binoculars. "Anne, there's one of those horned structures, as you call them, that looks in pretty good condition. Pretty much as Sean just described he saw in Cameroon. Why is that?"

Anne knew exactly where he was referring to. "That will be the Amazon's House. It is the only one of these structures that has been restored. Even the turf roof is in good condition. Seems the sheep know better than to get up and wreck that roof." Anne knew there was something special about the building, not because it had been restored but by the way the sheep behaved around it. If she hadn't been scientifically trained she would say they were showing deference. They trashed every other turf roof they could climb onto.

"That's interesting, it looks like the tide has come way up higher than usual here as well. Much higher than at Village

Bay." Anne noticed a strand line on the turf at the foot of the glen. "The tide must have risen 30 foot this morning, blimey! Hey, it must have been a tsunami. I thought there had been a small earthquake when I was up in the scree and a few biggish rocks fell down. There must have been an underwater landslip and a section of seabed shifted and tipped over the continental shelf. That would account for a tsunami alright." She omitted to tell the two men what, or rather who she had witnessed from the Hidey-Hole up in the scree. The ground had certainly shifted in the Featherstore that morning, she thought.

"'Enough, enough, let's get to work." Sean was impatient to start the business of the day. While the other two were discussing archaeology and tsunamis he had been studying the ground beneath them. The Glen was a U-shaped glaciated valley so if they fired from the center the ground rose in front of them in three directions. If they shot toward the sea, the bullets would fall harmlessly enough. They would have to conceal themselves though. He thought the horned structures would be pretty good places to shoot from. The sheep wouldn't know what hit them and, with sound moderators on their rifles, the others wouldn't hear either. The three of them got back onto the Argocat and Sean carefully drove through an opening in the Turf Dyke eroded by years of sheep feet. They had to hang on as the eight-wheeled vehicle negotiated the steep concave slope into the glen. Just as the ground levelled out a white Snowy Owl flew up from a ruined cleit beside the burn. "That's the bugger that put the shite up me last night!" They drove the multi-purpose vehicle down near the foot of the glen. "I reckon that one will do, Sean." Gavin pointed out one of the horned structures with its corral walls virtually intact. They could shoot safely in any direction, as long as no one came walking through the glen, which was highly unlikely. Sean gave Anne a large shiny whistle which he used when refereeing Youth Club football matches back home. "You hide yourself over there in that other compound and if you see anyone coming, give a good blast on the whistle and we'll know to stop firing, OK?" Anne was OK and actually quite interested in seeing how the sheep reacted. They never showed any interest when one of their own died from natural causes, just carried on grazing around the body. "We've never shot sheep before, so we don't know how the flock will react. Just have to see how it goes."

The Soays had scattered as the Argocat came down the glen. They had never seen a vehicle of any type driven off road before but now were settling down to graze high on the north side of the glen. That was good, Gavin had said. The sheep would be well lit by the sunshine from the south and clearly visible. Shooting into the sun would be next to impossible with telescopic sights.

Anne walked over to the adjacent compound and settled herself in. No problem with wind or rain but there were the Skuas to contend with. They were getting interested in what was going on close to their nesting territory. Due to Bonxie attack, men rarely ventured into the glen and never on their own. She waved back to the Sean and Gavin, indicating that she was safely at her watching place and they could begin the cull. The rifles were unpacked from their slips and magazines loaded. The sound moderators had been left on as the stalkers had not wanted to have to recalibrate the sights each time they took them out. They would just have to take into account range and windage. As there was no wind to contend with at all, it should be an easy job. They had their sights set for around 100 yards as they didn't want to shoot beyond that range and risk not getting a clean kill. Ideally through the heart or better still a head shot. Resting his rifle on the compound wall, Gavin was preparing to take aim on a brown ewe with a creamy belly about fifty yards in front of him. A sudden rush of air passed his head as the crosshairs settled just behind her shoulder. A heart shot was preferable to a head shot, less chance of missing but not so good if you wanted to butcher the carcass afterwards. The attacking Skua twisted and turned above him and came in for a second pass. This time it put its feet out and gave the stalker a hefty slap on the head. "For fuck's sake!" Gavin stood up cursing and reached for his cap, still folded up in his jacket pocket. The incident caused Sean some merriment until exactly the same happened to him. The sheep grazed unconcerned. "'Hey Anne, can you do something about these fuckers? They are really pissing us off!" Anne called back, explaining that that was what Bonxies did. Nothing she could do about it. They were at St Kilda now, so they would have to get used to it. Grumbling the two stalkers tried again, settling down in the compound after taking Anne's advice to extend a walking pole fully above their heads. The Skuas were wary of careering into the poles and kept their distance but were still making aggressive passes over the heads of the two stalkers. "OK, pal, let's try again, shall we?"

Sean wanted to make a good job of this. Making a botch of culling sheep wouldn't look too good on his record. Taking aim on a three year old tup, he made absolutely sure of a clean head shot at no more than 50 yards. There was absolutely no wind to take into account and as the cross hairs came down onto the unsuspecting rams head, his focus was just in front of the ears. Sean held his breath and squeezed the trigger. The sound of the bullet hitting the ram's head was louder than the report of the silenced rifle, but to Sean's horror he saw the animal run away, gouts of blood pouring from where its nostrils should have been. Even as close as 50 yards, all he had managed to do was badly injure the beast. He ran out from behind the compound wall to follow and finish off the ram but was knocked to the ground by a violent blast of wind. Before he got back to his feet a second bullet hit the ram behind its left shoulder and the animal dropped. Gavin had seen the botched shot and while Sean was safely on the ground he put an end to the ram's suffering. "Christ! I thought you two were professionals? Even my dad is a better shot than you, Sean!"

Anne hated to see the tup injured and had expected better from the stalkers. "It's the bloody wind out here, it came from nowhere. There are no trees here, you can't see the leaves move as a warning." Anne was incensed, "Well I am not hanging around to see you two make a botch of this. Either shoot them cleanly or not at all. You are going to have to do better than this if you're going to cull the flock around the village." She stormed off, back up the glen toward the ridge. She turned right at the Turf Dyke and followed its line until she took cover amongst the cleits near the Lover's Stone. This rock overhanging the southern cliffs of the island was a favorite haunt of hers and from this position she could look down unseen and monitor whatever Sean and Gavin did next.

The shooting of the tup had made one group of ewes and lambs uneasy and they herded themselves through the narrow entrance of the corral in front of the Amazon's House. It was if they were seeking sanctuary but the reason, so Sean and Gavin thought was to shelter from the gusting winds that could certainly now be felt if not seen blowing around the foot of Glen Mór. The stalkers looked at each other. "You thinking what I'm thinking, Gavin?" Sean had spotted the opportunity he needed. Gavin agreed, "Yep, let's get it over with." They started the engine of the Argocat and very gently drove it across the rough turf and blocked the entrance to the Amazon's House compound. Once again they picked up their rifles and rested them on the body of the Argocat and aimed into the compound. For the restless sheep there was no way out over the high restored walls. They instinctively resisted escaping into the unknown darkness of the stone chambers behind which might have saved them. Skuas retuned with a vengeance. They had teamed up, as they always did when faced with a determined intruder, and rained one blow after another on the heads of the stalkers who had left their walking poles at the ruined compound across the glen.

Sean had had enough, "Fuck this for a lark!" He reached into the rifle box on the Argocat and pulled out his pump action 12 bore shotgun and fitted its ready loaded 14 round magazine. Angrily firing at the circling Bonxies one after the other fell injured or dead around the walls of the Amazon's House. The sound of repeated shotgun firing echoed round the glen and only after the fourteenth shell had been fired did the echoes of gunfire die away. Anne watched the slaughter of Skuas with horror. Not only horrified at the violent deaths of so many protected birds but also in the knowledge that the Morrigan's retribution would inevitably follow. No amount of milk poured over the stone beside the quarry would appease this sacrilege. The remaining Skuas retreated to watch from safety on the higher slopes of Mullach Bi. They were intelligent birds and knew that their most venomous attacks would be no match for the Sean's shotgun. They also went to ground, Anne had previously noticed, before high winds made flight in the glen impossible.

When Sean began firing at the Skuas, the trapped sheep panicked and all but one escaped from the enclosure. One elderly ewe lay on the ground, panting with fear. She expired as Gavin walked over to her. "Well, that was bloody clever Sean. Now they have all escaped. Gone round the corner toward the headland, below where you had your fright last night."

Gavin was not impressed at the unprofessional way Sean had handled things so far but sought a way to save face for both of them. "Tell you what, Sean, why don't you load that blunderbuss of yours with buckshot, we've got plenty in the ammo box. I'll drive the Argo and we can try to herd them into a corner. They are bound to run now, so rifles won't be much good but with the SG buckshot you should be able to bring them down without making too much of a mess of it.

Running toward the promontory of Gob na h-Àirde, the sheep would arrive on a relatively level and open acreage of rough pasture. They would have 360 degree vision but on the narrow headland they would also be trapped with a two hundred foot drop to the sea behind them. Gavin knew that and zig-zagged the Argocat like a sheep dog working his flock. The sheep huddled together at the narrow end of the level ground, beyond which lay the path to the Tunnel, a sea cave open at both ends which ran beneath the headland. As they came within 25 yard of the huddled flock Gavin gave Sean the signal to begin firing.

From her vantage point near the Lover's Stone, Anne could not see what was happening beyond the glen but the violence of Sean's shotgun firing again horrified her. The air in the glen was clear and still, yet she sensed movement among the rocks off the path to the Cambir, the high headland enclosing the south side of Glen Bay. The sound of firing ceased for a few seconds while Sean reloaded his magazine. Then it began again. Whether it was the toughness of these feral sheep or their wool that absorbed kinetic energy from the buckshot, many sheep were being injured rather than killed outright. Anne saw one older ewe limping badly and coughing painfully as she attempted to lead younger and more inexperienced sheep to safety back in the glen. She watched as the Argocat come round the corner of the hill and saw Sean blasting at the group until his magazine emptied again. The sheep staggered and fell but through her binoculars, Anne could see that many of the Soays were still being left lying badly injured. She ran toward the slaughter in a vain attempt to try and stop it. Gavin and Sean were enjoying this now, roaring round in their off-road vehicle shooting at anything that moved. A blood lust had taken over, as Anne was to report later.

The spinning vortex roared down unseen from the Cambir and headed across Glen Bay to where the cull was taking place. Anne had no idea of the size or power of the spinning wind until it crossed the bay. The column of water must have been one hundred and fifty feet high, at least twenty across and it was heading straight for the Argocat, now racing toward sheep trapped at the neck of the headland. At the last moment Gavin saw it coming and tried to outrun the wind as it made landfall. Approaching the edge of the cliff above the northern end of the Tunnel the stalkers, like the sheep they were chasing down, had no room to maneuver. "Gavin! What the fuck are you doing?" Sean had dropped his shotgun and was hanging onto the Argocat for his life as Gavin raced the machine across rough ground along the cliff edge. Left and right he drove but the spinning vortex matched his every move before suddenly hurling its energy onto the vehicle and its occupants. The machine was picked up and hurled high into the air. Gavin fell from the driver's seat while Sean hug on grimly to the anti-roll bar as the Argocat smashed into the high cliff below Conachair. Anne had stopped running and stood both amazed and terrified at what she saw. No-one would ever be able to descend the 1200 foot cliff to retrieve either Sean or the machine that lay smashed on top of him. She could see Gavin's body lying on the turf at the edge of the promontory. There was a chance he had survived the fall but she had to see to the sheep first.

Many sheep lay dead on the rough pasture, some with terrible wounds. A few were still alive but with shattered limbs and blood stained fleeces. As she surveyed the aftermath of the one-sided battle, the spinning column of water returned, noticeably smaller with much of its energy spent. It circled around her before turning right along the cliff path to the small stone walled enclosure, built by St Kildans, above the Tunnel centuries previously. The vortex shrank further before disappearing with a hiss into the cleft surrounded by the improvised walls. Anne heard the wind sigh into hidden caves beneath her and apart from the breathing of the Atlantic, all was still and quiet once more. The injured animals made no discernible sound as she approached. When she found a sheep injured but alive she lifted its head and, with her razor sharp pocket knife, deftly slit its throat. The sheep died quickly and humanely as she had been trained when working as a volunteer shepherd. Finally, after giving priority to dispatching the injured sheep, Anne walked slowly over to Gavin. He was lying in an unnatural position, even though still breathing, his spine was obviously broken. Gavin was barely conscious as Anne lifted his head and slit his throat. Gavin's blood poured onto the turf to mingle with that of the slaughtered sheep. He died just as quickly and humanely, Anne considered. At least she was being professional about this, she reminded herself. Rather than have to explain the circumstances of Gavin's death as any different to Sean's, Anne dragged his lifeless body to the cliff edge and tipped it over. The stalkers worked together and they died together, that would be her story. The trail of blood to the cliff edge would soon be washed away by rain and salt spray. As his body hit the water two hundred feet below a great sigh, almost of thanks, Anne thought, came from the crevice in the rock where the misty vortex had disappeared.

Anne walked back along the narrow strip of coastal pasture toward the glen. She took a drink at the Well of Virtues, Brighid's Well as it had been known before the missionary men landed, then continued until she came to the waterfall at the foot of Glen Mór. There she squatted to wash the blood off her hands and pocket knife. She spotted a suitable stone at the stream's edge and honed her blade back to its usual sharpness. When it came to dispatching injured sheep, she wanted death to be as quick and painless as possible. With traces of blood removed she began the long climb out of the glen toward the ridge road. Anne did not follow the tracks of the Argocat, where the three of them had driven down earlier. She felt an instinctive repulsion to following in the tracks of the machine complicit in the slaughter behind her. As the ground began to rise in front of her she bore left, heading for the point where the line of cleits from Mullach Geal terminated. From experience she knew it was the least exhausting route out, the men had at least done one thing right in the past. There was no urgency to for her to return, the stalkers were gone and the remaining sheep peacefully grazing again. It always surprised her how quickly they got over traumatic events. The right attitude, she thought. Looking back she could see the Skuas had settled back on the small lochan, bathing contentedly. There being no further wind she decided to return via the summit of Conachair. The views across to Boreray would be impressive and with the sea so calm there was good chance of seeing whales too.

At the S-bends she saw the dents in the crash barrier. Heavy dents where large machinery had hit it and she saw the olive green scuff marks where the small Argocat had scraped along the steel guard rail the night before. The Snowy Owl was often seen near this place but she doubted it would return for several days after the commotion in the glen that morning. The owl had probably sought refuge on Soay, though it would return once it got hungry. The oversized St Kilda Field Mice were a satisfactory substitute for the owl's usual diet of arctic Lemmings. Continuing along the road toward the defunct radar station at Mullach Mór, it was strange not to see the communications mast towering over the small buildings. It was the silence that struck her for up there at around 1000 feet above sea level there was always a breeze, it was never totally still at the top of the hill and in the past there been the sound of wind in the wires to guide her in the mist. Now the mast and its supporting cables lay in a tangled heap to the right of the buildings. In a way, she thought, it was lucky the mast hadn't fallen down into the glen. The wind must have blown uphill and sent it crashing toward the Base. Turning right toward the short slope to the summit, Anne crossed the last peat beds worked on the island. It was easy to imagine why the human community here failed in the end. She didn't count the military community as such, with ten men for every woman at best, it couldn't be considered anything more than a male colony. She imagined the hardship of trying to keep warm and be able to cook meals dependent on walking to the top of this hill and carrying the peats back down again. The line of cleits along the ridge bore testimony to attempts to dry out the fuel before it was carried down in creels to the village. It had been a Spartan existence and one in which only the fittest survived. Charles Darwin had been right when he described the survival of the fittest. It would be like that again when the, her, new community was established, they would follow the island's rules and only the fit would survive. It was good, she thought, that historically more girl babies survived tetanus than boys. Only the fittest boys would survive into manhood to fulfil their limited purpose.

Connachair's Bonxies watched her as she climbed the slope to the summit. This tribe of Skuas had not been involved in the mayhem below in the glen. They had their own territories and would fight off invaders from another group entering their nesting ground. They were known to be cannibal when the opportunity presented itself and if it hadn't been for the bounty of newly dead sheep to feast on in Glen Mór these Skuas would have soon dined on their fallen comrades. Standing at the summit, the light breeze from the west rustled her long dark hair. Looking across at Boreray and the Stacs, the whiteness of the gannet colony shone out, millions of white birds and their droppings reflecting the mid-day sunshine. The whiteness and purity, she considered, compared strikingly with the rusty tangle of metal, broken glass and concrete lying on the moor behind her. It had been hot work climbing to the summit and she took a drink from her water-bottle, filled from the Manse kitchen earlier that morning. The day was barely half-way through yet so much had happened. Gannets swirled around Boreray, some breaking off to fly in tight lines toward distant feeding grounds, tired stragglers being picked off by Bonxies.

Survival of the fittest again she thought. Anne's gaze followed the line of the cliff path down to the Gap and was she surprised to see her father standing at the edge and like her appeared to be gazing out toward Boreray. Patches of white flowered heather lined the path as she made her way down the steep slope toward him.

"Hi Dad, what brings you up here? Your back must be a lot easier today." He was equally surprised to see his daughter walking toward him. "Hello Anne, I could ask the same of you. Aren't you supposed to be over in the glen helping with the cull? I heard all the shooting but it stopped a while ago. Did it go alright?" Anne decided to leave giving her father much detail about what had actually occurred in Glen Mór that morning. "Yes, Dad. There are a lot of dead sheep down there." She asked him about the night before. "Yes, I had a great time with Don and Lachie. I slept on their boat, I mean really slept for the first time in weeks. Just being away from this island, even just by a few feet, made such a difference. To be honest I was glad to get away from your mother for a night too. I think it does us all good to have a break sometimes. They are such a good pair, those two and to think I got so wound up about them." Dave had forgotten Anne had not been present at the altercation at the top of the slipway where Deborah had pushed him, but she knew exactly what he was talking about. "I believe Dan is leaving with them tonight. Then the Featherstore will be free and I think I'll move myself in there and leave the Manse to you girls, eh? We prophets need time to ourselves, don't you think?" Dave was making a small joke at his own expense and Anne appreciated that. He had been a good father to her but now had the good sense to voluntarily stand aside. Smiling at him, she thought it was good he jumped before he had to be pushed. "Erica suggested I went off with Dan but I feel so much better now. I'll stay and do my bit, whatever I can until my back recovers properly."

Gazing out toward Boreray they both marveled at the whiteness of the Stacs that afternoon. "There are Angels over there, Anne. That's where we need to be, not on this godforsaken island, if you'll pardon my expression." She smiled again, "Yes, Dad. I do believe you're right!" Anne linked arms with her father and the pair made their way back to the village. At the bottom of An Lag, Anne told her father she'd leave him to make his own way back from there as she needed to go and speak to Erica.

Knocking on the door of Erica's blackhouse, she entered to join her sister at the table. "Sit down, Anne. All over in the glen for today, is it?" Erica was interested to know how the cull had gone. "Yes, that's what I wanted to talk to you about." There would be no mention of her slaughtering Gavin but obviously something had to be done. If she had her way she would have let things be. Nature had taken its course and the fittest survived. She began to relate what had happened and when she told Erica how Sean had blasted the Skuas as they tried to defend their territory, her sister's face noticeably darkened. Then chasing the sheep in the Argocat and making a complete hash of culling them and how she had to intervene to put so many out of their suffering. "Where are Sean and Gavin now, Anne?"

Erica had been intending to have them off the island that very evening regardless of what Dave or anybody else thought. Murdering male bastards had no place on their island and she told her sister exactly what she thought. "I agree, Erica. But they are gone now and won't be back." Anne was matter of fact about it. "What do you mean, how?" Anne related the outcome of the cull as she wanted it understood. In their bloodlust the two stalkers had driven too close to the cliff edge at the back of the Tunnel. There had been one of those inexplicable gusts of wind which had picked up the Argocat and thrown it against the rock face. Both men and their machine were now at the bottom of the sea.

"Where the crabs can feast on them for all I care!" Erica was outraged but realized the men would be missed at the end of the day when they failed to return. "We'd better let Mum know about this, she'll have to let that Josephine woman back at the Trust know what's happened." The sisters walked through the village to give Deborah the news. They had agreed not to let Dave know initially as they were unsure of his likely reaction. The last thing either wanted was a Biblical rant doubtless connected to lambs of God and divine wrath. Deborah was the level headed parent at the moment. Anne again remained silent about what she knew about her mother's instability, or so she thought.

Erica and Anne walked into the Manse and found Deborah in a surprisingly jovial mood. "You'd better sit down, Mum. There's been an accident." Deborah knew it couldn't be Dave. He was outside showing a renewed interest in the walled garden. Anne explained what had happened near the Tunnel. It was a long and hard walk there and back and Deborah had only been once just shortly after the family arrived on the island. Her knowledge of the topography was sketchy.

"You are saying the Argocat was blown off the cliff edge. Anne, are you sure they are dead?" Anne nodded, "Absolutely Mum. They stood no chance and retrieving them will be next to impossible. It wouldn't surprise me if the currents down there have taken them over the edge of the continental shelf. They could be lying under a 1000 feet of water by now." Deborah needed advice on what to do next. "Let's go and have a word with Don and Lachie and see if they have any ideas on what we should do." The sisters followed her down to the jetty where she found Don checking the fuel filters of *Beluga*'s twin diesel engines. "We have just helped ourselves to some of Her Majesty's diesel and there might be a bit of water in it after all these months. We don't want to break down on the way back."

"Don, we need your help. There's been an accident and we think the stalkers are probably dead. The Argocat was blown over the cliff above the Tunnel and there's no sign of either them or the machine. Do you think you could take us round there in the boat to see if we can do anything?" Don let out his breath in a hiss and looked pale. He called Lachie up from inside the boat. "We are going to have to go round to the Tunnel, Sean and Gavin have gone over the cliff." Lachie was equally shocked. "Bloody hell, do you think they are OK?" Don shook his head, "I doubt it and they are probably both dead by now. There is a problem Deborah. The currents off that headland are treacherous and I don't want to risk damaging the boat on the rocks. The tide races through the tunnel and if the charts are to be believed a channel has been scoured all the way to the continental shelf. Anything or anyone falling in there would be swept into the abyss well before we had time to get round there." This was just what Anne wanted to hear. Erica didn't show undue concern either. "What we need to do now is go out beyond the mouth of Village Bay and call the coastguard and let them deal with it. I can't call from here because the VHF signal is blocked by Oiseval." The hill of Oiseval blocked all line of sight transmissions between the village and the outside world. Yachtsmen, anchored in Village Bay, had regularly requested to use the telephone when the Base had been active. Don with his of local experience knew they had to sail out from the bay to be able to call out. He invited the three women to come with him, Anne in particular would have to give an eye witness account of what had happened. Lachie issued the women with life jackets and untied the mooring ropes. Don reversed the *Beluga* out from the jetty before turning the vessel and heading out toward the small island of Levenish at the mouth of the bay. "Got to be careful with shallow rocks round here, we don't want to be joining the boys just yet, do we?" Don's graveyard humor wasn't out of place. The boatmen faced death every working day, if their passengers only knew. So many uncharted rocks around the islands and ferocious tidal races to contend with. In some places a malevolent wind blew against tides in the shallow seas creating columns of angry water that waited to drown unwary sailors. Don didn't think that after several hours the accident constituted an emergency so called the coastguard on their working VHF Channel 67.

"Stornoway Coastguard, Stornoway Coastguard. This is MV *Beluga*."

The call was sent twice and once he had finished sipping his tea, the duty operator answered the routine transmission. "MV *Beluga*, MV *Beluga*. Stornoway Coastguard, how can be of assistance Don." Don was slightly hesitant about broadcasting bad news. "Ah, yes Andy. We have an incident at St Kilda to report. I'll pass you over to the young lady here who can tell you all about it." Anne winced at the condescension but took the handset from Don and proceeded to tell Andy, the duty coastguard operator what had happened. Andy knew the waters as well as Don and agreed the stalkers would have stood no chance. There was no point in sending the helicopter out from Aberdeen as there would be no-one to pick up dead or alive. He would pass the matter on to the Police and all he could suggest was that the Health and Safety Executive might want to visit as it was technically a workplace accident. Don shook his head, it was highly unlikely HSE would come out so far to investigate what was obviously just a tragic accident, no more. Anne's statement should suffice and considering the currents, Sean and Gavin would be listed as lost, presumed dead at sea. It would be up to the Western Isles Trust to inform their families and look into their own safe systems of work should stalkers be employed at St Kilda in the future.

Once the call to the coastguard was finished, Don turned the *Beluga* around and headed back to the jetty. They tied up and Anne was asked to remind Dan to be down at the jetty with everything he wanted to take no later than 0800 next morning. As before, Don and Lachie opted to stay on board rather than brave the frosty atmosphere in the Manse.

Sitting round the table that evening the family discussed the traumatic events of the day. Dave had returned from the Gap, convinced of the existence of Angels on Boreray, but opting not to share his belief in Deborah's presence. Deborah was visibly still shaken by the accident. "One moment they are here, those two young guys, and the next they are gone." Anne tried to explain, "But Mum, they got it all wrong. It was complete mayhem down there. Something got into them, bloodlust maybe, but they were driving round like lunatics in that machine firing at anything that moved. I'm glad they told me to keep well out of the way. There were so many injured sheep that I had to dispatch afterwards." Anne explained most of what happened in a clinical, dispassionate way. Erica was less restrained. "The bastards, if I had seen them firing buckshot indiscriminately like that I would have taken our own rifle and put a stop to it. A pity you didn't dispatch them as well, Anne." Dave intervened, "Now then girls, *Vengeance is mine said the Lord.* I agree it was a botched cull so what we will have to do in future is somehow keep the sheep out of the village area. Up on the hill and over in the glen, they will be a good resource for us. Just not in the vegetable gardens" He was trying to remain pragmatic over the incident. "You could try just asking them to keep out?" Anne was being sarcastic but thought to herself that when the time was right she would go down to the glen and do exactly that, ask for the sheep to be kept out of the vegetable gardens. "So what's Dan up to tonight then?"

Dave had been aware that Dan was planning to leave in the morning. Erica said she had seen him sweeping out the Featherstore and having a general clean up. Although Dave was planning to move in there himself he hadn't been aware

Deborah had been thinking the same thing. As far as she was concerned, their marriage was over and she didn't want him sleeping under the same roof, let alone in the same bed with her. She would tolerate his presence for just one more night. Erica knew from the earlier conversation with Sally that all was not well between her parents but tactfully kept the knowledge to herself that evening. She suggested they should invite Dan over for a last drink before he set off in the morning. "I don't think that's a very good idea, Erica. He'll want to get himself sorted out and if he gets drinking he won't get his act together in the morning." The last thing Deborah wanted was for Dan to mess up her plans now. Anne remained impassive, now was not the right time to let on what she had seen from the Hidey-Hole. Erica expressed a desire to see him off, even if no-one else did. "Well if it is all right with you miserable lot, I'll go over to the Featherstore later and be sociable with him." Erica knew nothing of Deborah's seduction and simply expected Dan would be glad of some company on his final night on the island. After the meal was cleared away, Erica went back to her blackhouse, lit the woodstove for residual warmth when she got back then walked back to the Featherstore to find Dan. When she got there, she was amazed how spotlessly clean the apartment was. Dan was still scrubbing at some stubborn dirt in the corner of the sea-facing bedroom window. "Blimey, Dan! What's come over you? You'll lose your credibility as the island slob at this rate." Dan looked up. "Just a minute, Erica. Let me finish this corner then I'll be with you." She explained the purpose of her visit. "I just wondered if you'd like to come over to the blackhouse for a drink. Hey, have you eaten tonight?" Dave hadn't had anything all day. "Er, no, not yet. Actually I would like to come over to yours, Erica. There's just been too much stuff going on around here today. I could do with somewhere to chill for a bit." She thought he had cleaned enough. "Come on then, put the dusters away and I'll make you some supper."

The two of them walked the weed strewn seafront road to the firepond and followed the burn up to the end of the Street and Erica's blackhouse. Standing outside for a moment, Dan took a long glance across the bay toward the *Beluga* tied up at the jetty. This was his last night on the island. Last night on this island of crazy women, he thought but kept it to himself. But Erica was alright, the least crazy of them. He followed Erica inside and sat down beside the warm woodstove. What a luxury after the cold Featherstore. It would be appalling in there when next winter came and apart from damp and cold, he badly needed to get away from Deborah. "Aye. I'll be off with Dan and Lachie tomorrow. I heard all the shooting, did the start of the cull go well? Mutton for you lot and I'm going to miss it!" It hadn't occurred to Erica that, being so busy cleaning the Featherstore before he left, Dan might not have heard about the accident. "Oh God, Dan. Don't suppose anyone's let you know. There was an accident down in the glen. Sean and Gavin were lost." He was surprised, "Lost? What do you mean, Erica?" She explained what Anne had told them. "I didn't see it myself so I only have Anne's word for it, she was down there with them. In the frenzy of chasing sheep, the Argocat went over the edge. Don and Lachie reckon they must have been swept out and over the edge of the continental shelf. We won't even find their bodies." Dan was dumbstruck. All he had been thinking about was his being used by Deborah and then dumped. These men, great guys in his opinion, had been killed and he had been the last to know. Didn't anyone here even think to tell him, was he so insignificant around here? In the grand scale of things, his being shagged by Deborah was pretty insignificant compared with the accident but he still couldn't bring himself to engage with much more than his own hurt. "Isn't there anything we can do?" he asked. "It's been done, Dan. Anne was the only eye witness and she spoke to the coastguard from the *Beluga*. They had to go to the mouth of the bay to make the call, you might have seen them go out for a short while." He had seen the boat go out. "Yeah, I thought maybe they had gone fishing or something."

Erica continued, "Apparently the coastguard reckons there's nothing can be done either, other than fill in reports when the time comes. The Trust will no doubt have some serious paperwork to do but as far as we are concerned it was a tragic accident, like all the others that have happened in Glen Mór." Erica spared him her hope that the crabs would have a good feed over the next few days too. She passed him a can of Tennent's and went to begin making their meal.

"Afraid I am still on mutton from the sheep that dad shot. When I get round to it, I'll make a smoker. Then I can cure the odd leg of mutton and hang it up, really ethnic or what?" Dan was a little surprised at Erica's levity following the accident but accepted that there was nothing any of them could have done. If anyone should be upset, it should be Anne. Having witnessed the event she seemed the coolest of all. Of all the women on the island, she was the most unfathomable, he concluded. "Is your sister OK? I mean she must have seen everything." Erica shrugged, "Oh, don't you worry about her. It's just another ecological event as far as she's concerned. Men, guns and machines; testosterone mixed with releases of kinetic and fossil energy. She will be fine, like water off a duck's back to her. She'll be more concerned about the Skuas they killed at the start of the carnage." Dan admitted to Erica that he thought killing Skuas might not have been such a bad thing. They had always attacked him every time he tried to go into the glen to plan his now abandoned guided walks program. He had given up any desire to venture further than the end of the line of cleits on the northern side of the glen. "I think I'd better forget you said that, Dan, before we fall out over it. The plan, as I understand it, is find a way of keeping the sheep out of the vegetable gardens while using them as a meat resource. Anne thinks she knows a way to do it but isn't really letting on. She thinks she can draw on some kind of divine support. Fuck! She sound's as crazy as Dad sometimes. What is this family all about?" What indeed? Dan thought and thank fuck he would be away from them all in the morning.

There was a knock on the door and Sally stepped into the open interior of the blackhouse. While listening to Dan, talking as he ate his mutton sandwich, Erica had lit a couple of hurricane lamps sitting in alcoves she had built into the wall. In spite of the low energy LED lights, she preferred the ambience from the oil lamps. "My, what a cozy scene I see before me, got room for a *ménage à trois* or is this a private party?" Erica feigned indignation, "Don't you bloody start, Sally! Anyway, to what do we owe this dubious pleasure? Come in and join us." Sally moved to the center of the room. "Sit yourself down but keep your hands off Dan, he's mine tonight. Poor bloke didn't know about the accident till just now. Bit of a shock to lose a couple of mates like that." Dan was shocked but also at the flippant way the two women dealt with the deaths of Sean and Gavin. A couple of men die, oh well there'll be a more along soon. It was scary that life out here in the North Atlantic life, well male life at least, seemed so cheap to these women. Erica produced three more cans of date expired lager and they sat down to chat.

"How are you feeling now, Sal? After Dad's little *faux pas* this morning?" Erica was still concerned over her father's behavior. "Oh, I'm OK now. Just a bit worrying at the time." Dan was looking puzzled so Erica thought to explain another event he had missed that morning. "Dan, you are off tomorrow but I must ask you to keep this to yourself, OK?" Dan nodded his agreement. Whatever was about to be revealed would go no further than the three of them.

"Well, as you know Dave is struggling with lower back pain and Sally gave him a massage to ease things for him." She looked at Sally in a conspiratorial way before proceeding. "So after Dave has his massage, he gets up nimble as you like and makes a grab for Sally dressed in no more than his underpants."

Here she couldn't contain her giggle. "And apparently he had an erection like a flag pole!" The two women collapsed in giggles at the description of the ever so pious Dave damn near erupting out of his boxers. Even Dan had to laugh with them, it was so preposterous. "Come on Dan, your turn now. Tell us a joke!" Sally was in a good mood and wanted to forget about the unpleasant events of the day as soon as possible. Dan decided against telling jokes, most of his once large repertoire long forgotten since arriving at St Kilda. There hadn't been much, if anything, to joke about lately, as far he was concerned.

"Well ladies, there is one thing……." he was cautious but overcame it seeing Sally's interest. "Yes…..? Come on Dan you can tell us, can't he Erica!" Erica grinned at what salacious titbit might be coming. "Actually Dave isn't the only one who's been making passes where they shouldn't have been made." Dan was getting into his element with the two women waiting for him to divulge his juicy secret. He paused for effect before telling them about his morning with Deborah.

"You're telling us that after making Dave's life a misery, she went over to the Featherstore and shagged the living daylights out of you! You are kidding us, surely not Deborah as well?" Sally was incredulous. "Yes, there was no stopping her. I didn't have a say in the matter, she just took me." Sally's disapproval was clearly insincere. "Dear, oh dear, young man. What's up with that family, what are they like! A couple of latent swingers by the sound of it. They ought to lighten up a bit with all this free love going on. So who's Anne shagging when she goes off down Glen Mór for the day ha, ha?" Dan and Sally were having fun recounting their wayward adventures with Dave and Deborah but Erica failed to find the banter amusing. "Hang on a minute, you two. It's my parents you're having a laugh about. OK, it may be a bit ludicrous to think of Dad losing the plot in his underpants but Mum making a lot more than just a pass at you Dan is downright revolting." Erica got up and began pacing the room thumping her fists on any available surface. "It's just not funny, Dan. How do think it makes me feel to think of my mother and .... you! You are a man, like it or not, and you could have said no. Just say no! We were all taught that at school and you let her make a complete fool of herself. Why didn't you say no, Dan?" He was backed into a corner. "It wasn't like that, please believe me. It wasn't something I wanted, she made me do it." Erica was scornful, "Oh, yeah, right! Blame my mother now, why don't you. Christ, you are such a pathetic weakling Dan! Go on, just fuck off out of my house and make sure you're on that boat in the morning and don't come back!" Sally tried to sooth things in the blackhouse as Dan got up to leave. "Hey you two, that's enough. It's hard enough out here without falling out with each other. Erica, at the end of the day they were two consenting adults. I didn't consent to what your father had in mind, it's me who should be up in arms not you." Dan had his hand on the door latch. "Well, if you'll excuse me I'll get my sorry male head out of here and leave you to argue amongst yourselves. Jesus, I have had enough of this place. Two great guys got killed this morning, I don't give a toss who's shagging who and neither should you. Good night!" Dan had had enough and mild natured as he was, his temper was at snapping point. Getting away from the island and its crazy inhabitants would be the best move he could make. Erica had had enough too. "Sally, if you don't mind, could you just go as well please? I've really had enough for one day. It's really nothing you've done or said, I just need some space tonight, OK?" Sally finished her beer and got up to leave. "See you tomorrow, Erica? Sleep well."

With Dan back in the Featherstore and Sally in the Factor's House, Erica collected her thoughts on the day's events. She could smirk at her father's behavior, but not her mother's. Dan was kind of, well her friend if not her actual lover. Now that could definitely never happen and after he was gone the only man left on the island would be her father. She did like Sally and sensed things could develop with her but it wasn't what she wanted. She decided a smoke would calm her nerves and rolled a spliff from the grass she had bought from Lachie. Taking it outside, she sat on the low wall in front of her rounded cottage and lit up. It was peaceful in Village Bay that evening. Just a slow gentle swell breaking quietly on the beach. The distant call of seals could be heard coming from the Dun gap. A bit like dogs she thought, but their howls were nowhere near as lonely sounding. The grass was excellent and doing her the world of good apart from the dryness in her throat. She fetched a glass of water from the bucket she had filled at the well Anne where had tripped over. Normally she would have drunk rainwater but had run out until the weather broke. They had had surprisingly little rain so far that year. She couldn't be quite sure when she first noticed it but there seemed to be some commotion in the Dun gap. Erica could hear the song of the seals turn into disgruntled barking and growling as they were sprayed with cold seawater while dozing on the flat rocks. A vortex, a column of water was spinning between Dun and Hirta and edging into Village Bay. Slowly exhaling she watched as the water spout appeared to try not to further disturb the dozing seals. The light was fading but it was still possible to see the animals look up, grumble and settle down again. The water spout spun across the bay before hesitating in front of the Featherstore. It then curled around the end of the jetty and Erica saw Don quickly go to the aft of the *Beluga* and lash down his inflatable tender. As if satisfied with the men's preparations to leave the island, the spinning water-devil followed the curve of the beach before disappearing into the half submerged Cailleach's Cave below Ruiaval.

Erica rubbed her eyes and pinched out her joint to save it for another time. She really felt dry and finished off her first glass of well-water before pouring and drinking another straight off. Had she really seen a water-devil on such a quiet night? When strong winds blew down from the hill they could be expected or over in Glen Bay at almost any time, but here on a tranquil evening in Village Bay, she must be imagining things. It was time to hit the sack and start afresh in the morning.

Dan had his belongings down on the jetty before Don and Lachie had barely surfaced. "You're keen, alright. Anyone would think you'd had enough of this island!" Inscrutable as ever, Don didn't miss much and could sense Dan's urgency to get away from St Kilda. He had factored this into the leverage regarding the unpaid debt earlier. Now Don was pretty eager to get away himself. The business of the two stalkers was unsettling. There was really nothing any of them could have done after such an accident, which was the hard part about it for him. To simply write off two men's lives could never be easy, though he thought it strange that Anne, who had witnessed the event, seemed almost totally unmoved. She was very matter of fact about it. These women were an odd bunch, no wonder Dan was eager to get away. He was invited on-board for coffee and waited while the other two ate their breakfast. He felt hungry watching them eat bacon sandwiches and asked if he could make himself one. He hadn't wanted to make breakfast in the Featherstore after spending so much time cleaning the kitchen area. He had been determined to leave a good impression when he left but had no idea that Dave would be moving in there as soon as he departed.

With the *Beluga* readied to sail back to Leverburgh, Dan left Lachie in charge and walked up to the Manse to say goodbye and arrange a time for their next visit to St Kilda. Knocking on the door, he went in without waiting to be called and found a frosty atmosphere between Dave and Deborah. They both looked up and Dave was the first to speak. "Ah, good morning, Don. So you are off then?" It was clear he was. "Aye, yes. I wanted to arrange a date to come back with you before we leave. Dan's on-board already so we can get off promptly. So, when would you like us back?" Deborah spoke this time. "Don I think if you came back next week sometime that would suit us, fine." Don was surprised to be asked back so soon. "Next week! Isn't that a bit early?" Dave couldn't see the urgency. He had no idea of his wife's plans to send him away. Deborah had made her mind up that, apart from the issue of their struggling marriage, he would be better away from the island for his own, and their daughters', sanity.

"Yes, Don. Come back in a week's time. I'll email you if there is any change of plan." He nodded, "OK then, good job you can still crank up that generator. You ought to get yourself a satellite phone in case one day it doesn't start. I could get you one and bring it over next week, if you like." It seemed Don was intuiting Dave's exit from the family. Having no practical knowledge of things mechanical herself, Deborah agreed it would be a good idea. As much as she respected her daughters' practical abilities, she didn't think they extended to fixing the generator. It would be better to have some way of contacting the outside world if push came to shove. "I'll let you know how much you owe me when I come back, OK?"

Don was eager to get back to the boat and set off so said his goodbyes to Dave and Deborah and left the Manse for the jetty. Lachie had already warmed up the engines which ticked over, burbling, waiting for him to take charge and open the throttles for the trip back. Don untied the mooring ropes and stepped on board to take the controls from Lachie. Though more than capable, Lachie handed control of the boat to Don who, as well as being his personal friend, owned the boat and paid his wages. Twin propellers churned the water and pulled the *Beluga* away from the jetty before Don pushed both throttle levers forward and turned the boat toward the mouth of the bay. With changing weather on the horizon, as the boat left the calm of Village Bay it began to rise and fall on the increasing swell. "Sea's running from the north-west, Dan. Hope you are a good sailor!" Lachie joked with Dan who was already failing to see the funny side of the boat's rolling motion as it crossed the swell. "You'll live, man. They reckon it's worse on the way out to St Kilda." They, by which he meant his paying passengers, rarely survived the crossing totally untouched by sea-sickness. From being a bit green about the gills to needing a full day lying down to recover, the *Beluga*'s charter passengers had always been a varied lot. The one thing they had in common was the ability to pay around two-hundred pounds for a return day trip into realms of their imagination. St Kilda was like that.

18 REVELATION

With Dan out of the way, Dave thought Deborah looked radiant. He hadn't seen her so bright and positive about life for a long time. The atmosphere in the Manse had improved beyond recognition and he had begun to think that all would be well with their venture to resettle the island. He still kept up his Bible readings which now appeared tolerated by the women around him, even appreciated by his youngest daughter. It never occurred to him that apart from Anne, his readings were being considered a harmless irrelevance. Dave was using biblical scriptures to justify his ambition as island patriarch. Anne had other ideas.

The *Beluga* had been gone two days when Anne chose her moment. It came as the family sat down for their evening meal. Dave had finished his short reading and started a more general conversation regarding the day of the stalkers' accident.

"That day even started oddly, we were bickering with each other from the word go and I had a murderous bad back." Deborah had heard the gossip and thought it a good moment to embarrass Dave in front of his daughters. "And you made a fool of yourself with Sally, so I heard!" Dave's feelings of familial optimism evaporated in an instant. He felt the ground shift beneath him as his wife made his foolish pass at Sally known to all of them. How she knew, he had no idea. What Deborah hadn't allowed for was that his daughters already knew and while not condoning his behavior, though it understandable given the circumstances.

"Mum, Dad had a terrible bad back and went to seek help from Sally while you were occupied in the Featherstore. Isn't that right?" Anne met her mother's surprised expression with dispassionate full eye contact. She continued to speak with carefully calibrated scorn in her voice. "You've told us about Dad, it was something we all knew but chose not to make anything more than a joke about. Two men died that morning which was pretty serious, in case you have forgotten. So if we are reduced to salacious point scoring, why don't you tell us what you were up to with Dan the other morning?" Deborah was on the defensive. No-one was eating waiting for her to answer. She looked at Erica and at once understood that both daughters already knew what had been happening in the Featherstore. "But....how did you know?" She was genuinely shocked that the whole family seemed to know about her affair with Dan. All except Dave who was beginning to look thunderstruck as the implication behind his wife's obvious discomfort wormed inside him.

"How did we know what? What has been going on, Deborah?" Erica answered first. "While you were having your back seen to, Dad, your wife was busy shagging the daylights out of Dan!" Erica could barely disguise the disgust she felt for her mother. As far as Erica was concerned, her father was a special, if damaged, man and worthy of at least some respect from his wife. She had seen enough family breakdown in Edinburgh, now it was happening here. Anne sat back, a small smile quivering around her mouth. It was going just as she had planned. "'I think your God might have forsaken you somewhat, Dad. What does the Bible say about unfaithful wives then?"

Dave was put on the spot in front of the women. It seemed his daughters held some grudging support for him in his predicament and it would be good if he could remain magnanimous, however hard that be. "Dan was a foolish young man to allow himself to be used like that. Proverbs 7 describes a

Young man void of understanding who was forced by the *flattering of her lips* to go to her *as an ox goeth to the slaughter, or as a fool to the correction of the stocks."*

"Yes," Anne continued. "I have been reading that bit too, Dad. It also says,

For she hath cast down many wounded; yea, many strong men have been slain by her. Her house is the way to hell, going down to the chambers of death."

Erica was as surprised as her father at her younger sister's knowledge of the scriptures. In an attempt to diffuse the situation she tried to introduce some levity.

"As a fool to the correction of the stocks. It sounds like the fool was the one who went to Sally's massage parlor if you ask me!" Erica thought carefully before continuing. "But, Mum, why did you do it? Why risk our family for a few hours of pleasure with that, what can I say, *young man void of understanding."*

She had wanted to say with that complete prat but thought to humor her father if possible. Dave remained silent for a while waiting for his own moment. A decision had to be made, he knew, but one that did not make him look any more foolish than he already felt. Deborah was waiting for the outburst of rage she felt must surely follow but it appeared Dave was expressing empathy with Dan.

"I'll refer to Proverbs again. Chapter 6, verse 32,

But whoso committeth adultery with a woman lacketh understanding: he that doeth it destroyeth his own soul."

It was Deborah who exploded. "Damn the lot of you, you're all on his side. You know we have hardly made love since we got here and now it's all my fault. Christ, he has sympathy with Dan who at least managed to treat me like a woman! And you Anne, why have you been reading that patriarchal garbage?" Dave answered instead, "I hope the blasphemy made you feel better, Deborah. I am truly glad that Anne has chosen to read and gain some understanding from the scriptures. Erica, I feel could make a good Quaker but you Deborah could do no better than make a start by picking up the Bible yourself."

She was incensed, "Jesus, if I pick that book up at all, it will be to throw it into the cess pit where it belongs." Deborah was past caring, it seemed they were all against her but at least she had known, well if not exactly love, she had known physical affection not just pie in the sky twaddle about Gods and Goddesses preferred by her own family.

Dave had come to a decision and explained that he would go and stay in the Featherstore for a few days and think things through in peace. Erica had her blackhouse retreat and it just left Deborah and Anne to share hostility in the Manse. The meal was hastily finished, they still needed to eat, before arrangements for separate accommodation were finalized. Anne went to her bedroom early, giving the appearance of wanting to keep away from her mother. In effect she couldn't have cared less about what was going through her mother's mind that evening. Dave was grateful that Dan had left the Featherstore apartment in a clean and tidy condition before he left. If anything he was relieved to be on his own where his dreams would not be continually challenged. Deborah knew instinctively that it would be a waste of time trying to talk anything through with Anne. Was she really her own daughter behaving like, well like some kind of family psychopath when it came to things emotional? Talking to Erica would be a waste of time for much simpler reasons. Her eldest daughter had branded her with shame. Tearfully she realized the only woman she could talk to was Sally.

"Don't beat yourself up too much over it, Deborah. This island has a strange effect on women at times. I've seen it before when the young lasses used to come out on conservation holidays. Once away from the social constraints of the mainland there was no stopping them and the guys working here weren't going to say no, were they?" Sally explained powerful effects of the ocean, the moon and tides had on everyone, especially women visiting the island for the first time. Their bodies had to acclimatize to a raw power of nature rarely encountered in modern life. "It's your age too, Debs. You're approaching the end of your fertility and it is quite common for women of your age to go off the rails a bit and have a last fling. Think yourself lucky you are married to Dave. A lot of divorces happen in middle age due to lack of male understanding of what their wives are biologically experiencing. From what you have told me, it sounds like he is more concerned about the effect you had on Dan. Bloody loved every minute, if I know young men!" They both laughed at this, though Deborah knew that for Dan it was a little more complicated. "Well, it's too late for the morning-after pill but I ought to give you a pregnancy test sooner rather than later." Deborah's thoughts focused. "You think that's a possibility, Sally?" Sally reiterated the power of the natural elements around them and this reminded Deborah that she did unexpectedly 'come-on' just before making love with Dan. It could be a possible. "You could look at like this, I know it sounds daft but maybe this place badly needs children after such a barren century. Bring me a urine sample as soon as you can and I can give you an answer in a few minutes. I've had to do a few of these tests in my time." Sally gave Deborah a knowing wink which put her at ease. "If I bump into Dave, I'll have a quiet word with him, but from what I am picking up I don't think any lasting damage has been done."

That evening Dave lay on his single bed in the Featherstore, overlooking the sea. He was deep in thought, not so much about the revelation of Deborah's unfaithfulness with Dan but more on his own situation at St Kilda. It been his last great opportunity to make something of himself, restore the island community that had fell apart in 1930 to be replaced by a predominantly male military community recently evacuated due to what seemed mostly alcohol related psychological problems. There had been a security lapse which allowed a terrorist attack but that should have been more of a wakeup call rather than a cause for evacuation. It was odd that the men never ventured into Glen Mór. It did feel an eerie place to him after the small plane crash on the day of their arrival. Those hunters never stood a chance and it was an accident that shouldn't have happened. A bit like Sean and Gavin, both experienced stalkers. It should never have happened to them either. He knew he wouldn't be going over the hill to the glen anytime soon. His back wouldn't let him climb any further than the Gap and further stone walling was out of the question for the time being. A brief adrenaline rush hit him when he remembered Deborah and Dan, probably copulating on the very same bed he was lying on now, but he quickly dismissed the thought, put it in a box and sealed the lid as tightly as he could. What had happened, had happened and he was now being tested by God. Abraham had been expected to slaughter his beloved son to prove his faith. Forgiving an errant wife would be easy compared with that. "Thank you, Lord. You've let me off lightly this time." His words echoed in the empty room as he poured himself a glass of water from the jug Anne had filled for him earlier. As he drank the water, his thoughts returned to the Angels he had seen beckoning him towards Boreray.

Deborah walked up to the Factor's House carrying a small plastic pot under her jacket. She had just passed her ovulation date and needed to be tested now, but she didn't want it to look too obvious what her second recent visit to Sally might imply. Once inside she passed the container to Sally who placed it on the kitchen counter. "Just a minute and I'll go and get the testing kit. It hasn't been used for a few years but there's nothing there to go off. We'll soon know the outcome." The testing kit consisted of a box of individually wrapped EPT sticks. Sally unwrapped one and dipped the end in Deborah's urine sample. "Got to hold this in here for twenty seconds, then wait two minutes, OK." Sally replaced the cap over the moist end of the stick and they waited for two minutes. To Deborah they were the longest two minutes ever, but as Sally suspected, a blue line appeared in a small aperture on the side of the testing stick indicating that, indeed, Deborah was pregnant.

"Well Deborah, you are going to have to consider your options and sooner rather than later. First of all think of yourself, do you want to have this child, at your age? There'll doubtless be grandchildren coming along soon. I can't give you a termination out here but I can arrange for the procedure to be done in Stornoway, but it has to be your decision, no-one else's. There's Dave to consider too, assuming you are going to stay together. How would he feel about bringing up Dan's child? It's not every man who could be happy with that and the last thing a child wants is to be resented by one of its parents. I am not going anywhere near the guilt thing but repercussions could be long lasting. I suppose we have to think of Dan too. If you carry the child he would probably go either of two ways. He could want nothing to do with the child or live a life of angst wanting to be a good father and I assume that is not a scenario you are seriously thinking of?"

Deborah was certain about that, "Most definitely not, I am afraid, Sally." Dan had served his purpose and there was no way Deborah wanted him back on the scene.

"As for the child, he or she would need a loving family, even if that family was just you, or a foster family until adoption could be sorted out. Due to your age you should also consider amniocentesis. Testing for Down's syndrome. It was becoming clear to both women that in her moment of passion, Deborah's maturity had played no part when it came to thinking about the consequences.

"There is one other thing you should seriously consider too. There have been no babies born at St Kilda since the 1920s. I must emphasize this to you, Deborah. This island has a tragic history of infantile tetanus, the eight-day sickness. There was nothing wrong with the fecundity of the population but between 70-80% of new born infants died of tetanus within the first two weeks of life. Most succumbed within eight days hence the local name for the disease. At its height, the population reached two hundred souls, never anymore and way before birth-control was ever thought about. The 'Eight-Day Sickness' was considered God's way of keeping the population at a level the island could support. You've seen the way the sheep breed until they starve. Out here, infant mortality has always prevented the human population going the same way. By the end of the nineteenth-century it was known for some St Kilda women to leave the island to give birth. That way they avoided, not divine retribution for their carnal sins but avoided nature's way of conserving the meagre resources available to all species out here. For land animals, humans included, it really is life on the edge here. So whatever you decide, Deborah, I must strongly advise you to leave the island. If you opt for a termination, then you need to leave the island as soon as possible. You probably need to have a heart to heart talk with Dave, too."

Deborah let the words sink in. "It puzzles me, Sally, why Dave shows so little interest in all this. It's as if he doesn't really care about my affair with Dan. I wish I could make him out, I really do." Sally continued her advice, "Talk to him Deborah, that really is the only way if your marriage is going to survive."

A few days later, Deborah decided to bite the bullet and walked over to the Featherstore to speak with Dave. It felt odd knocking on the door to speak with her own husband. Oddly the intervening hours had taken the sting out of the situation between her and Dave. Having a serious talk with her husband didn't feel too daunting, especially as her knock was acknowledged by a cheery response from inside. "Come on in!" Dave welcomed her. Entering, she saw Dave sitting in the worn armchair by the window. An oil lamp illuminated the large Bible he had taken with him and had been avidly poring over before she knocked.

"Hi, Debs! I wondered when you'd be over to see me. Think I have had enough of my own company for a while. Mind you it has been great sleeping in here with the sound of the waves and the seabirds right on the doorstep. I haven't really missed the Manse with its generator and mod-cons. You know, Dan left this place really clean and tidy."

Deborah came to the point quickly. "Yes, I gathered that. To tell you the truth, Dave. I wanted to have a talk with you about Dan and what went on, and why. I am taking a risk, I know, but you seem so relaxed about what happened, I am hoping we can talk about it?"

Deborah walked over to her husband and rather than tower over him, she drew up another chair and sat down beside him. "'Don't worry, Debs. As they say, the Lord moves in mysterious ways. He is testing me through this situation. By accepting without recrimination, I hope I am becoming a better man in the Lord's eyes. At the end of the day, I still have my Faith and there are plenty of references in the Bible about forgiveness for fallen women. Consider Mary Magdalen, how she cared for Christ in his hour of need." Deborah contained herself. "It's not forgiveness I am here to talk about, Dave. There are some practical issues we need to discuss. I am pregnant and not by you." If Dave was shocked by Deborah's revelation, he barely showed it but began turning the pages as if looking for the appropriate scripture. Deborah was quicker than her husband.

"I know what you are looking for Dave, it's in Luke, right at the beginning if I remember rightly. Elizabeth the wife of Zacharias became an older mother and gave birth to John the Baptist." Deborah had rehearsed this moment over and over in her mind before walking to the Featherstore. She knew her husband would seek Biblical justification for the situation. Dave quickly found Luke 1 and scanned the verses.

"Well, Debs, you are spot on. Elizabeth was favored by God and a close friend of the Blessed Mary, Mother of Christ. This was meant to happen! Though something similar happened with Abraham and Sarah, didn't it?" She humored him, "If you say so, Dave." Deborah had not researched further than Elizabeth and John the Baptist.

"Now, Dave. I'd better tell you the options Sally gave me, or should I say gave us? We have to take this seriously for our own benefit and for, er...wee John's sake too. Let me finish what I have to say before you give your opinion, OK?"

Deborah proceeded to tell Dave the options as she understood them. She could have an abortion as soon as possible and the problem, if that is what it was, would be over. She would be left with an emotional stain but no further consequences. She could go ahead and have the baby which could lead to Dan wanting to be involved. The baby would be at risk of Down's syndrome due to her age, but she could be tested for that. She ought to have the baby off island due to the statistically high risk of infantile tetanus. Apparently the St Kildans considered infant mortality an act of God, natural population control. There was the child to consider, he or she had to grow up in a loving family, either their own or with adoptive parents. Whatever the outcome she would have to leave the island for a while, either for an abortion or to give birth inside a hospital safely away from the scourge of tetanus. Dave took only a moment to consider.

"You must stay and have the child on the island, Debs. The

St Kildans were right, it will be God's will whether the child, who we will call John, lives or dies. Just think, he will be the first child to be born here for a hundred years!" Dave was excited at the prospect of not only a child for the island but also for the direct intervention of God. Deborah had other thoughts.

"You are wrong, Dave. Firstly the child could easily be a girl and I'm not taking the risk of him or her dying of tetanus. I have thought long and hard about it and have decided I do want to go through with this pregnancy. Let's be honest, it has nothing to do with you. No it was not an immaculate conception, before you get any funny ideas, but the child is mine and I intend to have it away from here. Sally will arrange things for me.

"Ephesians 5:22-23 *Wives, submit yourselves unto your own husbands, as unto the Lord. For the husband is the head of the wife, even as Christ is the head of the church: and he is the savior of the body.*"

Deborah's patience was exhausted. "In your dreams, Dave! I will have this child, who I hope will be a girl, and I will have her in a hygienic hospital on the mainland. If that is your final opinion, I'll bid you goodnight!" Deborah stormed out of the Featherstore slamming the door behind her as Dave searched for further scriptures to support his insistence that Deborah stayed and subjected her pregnancy and delivery to the will of God.

He returned to Hebrews 11 and read more about Sarah, wife of Abraham who gave birth to his son Isaac at a late age. "Of course, that's it!" Dave spoke his thoughts aloud. Sarah gave birth to Isaac and Abraham was then tested by the Lord to be prepared to slaughter his son as sacrifice to prove his worth. It came right at the last minute when God spoke and allowed Abraham to spare his son. God wouldn't really allow Deborah to leave the island, taking his son away. He would throw up a great storm to prevent Don's boat arriving or some other such thing to prevent her leaving. All he had to do was go along with her plans to leave it until God spoke and all would be well. Dave was satisfied and closed the Bible. He poured himself a glass of water from the plastic jerry-can he had refilled at the well that morning.

Back in the Manse, Deborah was fuming. "OK, Anne. You seem to know all about everything. I am pregnant! Sally confirmed it for me this morning and of all the options one thing is for certain. I am going to have to leave for a while. I might even decide to stay away for good as I will have a child to look after in a few months' time. Your father, of course, wants me to stay here and give birth on the island. He couldn't give a monkeys whose child it is but he is certain it will be a boy and it will be God's will whether he catches infantile tetanus or not. Over my dead body, Anne, over my dead body!"

Her daughter showed little reaction to the news. "So when are you off then, Mum?" Anne seemed almost as unconcerned about it all as her father. What was the matter with this crazy family? There was going to be a new baby and nobody gave a toss that it was the result of an affair she had had with Dan. Well that wasn't strictly true. Erica resented her for it though she reckoned that was more female jealousy than anything else. She had to smile at the idea that as a middle-aged woman she had beaten her nubile daughters to the bed of the only young man on the island. What she hadn't realized that the poison of female rivalry ran deeper than she could imagine. Anne was only too delighted that her mother would soon be out of the way for she had been reading the Bible too. In fact Anne had decided it was high time she spent more time with her father and that they read the Bible together rather than study independently. It was all part of her plan.

"Sorry Mum, I was a bit blunt then, we don't really want to lose you. I know you and Erica don't see eye to eye at the moment so if you want someone to talk to, go ahead."

Deborah felt tearful, "Thanks, Anne. I have just had about enough. My emotions have been going wild just lately. One minute I am as horny as hell and the next I am a man hater. What's going on?"

Anne thought for a moment before replying. It was actually a bit close to the way she had been feeling too. Her mother was obviously needing to cry, she hoped it wouldn't set her off as well.

"Sit down, Mum. It's going to be OK. It would be easy to say it's an age thing with the menopause just around the corner. As a scientist that's what I would say but as a woman I think there is more going on out here than we realize." Anne explained how she had felt too at the last spring tide. She had a huge period and was alternately horny and tearful afterwards. The small tsunami seemed to add to the effect the big tide range had on her. She had kept out of the way to avoid getting into unnecessary arguments and had been spotting birds in the bay from the Hidey-Hole. That's when she had spotted her mother with Dan, but tactfully thought not to mention it again.

"The movement of the tides affects us, Mum. More than we can imagine. Back in town the same thing happens but there are so many other distractions. Out here we get it full on, is it any wonder we go a bit crazy. Sally says you get used to it eventually and settle back to normal. I wonder if there were more people here we wouldn't be affected so strongly. Maybe it is one of nature's ways to get us to repopulate this island?"

Deborah remembered Sally had suggested much the same thing. "Oh well, that's alright then. Lots of women use the excuse of things happening to them beyond their control!" They both had to laugh at Deborah's implication and Anne's thoughts went straight to Sally and her massage table.

"Sally once said there was something in the water out here that makes people go a bit crazy, maybe she is right? She reckoned the military guys out here were doing relatively fine until that new borehole was commissioned. Doesn't it look pretty with all the Butterwort growing around it? It will die down soon and the dried leaves will probably fall down the well. Could be that's what she meant?"

Deborah thought for a moment before replying. "No I don't think so, the Butterwort, or Mothan as it's called round here, contains a powerful anti-biotic. Probably do us the world of good! It was used as a cure-all by the St Kildans in the past. Supposed to bring us good luck if we chew it, so we had better start munching, I reckon." Deborah had read the tales of Roderick the Imposter, a rogue minister who modelled himself, ironically in the light of current events, on John the Baptist. After his carnal method of saving female souls had been rumbled he had been sent to Dunvegan Castle for sentence. On the way, so the story went, he chewed copious amounts of Mothan and got let off with not much more than a slapped wrist and being told to behave himself in future. She had been reminded of this tale after coming up with the John the Baptist ruse to placate her husband.

"So what am I to do, Anne? My maternal instincts tell me to have the child, yet my common sense warns me it might be born with Down's syndrome. By the time I can have the amniocentesis test, it will be too late for a termination. Then shouldn't Dan have a say in this decision?' Anne was unequivocal, "Dan's a prat. You can leave him out of the picture, Mum! He won't want to know, I'll tell you that much." Deborah explained her father's thinking to her daughter. "Your father wants me to stay and have the baby here and whatever happens will be God's will. He started citing the biblical story of Abraham, Sarah and Isaac. Think he could relate better to that old patriarch than to the related tale of Elizabeth and Mary I told him about to start with."

Anne was approving, "You are bit cunning yourself, Mum. Clever shot to use the Bible to justify your actions to Dad." Deborah continued, "But anyway, Anne the upshot is that I feel I want to have this child and I need to get off the island rather than put my baby at 70-80% risk of infantile tetanus or subject it to the will of God. So when am I going? As soon as Don brings the *Beluga* back here, which I believe is next week sometime." Anne, as Deborah should have suspected knew more than she let on.

"Yes, Erica was talking about that. He's bringing her a small house cow. She's really looking forward to it."

Over the following few days Deborah busied herself with preparations for her departure. Dave kept himself out of the way and showed no obvious concern over his wife's arrangements to leave the island. He was wrapped up in a world of his own and took long walks over Conachair, stopping to gaze northward toward Boreray. He spoke with his wife over superficial domestic arrangements but there was no discernible bitterness displayed over the forthcoming separation. As far as he was concerned, it was God's will. They seemed to have acquired what they both wanted. Deborah was carrying her late conceived child and Dave had finally found and connected with God. Erica and Sally continued to meet at the far end of the village for drinks and chat in the blackhouse and Anne returned to her habit of spending long hours walking around the far side of the island, usually in Glen Mór. The family rarely saw each other, taking their separate pathways and the island remained peaceful while they waited for the arrival of the *Beluga* from Harris.

19 RESURRECTION

The *Beluga* arrived the following Wednesday. Don could never predict exactly when they would arrive unless there was a prolonged period of calm weather, an unlikely happening at St Kilda. Dave was away up at the Gap when they arrived but as soon as they heard the twin diesel engines slowdown in the bay, Erica and Sally ran to the jetty to meet the boat. The arrival of the first cow on the island since 1930 was a cause for celebration as far as Erica was concerned. She had left the choosing of the cow to Don. Like most Hebrideans he had a working knowledge of livestock husbandry. He knew that the heavy commercial beasts would be a handful on the island, not least for their size. They would need shelter in harsh conditions and even the derelict Bull's House could not contain a modern breed. Don had chosen a Dexter, the small breed from Ireland thought to have been bred by the Celts. He had thought getting the beast off the boat and onto the jetty would be a problem but the cow proved nimble and, glad to see firm ground after the three hour sea crossing, jumped ashore unaided. The animal paced the jetty taking in its new surroundings. When Erica approached, the cow was at first nervous and wouldn't let her take the halter thoughtfully left on by the previous owner, a crofter from Luskentyre. Erica and the cow faced each other along the jetty. Luckily the railings erected to prevent tourists from falling off the edge deterred the cow from jumping. Don and Lachie grinned as Erica tried to coax the animal toward her. Only after a gently swirling breeze lifted strands of dry seaweed off the jetty did the cow relax and let Erica take the halter. The bond had been made and Erica led the Dexter up to graze in front of the empty Base.

"You can let her go, Erica. She trusts you know and if I was you I would bucket train her. Douglas raised her to the bucket so she will know what to do. She must be hungry now, didn't like the crossing much." Lachie hadn't liked cleaning the mess after she had repeatedly scoured on the crossing either, some coarse grass inside her would soon sort that out, Don advised. The Soay sheep were curious. None had ever seen another grazing animal but soon accepted her. "There's just one thing you need to watch out for, Erica. She wasn't raised here so there is a possibility she could pick up something she has not been vaccinated against. I was going to warn against Red-water Fever but as there are no ticks on the island, that's most unlikely. From what I know, I don't think the St Kildan cattle suffered any more or less than any others from bovine diseases. She's three years old so worms shouldn't be a problem. Her last calf was only a month ago so she'll milk fine for a while but you will need to have her artificially inseminated or get yourself a bull in a few months' time. Let me know what you decide and I'll arrange it for you. Just remember to choose semen from a Dexter bull or another small breed to avoid problems when she comes to calve." Don was happy to advise Erica on anything she needed to know about keeping the island's first house cow for nearly a century. Right now, Erica was entranced and desperately wanted to give the cow a name. The small beast looked at her and lowed. "That's it you midget. Bridget the midget!"

Sally remarked that there was an old pop song about Bridget the midget. "Don't suppose that's a very nice thing to call her but Bridget is an apt name for the Hebrides. She is the patron saint of boatmen and cattle amongst many other things, so I reckon Bridget it is then." Erica wanted to use a Gaelic name for her cow. "Brighid she is out here, please Sally!" Erica had fallen instantly in love with the small cow now earnestly grazing nearby. She announced that after she had been milked she could shelter inside the blackhouse when the weather was bad and no, she wasn't going to build a pallet bed for Brighid when Lachie teased her about molly-coddling the beast.

Deborah had got everything packed that she needed to take. In the unlikely event she would want to return with her child to St Kilda, the rest of her belongings could stay. Dave had seen the cow being unloaded on the jetty and made his way down through An Lag, passing the sheep fanks and thought what a good place it would be for a few small cattle like that Dexter. South facing and out of the wind and excessive salt spray, the grazing would be sweet. If he could keep the sheep out, he was sure a few Dexters could be raised in those stone walled enclosures. When he reached the slipway he saw Deborah passing her large rucksack and wheeled hold-all onto the *Beluga*. It looked like she really was leaving him. Engaging his mind on livestock farming had briefly taken him out of his religious bubble but the reality of watching his wife readying to leave hit him hard. Tears were running down his cheeks as he walked up to her on the jetty. Putting his arms around her he tried to give Deborah a hug but she froze before shrugging him off.

"Bit late for that, Dave. Perhaps, if you had shown me some affection earlier I might have stayed. Come on Dave, you have your God now. He's probably more use to you out here than I ever will be. I'll be in touch and let you know how we get on, the child and I. I'm not promising but I might consider coming back after I have had the baby. We'll just have to see how things work out. Look, dry your tears Dave and I'll give you a hug before I get on board." She held him close while acknowledging her own fierce determination to move on. This man in her arms felt like a small boy to her now. Lost in a boys' own fantasy world justified by an imagined God. It felt good to be leaving, bringing up a child out here might have been OK for a younger woman, but not for her. She released Dave from the embrace and looking at him, realized that he had already disengaged from her emotionally. "God is testing me, Debs. He is testing me and I will not be found wanting. Go in peace and let me know how you get on. You will be warmly welcomed when you come back. I don't think the Prodigal….." She cut him short, "Prodigal daughter I think you meant to say. Thanks, Dave. It is good to know there will always be a place for me here if I need it. Now it's time to be off."

She kissed her husband lightly on his heavily stubbled cheek and stepped down lightly onto the deck of the *Beluga*. Don had already started the engines which were ticking over as Lachie released the mooring ropes from the iron bollards on the jetty. The boat gently reversed out over the kelp becoming exposed by the falling tide. As the boat disappeared around the Point of Col heading back toward Harris, Dave allowed himself a few wracking sobs before switching off from the situation. "1 Corinthians 7:12-15 I will not put you away and you are not in bondage to me, Deborah," he cried aloud.

Dave soon realized he was now the only man on the island. He had listened to the Lord and led his family away from the mess of mainland life. Now like Lot, his wife had turned back and he was left alone with his daughters, and Sally the paramedic nurse. Before the boat had left Don had spoken with Dave to advise him they couldn't come out the following week because there were missile trials taking place and shipping had to avoid the sea area to the east of St Kilda while the exercise was going on. The weather forecast was good so he hoped the Range would get it all over with quickly but, he had added, given past form the lads at Rangehead usually made a meal of things. That, in his opinion was real reason why they had been pulled back from St Kilda if the truth been known. With Deborah gone, Dave sensed a vacuum. A vacuum that needed filling and the scriptures were the obvious source for advice. He had found solace in Timothy on more than one occasion. Timothy understood and he turned to him again.

1 Timothy 3:5 *For if a man know not how to rule his own*

house, how shall he take care of the church of God?

He hadn't done too well in ruling his house so far but there was still time. He could see no reason not to take a second wife. Thinking of Abraham, as he often did, he had read of Abraham's two wives not to mention his several concubines. There should be no problem and he might even have a divine right to another wife while Deborah was away. After all it had been she who had committed adultery after all. There was only one available woman on the island and he decided to chance his luck with her once more. This time, however, he would be more of a gentleman. For the time being he stayed in the Featherstore, leaving the Manse to Anne who was only too pleased with the arrangement. That evening he walked up to the Factor's House and knocked on Sally's door. Proverbs 18:22, he thought. If I find myself another wife I will return to the favor of the Lord.

"Hello Dave, what can I do for you so late?" It had taken Sally a while to answer the door. It was cold in the Factor's House now that the power-station stood lifeless but the back boiler in her fireplace still produced enough hot water for the occasional luxurious soak. She was in her dressing gown, having reluctantly left the warmth of her bath-tub. Her other comfort that evening had come from the near emptied gin bottle, quickly hidden in the airing cupboard before she answered the door.

"Well first I'd like to apologize for my behavior the other day. I don't know what came over me like that. To be honest, I suppose I was feeling pretty desperate for affection after months of coldness from Debs." Sally immediately suspected Dave's motive for the evening call was more personal than professional. She came straight to the point. "That's OK, Dave. Perfectly understandable given the circumstances, but I am afraid that if you are looking at me for comfort you are barking completely up the wrong tree." He hadn't expected her to spot his motive so easily or be so blunt about it.

"What's that supposed to mean, Sal?" She invited him inside. "Sit down, Dave. Oh God, I didn't want to have to explain but now Deborah has left, I suppose I must. I don't tell many people this but I used to be married and lived on a croft near Tarbert. My husband and all his family were staunch members of the Free Church. Don't get me wrong, they have some excellent values when it comes to supporting family life but when I needed help the Free Church proved inflexible and unforgiving. I was banished and considered an abomination just because I had an affair, with a woman." Dave was taken aback, he hadn't expected this. He was now a single man and he wanted to begin courting a single woman. In his eyes it should have been simple.

"I have four children who they've managed to turn against me. We haven't been in contact for years. My husband divorced me on the grounds of adultery, he couldn't bring himself to admit his wife was if not actually lesbian, had proved to be bisexual. Not only was I banished but after our divorce, he was given custody of the kids. Apparently I was considered too deviant to be trusted with their upbringing. Can you imagine what that was like? To lose my husband, my children and wider family network simply for following a perfectly natural inclination that could have harmed no-one. It turned me against men and their precious Church, I can tell you. I will never understand what was so wrong that I would be considered an outcast. Come with me…"

Sally led Dave into the bathroom and opened the cupboard behind the door. The shelves were stacked with Gin bottles, mostly empty. "Those are my friends, my lovers now. The only friend I can rely on now is alcohol and when it's finished I don't know what I'll do. I am medically trained so I know what the stuff does to you. I am physically dependent as were so many of the guys who worked out here. Yes, I know I cover it up well and I'd appreciate it if you didn't spread it around. Erica knows of course but no-one else does. She has been a real pal to me as I am sure you are aware and no we are not a pair of lezzies before you start worrying about it, just good close friends. There is a difference, you know."

Dave did not know what to say. The wind had been taken completely out of his sails. A slap in the face he could have understood but here was Sally showing herself to be a far more complex human being than he had ever imagined.

"Sally, I am so glad you told me this. It explains a lot I didn't understand, or failed to see before. You have been open with me so I will admit that it had been on my mind to ask you to marry me when I came up here?" Sally was shocked this time. "What, Dave? I thought I was the crazy one!" He explained his position to her, as he saw it. "The thing is that from what I have been reading in the Scriptures, without a wife I am a less of a man in the eyes of God." Sally was again straight to the point. "That's complete and utter bollocks and you know it, Dave! So you thought that by marrying me everything would come right for you. Marrying me would be the worst thing you could ever do. Could you afford my Gin bill? Because I can't!"

Dave continued, "Sally, Abraham had two wives and it did not displease the Lord." She was getting annoyed with him. "Did you hear what I said, Dave. A thousand times no, I am not going to marry you. Not now, not ever. Jesus Christ I need a drink." Sally reached into the cupboard and pulled out the half emptied bottle she secreted when Dave unexpectedly knocked on her door. Putting the bottle to her lips she took a large gulp. "You are welcome to join me if you bring a bottle to share but I expect you'll want to go home and think about your situation. You know, I reckon everybody who worked at St Kilda had something to hide, to run away from. What was your real reason for coming here, Dave?"

Dave walked back to the Featherstore, his head spinning from Sally's revelation. Part of him accepted what she said had been spot on, but he couldn't imagine what he was running from. To the contrary he was trying to reach a better life. This was just another test and he quickly dismissed his niggling doubts as he had done when Deborah left earlier in the day. The Bible remained where he had left it on the table in the Featherstore and he sat down with water rather than alcohol to seek his solace from the Scriptures. He could not imagine a time when he would feel lonelier. That day his wife had left him and once more he had made a complete ass of himself with Sally. It should have been straight forward but it wasn't. Here he was on an Atlantic island that should have been the key to an idyllic future. The trouble was people ruined the dream by not sharing in it with him. His two daughters thought like him, he was sure. Erica was a hands-on young woman who any man could be proud of and even enigmatic Anne had shown an interest in the Bible lately. There was a chance this could work out in the end but it would depend on his step-daughters. He would invite them round and together they could make plans. At the end of the day, he was now their father and his opinion should be respected.

Sally walked over to Erica's blackhouse to discuss Dave's latest attempt to win her over. "It's really getting too much, Erica. I hope he understands now why his paternal ideas are so crazy. That sort of thing just doesn't apply out here. It never did. If he tries it on with me one more time I am going to have to leave, I can't take it anymore." Erica thought about her father and his problems for a moment. "Yeah, he is becoming a bit of a worry. A horny old man with a bad back, perhaps you should invite him back and give him the treatment, Sal?"

"What! You mean just like in the old days out here?" Sally raised her eyebrows at the thought. "Yes, he is a kinky old sod, he'd love it – and I did pick up somewhere that he had enjoyed a previous session with you. Instant cure for his bad back or something like that," laughed Erica.

Sally was thoughtful and considered the wisdom of Erica's suggestion for a moment. Her treatments had been much appreciated by the men from the Base in the past and no trouble had come of it. "Well, why not? The only thing Erica, is I'd like you to bring him along so I appear professional, on the surface at least." Erica grinned and couldn't suppress a giggle at her father's expense. "OK, I'll get him. You can get things ready in the Factor's House. Don't forget to light the fire for him!"

The two women walked along the street together planning how they would take Dave's mind off things and with a bit of luck, after the evening was over, he would stop bothering Sally. Sally popped into the Factor's House while Erica continued the length of the street to the Featherstore. Knocking on the door, she went inside without waiting to be invited. Dave was poring over pages of Genesis and looked up, surprised to see her standing there.

"Dad, Sally and I have put our heads together and come up with an idea you might like the sound of. She is offering to give you another treatment for your back, and by treatment I think she could be meaning something more than a simple massage. She used to do this for the men of the base sometimes when she was employed out here." Dave was intrigued and wanted to know more.

"Men had problems out here, as you already know. Young and not so young men away from their wives and girlfriends for a month, sometimes longer, needed to have an outlet for their, shall we say, energies. We reckon this what has been getting you down and I doubt any amount of Bible study would substitute for a pair of female hands in the right place." He could hardly believe what he was hearing from his own daughter.

"Erica, are you saying what I think you are saying?" She replied positively, "Yes, Dad. It will all be very clinical, nothing to get concerned about. Trust us, we have only your best interests at heart."

Dave thought it quite a coincidence. Here was his first born daughter suggesting some kind of sexual service just after he had been reading about Lot in Genesis 19. The similarities were striking. Lot's wife had turned back from the wilderness and been turned to a pillar of salt leaving only two daughters to continue his line, which they had apparently done willingly, so the Bible said. He felt aroused at the thought of such a thing manifesting itself right here and now.

Was Anne going to be involved too, he asked. "No, Dad. Just me and Sally. She was a bit embarrassed after what she said to you earlier and wanted me to ask you to come along. That OK with you?" She wanted to make sure you were happy with the plan. "Fine Erica, do I need to do anything?" She made one request. "Just put that Bible away, Dad. You won't need it again tonight." And with a bit of luck never again, she thought but tactfully kept it to herself. Her Dad was alright, but bloody hard work at times since they had come to St Kilda. He needed a woman's touch, which was all.

By the time Erica had led her father to Sally, she had a fire blazing in the hearth and the massage table was ready in the warm living room. "Take a seat both of you. Do you want to stay and help me, Erica?" Dave sat down in the armchair and to his further surprise, Sally poured him a large glass of gin. "There you are, old man. Just so you know I didn't mean to upset you earlier. It's not every day a girl gets asked to marry, is it?" It had actually happened quite a lot in the past during drunken evenings in the Puff-Inn, just another hazard of being a divorced woman working alongside heavy drinking and lonely men. She passed Erica a glass of gin too and the three chatted amiably, enjoying the warmth of the drink as well as the fire. "I'm feeling quite relaxed now, don't want to put you to the trouble of a massage. I'm OK, really."

Sally was insistent, "Dave, last time you had a terrible lower back. That was business, tonight it's going to be pleasure if you get my meaning." Erica couldn't suppress a giggle and snorted into her gin which was certainly having the desired effect. "Oh, come on Dad, loosen up. She is offering you, for free, the kind of massage businessmen pay a lot of money for back in the Edinburgh. You must have heard of the goings on at the Bad Moral Hotel!" He had heard of alleged goings on at the Balmoral Hotel and Dave blushed slightly at the implication, but secretly was beginning to look forward to what the two of them had in mind for him.

"Just get undressed down to your underpants, Dave. You can put this dressing gown on if you feel chilly or a bit exposed. Don't know why you should though, we both seen it all before, haven't we Erica? When you're ready just climb up on the bench and lie down, on your back this time."

The bench was close to the hearth and Dave felt quite hot being so close to the fire but encouraged by his daughter he had done what Sally asked and now lay on the bench staring up at the slightly smoke stained ceiling. Back draughts frequently blew down the chimney and this night was no exception. "One more thing Dave, to ensure you get the most out of this, I am going to ask Erica to strap your wrists and ankles to the bench. That way you won't be able to suddenly change your mind." Sally winked at Dave and Erica gently took his wrists and strapped them to the sides of the bench, then moved to his feet and strapped his ankles. Erica did think it looked slightly ridiculous, her father being strapped down to the bench in just his underpants and had to work hard to stifle her amusement. It was in the best interest of all of them that they broke his religious mania once and for all and so far he didn't seem to be protesting. For his part, Dave began to shiver in anticipation of what was coming. If God thought it was OK for Lot, then it was alright for him. He was disappointed when Erica got up to leave. "Right then, Sally. I'll leave him with you," she giggled. "You can tell me how you got on in the morning."

Sally walked over to the wall cupboard at the opposite side of the room and put on the white medical coat she kept hanging up there. It was surprisingly clean considering it hadn't been worn for such a long time. From the top shelf inside, she took down a box of latex gloves and put a pair on in front of Dave, who by this time had stopped his nervous shivering.

"Just what are you intending to do with those Sally?" She grinned at him. "Wait and see Dave, just wait and see. First of all we need to remove those pants, don't we?" From her pocket she produced a pair of surgical steel scissors and began to cut the material between the right leg of his boxers and the elastic waist band. Gently she lifted the material over to his left side, nearest the hearth. He looked in better condition than a lot of men she had seen in the past. No flabby beer gut to get in the way for sure. Dave was as well toned as he could be for his age. Hard physical work had had some benefit for him. Perhaps, she thought, if his back hadn't gone he could have worked out this religious nonsense in a more constructive kind of way.

"Just have to check under here first, Dave." Sally slid a well lubricated latex gloved finger into his anus. Dave struggled to rise from the bench but the straps held his wrists and ankles firm. All he could do was arch himself upwards as Sally's finger explored inside him. "Man of your age, Dave. He might have prostate trouble, just checking for you." She kept her finger inside him until he had no option but to relax. She slowly pushed her finger as far inside him as she could reach and began to slide it back out. She noticed the moisture on the end of his foreskin. I spite of his initial protest, it looked like it was going to work. She kept one finger in his anus and brought the other hand over to his penis and began to massage it. Strapped to the bench, naked and vulnerable, Dave became tearful as his erection rose. "There, there Dave. It's alright and you'll be so much the better for this when I am finished."

Sally was doing this for free. In the past she at least had been given a bottle of gin or whisky for her services, she remembered. Never mind, if it cures the old sod of his mania, that's all that matters. "Now let's make a good sinner of you, Dave." Skillfully she manipulated him, powerless in her hands, until he ejaculated copiously. Semen splashing across his stomach. "Wow, Dave. I reckon you needed that. It's been a long time since you came, that's for sure."

To her surprise, rather than letting out a satisfied sigh as had most of her previous clients, a sudden gust of wind blew smoke down the chimney into the room and Dave let out a howl of anguish as she withdrew her finger from his anus. Shaking and shuddering on the bench he began to froth at the lips.

"Fuck, Dave. Don't go having a fit on me, I'll get the straps off you." As the seizure took hold, Sally was unable to get him off the massage bench in time and with one wrist still attached he fell to the floor pulling the bench over with him. He looked a pathetic sight. He lay crumpled and naked on the floor, semen dripping from his now limp penis and one wrist still strapped to the bench lying across him. To make matters even worse, he appeared to have defecated as he fell. Quickly Sally undid the remaining strap and helped him get up. Thankfully it hadn't been an epileptic seizure but an extreme reaction to the emotional turmoil he had been experiencing.

"Look, you had better clean yourself up Dave. Here put

on the dressing gown and you can use my bathroom to wash yourself." Bewildered, Dave put on the gown and went to the bathroom. Luckily the blazing fire had heated up the water and by the time he re-emerged he looked presentable, if still dressed only in Sally's dressing gown. Sally had thrown the soiled latex gloves on the fire and hung up her white coat. The massage bench was folded up back in the closet and she had cleaned the mess from the floor. "Oh dear, are you alright Dave? I wasn't expecting anything like that to happen."

He surprised her again, "I'll be a lot better when I've got my clothes back on and another gin would be nice, Sally." She relaxed, "Phew, there's me thinking you'd be really mad at me for controlling you like that. A lot of men like it and just a few don't. I thought you'd be one of those when you screamed out. At least you look chilled now, that's the main thing."

His next comment was not what she expected. "You've certainly relaxed me, I'll say that. But the Bible says it should have been my firstborn daughter to take my seed. Tonight, it all went to waste. I read too about Onan the other day, Genesis 38: 8-10 and because he had deliberately spilled his seed on the ground rather than procreate, the Lord put him to death! I am glad you were in control there, Sally, and not me."

Sally was perplexed, maybe nothing had changed for him. Had she simply reinforced his perverse convictions? "Dave, nothing went to waste tonight. You came in here a tormented soul lost, dare I say trapped, in the world of the Old Testament. Now you are back with us, in the here and now, at St Kilda in the twenty-first century."

Discarding his cut boxers into the fireplace, Dave dressed himself and Sally poured him another large gin. She had already topped her own up. They sat opposite each other staring at the fire rapidly dying away before Dave placed another armful of scrap pallet wood on the embers. The fire soon blazed once more. "Tell me Dave, I'm intrigued about why you thought it should have been Erica who took your seed. Whatever made you think of such a thing? To put it bluntly wouldn't that be incest?" There was a knock on the front door which interrupted their conversation. Sally got up to see who was there.

"Oh, Hi Anne. What can I do for you?" Anne had slipped while walking down the slope from Conachair, just above the village. The scree slopes were good areas for finding unusual plants and she had been out botanizing earlier that evening. The slopes were inherently unstable and even the most agile member of the family had now taken a tumble. Anne was holding her left arm with her right hand as she came into Sally's living room. She was surprised to see her father sitting there in the room with an intriguing aroma of wood-smoke and the medical disinfectant Sally used to clean up the mess left by Dave's loss of bodily control shortly before.

"I've hurt my elbow, Sally. Could you take a look at it?" Reluctantly, Sally adopted a professional stance. "OK, take your jacket off and roll up your left sleeve for me." Anne's elbow was grazed and visibly red and swollen. Sally slowly moved the limb feeling the movement of the tendons and elbow joint. "I think you have just badly bruised yourself, Anne. It all feels fine in there but you'll probably be black and blue by the morning. I'll give you a tubular bandage to support your elbow for a day or two, but there's no serious damage. Just take more care next time, this is an unforgiving place and it could be your head you bruise next time. Might knock some sense into you!" Anne narrowed her eyes at Sally's joke but was curious as to what she and her father were up to.

"We were just discussing the Bible, Anne. Your father reckons it is quite alright by God to commit incest. Why don't you stay and join us for a drink, we might both learn a thing or two from this Bible of his."

Dave was put on the spot with both women eager to understand his argument. But he could direct them straight to the appropriate scripture and he asked Sally if she had a Bible he could borrow. "Well it's not on my reading list, for sure, but I think there is an old Gideon's Bible in the spare bedroom upstairs. I'll go and get it." When she came back, Anne was sitting on the arm rest of her father's chair sipping a small glass of gin herself. "Here's the Bible, Dave. I must say I find it hard to believe the Bible says incest is OK though." Dave turned to Genesis 19 verses 30-38. "Tell you what, I'll let Anne read it out to you. Then you'll know I am not making it up! It's about Lot and his two daughters Pheiné and Thamma after Edith, his wife, had been turned into a pillar of salt for looking back toward God's destruction of Sodom and Gomorrah." Anne took the book and began to read out loud.

'And Lot went up out of Zoar, and dwelt in the mountain, and his two daughters with him; for he feared to dwell in Zoar: and he dwelt in a cave, he and his two daughters. And the firstborn said unto the younger, our father is old, and there is not a man in the earth to come into us after the manner of all the earth: Come, let us make our father drink wine, and we will lie with him, that we may preserve seed of our father.

And they made their father drink wine that night: and the firstborn went in, and lay with her father; and he perceived not when she lay down, nor when she arose.

And it came to pass on the morrow, that the firstborn said unto the younger, behold, I lay yesternight with my father: let us make him drink wine this night also; and go thou in, and lie with him, that we may preserve seed of our father.

And they made their father drink wine that night also; and the younger arose, and lay with him; and he perceived not when she lay down, nor when she arose.

Thus were both the daughters of Lot with child by their father.

And the firstborn bare a son, and called his name Moab: the same is the father of the Moabites unto this day.

And the younger, she also bare a son, and called his name Benammi; the same is the father of the children of Ammon unto this day.'

"Dave that is pure filth!" Sally was amazed at what she had heard Anne read to them. "Whoever wrote that must have been the first recorded pervert in history. OK, I like the biblical justification for getting pissed but to justify an old man be shagged by his daughters, well that really is too much."

As a mother herself, Sally was genuinely shocked but Anne carefully considered what she had just read out. It wasn't quite so clear cut for her and she explained her scientist's reasoning.

"I'm not so sure, Sally. Erica probably wouldn't agree with me but livestock breeders sometimes mate father and daughter to get pure offspring. Take the sheep for example, we have the purest Soays in the world out here and genetic testing has shown inbreeding is common amongst them. Any malformed lamb would quickly die leaving healthy stock to continue the line. From a woman's point of view if there was no other man available, wouldn't incest be preferable to us becoming withered old crones before our time?"

The wind once more blew down the chimney sending smoke and ash into the room. "Oh, bugger! I've only just cleaned up after the last time. What's up with the weather tonight?" Sally was not totally surprised at Anne's comments regarding Lot and his daughters. "All I can say, Dave, is don't get any more funny ideas. Remember it will be three against one if you try it on!" Dave was not to be beaten, "Didn't you listen to the reading, Sal? It was the two daughters who tried it on. No one else comes into the story." To add emphasis, Anne, still seated on the armrest of his chair gently stroked her father's hair. "What are you lot like, I give up! Anyway I reckon it's time for my beauty sleep. Time to chuck you out."

Sally had had enough of being social for one night and didn't want to share her dwindling supply of gin any further. Anne and Dave walked back along the street arm in arm. Stopping outside the Manse, Anne asked her father if he would like to come back inside the Manse. She was pretty lonely on her own in there and it would be great if her father came home again. They ought to invite Erica over for a meal the following evening. Sally could come too if she wanted. After the dramas of the past few days they should all start afresh.

Erica had been preoccupied with welcoming Brighid to the blackhouse and surrounding pasture. The fields around the village were still lush due to over-manuring in the nineteenth century, the fields and the grass managed to keep pace with the sheep in the longer growing season since the climate had turned milder. Anne had remarked on this to Erica before and warned that the climate could easily tip the other way. The frozen winter they had just experienced might not have been a one off event if the Gulf Stream was shifting its course. In spite of earlier declaring she wouldn't do it, Erica brought Brighid into the blackhouse each evening and, following tradition, the cow was stalled in the lower side of the cottage where her dung built up surprisingly quickly. Ash from the wood stove was mixed with the dung though Erica drew the line at adding her own excrement to the compost. She was engrossed in her increasingly self-sufficient lifestyle and began to see less of her sister and father. Sally was virtually off the radar now the cow had arrived and Erica would spend most evenings indoors content with Brighid's company. Dan had introduced her to Mothan laced spirit and Erica continued by steeping the plentiful herb in whatever drink was available. Not being much of an alcohol drinker, she had experimented with making tea from Mothan and even considered smoking it. Leaves of the plant hung on strings near the woodstove to dry out. The herb in whatever form it was consumed helped her suspend her disbelief regarding they situation they all found themselves in. Deborah and Dan had already left and, if she was honest, her father was becoming a liability to the project. It wasn't meant to be like this and only she had managed, so far, to make a decent attempt at rebuilding St Kilda. There had already been two deaths, her mother had left and her father almost invalid due to his back troubles. He sought solace in the Bible and now increasingly in the company of Sally who seemed to exert some kind of hold on him. As for her sister, she seemed implacable and inscrutable as ever. It was a shame Dan had had to leave but, after the business with her mother, inevitable under the circumstances. Erica was deep in thought over a steaming mug of Mothan tea when Anne knocked on her door.

"Anne! What brings you here?" She hadn't seen her sister since the night at Sally's. "I thought I'd let you know Dad has moved back into the Manse and we are hoping to have a family meal and try and start afresh after the dramas of the last few days. Will you come and join us?"

Erica was curious. "What about Sally, is she going to be there?" Anne shook her head, "No, I asked her but she declined saying she would rather stay out of our personal business. There was bound to be family stuff to discuss and she thought it would be easier for us without her being there." Erica nodded, "Yes, I would agree with that. She seems to have some kind of hold over Dad at the moment. Did you know she had her children taken away from her following a lesbian affair? Just shows you how intolerant the Western Isles can be of anyone behaving differently to roles prescribed for them in the Bible. Then poor Dad, ineffectual since his back went, has to rely on guidance of that Bible to get through his days out here. What a turn around, Anne." Her sister wasn't so sure.

"Hold on, Erica. You can't blame the Bible for everything. It's down to individual interpretation in the end. I have actually been reading the Bible a bit with Dad too and some of it makes a lot of sense." Erica rolled her eyes, "Not you too, Anne! Well you won't get me organizing my life around that drivel. Anyway when's this meal going to take place? I could do with a change of scenery and by the way, what are we eating?" Anne knew her sister too well.

"Thought you'd ask that so, as the best shot here, could you cull one of the old barren ewes and we can have mutton stew. Dad said he could do the butchering but thought it would be good to involve you by doing the killing. I took the liberty of bringing the Tikka and some rounds with me. It's just outside the door waiting for you." Erica went outside and saw the rifle in its heavy duty slip propped against the blackhouse wall. She brought the weapon inside and leant it up in the corner of the room. "Thanks, Anne. That will be no problem. Quick and clean with one head shot, not like those barbaric lunatics with their shotgun. In fact I might as well do it now, there's one old ewe been hanging around the end of the street this time of the morning for quite a while."

As Erica predicted, the old ewe was grazing slightly away from the hefted group of younger ewes and lambs at the west end of the village. She was at the top edge of the burn with rising ground behind her. "Perfect, pass me the rifle, Anne." Anne unzipped the rifle from its slip and passed it to Erica who worked the action a couple of times. Her father had obviously oiled the mechanism when he put it away last time after he culled sheep from his vegetable garden. Erica took one cartridge from the pocket of the gun-slip and slipped it into the breech. No need to bother with the magazine on this occasion. She put her elbow through the sling and leaned her forearm against a protruding stone on the blackhouse wall. Erica took aim and as she slowly exhaled, squeezed the trigger. The crack of the rifle echoed around Village Bay. The other sheep looked up briefly before returning to their grazing. One shot aroused curiosity, anymore would have generated alarm and scattered the flock. The old ewe was nowhere to be seen having leapt into the air to fall lifeless beside the burn. "Well shot, Erica! Now can I borrow your wheelbarrow, please?"

Anne took her sister's wheelbarrow over to the burn and dragged the ewe up from the waterside. It was lucky the ewe hadn't fallen in the stream or, with wet fleece, she would have been far heavier to drag up the bank. With the ewe in the barrow, Anne called back to her sister, "So, tomorrow night then, Erica. You might as well keep the rifle up here for now. You can pick up the rest of the ammo tomorrow." She wished Erica goodbye and headed off cheerily, with the ewe in the wheel-barrow, toward her father waiting in the Manse.

The following day passed quick enough for the three of them. Sally had taken herself for a long walk to the far side of the island, intending to keep well out of the way. Her obsession, as she realized it was, for wanting to control Dave needed thinking through. She was no fool and needed to consider whether her desire to control stemmed from having had so much taken away from her following divorce. It wasn't too bad when the Base guys were there. Her controlling urge was diluted among them, but now with just one man she would have to watch herself. It wasn't his fault she had lost her children, but it was the fault of her ex-husband, another God fearing man. Dave was far happier back in the Manse with Anne. He hadn't needed much encouragement to return to the family home now Deborah had left. In fact he thought it better in almost every respect living with Anne. Her chirpiness and obvious contentment such a contrast to the last days with

Deborah. He had skinned and butchered the ewe and everything was ready for their evening dinner. Just a pity there were no fresh vegetables, rather than tinned ones fetched from the Base store room. Next year, he thought. Next year things would be very different.

Father and daughter worked together to clear and lay the kitchen table. Anne had managed to find some wild flowers amongst the rocks and placed them in a clean jam-jar at the center of the table. She even added a sprig of Mothan picked from around the well. A pair of candle sticks were borrowed from Cottage 1 and a couple of bottles of wine retrieved from the Puff-Inn. It was going down, but the old Puff-Inn cellar would keep them going a bit longer. All in all, Anne had to admit, the Manse was beginning to feel very homely. If what she had in mind came to pass, next year the Manse would be homelier still. When Erica arrived after first settling Bridgid into her stall, the light was fading. There was always so much to do and she had to make use of the available daylight. She knocked as was customary before entering the Manse. Dave and Anne were already seated at the table, both had already a glass of red wine each. The mutton stew was simmering on the electric cooker, the gentle burble from outside indicated the generator was not running under a heavy load.

"Come in and sit yourself down, Erica. Welcome home my firstborn!" Dave was in a jovial mood. In his opinion it had been bliss working with Anne to get everything ready for the evening. The wine she poured him had helped too. He poured Erica a glass and Anne got up to serve the stew. Three bowls of mutton and vegetables were soon steaming on the table and it was Anne's suggestion that they said Grace before starting their meal. The three of them held hands and, in deference to Erica, she thanked their gender neutral Maker rather than God for the food on their table.

"Right then, tuck in folks." Dave encouraged them to start. Anne served her sister and father with as much as they could eat and importantly kept their glasses topped up, especially her father's. When the meal was finished the three of them retired to the living room at the back of the Manse. The generator briefly labored as Anne switched on the electric heater, feeling a late evening chill in the room barely used since Deborah had left taking her own chilliness with her. The long defunct flat screen television on the wall remained blank but Anne suggested a Bible reading before turning in. She rather hoped Erica would stay the night with them, it was in her plan. Dave, in spite of consuming the best part of a bottle and a half of Merlot, was eager to read to his daughters.

"Tell me Anne, which passages would you like?" She answered straight away. "Genesis Chapter 19, of course Dad." Anne had used Biblical justification to convince her father but, in spite of the past closeness between them, she couldn't be sure of Erica. "You know, the story of Sodom and Gomorrah with Lot and his daughters. It's the best bit in the Bible!"

Dave had to laugh at Anne's impropriety but began to feel quietly aroused. Erica had heard of Sodom and Gomorrah but beyond Lot's wife being turned to a pillar of salt had no idea of what was coming. Dave had brought the large family Bible from the Featherstore when he moved back in. In spite of his obvious drunken state he composed himself before reading Genesis 19 to his daughters.

When he had finished reading, Anne made her intentions plain. "Isn't that great, Erica. It means we can sleep with Dad and it's OK with God. You'd think we'd be sent to Hell but apparently not. I am so exited Erica. I made up the double bed for you and Dad and I'll be in there with him tomorrow night. Next year, we won't just have vegetables, Dad, we'll have babies! St Kilda will live again."

"Christ, Anne! That is the sickest thing I have ever heard. Are you behind this, Dad?" Dave smiled at her, "No Erica, it wasn't my idea but I think it's a great one! Come on then girls, I believe you as my firstborn should be first, Erica." She was scared as much as angry. "In your fucking dreams! You are crazy to even imagine I would go along with this. Anne you have been plotting this for days, haven't you?"

She needed to at least understand what was going on and Anne tried to explain. "But Erica, we need children to rebuild St Kilda. We can't do it on our own and there is no other man available. It's OK, it really is. The Bible says so, isn't that right father?" Erica got up to leave. "I am out of here, right now and, if there was a chance, I'd be off the island tonight and away from you perverted lunatics. Anne, think what you are doing. You are the ecologist, you know the risks." Anne was smiling as Erica left, slamming the door behind her. She heard the porch door slam a moment later as her sister stormed off into the night. "Don't worry Dad, she will be alright in the morning. So it looks like it's going to be me first, doesn't it?"

Dave was dumfounded. Drunk as he was it would be a very major step to go along with this and sleep with his daughters, even if scripturally sanctioned under their present circumstances. Anne could sense his slight resistance and snuggled closer to him on the settee. "Come on Dad, or should I just say Dave. You won't regret this. How long has it been for you? I can barely remember the last time I had a man, never, I would say as back in Edinburgh Dan was just a boy then." Anne had never slept with Dan but she knew her father saw him as a rival and would want to purge the memory even if it been Deborah making all the moves in their affair. Dave had had a lot to drink and his voice was slightly slurred when he rose unsteadily to his feet.

"I need to go to bed, Anne. This is all a bit much to take

in." She persisted, "Let me help you, I've made the bed for us."

Anne, who had hardly touched her wine, gently led her father into the double bedroom and sat him on the bed. "I'll just go outside and switch off the generator and be with you in a moment. Here's a candle from the table. Be careful you don't knock it over, OK?" Anne went outside and switched off the generator. The stars were bright that night as the rising wind had blown the clouds away from the island to stream out over the Atlantic. The sky was clear and open, it was beautiful with only an occasional sleepy seal call to disturb the night. What a night this was going to be, what a fateful night, she thought.

Anne went back into the warmth of the Manse, the electric heater clinked as it cooled down and she went into the double bedroom to find her father had undressed himself and was now fast asleep and snoring in bed. She undressed herself and climbed in to join him. She would let him sleep for a while and curled around him, spooning she had heard it called once. Dave awoke in the early hours to feel Anne pressed against him. Her young breasts pressed into his back and her pubic hair warm and soft against his buttocks. This was meant to happen he convinced himself. Anne awoke from her own light sleep and nibbled at the back of his neck. He turned and they kissed, passion rising in both of them. He put his arms around her and she responded fiercely by clinging to him, her breasts pressed against his chest this time. She pushed him gently until he was on his back and lifting the duvet, she kneeled over him her nipples brushing the greying hair on his chest. "Just lie there and let me do this, Dad."

His erection stiffened as she guided him inside her and lowered her buttocks on to his thighs. He moaned as he handed control to his daughter. In the darkness she was smiling but Dave had closed his eyes and failed to see her delight. As she gently rose and fell she could feel him swelling even more inside her until with a shuddering gasp she felt his warm semen ejaculate inside her. Anne's purpose for him at St Kilda was finished but she wouldn't spoil the night for her father now. He was asleep again by the time he had subsided and she lifted herself carefully away to lay beside him. She had used her father for his seed alone, but even so she loved him and settled down to sleep beside him. Anne held her hand tight between her legs, she didn't want any of her father's seed going to waste as a damp patch on the sheet.

Dave awoke to find Anne dressed and standing beside him offering a mug of hot tea. "Morning, Dad. Here's a cup of tea for you. How's the old head this morning?" Slowly, Dave sat up in bed. Anne rearranged the pillow behind him. Realizing his nakedness and semi-dried stickiness around his groin he made sure to pull the duvet up around himself. Anne didn't appear to be embarrassed in the slightest to see him there, but he was confused about the night's events. He knew Anne had made love to him, yes it did feel like love. Was it wrong or was it right? I didn't feel wrong when he thought of it as a man and woman making love, but as father and daughter? Wasn't that the old cliché about isolated highland and island communities? The reality might not be so funny. Genesis 19 had said it was OK but he would have to check further passages on this subject when he got up. "Breakfast will soon be ready, Dad. No bacon and eggs I'm afraid but we can stretch to beans on toast. Erica made some bread yesterday and left a loaf with us before she went home." Erica, Dave remembered, had left under exceedingly strained circumstances. Would she even speak to him again after last night? What was happening here? He needed the Bible. Dave quickly got dressed and ate the beans on toast Anne had made, then began scouring the Bible still laying where he left it on the kitchen table. There were plenty of injunctions regarding sex with in-laws but nothing specific to sex with daughters. It was either OK or so totally wrong it was beyond redemption. He just couldn't tell. Anne seemed very happy this morning, no sign that anything was wrong at all. She was not confused so why should he be? In fact Anne seemed happier and more relaxed than ever that morning. She came and joined him at the table and he thought it was time to ask the question.

"Anne, about last night. Why did we let it happen?" She was confident, "Because I wanted to, Dad. I am a grown woman now and I have been so excited about resettling this island, starting our own new community. I am sorry if you feel I used you a bit, suppose I did really. It won't happen again as I am sure I conceived last night, I know I did." Dave felt his stomach churn. "You mean you took me for my seed, the only available sperm donor and that's it?" Dave was incredulous that his daughter could be so scheming. Resettling St Kilda had been his dream, with him at the head of the family, not Anne. Not a sperm donor either, to be discarded once the deed had been done. He felt sick when he realized how Anne had manipulated him to get her way, quoting Genesis 19 as justification, deliberately getting him drunk. At least Erica had had the good sense not to go along with her scheming but where was Erica now? Smoke was coming from the blackhouse chimney pipe so it was likely she was at home. He left Anne clearing up in the Manse and walked the length of the street to speak with her. It was odd that Brighid hadn't been put out that morning. He knocked on the blackhouse door and waited for an answer. "Who's there?" He could hear Erica coming to the door cautiously and waited for her to let him in. She stood in the doorway, blocking his entrance. Her eyes were red from crying. "Dad, what have you done, what have you done?" Dave tried to explain what had happened.

"But Erica, I was taken advantage of. I couldn't have

imagined just how scheming your sister has become." Erica viciously cut him short. "Dad, that is just typical. Blame the woman when all you had to do was say no. You knew how wrong it was but you just let her use you. Yes, you heard me. You have been used by your own daughter. God help all of us and as far as I am concerned, I never want to see you again. What you did was unforgiveable, not just in my eyes but in the eyes of your precious God too, I expect. Please just go and leave me to get on with my life in peace.

Dave turned away dejected. His wife had left him, one daughter had used him and the other rejected him. There was only one person left he could talk to and he made his way to the Factor's House. When he got there, Sally was waiting outside for him on the porch step.

"I'm sorry Dave, but I don't think I can see you today. I'm too mixed up, I shouldn't have been playing games with you. I need to sort my own head out before I try and help you again." The ground twisted and shifted beneath him as Dave staggered back toward the Manse, but he knew he didn't want to go back there with Anne inside. He turned and went into the Kirk and picked up one of the pocket bibles in the schoolroom. He read from Genesis 28, he would go again to his father's house in peace and the Lord would again be his God. Like Jacob, he must have been dreaming all this. He took the short walk up through An Lag to the cliff edge at the Gap three hundred feet above the ocean. He saw Angels ascending and descending the ladder reaching four miles out to Boreray. Without hesitation, Dave stepped off the edge and onto the ladder to join them.

20 DEPARTURE

The atmosphere in Rangehead was tense. The success of forthcoming multi-national sea-trials, led by the US Atlantic Fleet, were vital to the future of the Hebrides Range and by extension the future of the Hebrides economy in general. The fact that the control room had lost contact with one of several sea-skimming Banshee target drones was more than embarrassing considering the recent debacle at St Kilda. The British developed Banshee had been in service since the 1980s when various navies found themselves vulnerable to attack from sea-skimming missiles. The Banshee 300 had somehow developed a control malfunction and was now racing toward the St Kilda islands, skimming the Atlantic swell to mimic an enemy attack from beyond the horizon. It should have been skimming the sea toward a US cruiser out to the west in the direction of Rockall. The UK Rapier missile, fast as it was, needed to hit its target to explode. With dummy warheads used for training purposes Rapiers simply punched target drones out of the air and damaged Banshees would be retrieved from the sea and patched up to fly again. There was no real danger from an out of control and unarmed fiberglass drone, it would eventually run out of fuel and fall to the sea, where the small, bright orange unmanned aerial vehicle would float and be retrieved to fly another day. This Banshee, however, was being tracked toward St Kilda and it looked likely that the guidance mechanism had malfunctioned. Rangehead suspected the guidance mechanism had actually locked and the drone would be likely to enter Village Bay within the next few minutes and crash ignominiously into the old Base buildings. Rangehead did not want to risk firing a Rapier which might impact on their own empty property. There was also the small matter of the Trust's custodians to consider, dummy warhead or not. The Americans had a much faster and more reliable missile defense capability and, reluctantly, Rangehead asked for help from the US Atlantic Fleet. The exercises were being overseen from a Nimitz-class aircraft carrier and when the request from Rangehead was received, it came as no real surprise. With one thing and another, the American military had come to expect overstretched British defense systems to prove unreliable. Knocking down one of their Banshee drones from beyond the horizon would be a useful training exercise for the carrier's MK 29 Sea-Sparrow launch system team.

Erica's house cow was grazing near the power station when she glanced seaward, hearing the sound of the approaching Banshee. A few accompanying Soay sheep also briefly looked up before resuming the morning's grazing with their new flock leader. None of the sheep had ever seen a cow before and for the time being followed Brighid as the alpha female. Ovine behavior would no doubt return to normal when the rutting season commenced. That was Anne's advice to Erica who had expressed some surprise at Brighid's woolly followers. The sound of the approaching Banshee soon became clearly audible to the sisters too as they discussed their father's tragic accident. In the light of his death, Erica had pushed her sister's seduction to the back of her mind. They went outside Erica's blackhouse in time to see the bright orange drone pass Levenish, apparently heading straight for them.

"For fuck's sake! What's that coming toward us?" Erica looked at Anne, who for once seemed lost for an answer. As the Banshee entered the mouth of the bay, a blast of wind angrily roared down from the ridge creating a water-devil out in the bay. The spinning column of water intercepted the Banshee as it passed the end of the jetty, within meters of the old power station. The water-devil tossed the Banshee away to career wildly into the basalt cliff below Ruiaval just as the Sea Sparrow screeched through the Dun Gap. The US fire team were enjoying this one and wanted to show off their control skills to the embarrassed Brits. One minute the Banshee was there on their screens, the next it was gone, smashed into a thousand pieces sinking to the sea floor. This Banshee was not going to be retrieved. The Sea Sparrow with small but live warhead missed its target and careered across the bay to smash through the rusted curtain doors on the seaward side of the power station. The explosion inside sent shards of shrapnel spraying out toward the grazing animals. As internal diesel tanks ruptured fires broke out simultaneously, rapidly growing in intensity.

Erica screamed and ran toward the scene of fiery destruction. "Brighid! Bastards! Bastards! Fucking bastards!" It took Anne a moment to catch up with her sister now kneeling by the head of her injured cow. One of the animal's hind legs was clearly broken and lying on the ground she lowed in pain as the black smoke from the burning power station drifted over them. Anne reached for the knife in the sheath attached to her belt. "Anne, what are you doing?" Erica's voice was as menacing as it was questioning. "I'm going to put her out of her misery, Erica. I've done it many times for the sheep. A grazing animal with a broken leg will suffer for days and never be able to eat properly. If infection doesn't kill her, starvation will and here the Bonxies will soon have her eyes out. Let me slit her throat, it really is the kindest thing to do." Anne went to cut Brigit's throat when a heavy punch from her sister knocked her sideways. "If she needs putting down, I'll do it!" There really was no argument over euthanasia being the only option for the injured Dexter cow lying on the ground surrounded by twisted metal and broken concrete. Anne let her sister run to the blackhouse and fetch the Tikka rifle while she quickly slit the throats of several badly injured sheep lying nearby. Erica walked back slowly with tears running down her smoke blackened cheeks. "Stand aside Anne, I don't want any more accidents."

Erica loaded the rifle with a single hollow-point round. With the safety catch on, she lay the gun on the ground and kneeled to gently kiss Brighid on the forehead exactly where she would place the muzzle of the rifle. At such close quarters the telescopic sights would be useless and it had to be a final painless end for the animal. She released the safety catch, placed the muzzle on the still moist patch on Brighid's forehead and fired. The hollow point bullet expanded inside the animal's brain and the deformed lead slug span down through the cow's body to exit through her abdomen. Through the gaping exit wound the intestines could be seen still heaving with the shock of the impact. With a heavy sigh, Brighid died and with her died Erica's hopes for the resettlement of St Kilda.

The carrier reported back to Rangehead that the Banshee had been destroyed. They omitted to say that the drone had disappeared from their screens seconds before impact. The problem was solved and now perhaps they could all get on with their exercise. It was only when the fire spread to the Base that the smoke could be seen from Rangehead. From the observation post above the 'Lady of the Isles' monument a large fire could clearly be seen on the western horizon. Plumes of black smoke billowed out and as evening fell, the glow of the flames beneath could be picked out reflecting from the acrid cloud. There was nothing to be done that evening and Range Control certainly did not want any more American intervention on their patch. A phone call to Don secured the Beluga to take an inspection crew out at first light next morning. Reluctantly it was agreed that they needed to inform the Americans that the Beluga was going out and would they please refrain from firing on it, it was not a training target. Range Control attempted to remain as discreet as possible and Don was asked to pick up the inspection team by dingy from the beach below Rangehead before crossing over to St Kilda. Once aboard, Don, who was grateful for the extra business, set off for the islands.

Anne had dragged the dead sheep to the low cliff edge in front of the power station and tipped them into the sea the previous evening. She had wanted to do the same with Brighid but even had she been strong enough, Erica was firmly against her sister disposing of the cow that way. There was no obvious answer and Erica had stayed with her all night to keep early morning Skuas away from the carcass. Something had to be done with the body, she even thought of butchering the dead animal but there was no way of storing such a large amount of meat with things as they were. What would St Kildan's have done? Probably divided up the meat amongst the island families so that each would have a manageable amount to deal with. Here today, it was impossible with just Anne, Sally and herself to feed. Erica was sobbing when some two and a half hours after leaving South Uist, the Beluga roared into the bay. The devastation in the aftermath of the fire was clear to see. While most of the sturdy power station building still stood, it was blackened by the intense diesel fire which had spread and destroyed the flimsily built Base buildings and left the sturdier Manse uninhabitable. Anne had temporarily moved into the Factor's House with Sally, neither of whom wanted it to be a permanent arrangement. Anne thought to leave Erica to grieve over Brighid, not realizing her tears were as much of frustration at the failure to even begin to rekindle a sustainable community at St Kilda. Anne had fetched her sister some fresh water from the well behind the cottages, safely away from the fire. As she drank Erica's swore that, once again, men had caused everything to go wrong on the island and now here they were back again to gloat over the success of their missile strike. Erica rubbed her sleep deprived eyes and stood up. That was it! The men had fired a missile at them to deliberately prevent her rebuilding the community. They didn't want women here at all, it was so fucking obvious! Well they had three women here to deal with and they meant business. Erica picked herself up and ran back to the blackhouse to pick up her rifle and this time collected several clips of ammunition. They were not coming ashore, no way!

Don had spotted Erica running toward her blackhouse. "There's Erica, at least she's OK. I wonder where the others are." The Beluga headed toward the jetty. Don was intending to disembark the inspection team so they could send back a preliminary report as to what had happened. There was an element of *schaden freude* that the Americans had fouled up on shooting down the Banshee. That was the obvious first conclusion but the Trust would have to be informed too. After all, it was their island in spite of a sizeable chunk still leased out to the British military. The lease required removal of all military buildings on termination of the lease and the Americans would certainly have to contribute to the astronomical cost of demolition now they had already started the job with their missile strike.

By the time the Beluga was alongside ready to be tied up Erica was standing on top of the decrepit gabion sea wall shouting at the men to clear off. She was waving the rifle in one hand and pointing at the boat to emphasize her anger at their presence. "You bastards! Do you think you could get rid of us so easily? I don't give a shit about the buildings but why did you have to go and kill Brighid?" Don heard her last words of the rant aimed at them and decided to step ashore and find out what had happened. He was as concerned as Erica if something had happened to the cow. "Get back, Don! Get back or so help me, I'll shoot you."

Erica levelled the Tikka at Don as he stepped onto the jetty. He raised his hands and stepped back on board. "Well gentlemen it seems we have a problem. Apparently we are not welcome any more. She's a friend of mine so I recommend we leave it for now and come back another day when things have calmed down." The team supervisor was adamant, "Not likely, Don!"

The senior member of the inspection team from Rangehead expressed his concern that after paying Don around £200 a head for the return trip, the guys were going ashore and that was that. The inspection team gathered together at the top of the steps waiting for instructions. Erica still had them covered and the team found it more than disconcerting to be faced with an armed stand-off situation after what should have been a leisurely day assessing damage caused by the US Navy's Sea Sparrow. Ian, the supervisor looked up at Erica with a mixture of pity and frustration. "Come on, girl. Put that thing away and we can get on with our work. Then we'll go and leave you folks in piece."

Ian had walked barely a couple of steps when the first shot rang out. The bullet hit the concrete close to his feet and ricocheted noisily out across the bay. "Now fuck off, the lot of you! Come any further and you're dead!" Erica screamed out. Ian made the quick and correct decision to retreat, ordering the men back on board. "Jesus Christ, Don! That woman's mad." Don wasn't going to disagree with his paying customers. "Aye, and she's a crack shot too. She meant to miss just then. I don't want to be around when she aims to hit us."

Don reversed the Beluga away from the jetty before turning the boat eastwards back toward the Uists. The swell was building and the boat lurched unsettlingly toward the mouth of the bay. Whether from nervous tension or sea-sickness, Ian suddenly threw up. As usual, Lachie assisted Don with domestic arrangements at sea and he should have spotted the signs and passed Ian a sick bag, conveniently contained in a plastic beer glass. This time he groaned and reached into the cupboard beneath the cockpit to retrieve the mop and bucket. He took a backward glance to the island and saw Erica had run along the shore to watch them from the 1918 naval gun emplacement. "She's still watching us, Don. Thank fuck that old cannon's just held together by rust or she'd be thinking of blowing us out of the water, I reckon." Ian, who by now had been given a fresh sick bag, asked to use the VHF radio to call Rangehead. Don passed the handset to him.

"We had to abort the inspection. You won't believe it but we were shot at by a lunatic woman with a hunting rifle. Can you inform the Police and let them deal with this. We can go out another time when she's safely off the island." Don butted in to the conversation. "There's no need to involve the Police, Ian. She'll be OK in a day or two. That island gets to you and I have taken quite a few off suffering from depression, having thrown punches at each other – after a heavy night. You don't know what she's been on and the killing of her cow must have tipped her over the edge. Just leave her be for now and I'll talk to her before the team go ashore next time." Ian would have none of it. "No way, man. She's a danger to herself as much as us. I am going to let the Police deal with it. Crack shot or not, I doubt she's got a permit for that thing so it shouldn't be a problem to get her put away for a while."

When the duty officer in Tarbert received the complaint, he could barely believe his ears. This simply did not happen in the Hebrides. There was no armed response unit in the isles and even if there was, how were they going to get to St Kilda? He would have to contact the mainland. It appeared the nearest armed response unit was based in Glasgow and trained in anti-terrorism and gang related firearm incidents. Urban firearm situations were their forte and he could just imagine their collective groan at being sent to deal with not only a rural incident but one at the outermost of the Hebridean islands. The firearms unit would have to be helicoptered out and it would cost the Glasgow council tax payers a small fortune. St Kilda was such a bloody expensive place to get to. Don's passenger business pretty well kept the Tarbert economy afloat but it would take too long to get the Glasgow boys out there on the Beluga.

Erica walked back to her blackhouse, satisfied for the time being that the Rangehead team had gone. She had ran up to the Gap to make sure they weren't going to land in Glen Bay and sneak back to the village over the hill. Anne and Sally had seen and heard the commotion and were waiting outside the door for her. "Come here, Erica. You need a good hug, a bloody good one." Sally held Erica close and let the emotion inside her pour out. Erica was sobbing uncontrollably as Anne took the rifle from her and put it away indoors. The three women went inside to talk about what to do next. Sally and Anne were silent for a while, not knowing what to say. Erica's well controlled shot had taken them over another threshold. Things could not be the same again and Erica knew that as much as any of them.

Sally spoke first. "The Police are bound to be involved, Erica. I know Ian and he doesn't let go of things like this. Don would have been alright about it but I am afraid we will probably be visited again in the morning. There's no way they'll get themselves together in time to come out today but they will be here in the morning. Whatever you do keep that gun hidden and let me do the talking. I am a qualified nurse and you are having a bad bout of clinical depression, OK? We should be able to get you placed under medical supervision for a few weeks and then get back to normal. One thing I would say is that I think it is time you called it a day out here. We have tried to resettle St Kilda but it's lead to deaths and chaos. Time to admit defeat, don't you think girls?" Anne didn't say a word. What could she add? She could hardly admit to the thrill she felt at imminently having the island to herself and her child to be. Sally was sure to go off island with Erica when armed Police arrived in the morning.

"You are probably right, Sally. But I can't leave, not after we have tried so hard." Erica felt sick with tension knowing the challenge the morning would bring. At that very moment she was torn between making a stand against the undoubtedly male Police officers who would come to arrest her or leave quietly, accepting Sally's diplomatic diagnosis of severe depression. She was intelligent enough to allow herself the rest of the day and night to think things through before making her decision. "It's your call, Erica but we'll be in the Factor's House while you think about it." Being separate from the Base, unlike the Manse which abutted the military buildings, the Factor's House had escaped the fire started by the American missile. Anne and Sally walked back to the two bedroomed house where Anne had salvaged what she could of her belongings and moved into the spare room. Sally was uneasy about the arrangement but for the time being there seemed no other sensible option. They would all be leaving in a day or two and the island could be left to the sheep and birds.

The Police helicopter refueled at Benbecula before making the crossing to St Kilda. The intelligence had been good. Somehow, the officers had known about Erica's feminist leanings and thought to send out a couple of police markswomen who would hopefully be perceived as less provocation than male firearms officers. The helicopter flew well to the north of St Kilda before coming in low past Soay. It was unlikely the machine would be heard landing from the village. The two Police markswomen were quietly landed at Glen Bay before the helicopter circled the island to approach from Village Bay. The Police pilot approached cautiously, hovering over Dun and keeping out of accurate range of Erica's rifle. Anne saw thousands of distressed seabirds leave their nests in panic as the machine hovered over their breeding grounds. The Puffins would never return to their burrows after such a disturbance and countless chicks would be abandoned. Incensed, she ran to the blackhouse and screamed at Erica.

"This is all your fault, Erica. Look what they are doing, they're ruining the breeding site. They are only supposed to approach the helipad well away from the breeding grounds, down the middle of the bay, don't they know that rule applies to all helicopters, even the Police. It is up to you, Erica. Do something about it!" Erica had hardly slept that night and in her tiredness and confusion, she made her mind up. She would make a stand.

Picking up the rifle and placing an unopened box of ammunition in her day-sack she made her way to the Hidey-Holes in the scree slope of Mullach Sgar. It took about five minutes to get there and the police had already spotted her picking her way across the boggy ground, then up to the scree before disappearing from sight. They relayed a radio message to the two policewomen making their way up Glen Mór toward the ridge. "Suspect last seen on the scree slope above the beach in Village Bay. You should be able to look down on her when you cross the ridge. Meanwhile we will attempt to land at the helipad and let's keep our fingers crossed she has had time to come to her senses since yesterday."

The two police markswomen made their way up the glen under the watchful eye of hundreds of Great Skuas. The Bonxies did not attack as they would have done had male police officers approached, but they were wary. Rising beyond the Well of Virtues, the pair labored uphill passing the Amazon's House on their left. In spite of their police training these two women struggled up the steeply sloping glen. Urban training was no preparation for action on a volcanic island in the North Atlantic. They were both shaken by an unexpected blast of wind that lifted them off their feet to fall back toward Glen Bay. Picking themselves up and re-slinging their sniper rifles the two women eventually managed the climb to the turf dyke boundary at the top of the glen. Exhausted they sat down on the remains of a peat store cleit to recover. They were about to comment on the incredible view out to Soay when the radio message came through. Their potential target was last seen on the scree slope below them on the Village Bay side of the hill. They got up and walked the short distance to the military roadway, cracked and weed-strewn since the last MOD vehicle had left the previous year. Village Bay lay before them and the ruins of the Base clear to see. To the left lay more rusting steel and broken concrete following the opportunist terrorist attack on the radar station at Mullach Mór. The scree slopes formed a horseshoe around the bay. "How on earth are we going to find her in all this lot?" The other policewoman shrugged and spoke on her radio to her commanding officer in the still hovering helicopter. "OK, just stay in position until we can ascertain her position. We'll know soon enough."

The pilot cautiously flew the Strathclyde Police Eurocopter past the Dun gap and followed the cliff edge of Ruiaval to cross above the scree slopes of Mullach Sgar. He was intending to descend safely to the helipad above the beach. It was, he reckoned, foolish to risk flying in straight across the open bay with an armed and unstable suspect watching their every move, from where ever she happened to be at that moment. The pilot swore audibly in the noisy machine as Erica's first shot entered the belly of the helicopter. Fear gripped the other two unarmed officers on board and all three quickly smelled the leaking aviation fuel. "We are going to land, now!" The pilot yelled at them to brace as the machine made a rapid controlled descent to the helipad. The sudden blast of wind coming down from the hill took the pilot unawares and the helicopter lurched sideways across the beach. In attempting to turn, the main rotor made contact with the shingle bank heaped up by winter storms. The Police Eurocopter, its rotor blades mangled, span to crash on its side on the grey sand beach where the freshwater stream of the west burn, Abhainn Mór reached the sea. Securely strapped in their seats, the occupants of the helicopter, bruised and shaken, knew they had to get away from the machine and its leaking fuel tank. Erica watched as the three men ran for cover behind the earth bund sheltering the power station fuel tanks. She didn't want to kill anyone but the two police markswomen weren't to know that.

Sitting on the ridge at Mullach Geal the two policewomen saw the cautious progression of the helicopter above the scree, heard a rifle shot and saw the machine suddenly veer off to be hit by a gust of wind and crash land on the beach. They spotted their colleagues run for cover behind the earth bund surrounding the main diesel storage tanks. Eileen McCarthy whispered to her colleague Liz Stobart. "She must be down there. The guys in the chopper must have spotted her before they veered off. Pity they smashed the chopper but at least they look OK. She will be watching them and not expecting us coming down from above her." Sally had seen the crash and come running from the Factor's House with her medical bag. In the past she had been stationed at the helipad on flight days just in case such a thing happened. At least she had seen the guys get up and run away, they couldn't be hurt much which was a blessing. Panting, she arrived at the diesel tanks.

"Get down!" The pilot hissed at her to keep out of sight of the scree slopes. He explained how the chopper had been shot at, piercing the fuel tank and then a gust of wind had hit them at a crucial moment when he tried to land. At least they had made it to cover here among the diesel storage tanks. Sally was pleased there were no serious injuries to deal with and, getting her breath back, she retorted. "If she had wanted to kill you, she would have done so. Erica is a crack shot and she is letting you live so don't get any ideas about taking her on. Leave her to me now and I'll talk her out of making any more mistakes with that wretched rifle."

Erica watched Sally leave the cover of the earth bund and make her way, out across the open moorland, toward the foot of the scree slope. She knew where Erica would be hiding. The path was now hard to follow but in MOD times there had been a famous cross country run through a cleft in the hillside, the Chimney Challenge. Runners would be reduced to their hands and knees by the ascent. She knew that Erica would be in the Hidey-Hole near the foot of the cleft. She also prayed Erica would not open fire on her as she would be totally exposed as she climbed the slope toward her friend. She called out, "Erica, it's me, Sally. Don't shoot!"

She dropped into the hidden trench beside Erica to see her friend's tear stained face. "I didn't mean for the chopper to crash, Sally. Just wanted to warn them off, I thought they would fly off and leave us in peace. Those bastards, did you see what they did to the birds? Broke every rule in the book about flying in here. It was no wonder they got caught in that down draft." A dull explosion distracted both women and they turned from each other to see the damaged helicopter burst into flames on the beach. "Thank God those men got out in time Erica or you could be facing a murder charge." Erica burst into tears. "I don't want to kill anyone, Sally. Why can't they just leave us alone?" Erica collapsed into Sally's arms sobbing uncontrollably for the second time in as many days.

A large stone came clattering down from the scree above them as the two police markswomen took position. "Shit! Now she knows we're here." Liz was never one to mince words. "It's no wonder we are dealing with nutters in a place like this. Eileen, can you take her now and get this thing over with?" Having Erica in their sights, police firearms training kicked in. Having already downed the helicopter with her first shot, the policewomen were taking no chances. This was a terrorist situation as far as they were concerned and it was shoot to kill before anything else happened. Eileen had the cross-hairs of her telescopic sight squarely on the back of Erica's head as she peered out of the trench down toward the beach and burning helicopter. "Damn it Liz, there's two of them now but I don't think the second one is armed." She remembered her training. "I had better shout a warning or we'll be in deep shit with the PCA." Liz bellowed down to Erica and Sally. "Armed Police! Put down your weapons and come out where we can see you. There will be no further warning!"

Erica and Sally ducked back in the Hidey-Hole out of the line of sight of the policewomen. No one moved for several minutes. "You stay here, Eileen. Take her if you can and I'll move over there to get a second shot from the ledge if needs be." Erica watched as Liz made her way to the ledge at the side of the cleft dividing the hillside. She could have picked her off easily but made no attempt to do so.

Anne came out from behind a rock at the vantage point and cracked Liz's skull with one blow from a large stone. Liz tumbled silently to fall crumpled at the foot of the slope, her body battered in many places and as Anne had intended the damage to her skull would be indistinguishable from further multiple injuries caused by her fall. The impact of the falling body alerted a pair of nesting Arctic Skuas near the foot of the slope.

With her finger curled round the trigger of her rifle, Eileen screamed in pain as the impact of the attacking female Arctic Skua burst her right eyeball. She stood up, dropping her rifle as the male Arctic Skua hit her hard on the back of the head. Erica spun round and looked up the slope above her to see the police markswoman holding her face in her hands, blood running through her fingers. Anne was above her, higher on the scree watching through her binoculars as the pair of Arctic Skuas returned to their nest site, satisfied to have warned off the intruders. Sally scrambled out of the Hidey-Hole and climbed the scree to aid the injured policewoman. She also noticed the crumpled figure in black police waterproofs lying far below at the foot of the cleft. The woman must surely be dead down there but her concern was with the living now. She tried to lift Eileen's hand from her face, the one covering the burst eye, but with the other the policewoman pushed her away hard. Sally tumbled backward but luckily fell on soft turf at the edge of the scree. She quickly picked herself up spoke quietly, yet assertively to the injured officer. "I am a trained nurse, you must let me see your eye. I might be able to help and at least I can bandage it for you." When Eileen finally agreed to let Sally look at the injury, it was obvious that the right eye was damaged beyond any hope of recovery. The impact of the tearing beak had shredded the tissue of her eyeball. Eileen would never shoot again and would have precious little chance of remaining in the Police service after this incident. While Sally bandaged up Eileen's bloody eye socket as best she could from her field first aid box, Anne slipped away quietly to join her sister in the trench below.

The smell of trampled Mothan growing in the damp floor of the Hidey-Hole was overpowering as Anne climbed down to join her sister. Erica looked vacant, bewildered by everything that had happened around her that morning. "It's alright, Erica. It's over now. I couldn't let them shoot you, they would have too. They are trained killers and I was watching them, could even hear what they were saying. It would have been so much easier to take you out with this sniper gun than go through the bother of trying to arrest you. Anne had quickly picked up the sniper rifle dropped by Eileen when the Skuas attacked. Once you had fired at the helicopter, they had full authority to kill you. You are lucky she let me call the Arctics." Erica looked more puzzled than ever. "I really have no idea what you are talking about Anne. But thank you for saving my life. I just wish we didn't have yet another death on our hands." Anne felt no such remorse. "She slipped and fell, Erica, just slipped and fell. This scree slope is treacherous and those city cops were well out of their depth here. They should have kept off the scree and away from the Arctic's nest. It's not our fault, just a pity they didn't speak to us first rather than sneak up from Glen Bay. Had they been male police officers, the Bonxies would have seen them off for sure but it took the Arctics to recognize the maleness of their intention. Women acting out male roles, we will have to watch for that from now on." Erica was not listening, "Anne, this is the end. There won't be anything to watch out for from now on. I'll be arrested and taken away. Look the other police are walking up here now."

The pilot and three policemen had left the cover of the diesel tanks bund having deduced the danger up on the scree was over. They scrambled and slipped as they made their way to join the women. The senior officer swore quietly when he saw the crumpled body at the foot of the cleft, but was pleased to see Eileen receiving competent medical attention as they struggled toward the Hidey-Hole. The sound of high powered marine diesel engines made all on the slope turn around to see the Beluga roar into the bay, throttles wide open. "What the fuck? Didn't that man get the message or what?" Erica again picked up the Tikka and took aim only to have Anne roughly pull the rifle away from her. "No Erica, no. We are going to need these guns – and we are going to need Don and the Beluga next year. We can't do this on our own and Don's alright, he's on our side. Now give me the rifle."

The small cave on the hillside was known to very few apart from the student sheep researchers who used it for secret parties. You had to wriggle through the small muddy entrance but once inside you could sit, almost stand in relative dryness. An ideal place for their secret activities as the remains of candles and empty whisky bottles bore witness. Anne placed the Tikka and two police issue Heckler and Koch G3s with full magazines in the driest spot she could find in there. When she returned to her sister, the front of her waterproof jacket and trousers were plastered in mud. "Quick Erica, do as I say!"

They both picked up the two largest stones from the scree that they could manage and screamed as they hurled them over the cliff to fall with spectacular splashes into deep water at the front of the Cailleach's Cave. The screaming drew the attention of the policemen, just as Anne had intended. "Now what on earth is going on with you crazy women?" The senior policeman had had just about enough and was really pleased that Don had turned up. Tourism to St Kilda underpinned Don's business, he must have seen the fire on the horizon and come out to check what had happened. Now they would at least get back to Harris tonight, away from this godforsaken rock in the North Atlantic.

This time Erica spoke first. Her future liberty might depend on what she did and said now and she thought Anne's plan sounded feasible given their present circumstance. "We've thrown those fucking guns in the sea. I've had enough of shooting and death here. Just look at our home down there, can't you see the ruin your missile caused us. Enough is enough I just can't take anymore."

Erica sobbed convincingly in front of Sally and the police officers. Sally left the injured Eileen in the care of her male colleagues and went to comfort Erica. She whispered as she put her arms around her friend. "Good ruse, Erica. Even I can't decide between genuine depression and what you're making up now. Let's keep to the story that you are severely depressed, the police won't be bothered for now. They just want to get away from this place and when I write my report and copy it to them, you'll be just fine if you accept recognized treatment for clinical depression. After all, you didn't kill anyone, just put the fear of God into a few." Sally squeezed Erica's hand to secretly emphasize her tacit support for what she had been through. Anne was another matter and if anyone should be locked away, in her professional opinion, it should be the younger sister.

Sally supported Erica as she climbed out of the Hidey-Hole, her face streaked with mud and tears. The senior policeman muttered something about willful destruction of police property, meaning the rifles he believed had been thrown in the sea, but he had the more important matter of getting himself and his remaining officers away from St Kilda safely and as soon as humanly possible. When the group reached the foot of the slope, they met Don at the helipad. He had asked Lachie to stay on board and sail for help should he not return in a reasonable time. He fully understood the inherent danger of an armed, depressed woman facing trigger happy Glasgow police. Pity about the chopper, he thought. Such an eyesore lying there on the beach and not likely to add anything to the green tourist business he had just been discussing with Anne for next year. Anne had slipped away as the injured parties comforted each other and briefly proposed her idea to Don as she walked back with him toward the helipad. So much had happened since they arrived on the island, it was obvious that Dave's idea of a nuclear family resettling St Kilda wasn't going to work. Patriarchy was what had ruined St Kilda. Now it was down to women to rebuild the community. They would need men, of course, but on their terms. Anne was wise enough to accept that she couldn't do it all on her own but with Erica's help it could be possible.

"So gentlemen and ladies, I expect you'll be wanting a lift back to the real world, will Leverburgh do you? When we get closer in I'll give them a call and I reckon the 'Happy Landings' will be more than agreeable to feed you and put you up for the night. You can get the bus to Stornoway in the morning and then, if the plane hasn't broken down again, you can get the mid-day flight back to Glasgow, all at Her Majesty's expense I reckon. No doubt she'll be pleased that you got off here mostly in one piece." Sally gave Don a warning glance.

"I'm just going to the Factor's House for the inflatable stretcher. We have another casualty, Don. This one won't be walking off the island I am afraid. Now will you please take care of Erica while I go and get it. Two of you will need to remain here and carry the casualty when I get back, OK?"

By the time the stretcher was placed beside Liz, *Rigor mortis* was beginning to stiffen her body. "Quick as you can, boys. Straighten her legs before she gets too stiff." The two police officers wiped their hands on the grass after straightening out Liz's broken legs. Her trousers were soaked in urine her body had released as she fell dying from Anne's heavy blow. Her arms were placed by her sides with some difficulty and only prevented from springing up again by tightening the straps of the stretcher. "Don't worry boys, she can't feel anything." Sally was surprised at her own flippancy. She placed her woolly Beanie hat over Liz's blood matted hair and she looked to all intents and purposes as respectable as a corpse could be under the circumstances. "Rightio, let's get her down to the boat."

The policemen carrying her body were shattered by the morning's events. They had been looking forward to the scenic flight from Glasgow and what should have been a relatively straight forward arrest of a depressed female suspect. They had lost one officer, another badly injured and a multi-million pound helicopter totally written off. There was also the issue of a once functional MOD property left a smoldering ruin but that wasn't their problem. The stretcher bearers had to put Liz's body down several times to rest before nearly dropping her as they passed the stretcher to Lachie waiting on the Beluga. The stretcher was then attached to the small crane they used to lift their inflatable Zodiac tender on board and the body stowed at the rear of the open deck. Lachie was well aware that Don wouldn't take kindly to a leaking corpse inside the pristine saloon cabin of his boat. The rest of the group were already inside the Beluga by the time the stretcher was loaded. All agreed that Sally should take charge of Erica and get her into some kind of sheltered accommodation for the night before local police could interview her in the morning. It would have to be done, there was no doubting that, but Sally was well respected in Leverburgh and her mother's croft would be a good a place as any. Erica was clinically depressed, in Sally's professional opinion, but genuine or not Erica would need to keep up the act for a few days yet. The authorities would soon agree for her to resume normal life once it became clear what they had all been through out at St Kilda. Eileen had been given strong pain killers and Don joked as usual that passengers rarely felt seasick on the inward journey to Harris. They were all set to depart the historic jetty, leaving the wrecked helicopter and ruins of the Base and Manse still smoldering behind them when Erica asked the obvious question. "Where's Anne?"

Anne had last been seen near the helipad after walking up from the jetty with Don. It was Erica who spotted her as she took a last glance toward her restored blackhouse. The home she would now have to leave, for a while at least. It was still hard to understand let alone comprehend why it had all gone so terribly wrong for them. The Williams family had such high hopes of a new life away from the stress of 21st century Edinburgh, but the stress of living at St Kilda had proved unbearable. Was it the male approach to living in such an environment or was it the environment itself. According to

Sally, the environment had changed, it was becoming milder and wetter. A longer growing season meant weaker sheep were now surviving winters when previously they would have succumbed. Everything was growing so well, she had remarked once. Just look at the Mothan, she had more than once pointed out. The damper areas were awash with purple flowers. Milder conditions meant more midges and the insectivorous Mothan plants would thrive. Just a nuisance when rotted leaves got into the water supply.

Anne came out of Erica's blackhouse and stood gazing across the bay toward a small pod of dolphins playing along the edge of Dun. The deeper waters on that side of the bay were teeming with fish and the dolphins knew the right places to feed, as did the resident seal population. Back on the Beluga Sally wanted to go and check on her. "If you don't mind waiting for a moment, I think Erica and I should go and find out what Anne plans to do." Sally needed to find out to let Josephine at the Western Isles Trust know if Anne was planning to stay. "If she is coming with us, then she needs to get a move on." Don, Lachie and the police team were getting impatient to leave. The Police in particular didn't want to spend another minute on the island. An unexpected hiss of air leaving Eileen's corpse, firmly trussed in the stretcher on the deck, emphasized the point. Sally and Erica walked briskly over the fields to the restored blackhouse where Anne greeted them. Sally came straight to the point.

"We need to leave now, Anne. So are you coming or not?" Anne seemed distant, lost in thought. "Sorry, what was that? Leave here, why?" Erica explained, "You'll be on your own Anne, and I won't be back for a long while, maybe not at all if I get banged up in a psychiatric hospital or something like that." Erica really did sound depressed, negativity was so unlike her, thought Sally. But, if Anne wanted to stay then so be it. The island was unrestricted, had been ever since the 2003 Land Reform Act opened up so much of Scotland for the public to enjoy without fear of gamekeepers and stalkers giving them a hard time.

"OK, Anne, that's fine by me but just one thing. Take good care of my cottage, please. I put my soul into making that ruin a home and as we all know once empty, when life and fire goes out, it will quickly become a ruin once again." Anne made an enigmatic reply. "Don't worry, dear sister. This place will be ideal for us." Erica detected a hint of sarcasm in Anne's reply, but let it go rather than get her to fully explain. "Erica, you will be back and sooner than you expect. Stop fretting and go and get your, err, treatment over with. I'll have the fire lit when you return. Just please don't bring that friend of yours back with you." Erica had to think who she meant. "You mean, Dan? You must mean him and I very much doubt if he'd ever come back but who knows. Maybe even Mum will be back." Anne emphasized her opinion. "No way, she's a liability and I couldn't ever imagine her and Dan on the same island, could you?"

The sisters both laughed briefly at the thought of their mother's fling with Dan. "Poor boy, he wouldn't have known what hit him, until it was too late." Erica introduced a serious note to their banter. "It was such a shame Dad finally lost it though, Anne. The affair must have tipped him over the edge, literally. This is no place for the depressed which is why I will go and get my head sorted. Yeah, maybe see you sooner than you think. A fresh start would be a good thing to look forward to."

Anne explained her earlier discussion with Don about bringing paying visitors to St Kilda to help rebuild the community. There should be families out here but only families prepared to live in harmony with the island and its environment, not trying to brutally wrest their living from it as had been done over the past 150 years. She brought the conversation to a close. "Don't worry, I'll be just fine. And I will take good care of your cottage, Erica. In fact I look forward to restoring a few more with you when you get back."

Anne gave Erica a warm hug to send her on her way. Sally extended her hand only. She wouldn't trust Anne further than she could throw her and suspected her active involvement in the tragic accidents that happened over the past week or two. The stalkers, Dave's apparent suicide and the death of the policewoman now lying on the deck of the Beluga. With her affinity with the wildlife on the island, could she have instigated the Skua attack which left one policewoman dead and the other part blinded? No, that was a crazy thought!

"OK, girls, time to say goodbye. I'll probably won't be back any time soon but no doubt you'll see Erica back in a few months. So better luck next time, Anne. Don't get too fat eating all the food we're leaving behind. Don will bring you more out when you need it." Anne assured her, "We will be just fine, Sally. Don't worry about us. Don't worry about us at all." Anne was becoming distant again and Sally found her use of 'we' irritating. Who did she think she was, Queen of St Kilda? Sally linked her arm through Erica's and the two women made their way back to the boat. "She's a queer fish, your sister. There's no mistaking that. What's with the 'we' business? She will be on her own and no doubt loving it." Erica laughed at the thought and they were both in better spirits as they approached the boat. Sally cautioned Erica to appear depressed before they stepped on board.

"Thank God for that! Can we just go now before Liz out there decides to get up and stay too?" The senior police officer let out an audible sigh of relief as Don started the engines. Lachie untied the mooring ropes and they were on their way. Three hours to get back to the relative sanity of Leverburgh, he thought. And a stiff drink in the 'Happy Landings' before anything else happened. Anne made no attempt to see the group off, but did wave to her sister as the Beluga bounced over the swell at the mouth of Village Bay. She studied the ruins of the Base and decided to avoid the area as much as possible when she had salvaged as much as she could from the relatively intact kitchen area. There were plenty of fish and birds eggs to collect. Down in Glen Mór, Morrigan had said it was OK to go back to harvesting eggs as long as they didn't over pick any one area. Just a friendly warning, but she would send the Bonxies after her if she took too many. The Arctic Skuas were Morrigan's elite personal guards, Anne thought. The Bonxies her foot soldiers. Maybe one day that policewoman, Eileen would come to understand what it was all about and why she had lost her eye. The guns were safely hidden and Anne hoped she would have no immediate use for them but it would be good to keep them oiled and ready as you never knew who could come sailing into the bay. Vikings, Barbary slavers, German 'U' Boats or goodness knows who in the mid-21st century. As long as Morrigan was respected she would help them rebuild the island community, it was going to be good. As if to confirm this a sudden gust of wind ripped several more slates from the fire damaged roof of the Kirk behind the ruined Base.

It had been over a month since her last period and Anne was sure she was pregnant with her father's child. She went inside and sat at Erica's table. The large Bible was still there where it had been left and she re-read the account of Lot and his daughters. It gave her satisfaction to realize that as devious and violent as she had become, her life here was preordained. It was all written down there in the Scriptures, God's words were bearing fruit in her womb. Anne rested her hands on her, as yet, barely swollen belly. She spoke her thoughts out loud. "If you are boy, I will name you Ben, after Benammi to honor Lot your father……..."

ABOUT THE AUTHOR

Paul Sharman was born in 1952, growing up in the English city of Birmingham. Cold War fears were a major influence on his life leading to his chosen career in nature conservation and forestry. As a mature student he gained a PhD in Cultural Geography from University of Exeter in 2008. From 2010 to 2017 he worked as Ranger for the St Kilda archipelago, a Dual World Heritage Site in the north-east Atlantic approximately 100 miles west of the Scottish mainland. This is his first novel and inspired by experiences working at St Kilda. He now lives at Killerton in the County of Devon, south-west England.

Printed in Great Britain
by Amazon